KIKA HATZOPOULOU

MOTH DARK

PENGUIN BOOKS

To everyone making a different choice

PENGUIN BOOKS

UK | USA | Canada | Ireland | Australia
India | New Zealand | South Africa

Penguin Books is part of the Penguin Random House group of companies whose addresses can be found at global.penguinrandomhouse.com.

www.penguin.co.uk   www.puffin.co.uk   www.ladybird.co.uk

First published in the USA by G. P. Putnam's Sons, an imprint of Penguin Random House LLC, and in Great Britain by Penguin Books 2025
001

Copyright © Kika Hatzopoulou

The moral right of the author has been asserted

Penguin Random House values and supports copyright. Copyright fuels creativity, encourages diverse voices, promotes freedom of expression and supports a vibrant culture. Thank you for purchasing an authorized edition of this book and for respecting intellectual property laws by not reproducing, scanning or distributing any part of it by any means without permission. You are supporting authors and enabling Penguin Random House to continue to publish books for everyone. No part of this book may be used or reproduced in any manner for the purpose of training artificial intelligence technologies or systems. In accordance with Article 4(3) of the DSM Directive 2019/790, Penguin Random House expressly reserves this work from the text and data mining exception.

Set in Sabon LT Pro
Printed and bound in Great Britain by Clays Ltd, Elcograf S.p.A.

The authorized representative in the EEA is Penguin Random House Ireland, Morrison Chambers, 32 Nassau Street, Dublin D02 YH68

A CIP catalogue record for this book is available from the British Library

ISBN: 978–0–241–73309–7

All correspondence to:
Penguin Books
Penguin Random House Children's
One Embassy Gardens, 8 Viaduct Gardens, London SW11 7BW

Penguin Random House is committed to a sustainable future for our business, our readers and our planet. This book is made from Forest Stewardship Council® certified paper.

PRAISE FOR
MOTH DARK

'A world so unique and addictive that I devoured this in a matter of days. Whimsical prose and a slow burning romance unlike any I've read before.'
ALEXANDRA CHRISTO, author of *To Kill a Kingdom*

'Darkly dreamy, timely and expertly crafted. You will find star-crossed romance, a heady blend of science and magic and brilliant characters determined to end the cycle of violence.'
ALLISON SAFT, author of *Wings of Starlight*

'An achingly hopeful, breathtaking love story. It's the sort of book you want to linger in the dark with, and I absolutely loved every moment sunk within its pages.'
BEA FITZGERALD, author of *Girl, Goddess, Queen*

'Utterly enthralling and darkly whimsical, *Moth Dark* is a thrill ride of a book, with its tale of twisted timelines and unyielding love. Sascia and Nugau's story is certain to stay with you long after the book is over.'
A. B. PORANEK, author of *Where the Dark Stands Still*

'A lush, breathtaking and wholly unique fantasy, with a devastating star-crossed romance and a world that lifts off the page like a fluttering of moths.'
AVA REID, author of *A Study in Drowning*

'*Moth Dark* is everything I've come to expect from Kika Hatzopoulou – dark, twisty, romantic and completely, dazzlingly original. Unlike anything else I've read.'
SARAH UNDERWOOD, author of *Lies We Sing to the Sea*

'Decadent darkness, parallel worlds and a love that crosses so many boundaries. A unique fantasy that draws you in and doesn't let you go.'
NATASHA BOWEN, author of *Skin of the Sea*

'Beautifully written and deeply compelling – an absolute triumph of a book. Kika Hatzopoulou masterfully weaves together an engaging, unexpected plot with the kind of swoon-worthy romance that spans worlds and timelines.'
PASCALE LACELLE, author of *Curious Tides*

'Hatzopoulou makes a blazing mark in the world of contemporary romantic fantasy. Utterly exhilarating, mysteriously alluring and deeply beautiful.'
AMÉLIE WEN ZHAO, author of *Song of Silver, Flame like Night*

'Wildly imaginative, achingly romantic and impossible to put down. Get ready, readers: your next book obsession has arrived.'
ANGELA MONTOYA, author of *A Cruel Thirst*

'I was absolutely gripped by the fascinating, twisty, world of *Moth Dark*. Kika Hatzopoulou spins a story full of complex theories around genetics, time and gender with such deftly confident writing.'
ALWYN HAMILTON, author of *Rebel of the Sands*

'Hatzopoulou has crafted a multi-faceted jewel of a book. This story is resplendent, with complex world-building, achingly lovely writing and a tough-as-nails heroine I couldn't help but love.'
CLAIRE M. ANDREWS, author of the *Daughter of Sparta* trilogy

'I was utterly entranced by *Moth Dark*. Sascia and Nugau's connection is mesmerizing, and their love story both aches and captivates – tender and totally unforgettable.'
LESLIE VEDDER, author of *The Bone Spindle*

'Hatzopoulou at her very best. A unique and fantastical story threaded with a compulsive mystery. A feast for YA romantasy readers.'
RACHEL GREENLAW, author of *Compass and Blade*

'An enthrallingly original world, and an addictively intriguing story. The romance had me on the edge of my seat. I miss this world already.'
ESMIE JIKIEMI-PEARSON, author of *The Principle of Moments*

'Captivating, intricately crafted and brimming with wonder, *Moth Dark* pulls its readers into a deeply romantic, time-tangled tale. As poignant as it is powerful, this story lingers with you far beyond the final page.'
KIERA AZAR, author of *Thorn Season*

Also by Kika Hatzopoulou

Threads That Bind

Hearts That Cut

PART I

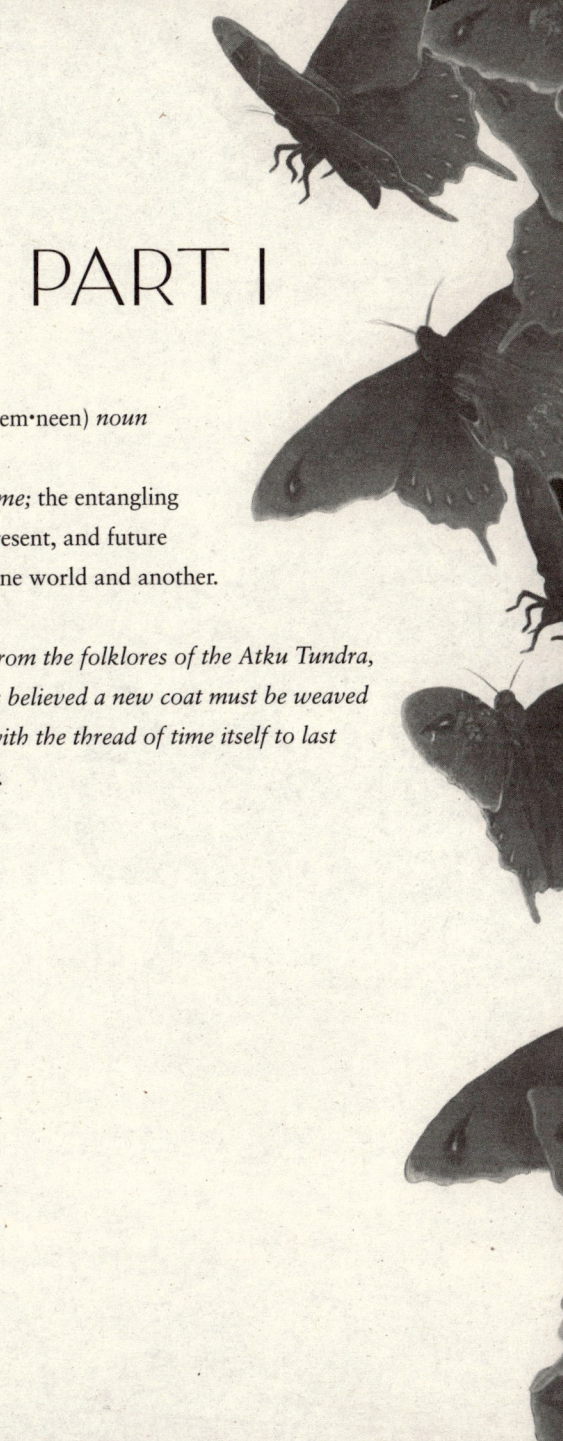

ymneen (eem·neen) *noun*

knotted time; the entangling
of past, present, and future
between one world and another.

*Archaic; from the folklores of the Atku Tundra,
where it is believed a new coat must be weaved
through with the thread of time itself to last
the winter.*

1

THE MAW

The Maw opens up between West 18th and 24th Streets, smack in the middle of Manhattan, a giant collapse sinkhole nearly half a mile across, its black so absolute it devours whatever preconceptions you might have had about darkness in one bone-snapping gnash. Nova-lights hang in a concentric ring on the concrete barrier, like a giant chalk line in an old-timey crime movie.

The body: the Maw.

The crime: existing.

On the observation deck at 21st Street, Sascia leans on the rail and watches today's visitors. There are the overeager tourists, pressing against the reinforced glass, smiling at their phone cameras. There are the kids, dashing about in Darkbeast masks. There are the tour guides and security guards droning precautions. If you pay close attention, you'll notice the gazes of this last group, the professionals, are carefully avoidant of what lies inside the barrier.

Sascia first noticed the feeling on her third day giving tours of the Maw six months ago. A sensation along her spine, a muted hiss in her ears. The instinct to just *bolt*. It was one of the security guards who put a name to it, after he noticed Sascia's hunched shoulders. *Feels like something's breathing down there, don't it?*

A monster in the darkness, lurking in anticipation.

But to Sascia, the Maw is far more than a crime to be feared. *Get your life together*, her dad had said after their massive blowout when it became evident Sascia was squandering her once-in-a-lifetime opportunity at an Ivy League education. Except Sascia's life *was* the Dark, and that wasn't socially acceptable, so she settled for the next best thing: running exclusive tours of the New York Darkworld to pay for her ridiculous remedial courses and ridiculous SAT retakes. The Maw is, in a way, her second chance.

"Its scientific name is NY18 Sinkhole," she says now to her latest client, launching into her familiar monologue, "but people call it the Maw, after that viral footage, you know, of the delivery guy on his scooter, racing away from the emerging Dark."

"Yeah," her client says, and dutifully quotes, *"Everything's disappearing into it—like it's a damn maw."*

Yvonne Coleman-Zhao is from Chicago, a first-year student at Juilliard, a violinist or cellist or something, and she's never seen the Maw before. Her eyes are big and unblinking, her body tense; she refuses to step any closer than necessary. (Chicago might have the occasional runaway Darkbeast, but it does not have a Maw.)

"The Pit of Shanghai is bigger, of course," Sascia recites, "and xenoscientists—scientists who study the Dark—believe there are cracks in the deep ocean that dwarf the ones on land, but, yeah, the Maw of Manhattan is catalogued as the second-largest host of Dark in the world. It is home to a number of monstrosities, as you can see." She gestures at the talon marks on the concrete barrier surrounding the Maw. "As you surely know, there are no humanoids in the world where the Dark comes from, but there's plenty of Darkcreatures, something akin to our own animals, and a few Darkbeasts, ranging in size from an elephant to Godzilla-level giants. Fortunately, no Darkbeasts have managed to burst out of the Maw in five years, since the Blackout. If something big is crawling through the Dark, movement sensors at the lowest ring of the barrier automatically turn on lights fortified with nova energy to the highest brightness and release light bombs to send the beast scuttling back."

Sascia pauses, because this is the point where most of her clients need to pose the question. Right on cue, Yvonne asks, "Does that happen often?"

"In New York? It happens three, four times a year." Her breezy answer is well rehearsed; after almost half a year on the job, she knows to offer the sense of safety her clients are craving. "Tradition says if the skyline blazes white and you're still alive when the lights switch off, you have to go get blackout drunk."

"Well, let's hope my parents never hear about that. It was hard enough to convince them to let me move to a city with an active Darkhole." The girl glances at the black-and-orange water bottle peeking out of the side pocket of Sascia's backpack—a gift from her father when they visited Columbia University last summer. "So you're at Columbia?"

Uh-oh rings like an alarm in Sascia's head. She doesn't want to have the college conversation, least of all with a bright-eyed first-year student. They're so full of dreams, opportunity ripe for the taking; dreams that Sascia should share, opportunity she should be taking advantage of. *I was recruited by the elite Umbra Program for Young Researchers at sixteen, offered an early provisional spot at Columbia a few months later, botched all my conditional exams at seventeen, and now, at eighteen, I have to complete remedial courses and retake the SATs* just doesn't have a good ring to it.

"Uh-huh," she drones instead. "But I'm taking a gap year right now." (At least this part's kind of true.)

"Oh, fun! And this is your side gig? These private tours?"

This is good money and me getting my life together is the real answer, but no one should have to say that aloud. "Hey," she evades, pointing at the entrance with her chin, "it looks like there's a big group coming. Do you want a photo before the place gets swamped?"

She opens her palm, but to her surprise, Yvonne doesn't hand her phone over. "Doesn't feel right," the girl mumbles, which earns her another point in Sascia's tally.

(The first one: pronouncing Sascia's name right, when she called to book a tour three days ago. Almost everyone goes for Sasha at first try.)

(For the record, it's: SAH-skee-ah.)

They descend the stairs to a typical late-October day in New York, orange speckling the green along the street, gray clouds peeking between the buildings. The air is thick with fried food and ketchup. Any good guide knows the drill: start with lesser attractions first, like the Darkgriffin sculpture installation at Washington Square Park, move on to the highlight of the tour, aka the Maw, then end the walk with a shopping opportunity at the flea market by the entrance of the observation deck. Street vendors line the cobbled street, booths heavy with Darkworld memorabilia, food stalls packed with Darkbeast-inspired delicacies.

"Sooo," Sascia drawls. "Like we discussed, I charge twenty for the one-hour tour. If you enjoyed it, I'd greatly appreciate you passing the word to your friends."

She notices the infinitesimal drop of Yvonne's eyebrows. Sascia's heartbeat heightens, her senses sharpen. This is the moment. It's why she tolerates the crush of tourists at the Maw and performs her parroted speech in every snippet of free time she has.

Yvonne says, "Oh. I thought—"

Sascia puts a puzzled frown on her face. "Yes?"

"I heard—"

C'mon, Sascia thinks with twin pangs of panic and anticipation. *Don't chicken out now.*

The girl's voice drops to a whisper. "Well, the person who referred me to you said you take your clients . . . *fishing*."

And there it is. Hook, line, and sinker. Sascia shrugs, but it's a hard facade to maintain. Her belly fills with self-congratulatory pleasure. "If they want to."

"I want to," Yvonne hastens to say.

"Fishing in the Dark is not exactly legal," Sascia warns, but Yvonne won't care—the ones who seek Sascia's services never do.

This is, after all, what her word-of-mouth campaign advertises: an immersive, collaborative experience, emphasis on *immersive*. Any proper tour company in the city can show you around the Maw and jabber about the legendary Darkgriffin and its many littler brethren. But only Sascia will take you fishing, so you can see (and let's be honest, *touch*) those littler brethren with your own two hands.

Yvonne says eagerly, "It's a hundred, right? For the fishing tour?"

"Depends on what you want to catch. Darkbeetles and roaches are eighty—"

"I want Darkfireflies," Yvonne replies without skipping a beat.

Sascia has to fight, like full-body wrestle, the urge to roll her eyes. She did it *once* for a visiting Harvard sophomore in June, and now that's all her clients ever ask for. Apparently, that girl was a sorority influencer or something, and she listed a Darkfirefly jar lantern as the must-have item for your dorm room decoration.

Luckily, Darkfireflies are essentially the most harmless, docile creatures to ever come out of the Dark. Catching them is both easy (which is great for Sascia) *and* spectacular (which is great for business).

"Darkfireflies are a hundred, yes," Sascia replies. "I've got a good fishing spot, but it's a bit of a walk."

Yvonne doesn't mind, so they spend the next twenty minutes walking uptown, during which Sascia makes sure to ask the girl lots of questions, carefully steering the conversation away from any facts about her own personal life. When they reach Hell's Kitchen and Sascia leads Yvonne into a narrow, dark side street, the girl is visibly spooked, lingering at the mouth of the alley.

"Don't worry," Sascia soothes. "I've done this dozens of times. It's perfectly safe. Look."

She removes the portable nova-lights from her backpack and arranges them in a circle at the end of the alley. With a click of the remote, the floodlights flick on, washing the brick and cement in white. The lights congregate over a manhole cover emblazoned with geometric designs and the word SEWER in narrow, square letters.

The legitimacy of it seems to settle Yvonne's nerves. She approaches and proceeds to gawk at Sascia's gear. A folding fishing rod (modified to hold bug bait instead of fish bait), a nova-gun (just in case), a waterproof canvas to sit on, and two small plastic specimen cups.

"What's that?" Yvonne asks.

"Our bait," Sascia answers, depositing the tiny Ziploc bag filled with gray dust next to the cups. "It's Darkflowers ground to powder, which research has shown is akin to pollen in the Darkworld. Scientists believe Darkfireflies love it."

(Tactfully, Sascia doesn't say *my* research, or *I* believe.)

She's almost set up, fishing rod extended, glue strips and bait hanging from its tip. There's none of the bone-chilling fear now. The big Dark is terrifying, but the smaller Dark, Sascia can handle just fine. In fact, she kind of excels at it. Her body is brimming with excitement, movements swift and focused, mind razor-sharp, and when she launches into her familiar fishing directions, she talks a little too fast.

"Here's how it'll go. I'll open the manhole. There'll be absolute Dark down there—this sewage line has been decommissioned by the city, which means there are no light wards. You'll lower the fishing line into the hole, and when you feel the tug, I'll turn off the nova-lights." At Yvonne's startled inhale, Sascia lifts her palms. "I know it's scary, but it's necessary. If we don't turn them off, the lights are going to instantly fry the Darkfireflies, and that's not what you're paying for, right?"

"Why am *I* holding the rod? What will you be doing?" A trickle of panic is leaking into Yvonne's voice. She has arranged herself neatly on the canvas so that no part of her trendy low-rise jeans, cropped tee, leather loafers outfit is touching the grimy cement.

Sascia's in her steady Doc Martens, trusty Levis, and an oversized hoodie. She doesn't care if she gets a little dirty; she kneels on the other side of the manhole and drums her fingers against the nova-gun. "I'm going to be aiming the gun into the Dark, monitoring any movement. Darkfireflies are absolutely harmless, but if we leave the door open too long, other things might come wandering."

"Christ."

This time, Sascia doesn't try to comfort Yvonne. The girl *should* be afraid—this is what she paid for. A roller-coaster ride, heart pumping, stomach dropping, the glorious thrill of danger. "Ready?" Sascia asks.

"*No*—"

Sascia heaves. The manhole cover dislodges with a *thwonk*.

In the hole, there is only Dark. Its abnormality doesn't register at first: It looks like any other lightless crevice. But after a few moments, your senses go into high alert. Your eyes don't adjust. Your ears pick up no sound: no pipes dripping, no rats scattering, no echoing shifts. There is an eerie lack of smell.

In the before, when darkness came to mind, Sascia could smell dust stirred up in the attic or basement, or dew coating golden leaves, or the smell of lavender detergent as she burrowed under the covers. This smells nothing like darkness used to. It smells *of* nothing.

The silence that follows is small and fragile. Sascia feels the girl's urge to fill it, with questions or prayers or blabbering, and she quickly gestures for Yvonne to lower the line into the sewer hole. The other girl obliges with only the slightest trembling.

"Now what?" Yvonne murmurs.

"Now we wait," Sascia replies calmly, as if she's not about to pop out of her skin with excitement. A hunger is gnawing at her insides, a longing for what is about to happen next. This intermediacy is killing her; she wants the line to tug sooner, the lights to go out faster, she wants darkness and beasts and *magic*.

"So," she asks Yvonne, "where were you?"

"When?" Yvonne's eyes, focused on the manhole, have gone big and glassy, and with the floodlights washing her in white, she is pure doe before the inevitable hit-and-run.

"May second."

"First Contact?"

"I've never met anyone who doesn't remember the precise moment."

"Hard to forget, isn't it?" The girl pulls her braids over one shoulder. "I remember walking into the living room, the TV playing at full volume, and seeing the Shanghai Darkdragon toppling skyscrapers in downtown Shanghai. I thought my parents had put on a movie. Then I noticed the news title. Heard Angela Herrera's voice, you know, *the gates of Hell have opened* and all that. I remember the screen going white when the air strike hit." Yvonne shudders. "Mom thrust a phone into my hands, told me to try my aunt, who lived in Shanghai at the time. But the lines were down and we didn't get through."

Yvonne stops there, and a stab of guilt courses through Sascia: Has she picked the scab on an old wound? It's a dangerous question, what happened on May 2. First Contact: when the very first Darkbeast, the hundred-foot-tall Darkdragon, tore out of the Dark and through the Xintiandi neighborhood in downtown Shanghai, shattering nearly a mile's worth of populated area and killing thousands.

But more than that, May 2 was the day humans became brutally and irrecoverably aware they weren't *alone*.

It's a dangerous question, but Sascia has yet to meet someone who doesn't want to share. The terror of that day, of the narrow confines of your world blowing up around you, however violent the explosion, however unhealed your wounds—it's a collective memory. Sascia has found that in these moments where they watch the ink-black swirl of the Dark, remembering the violent assault of the otherworldly on their lives, she and her clients find a sense of camaraderie. They all lived this, and there's a comforting togetherness in their struggle.

"Is your aunt all right?" Sascia asks.

Yvonne nods. "She was visiting her friend on the outskirts of the city. She contacted us when the power came back on, two days later—*oh*!"

The fishing rod is vibrating. Yvonne's fingers go white around its handle.

"Sascia! It's biting!"

A laugh escapes Sascia's lips. Here is the plunge part of the roller coaster: fear turning into exhilaration. She sets the gun's blast mode to maximum lumen, then carefully opens the empty collection cups, depositing one on her side and one on Yvonne's.

"I'm turning off the nova-lights now, okay? It's going to get very dark, but don't be fazed. Start pulling up the line and enjoy the spectacle. I'll handle the rest."

At Yvonne's soft "Okay," Sascia kills the lights. Shadows shroud the alley. Without the heat of the lights, the drop in temperature is startling, but Sascia likes it that way—it makes her fishing tours even more of an experience. In the manhole, the Dark is thickening, with a rippling liquid quality. The fishing reel starts gyrating quickly—newbies always spin too fast, but it doesn't matter. Darkfireflies are not fish; they'll come up no matter how suspiciously speedily their food is trying to escape them.

Then, abruptly, Yvonne's frantic reeling stops. "Oh wow."

Darkfireflies are swirling up the long column of the manhole. They're tiny things, their scaled bodies translucent, their wings crystalline. They fly in a murmuration, pirouetting in a synchronized spiral. Magnificent colors flow through them like a wave, blues and purples and soft whites that pulse with a bright interior force, more vivid than any natural phenomenon on Earth. It looks like the aurora borealis on drugs, distilled into a three-foot-wide hole in the ground.

"Go for it," Sascia tells the girl.

No further clarification is needed. Yvonne grabs the plastic cup and leans forward, taking a scoop from the surface of the hole. A dozen Darkfireflies are instantly swept into the plastic, and she screws the top on quickly. The kaleidoscope of light reflects in her irises.

Sascia watches her, utterly entranced.

It's not about the money, as her parents think. Not about the thrill of being the expert, as Danny teases. Sascia craves this, precisely *this*: a stranger's awe, a stranger's fear before the impossibility of a darkness filled with monsters. She wants to pluck a straw and drink up all of the girl's terror and wonder, wonder and terror, slurp, slurp, slurp, brain freeze be damned.

She wants to feel, even for a brief, lying second, what it felt like to stand in front of the Dark for the first time.

(Pass by it on the street enough times and even magic becomes mundane, Danny says.)

(But this should not ever be mundane, Sascia argues. *I mean, look at it.*)

From the corner of her eye, Sascia notices a ripple on the surface of the Dark. The lights have been off a little too long. She moves fast, single-mindedly: dives her hands into the surface of the Dark, the cup in one hand, its top in the other. She always grabs a sample of whatever her clients fish that day, for her own research. She's mid-scoop, her hands as deep into the Dark as she dares to go, when she feels it—

Fingers caress the back of her left hand. Sascia moves away, but the fingers close around her wrist. Panic drops like a stone in the pit of her stomach. She jerks her hand out of the Dark—the fingers come up with it. She can see them properly now, irrefutably: long, blue-gray fingers with pointed black nails. There's even a thumb, nestled into the grooves of Sascia's palm. The sensation is jolting, alarmingly familiar, horribly displaced.

A hand.

2

THE KEY WORD

Terror grips Sascia, instinct takes the reins. Her free hand drops the cup and fumbles around for the nova-gun. She doesn't fully register it's in her hand, that her finger is on the trigger, that she's firing a blazing hundred-thousand-lumen shot into the sewer, until her eyesight is bombarded with white.

The gray-blue porcelain skin of the hand blisters; between one blink and the next, it has retreated into the sewer. The few Darkfireflies buzzing at the top of the manhole make a frizzling sound, their lifeless bodies dropping unceremoniously back into the Dark.

Yvonne is splayed on the waterproof canvas, an arm over her face. "A little warning before trying to blind me?"

Sascia knows she's shaking, knows she looks completely unprofessional, but she can't pull herself together. "Sorry," she stutters, "something crawled out—"

"Yeah, I saw. Those long, pale tentacles . . . even I can recognize a Darksquid!"

Long, pale tentacles. Darksquid.

Sure, that could be it. But Sascia has faced Darksquids before in her fishing tours. She's seen their long tentacles up close, the pale gray of their boneless flesh. The Darksquids she's seen—they don't have knuckles. They don't have *thumbs*.

Dexterous opposable thumbs mean working with tools, foraging, skinning prey. Thumbs mean bigger brains and intelligent—no, *sapient*—life. But there's no sapient life in the Dark, no creatures as intelligent as humans. Studies are definitive: the DNA of Darkcreatures is not evolved enough for sapience. In modern terms, the world where the Dark comes from is still in its Mesozoic era—think dinosaurs and giant sharks, weird-looking bugs. *Not* humans, not for millions of years.

Holy hell.

Sascia is already dialing Danny's number. She tucks her phone between her cheek and her shoulder as she darts about, dragging the cover back, dismantling the fishing rod, and throwing the rest of her gear in her backpack.

"Pick up, pick up," she mutters under her breath. The rings are slow, sluggish—by comparison, her heart is running at twenty miles per hour.

"Thanks for everything," Yvonne says, matching Sascia's hurried strides to the mouth of the alley.

"You're welcome," Sascia says with barely a glance at the girl—and the cup of iridescent (and very illegal) fireflies clutched tight in her hands. God. Is the girl *trying* to induce a heart attack?

"Yvonne. You can't be gallivanting around with your *poached* Darkfireflies—and certainly not in broad daylight. Hold on." Sascia rummages through her backpack for a felt covering and a small plastic bag of pollen. "Feed them daily. Only take the covering off when the lights are out. When you grow bored of them—"

Yvonne's mouth scrunches.

"That's not an insult," Sascia says matter-of-factly. "You'll get bored eventually—everyone does. Take the lid off, put the cup in a drawer or a closet, and the little guys will just fly back into the Dark. Don't mess with them or hurt them. The Dark will remember and next time it has a chance, it won't send tiny pretty Darkfireflies for you."

Yvonne's brows shoot up, but she nods dutifully. "Sure thing. Listen—"

But Sascia's very much not listening, because Danny has finally picked up.

Her cousin snickers in her ear. "Done terrorizing the impressionable youth?"

She glances at Yvonne, who's still watching her expectantly, and marches around the corner of the alley. Quietly, she hisses, "Please tell me you're at the Umbra."

"No, I'm not spending my Friday night doing *homework*, Sascia. I left a couple of hours ago. Invited Tae for a bite to eat, but I don't think he even heard me."

"Oh, he heard you. Your crush is just an asshole, Danny. Listen, something happened."

Danny makes a *go-on* sound.

"I took a client fishing at the spot at Hell's Kitchen and something strange came out of the Dark. The impressionable youth thinks it was a Darksquid, but I was much closer and it looked like"—Sascia exhales—"a hand."

"A hand," Danny repeats.

"Fingers. With a thumb."

Silence on the other end of the phone. Then, a dead-toned "Sascia, are you messing with me?"

Sascia looks up at the brick and glass of the New York skyline, because suddenly she feels like sobbing. "I really wish I was."

But his reaction is heartening. Of course he doesn't believe her. Of course it's absurd. There are no humanoids in the Darkworld. The research is definitive, a fact that Danny knows far better than she does; he's majoring in xenoscience, after all. It's absurd and

Danny's going to laugh it off and everything will be normal again.

But he doesn't.

Instead, he says, "Hold on." She listens to the duet of his keyboard and mouse clicking. "There was a spike of Dark activity in that general area, timestamped 7:49. About two minutes ago. If the sensors picked it up, it was certainly larger than a Darksquid, but we won't know without a sonar reading. You've got yours with you?"

A whimpering "N-no" leaves Sascia's lips.

"Sascia, you've got to carry one with you at all times when you're fishing."

"But it agitates Darkcreatures."

"But it keeps *people* safe, which is the important bit. How close are you to the Umbra? I've got a spare in my lab."

Please, no. Only two people ever stay late at the Umbra Program labs on Friday nights. One is her cousin's asshole crush. The other is someone Sascia *really* doesn't want to see right now—or ever, to be honest.

Her whisper comes out in a hopeless plea. "Don't send me there."

"Sascia," Danny says soothingly. "You've got to. We need to know whether you've finally lost your marbles, or you just made the greatest scientific discovery of the decade."

She feels like stomping her foot and throwing a tantrum. But this is how things work in science, even if you're as crappy at it as the Columbia admissions team thinks Sascia is. You notice an abnormality, you make a hypothesis, you observe and experiment, then it's inevitably debunked.

This is the key word here. *Debunk*.

"Fine," she tells Danny. "I'll call you when I'm back at the spot."

He hangs up and Sascia sits frozen for a moment, staring at the black screen. She's entirely forgotten Yvonne is still there until the girl pops around the corner of the alley and extends a hand with a crisp hundred-dollar bill. "Here you go."

"Oh, right. Thanks."

Yvonne smiles wide, still high on the thrill of danger, sated with bottling the threat into a little plastic cup. "This was fun! If people ask, I'll send them your way." She makes to leave but stops. "Hey, I forgot. What's *your* First Contact story? Everyone has one, right?"

"Right." Sascia breathes in, recalibrating. "Same as yours, pretty much. Angela Herrera on the TV, calling and texting everyone I love."

But that's a lie within a lie.

3

A LIE WITHIN A LIE

Sascia is nine.

She's in the woods behind her grandparents' home in suburban Queens. She's wearing her puffy pink coat over her black velvet dress with the scratchy collar. There's mud on her good shoes, which she knows is going to get her a scolding later, but for now, the snow is so fresh, the woods so quiet. She simply *needs* to see if there are fish in the frost-sleek pond.

She tests the ice first—she's a kid, but she's not a fool, she's watched enough movies. The ice holds, even when she shuffles forward on her hands and knees, toward the center of the pond where there's a clear patch that she can take a look through. There's no fish, dead or alive. Only darkness. Maybe if she fogs the ice with her breath and rubs it with her palm, it will clear, like the windows of her dad's car do. She exhales and reaches out.

That's when the ice cracks.

She hears the sound and then, between one moment and the next, she's inside.

The cold is instantaneous. Water is pushing against her lips, trying to worm its way up her nostrils. Her puffy coat is heavy, dragging her deeper. She kicks her feet, reaches out with leaden arms. But she can't see anything, can't tell which way is up.

She's scared now. The air in her lungs demands release. *Save me*, she begs. But there's only darkness around her, its silence a death sentence. *Save me!* she thinks again, pleading, reaching, grasping at empty water.

A muffled sound reverberates through the pond. There's a flicker of light; bright spots of color float around Sascia's vision, a dozen of them, a hundred, little bodies that flutter against her skin. A current of movement breaks the stillness. Hands grip Sascia's elbows, and then darkness gives way to light, and she is out, she is breathing, she is *saved*.

Next to her on the bank, a figure is heaving. They're drenched to the bone, their face hidden beneath a long hood, their black cloak lustrous as polished gemstone.

The cold becomes maddening. Her vision tunnels, her lungs struggle, her limbs feel like they're made of iron. She thinks the figure stands. She thinks they carry her to the edge of the woods. She thinks she hears them say, "Thanks for getting me all wet, you menace."

But Sascia can only see white now. She's shivering, so very, very cold.

Next thing she knows, she's in a fort of towels, in the back of her father's car, and then a hospital bed. Every inch of her skin burns. Mom is crying. Everyone's asking questions.

Even weeks later, people are still asking questions.

Figures clad in black are a common trauma-induced hallucination, the doctor tells her parents while Sascia sits between them in the small hospital office. *You said there was a recent death in the family?* Sascia remembers her black velvet dress with the scratchy collar. The frost on the ground as they lowered the coffin into the dirt. Her grandmother's funeral was the first time Sascia saw the figure, but there have since been others, always cloaked in shadows, always watching her from afar. No one believes Sascia when she insists the figure is real.

When she's twelve, she sits in that same house in suburban Queens, sandwiched between her younger sister and her cousin, watching footage of the Darkdragon ravaging Shanghai. It's horrifying, mesmerizing, but Sascia's attention snatches on its skin: scaled and lustrous, as though cut from the core of the blackest gemstone—just like the figure's cloak.

Sascia isn't a kid anymore. She's never been a fool. But she can't help but feel that the figure in the onyx cloak came from this new, strange place, what the media have dubbed the Dark. They came to save her because she is special. She is worthy. She is magic herself. She knows it in her bones: this is the truth.

It doesn't take long for life to disappoint her.

4

CASE IN POINT

The elevator doors ding open to reveal the Umbra Program facilities. Sascia takes a deep breath, a gladiator facing a lion-filled arena. Her eyes cut straight to the corner office. Light leaks beneath the door—which is closed, thank goodness. She glances at the nearest desk next, where a lanky figure is hunched over a laptop. Empty coffee mugs and energy drink cans flank the screen, the loyal sentinels of Tae-Suk Ho's battle against sleep.

The Umbra Program for Young Researchers is made up of six of the brightest minds of their generation, but even among them, Tae is a supernova. He's eighteen like Sascia, originally from Seoul but currently studying here in the US. Like the rest of the students of the Umbra cohort, he has an affinity for the Dark. His design for a nova-light net to confine Darkcreatures got him into the Umbra at just fourteen, and into MIT at sixteen, where he's been majoring in xenoscience engineering.

Sascia is decidedly *not* in the mood to feel inadequate merely by existing in Tae's orbit tonight, so she takes the long way to Danny's lab, along the edges of the open desk area and through the kitchen. Her feet are soundless on the rough moquette as she grabs the spare sonar from Danny's desk. She should leave just as unnoticed as she arrived, but she can't help herself.

She slips into her own lab room and closes the door behind her, quiet as a thief.

Her presence is—as always—an invitation for mayhem.

At once, wings begin buzzing. The entire wall opposite the door is covered in glass, where a shadowed garden of Darkflora lies, blooms and leaves and gangly spiked ivy with flesh as hard as chiseled stone. Atop the otherworldly vegetation, hundreds of winged creatures press together against the glass, quivering with excitement at Sascia's return. Their colors blink in bright swirls and dots: violet and sky blue and pure white.

"Well, hello there," Sascia whispers.

The Darkmoths pulsate in reply. The soft sounds of their bodies are a balm; Sascia's fretful thoughts quiet down. She eases the backpack from her shoulders and walks to the glass separating the nest from the room.

"I've only been gone a few hours," she coos at them. "You can't possibly have missed me already."

Their joy is contagious; Sascia's mood immediately turns playful. She steps to the left—across the glass, the moths follow. She steps to the right—the moths mimic her. She stands tall and crouches low, then abruptly twirls around herself. Colors bounce off the walls as the Darkmoths repeat Sascia's impromptu choreography.

A laugh bubbles through her throat. "I've missed you too. All right, let's see what you've been up to."

She slips behind the desk, powers on the computer, punches in her password, and clicks to the camera records. An image of the garden appears on the screen. In it, the Darkmoths are static, perched on their designated spots. She zooms into the Manhattan area, rewinds to 7:40, and lets the recording play through in fast-forward.

It's a map of New York, her and Danny's garden, made entirely of moths and flowers. Darkmoths are a rare breed, even among the many peculiarities of the Darkworld. For one, according to world databases, they have only ever appeared to Sascia (and by extension, Danny). For another, they appear to be intrinsically linked to their home. A moth collected from the northeast corner of Central Park, for example, will choose to rest on a Darkflora sample harvested from that very same corner—a sample that Sascia and Danny will then place on the Central Park location on their map. And, last but not least, Darkmoths show an awareness that transcends space and distance—if there's a disturbance in Central Park, where the moth is from, the moth in Sascia and Danny's garden will react.

Just as it does now—at the 7:49 time mark, the stillness on the screen breaks. Color blooms as a moth feverishly flaps its wings. Zooming in, Sascia studies the stripes of its body, the twirling veins of its forewings, the dots at the center of its hindwings. It's sitting exactly at West 53rd Street, collected from the very same sewer hole Sascia just took Yvonne fishing in.

This is not necessarily bad news. It doesn't mean anything beyond what she already knew: that there was something in the sewer, large enough to disturb the Darkflora around it—and in turn, the Darkmoth in her map—as it crossed from the Dark into the human world.

Sascia spins around in her chair. Her moths have settled down again, each in their little chosen spot. She stands and walks to the moth sitting over the alley in Hell's Kitchen. Its antennae are short and its body pulses with neon purple, marking the moth as male—at least currently.

The unusual qualities of Darkcreatures have perplexed scientists for years. One such puzzle is what's been dubbed the Darknomaly: the fact that Darkcreatures seem to live alongside their distant ancestors. Two moths pulled from the same pocket of Dark on the same day might show millennia of evolution between them, yet they live at the same time.

Another is they can change their sex.

Sascia has seen it happen with her own two eyes: one moment a moth might be a large, pale female with feathered antennae, the next it might be a smaller, soft-winged male, and the moment after that it might be long-bodied and of unknown sex. The color of the swirls and dots that adorn their hard flesh, uniquely individual like human fingerprints (called, unsurprisingly, Darkprints), indicates their current sex. For lack of further information, scientists have been applying human gender binaries: across all Darkcreatures, purple signifies what humans consider male, blue female, and white something outside the binary, but there are an additional half dozen gradients of these three whose meanings have yet to be deciphered.

In recent years, however, some theorists, including the Umbra Program's own budding anthrozoologist, Shivani Kaur, believe that there's an element of choice in Darkcreatures' shifts between sexes. They bring gender into the conversation—*The Dark is genderfluid on a molecular level*, Shivani likes to say. (Of course, the straight while males of the science world aren't keen to accept that, but when did that ever stop the queers of the world?)

A sharp knock announces a visitor mere seconds before the door opens and the light is flicked on. White washes over the room—immediately, her moths are aflutter. Thumps echo on the glass as the bugs fly around, startled and agitated.

"Hey! This is a no-light lab!" Sascia bursts out. She knows who the newcomer is, she knows she should be respectful, but she doesn't care. She sidesteps him and hits the light switch by his shoulder, sinking the room back into semidarkness.

"Miss Petrou," Professor Carr says in his low, emotionless tone. "That blackout glass was manufactured precisely to keep your moths safe from light sources. It cost this program a small fortune, so I suggest, once again, that you start putting it to use."

Sascia finally graces him with a look: his neatly shaved jaw, the gray at his temples, the well-tailored suit. She knows damn well how much the glass cost, because the miserable man likes to mention it every time he visits her lab.

That biting bitterness must jump-start something inside her because she snaps, "And once again, sir, I have to tell you my moths don't *like* it."

The professor doesn't immediately reply. Neon reflections catch on his glasses as his head tilts to examine her. "*Your* moths?"

Well, shit. She becomes suddenly aware of where she is: *his* elite program, *his* lab. *His* moths, if they want to get technical about it. (Or legal; her employee contract dictates that any work produced in the facilities lawfully belongs to the Umbra Program.)

Sascia has to fight that all-too-familiar urge to block her moths with her body, power down the entire room so that they can escape back into the Dark, away from Professor Carr's disapproving pucker. She tries to keep her voice laid-back. "Did you want something, sir?"

"I noticed you coming in," Carr says. "I know how averse you are to working overtime. It struck me as odd."

For a second, Sascia thinks about telling him the truth. His expertise on the Dark is unparalleled. As one of the founding members of Chapter XI, the international group that oversees the study and management of the Darkworld, he has both the tools and influence to properly explore the possibility of humanoids in the Dark. In mere hours, he could assemble a team of the best xenoscientists in the world, with military support to boot.

But his objective—*everyone*'s objective—would be a dead body. A safe, unthreatening body to dissect and analyze, and Sascia can't give them that. Not now, not ever.

So she lies, yet again. "I forgot my textbook, sir."

Deftly, she flips open the front pocket of her backpack, showing him the textbook she's been carrying since this morning's class.

His face is marbled stone. "Miss Petrou. Despite what you may believe, I have only ever tried to help you. I offered you a place in my program and secured you a spot at Columbia University. I have long believed you are capable of extraordinary things—*if* you put in the work. Remind me, what were the provisional requirements you had to meet to secure your spot?"

Sascia exhales slowly through her nose. "A 3.9 GPA and 1500 SAT score."

"And tell me, after nearly two years of knowing these requirements and supposedly actively trying to fulfill them, what were your scores last winter?"

"3.2 and 1320."

Professor Carr is statue-still, no blink, no nod, not even a satisfied smirk of his mouth, which Sascia finds maddening. If he looked and behaved like a villain, it'd be so much easier to convince people that he *is* a villain. Instead, he's this: her gracious mentor, her benefactor, the fairy godmother of her second chances.

"I won't remind you what's at stake here, Miss Petrou," he says. "I am certain you know. You're a clever girl, after all."

Well, he's done it. Sascia is fuming so hotly she's surprised her clenched teeth don't meld together. The sheer *audacity* of throwing this line back at her.

When Carr first invited her and Danny to join his elite cohort of teenage prodigies experimenting with the Dark, it had seemed like a dream come true. With the Umbra Program's state-of-the-art tech and boundless sources of information, Sascia and Danny could turn their map into a citywide alarm system that could surpass the accuracy of the army's best sensors. Except, they soon discovered, the moths only appeared to Sascia. Only obeyed Sascia. Without her, the alarm system simply didn't function, and no investor was going to fund a teenager with a dream. The Umbra's founders wanted *credibility*. And so Carr secured Danny a spot at Princeton to study botany and plant genetics and a spot at Columbia for Sascia, to major in entomology. Hand-picked by an Ivy League school before she'd even turned seventeen—Sascia's parents were elated.

Then Sascia, being the dud that she is, failed each and every term of her conditional acceptance.

Fresh out of the big *get-your-life-together* fight with her father, Sascia already had her speech prepared when she spoke to Professor Carr. She wanted a second chance. *I can do this*, she had promised Carr (and her father) (and herself). *I'm a clever girl, after all.*

And now here they are, facing each other again six months later, and those same words have come back to bite her in the ass. As if cleverness matters at all when the rest of the world has already decided you're a screw-up.

"Yes, I am," she bites out. Because she *is* smart. Case in point: not telling him about the possibility of the greatest discovery in xenoscience.

"Then, Miss Petrou, I suggest you start acting like it," he says. And with that final slap on the wrist, he slips out of the room.

5

A BEETLE AGAINST GLASS

Sascia calls Danny when she's back out in the streets. She doesn't mention her run-in with Carr or the tender mark his reprimand has left. She doesn't say much at all, really, and it doesn't matter—Danny is an expert filler of silence, one of the many things Sascia loves about him. He talks about his horrible botanical anatomy professor and the latest paper he has them writing, then launches into a word-by-word recital of the texts he exchanged with Tae last night on their shared project.

Trepidation swathes her body with every step toward 53rd Street. It's night proper now, and the skyscrapers have turned into looming behemoths of shadows. At the mouth of the alley, Sascia takes out her nova-gun, walking sideways with her back to the brick wall, like a cop in a TV show.

The alley looks just as she left it, secluded and quiet. The manhole lies still. Thank god she doesn't need to open it to run Danny's tests.

The tiny monitor of the sonar shows the cavernous insides of the sewer, the very top layer of the Dark before it plunges into depths that no human technology has been able to map yet. Gradients of green, yellow, and red mark the spots where Darkflora or Darkcreatures roam—but all small enough not to be a concern.

There's an imprint of something larger a bit farther down, in faded colors on the sonar. Whatever was in there has retreated.

"It sounds like nothing's down there, cuz," her cousin says with chirpy finality. "Come hang out with me. I'll order conciliatory pizza for you."

This is good. This is just what Sascia wanted. Her hypothesis debunked, the world returned to order. Why, then, does she feel just a tiny bit disappointed?

She breathes a laugh. "That actually sounds terrific."

"See you in a bit, nutjob."

After she hangs up, Sascia shoves the sonar into her bag and takes one last look at the manhole. *Bye-bye, creepy sewer*, she thinks. She has no intention of ever fishing in this spot again. She's going to eat pizza and play *Zelda* with Danny and erase this entire day from her memory.

She's almost to the mouth of the alley when she stops, a sigh on her lips.

She can't help it. She turns back.

Like a beetle, her dad had told her once. *You keep throwing yourself against the glass, again and again, instead of flying out the open window an inch to your right.*

He meant it as a warning, but Sascia had found herself surprisingly delighted by it. She really did identify. Beetles look like absolute fools, sure, but they don't give up. They might get concussed, but after a thousand launches against the unbreakable, they'll eventually find their way out. Sascia sees no shame in that.

She cocks her nova-gun and, with her free hand, removes the sewer cover in one smooth, swift movement. The Dark welcomes her, black and cold and odorless.

Is she really going to do this?

(Hell yeah) she is.

She plunges her hand in and keeps to the rim of the hole, fingers skimming over the petals and spiky leaves of the Darkflora in the sewer. At her touch, petals and leaves become rock-hard, the thorns elongate. They're merely testing her—most of the time, humans are not perceived as threats by the Darkworld flora. (The fauna, on the other hand, is a different story entirely.)

A small mouth nips affectionately at the tip of her index finger—a Darkmoth. Sascia could recognize a moth with her eyes closed. They have this specific way of approaching her, all velvet-soft wings and tingling antennae, a kind of gentle curiosity that no other creature of the Dark has at first contact.

"Hello, little friend. I didn't mean to intrude."

Concentric ripples shape the surface of the sewer as half a dozen moths burst out in a whirlwind of bright colors. Their wings tickle her cheeks and neck.

"All right, all right," she huffs around a smile, "calm yourselves—"

Her skin tingles. A different sense replaces the soft membrane of wings at her fingertips. It's smooth and hard and warm as skin.

In her head, her father warns, *A beetle against glass*.

Sascia moves fast: she snatches the creature's limb and pulls, bracing her legs against the grimy cement, nova-gun cocked and ready. Her arm breaks through the surface of the Dark and she *is* holding a hand, a proper hand with fingers and a thumb. A wrist follows, and an elbow. As Sascia hoists herself up, the creature follows, unveiling itself: shoulder and head, porcelain gray skin, long ears peeking through jet-black hair, striking violet eyes.

Vines and sharp-edged leaves are tangled in the creature's shaggy, shoulder-length locks. Neon-colored blossoms pepper the black-scaled suit of armor that covers its torso. Strong brows and cutting cheekbones frame an angular face. It's a wild, ravenous beauty, that of thunder cracking in bloated rain clouds or the ocean frothing in stormy rage.

On its cheekbones, swirls and dots shape a Darkprint unlike anything Sascia has seen before. The outline reminds her of a snowflake, all points and angles. Its color is a bright purple, presenting the creature as male, but Sascia wonders distantly, through the shock, how sentient creatures' Darkprints might reflect their gender. No one has had the opportunity to ask them before—she hesitates to call this creature a boy without confirmation.

"*You*," hisses the creature from the Dark.

Me? Sascia shivers at the vitriol in the creature's voice, but a small part of her is elated. *Yes, me. Me, me, me.*

"Who are you?" she whispers. "What do you want?"

"I am a prince of Itkalin, commander of the Queen's army, and lord of the Jagged Blade. But today, I am the one who will deliver your sentence."

Sascia stumbles back and falls on her ass, the gun forgotten in her palm, her mind reeling from the impossibility standing before her. There is a creature, *an undoubtedly humanoid creature*, who just came out of the Dark—no, whom Sascia just *pulled* out of the Dark. A prince, a commander, and a lord, who will deliver her sentence. He looks like a nymph from an art museum or a regal elf from a fantasy film, except a thousand times prettier than any chisel or CGI could conjure. In his hands, he holds a scythe made of razor-sharp black crystal.

"You have been judged for your actions in the Battle of Feathers," the elf prince says, "and you have been found guilty of treason. You die tonight."

And he swings the scythe at Sascia's throat.

6

YIELD

Sascia rolls away on instinct, and the scythe clashes on the street with a screech. It should break—if it was regular crystal, it would most definitely break—but instead it bounces off unharmed, chipping away a small piece of concrete. Sascia scrambles to her feet and makes a dash for the mouth of the alley.

Behind her, she hears the swish of the scythe through the air, connecting with her bag. Holy hell, that was close. She only now remembers the nova-gun in her hand—not much of a clever girl, after all. She aims the gun over her shoulder, shuts her eyes, and fires. Her lids blast white from the shot, and a snarl follows a few seconds later. The creature is still in the middle of the alley, an arm up to protect himself. The flesh of his wrist sizzles charred and ashen from the power of the nova-light. Petals rain down from his armor, fluttering to the ground in scorched bits, but otherwise, he is wholly intact.

For a moment, their gazes meet: Sascia's wide with terror, the creature's narrowed into threatening slits.

"I tried to tell you in every way I could," he hisses, lowering his singed hand from his face, "darkness and light can only ever be enemies."

His arm swings back for another strike of his scythe. Sascia abandons all reason and succumbs to pure animal instinct—she *bolts*.

Her boots stomp the street, her body bumps against the parked cars and trash cans strewn along 53rd Street. She looks frantically around the empty neighborhood. Damn her impeccable research and damn this perfectly secluded fishing spot! She needs people right now, a hundred people with a hundred nova-guns, but there's no one and nothing around that could help her.

The boy from the Dark is in pursuit and gaining on her—she catches glimpses of his neon purple Darkprints reflecting on the windows of the cars she sprints past. She fires two more blasts without turning or breaking her run. But his footfalls still follow, still so damned close.

When she rounds the corner, familiar landmarks flash past her: the deli where she sometimes stops for a slice of chocolate cake, the ramp one of her clients locked their bike on, and that—isn't that frenzy of pixels the Times Square Tower? She's just come out to Seventh Avenue, which means Times Square is just a few streets away. There will be people there, lots of them, and sufficient light to perhaps at least slow the creature down.

Too late, she senses a shift in the air, a whoosh of movement. She dashes left at the last moment—the scythe grazes her shoulder instead of her head. Her flesh stings, blood slicking down her arm. Her lungs are laboring now, her thighs burning, but she bursts into a final gallop, because salvation is right there in front of her.

Times Square is—blessedly, thankfully—a pandemonium.

The famous red steps are full of tourists snapping pictures, with more loitering at the bottom for their turn. People are queuing before food stands, or browsing shop windows, or crowding around street performers. There must be hundreds, if not thousands—

But *none* of them is really paying her any attention, because this is the living, beating heart of New York and no one bats an eye at a girl running from an elf wielding a crystal scythe. It's Times Square: the place is a cosplayer mecca!

She needs to figure something out, fast.

A glance back shows her the prince is slowing, forced to zigzag between tourists. He's not hurting any of them, has in fact tucked his scythe close to his body so that the sharp curved blade is towering above everyone's heads. His eyes are locked on Sascia, shadowing her every turn and shift. He really wants Sascia dead, her specifically, for some unfathomable reason she does not have the presence of mind to go into right now.

But she can use this. If he isn't intent on hurting anyone else, maybe that's how Sascia can stop him. There's an NYPD precinct at the other end of the square, with cops always posted around it. If she evades him long enough to get there, they'll help. Her nova-gun barely slowed him, but what about those nova-rifles police carry? Or regular guns with regular bullets?

It's worth a try. She faces forward again—

And runs straight into a guy in a Mickey Mouse costume. They tumble head over heels, taking down the kids he was getting photographed with in the process. The nova-gun flies out of her hand, disappearing among the feet of the passersby.

"Watch it, lady!" the guy trills.

Parents are dragging their kids away, the Mickey Mouse guy is rolling in his costume, trying to pull himself upright, and Sascia is sprawled in the middle of the street.

The boy from the Dark has stopped a few feet away. People are giving him a wide berth. He looks down at Sascia, slumped on the ground like a limp doll.

"There's no point in running." His voice is bone-chilling ice. *"Yield."*

Like hell Sascia's going to yield.

His scythe comes for her—Sascia sends a silent prayer to the Dr. Martens manufacturers and kicks the heel of her boot at its blade. By whatever miracle, the thick plastic of her sole proves a match for the crystal of the scythe. The blade jams into the boot and Sascia uses the creature's momentary confusion to kick his wrist with her other foot. The scythe dislodges from her sole and flies from his grip. Sascia twists to her stomach and scrambles over Mickey Mouse guy's limbs in the direction she saw her nova-gun slide—it's there, thank god, among the shifting feet of the onlookers gathered around them.

She lunges for it, just as the creature's hand clamps around her ankle. Concrete bores into the soft skin of her palms as he drags her toward him and retrieves his scythe in one smooth move. Sascia clenches her teeth, mind pulsing with adrenaline. In a burst of energy, she snaps up the nova-gun and flips to her back, facing him.

They come to a stalemate. Him, with the scythe inches from her neck. Her, with the nova-gun aimed square at his face—from this close a distance and set at maximum lumen, she could do some real damage, and it looks like he knows it.

Strangled cries ebb and flow around them. The crowd is backing up, no longer entertained by their fight. Nothing stands between the Darkcreature and Sascia now. Death is only inches away, at the tip of a scythe made of the blackest onyx.

She should pull the trigger; guns are fast, unavoidable. There's a good chance the blast will hit him before he has the sense to push his blade into Sascia's skin.

Yet she hesitates.

Her mind reels like the gyrating lights of a police car. Red for fear and panic and self-preservation. Blue for awe and wonder and beauty—here is a person she pulled out of the Dark, an elf from a fantasy film, a nymph out of a heartland forest. How can Sascia hurt him? She who has loved the Dark all her life—how can she be the one to harm it?

Her index finger lifts from the trigger. Her arm goes slack; the nova-gun drops. In her periphery, she can see the crowd's reaction, hear their cries of panic—but she only has eyes for the prince.

The lines on his brow unravel, loathing giving way to confusion. A muscle flexes at his jaw, disfigured by a long scar that starts at his ear and disappears into his collar.

A hissed question tears out of him. "Why won't you strike?"

The column of the scythe trembles. He steps forward. His blade hovers over her skin, the promise of blood thick in the air. Shrieks erupt around them—Sascia's screwed.

For the sake of wonder and beauty, she is absolutely screwed.

Then someone yells, "Freeze!"

Someone yells, "Drop your weapon!"

Cops break through the crowd, handguns and semiautomatic nova-rifles all aimed at the creature. They form a wall, closing in on him, and within moments, Sascia is behind it, sheltered, safe. Someone hauls her up by the armpits. She flips her hood over her head, trying to disappear into herself.

"Part!" the creature demands of the crowd. "I have no quarrel with you."

The cops bark frantic orders in reply.

Sascia senses what's going to happen. The crowd withdraws in dread, Sascia strung like a puppet among them, and the cop on the farthest left shouts a command, spit spraying from his mouth. He shoots first. The other officers follow. Gunshots split the air.

The creature straightens his back and flexes his fingers.

All around him, the shadows between the paved stones, the black around the giant screens, the darkness beneath every car and taxi, every foot and stroller, down every alley and side street—in the space between seconds, it all streams toward him, pooling around his feet, rising in front of his body.

He has called forth the Dark, as though it is his to command, his to wield. It coalesces before him, shadow shifting into solid black, a thick, shiny wall of it—the bullets ring against it and are instantly swallowed into its depths.

The creature steps through the wall of black, shadows clinging to him like a pet cloud. Moths flitter around his face. His chin is tucked into his chest, his eyes dangerous slits beneath his brow. *He's beautiful*, Sascia finds herself thinking. Skin hard and smooth as porcelain, hair like streaming onyx, face sculpted in the image of an ancient god. He is power and danger and *magic*.

Hurried movements and sharp orders draw Sascia's attention. A young cop at the very back is hunched over a casket, assembling a weapon. Long snout, wide barrel, 500,000-lumen strong. A Dark-killer, military grade.

"Shield your eyes!" the young cop warns the crowd.

Stop, Sascia thinks. *You'll kill him.*

The machine gun shoots a missile of nova-light at the creature's chest. The stream of white is nearly a foot wide—nothing made of Dark can survive this kind of blast.

But the creature acts fast. He wraps the Dark like a cocoon around him. When the blast hits it, there's a deafening crack that makes Sascia's ears pop.

Every jumbotron, streetlight, and car headlight in the square dies instantly, as though the collision of the blast against the prince's cocoon was an electromagnetic pulse. The square descends into darkness, broken only by the flaming red of the grills in the hot-dog stands.

Sascia looks around frantically. There is nothing where the Darkcreature's charred corpse should be, nor anywhere else on the square. Against her instincts, against all reason, Sascia *hopes*—that he's alive. That he escaped.

The crowd gawks, equally perplexed, but Sascia has regained some of her senses. She is the girl who pulled a humanoid monster out of the Dark, then was chased through Times Square by him. This could go sideways for her very, very fast. Life might have just proven she's not as clever as she thinks, but at least she's still quick.

She slips through the crowd before the cops even think to turn their attention to her. She tugs her hood lower over her face and hurries down Seventh Avenue while sirens blare past her.

She takes the long way home.

SASCIA LOCKS THE DOOR of her bedroom and slides to the floor. For a few moments, she closes her eyes and breathes, counting her inhales and exhales.

Then, out of nowhere, something buzzes in her ear.

A panicked cry leaps out of her. Her hand shoots to the folds of her hood. Velvet wings meet her fingertips; cupping the thing in her palm, she raises it to eye level.

It's a moth, bigger than the ones she's been studying in her garden. Its forewings shimmer with a white Darkprint. A fringe of hair curves over its eyes and its antennae are long, oval, and feathered, their tiny touch tickling the soft pad of Sascia's palm. Where the hell did it come from?

Sascia's pocket vibrates—startled, the moth shoots toward a patch of shadow beneath her desk and disappears back into the Dark.

It's a text from Danny: Where are you?

Then: There's some insane news all over the internet.

Then: Tell me that's not you, along with a link to a video of a guy holding a Mickey Mouse head under his arm, describing the anonymous person who collided with him while being chased by a scythe-wielding humanoid monster that could control the Dark.

Sascia doesn't text back.

It's me seems too irreverent an answer.

7

SUGAR WATER

Sascia is twelve, sprawled on a straw beach mat with Danny and her little sister, Ksenya.

The world is painted in bright tones: the sun is too yellow, the sand shimmering gold, the sea bright blue, the pines that cluster over the cliff glistening like emeralds. Danny's reading the latest news off his phone. The United Nations Security Council has created a Darkworld initiative, Chapter XI—"chapter eleven," they have to explain to Ksenya, who doesn't know Roman numerals—named for the eleventh major world extinction scenario: the Shanghai Darkdragon attack. (The obvious question is *why didn't they tell us about the other ten?* But the answer is equally obvious. If the post-Shanghai Dark Panic is any indicator—the market collapse, the immigration waves, the exorbitant air ticket prices—people can't handle near-apocalyptic events with a clear mind.) Boqin Shen, the xenoscientist who discovered nova-light wavelength and built the nova-bombs that took the monster down, has been named the Chapter's director.

Sascia, Ksenya, and Danny were shipped to Greece as soon as international flights were running again after May 2. Yaya Vasso, her dad's mom, insisted on hosting Danny too, as she does whenever they visit. Greece in the summertime is the safest place there can be: daylight for more than fourteen hours, nights in their extremely well-lit beach house. But it's been almost six weeks now, and Sascia is bored.

She suggests swimming to the caves on the cliffside, but neither Danny nor Ksenya want to join her, so she ventures out alone. The sea is tranquil smooth, the cold water refreshing on her skin. It's dark inside the caves, which would make Yaya Vasso go absolutely feral if she knew, but Sascia finds it soothing. This is darkness like it used to be: unpleasant but not dangerous, ghostly but not filled with monsters. Sascia waits for her eyes to adjust, all prickled skin and hair sticky with salt.

She wonders if they'll fly back in a few weeks to find life resuming as normal: homework, track practice, walking her sister to piano lessons, helping her mom prep food for their family's restaurant. She wonders about the Darkdragon and its lustrous, rigid scales—black gemstone made flesh. If only she could touch them, she thinks, she would be able to tell if it was the same material, the same *skin*, as the cloak of the figure that saved her all those years ago and that she's been seeing ever since.

In the cave, the rocks are jagged, digging into her heels. She doesn't notice how much darker it's gotten. (There's bright yellow at her back, the lurid Greek sun—how can you feel fear with summer guarding your back?) Her foot meets a puddle and goes in, and in, *and in*, far deeper than any rock crevice has a right to be. The puddle is pure black, its surface thick like tar, its substance light as air.

This is not normal darkness. This is more. This is the Dark.

She should go back, should tell her Yaya, should alert the local precinct. Instead, Sascia squats before the puddle and sticks her fingers in. It's a dare to herself, a claim to bravery, and her heart hammers against her ribs.

She expects to find lichen and rock, but instead her fingers skim something velvet and fleeting. A twist of her fingers cups it in her palm. A Darkbug—similar to regular bugs, but with a touch of magic: bioluminescent veins ricochet across its flesh, blue as the sky.

She walks toward the mouth of the cave to examine it in the sunlight, but the bug—a moth, her *first* moth—tears fast across her palm and up her forearm, which is still in shadow. The edges of its wings whiten like ashen wood.

Sascia cups the moth in her palms, shielding it against her chest, in the darkness of her own flesh.

DANNY SWIMS OUT TO the cave with her the next day. They don't tell Ksenya—her sister is two years younger and finds the Dark far more terrifying than awe-inspiring. Danny, however, is appropriately amazed. They place the moth in one of Yaya Vasso's Tupperware containers; in their tiny bathroom, they hang towels over the windows and stuff them under the door, then switch the light off. The moth reflects neon blue on the tiled walls as it skitters about.

Danny uploads photos of it to a forum. Darkness is awakening, all over the world. There are sightings of flora, of tiny bugs and lizards. A (supposed) biologist from Istanbul advises them to return the moth to where they found it: it needs its sustenance and nutrients, whatever they may be. In that stuffy food container, it's going to die.

That upsets Sascia; for three days, she tries feeding it sugar water and every other bug meal she can unearth on the internet, but nothing seems to work. Her moth moves less and less, its wings sad and drooping. Danny isn't as concerned. The photos have made him somewhat of a celebrity among the local kids. Alone, Sascia returns the moth to its puddle in the cave, where it seems to instantly grow stronger.

One day, Danny invites their new friends to the cave. They pass the moth around like a holy item. Later that night, they light a bonfire on the beach, where Sascia meets Penelopi, the prettiest girl she's ever seen. They dare each other to take a vomitous sip of Penelopi's father's strong tsipouro and wiggle their toes in the sand and kiss. It's Sascia's first kiss; she feels euphoric.

The next morning, she swims to the cave. Its mouth has been sealed with concrete, the gray paste growing like a cancerous mass from the dark stone and green moss. One of the kids tattled to their parents. It's all right, Danny says. They held the moth in their hands and got pictures and now when they visit, they'll have friends here—that's all that matters.

For the rest of the summer, Sascia hangs out with the group and learns scandalous Greek swear words and kisses Penelopi and breaks up with Penelopi and kisses Andreas instead. At night after bedtime, she pulls out the Tupperware from her drawer and holds it up to the light. At certain angles, she can see the neon streaks the moth left on its walls.

A week before they're meant to fly home in late August, they wake up to footage of a giant Darkgriffin bursting out of a sinkhole in the middle of Manhattan.

They've already given the hole a name: the Maw.

8

WRONG PLACE, WRONG TIME

It's been a week since the elf prince exploded in a blast of Dark in the middle of Times Square and it is (understandably) all anyone's willing to talk about.

Danny leans on the armrest of his wheelchair, chin in hand. The blue of the screen reflects in his flat stare, bushy eyebrows squished together beneath a fringe of unruly curls. On the TV in front of him runs a montage of footage from the last week: increased military presence in high-risk areas, the launch of a new set of NovaCorp weapons, nova-bombs hurled daily into the major Darkholes of the world—even though no one really knows whether they actually work, because they're timed to detonate after they've disappeared into the Dark.

An old interview by Director Shen of Chapter XI has resurfaced, where he was asked about the possibility of sapient life in the Dark. At the time, his calm, considered reply had been *Peaceful coexistence would be our top priority,* which is not sitting right with the public now that sapient life has been revealed to wield a scythe and hunt a human through Times Square. People are marching in the streets, half of them in support of Shen's pacifist sentiment, half of them calling the attack a declaration of war. The round-cheeked newscaster drones on about eyewitness reports and expert testimonies, the Darkhumanoid's intentions and the Mystery Human's identity.

Danny's gaze drags to Sascia, where she sits on the floor beside him. He cranks up the volume and whispers, "Have you figured it out? What happened that day?"

"Is that really necessary?" Sascia gestures at the TV. "Our building is not wiretapped."

"Listen. It's a miracle your elf prince's weird blast took out all devices in a mile-wide radius. But just because your face is not on the news doesn't mean the authorities are not out there. Watching. Listening."

"It's been a week. If they knew I was the mystery human the elf prince was chasing through Times Square, the *authorities*"—she air-quotes the word to show Danny just how ridiculous he's being—"would have barged through the door by now."

Danny eyes the front door, barely visible among the mismatched furniture, piles of packages, and hanging racks between them and the hallway. (It's a cozy place, her family's apartment, but it is *not* tidy.) No one barges in. A blade of rheumy late-October dusk light cuts through the living room wall. The newscaster drones on.

"How can you be so calm about this?" Danny finally asks.

"Do I look calm? I don't feel calm."

Ever since the attack, she's been a paranoid, fidgeting ball of nerves. Every flicker of shadow is the elf prince, returning to deliver on his death threat. Every siren is Chapter XI, come to arrest her. Every buzz of her phone is a message from Carr, kicking her out of the Umbra, taking away her moths. Perhaps she's reached capacity with all that terror and now she's just numb.

She forces herself upright and steps to the hallway. "Come on. We have to get going."

"What I don't understand is *why*," Danny continues, wheeling himself after her. "The elf spoke English, right? Which means he's been in the human world before, long enough to learn the language. He's been here *undetected*. So why reveal himself now? Why let himself be seen by thousands of tourists? Why—well, you know."

Sascia has been shoving her arms through her jacket, but now she pauses mid-sleeve. She does know what he means, but neither of them says it out loud.

Why *her*?

(She thinks about that moment the prince stepped out of the Dark. *You*, he had hissed at her. *Yes, me*, she had thought. *Me, me, me*.)

"I've told you everything he said," Sascia says. Every word the elf prince spoke had been burned into her brain. "Apparently, I've been judged for my actions in the Battle of Feathers and found guilty of treason."

"But what's the Battle of Feathers? And treason for what?"

"I have no idea." She's been trying to puzzle it out for a week. "Maybe something I've done is a crime where he comes from. My research, my moths. Maybe even pulling him out of the Dark."

"So your theory is that this elf prince chose to very publicly announce the existence of his kind because, out of all the people in the world and all the potential reasons to be enraged, he needed to punish *you*."

Sascia bends over to slide her white Chucks on, her hair a curtain between them. She doesn't want Danny to see the disappointed pout on her face right now. It's not fair of him to phrase it like that.

"I'm not deluded," she bites out.

It's a loaded word for her: doctors used it, first when she claimed a figure in black saved her from drowning, then when she reported seeing the same figure throughout her childhood, always lurking in faraway shadows that no one else seemed to spot. Eventually, rumors of her "deluded" claims made their way to her school, at which point she stopped mentioning the figure's appearances entirely.

"*Ofcoursenotcuz*," Danny says in a worried rush, all too familiar with her sentiments on that particular word. "That's not what I meant at all. I'm only trying to say, have you considered the possibility that it might have just been a coincidence? A case of mistaken identity? Of wrong place, wrong time and all that?"

The answer is yes.

Of course she has. But the elf prince had looked at her and recognized her. He had spoken as if he knew her: *I tried to tell you in every way I could, darkness and light can only ever be enemies.* It doesn't feel like a coincidence or a mistake, even though it does chafe. Once upon a time, she had wished and wished to be chosen by the Dark—and now all clues point to the fact that she *has* been chosen, just as its enemy. (How narcissistic, she thinks, that the idea still sends a little thrill down her core.)

When Sascia straightens, she's rubbed the pout off her face and drawn on a smile, honest enough to reach her eyes. "You're right. I was probably just the first rando he happened upon. There's no way that even *I* could start a vendetta with elfkind without even realizing it, right?"

"Exactly." Tension drops off her cousin's shoulders.

"Should we go?" she says, eager to leave this conversation behind. "We'll be late for the meeting."

Professor Carr has called an emergency Umbra meeting, no doubt to discuss the pandemonium the existence of humanoids in the Dark has caused in xenoscience. The meeting is in an hour, which means she and Danny are already late; the 5:00 p.m. drive into Manhattan is brutal.

A few minutes later, the elevator whirs open on the ground floor—immediately, a desperate "Sascia! Is that you?" comes from the kitchen's back door.

"Don't," Danny warns.

But Sascia can't. "Yeah, Mom!"

Danny lets out a defeated groan and rolls his wheelchair to the ramp. "I'll start the car. Don't take too long, okay?"

The door on Sascia's right opens, revealing a messy restaurant kitchen. Her mother nails her a *stop-right-there-criminal-scum* look while her fingers keep furiously wrapping dolmadakia like it's Greek taverna doomsday. Her glasses are slick with condensation from the half dozen steaming pots around her. The whole place—damn, the whole *block*—smells Greek: dried oregano and sizzled garlic and fried fish.

Mikhail, the sous chef, glances up from his various chopping and stirring duties and gives Sascia a pleading smile, the meaning of which Sascia instantly interprets: her parents have overbooked the tables. *Again*. The familiarity of it all—the smells, the motions, her parents' inevitable blunders—eases some of Sascia's nerves. Here is a place she knows and belongs to, soothing in its simplicity.

Her mom nudges her head past the kitchen. "We need help with the table seating."

"Mom," Sascia says, "Danny is waiting in the car. We've got a meeting at the Umbra in an hour."

Her mother harrumphs. "What's that professor thinking, dragging you kids back into Manhattan during all this chaos? I thought we were still in lockdown."

"Lockdown lifted last night," Sascia explains. "And *this chaos* is actually what we're having a meeting about—"

"Sascia, the Umbra won't collapse if you're two minutes late. Go help your father."

Sascia stomps across the kitchen and into the main seating area, where the reservation book sits alone on the abandoned host stand by the entrance. As expected, it's a wild mess. They've got four parties arriving in fifteen minutes, none of which are assigned appropriate tables. Sascia crosses out names and overwrites others to figure out a better seating arrangement: the party of three at the table in the corner, the two families of four at the long table for ten (separated by bread baskets, free of charge), and the couple at the extra table on the veranda, which Sascia hurries to unfold and set a tablecloth on.

Her father spots her from across the packed yard and makes a beeline for her. "Smart!" he chirps over the noise. "I'll grab the silverware!"

Athena's Yard, her family's restaurant is called. Her great-grandparents arrived in New York from Pontus with barely enough cash to last a year, but they took one look at this corner apartment building and its disproportionately ginormous backyard and knew instantly that it would make an extraordinary investment: kitchen and indoor seating on the ground floor, tables in the beautiful yard, living quarters for the family on the second and third floors. And here Athena's Yard is, more than a hundred years later, having survived even the post-Maw recession six years ago that had every New Yorker abandoning ship for a smaller, safer town. Here the family still is; her grandparents moved to suburban Queens a couple of decades ago, and their daughters' families split the apartments between them, Sascia's on the second floor, Danny and his mother on the third.

When it's all ready, her dad pulls Sascia into a sweaty side-hug. "Oh, kardia mou. You're my savior."

A snort bubbles up Sascia's nose. "You're getting me all stinky."

"Stinky? *Me?* After a nine-hour shift at a Greek restaurant? Impossible." His arm sits comfortably on her shoulders as he marches her to the quieter corner of the host stand and thrusts his phone in her face. "Look at what Ksenya sent."

It's a picture of a lovely white beach with brilliantly blue waters, and Ksenya in her lime-green two-piece, smile wide, nose rosy with sunburn. Thanks to global warming, even October 31 equals summer in southern Greece, where Sascia's little sister has been staying with Yaya Vasso these past two years. Every other day, Sascia wakes up to a photo of the new beach that Ksenya and her friends drove to after school. She would be envious if she wasn't so goddamn relieved. Ksenya, sixteen now, is finally smiling, finally making friends, finally in a country without a single Darkbeast sighting ever.

"Next summer, we'll all go," her dad is saying. "It will be your Columbia enrollment gift. The four of us together again. Ksenya can take us to all her favorite beaches."

He's a carrot-and-stick kind of parent, her father.

One day, he's sitting you down at the sofa, getting increasingly frustrated by your evasive answers about your SAT scores and handing out ultimatums (see: *Get your life together, kid*) and the next, he's crushing you in a hug, laughter rumbling in his chest, praising your intelligence and gifting you vacations to Greece.

Sascia is used to it by now, but it is no less exhausting. "Sure, Baba. That sounds wonderful. Listen, Danny is waiting. I've got to go—"

"Yes, go, go." He claps her on the back. "All this studying, all this work. Don't think I haven't noticed."

And just like that, Sascia feels like shit.

Pure, nasty turd.

She's not sure when the shift happened, or how. But now this is who she is: a scammer. She cons her clients, manipulating their darkest curiosity for profit. She cons the professors of her remedial courses with half-hearted papers and minimum effort. She even cons her family, by pretending she has figured her stuff out. Pretending she's got a part-time job at a bookshop in Manhattan to make up for the Umbra stipend she lost when she failed to get into Columbia. Pretending she is over the shit in her past, grown out of her obsession with the Dark.

And now, apparently, she cons even herself, trying to convince herself she is not a coincidence or a mistake.

She sighs and heads for the door. There'll be time later to beat herself up over her lies—there always is.

9

THE STUFF OF FAIRY TALES

There's a clear-cut hierarchy in the Umbra Program. Case in point: the meeting room seating chart.

Professor Carr sits at the head of the table, a frown resting above his rimless glasses.

On his right sits Tae-Suk Ho, aforementioned supernova, sleep objector, and all-around kiss-ass. Tae is by far Carr's favorite (understandably so, loath as Sascia is to admit it). At just fourteen, Tae's tinkering with lumen technology resulted in the first-ever patent for mass production nova-light microtools, and two years later, Professor Carr invited him to the Umbra Program. (Danny also loves to rave about Tae's good looks: the long lashes and glossy dark hair, but being an insufferable know-it-all ruins all attractiveness for Sascia.)

On Carr's left sits twenty-year-old Andres Matthei, the Umbra's xenogeneticist. The only son of two geneticists from Santiago, Chile, Andres assisted his parents' team in hypothesizing the basis of what later became the Darknomaly theory—an attempt to explain the bizarre evolutionary anomalies of Darkcreatures. Andres is a six-foot-six giant with silver hoops in both ears, left eyebrow, and lower lip, the last of which he's currently spinning with his teeth.

Next to Tae sits Shivani Kaur, the newest addition to the Umbra, a seventeen-year-old aspiring anthrozoologist from New Delhi, India, who managed to domesticate a swarm of rodent Dark-creatures. Usually, Shivani is a dark academia girlie, all gray turtlenecks, plaid miniskirts, and woolen socks up to her thighs. Currently, however, she's in costume (Rogue from Δ X-Men), which Sascia finds delightful—who cares about very serious faculty meetings on life-altering Dark news when today is Halloween?

On Andres's other side sits a tablet, camera off but sound on as per usual. The furious *clickity-clack* of Crow's keyboard blends into the white noise of the city below the windows. Crow is the Umbra's resident jack-of-all-trades, from god-knows-where and majoring in god-knows-what. Sascia has never met Crow in person or seen her face, but she has deduced the girl is likely very young because of the memes she sends in the group chat.

"I'm sorry we're late, sir," Danny says, wheeling himself to an empty spot next to Shivani. If they weren't a devastating fifteen minutes late, Danny would be sitting in his proper place next to Tae, third in the unofficial Umbra ranking, but alas, Sascia's poor cousin is always doomed by association.

An emotionless noise leaves Carr's nose, completely closed to interpretation. Oh, he's in A Mood today, capital *A*, capital *M*, silent-treatment-style.

Sascia takes her seat. It's at the very bottom of the pecking order, of course, at the end of the table next to virtual Crow. Immediately, she slumps low in her chair, navigating her head behind Andres's bulky form and just out of Professor Carr's direct eyeline.

"Now that we're all here," Carr deadtones, "let us proceed with reassignments."

All five students perk up. In Carr-speak, reassignments mean new information has been released by the Chapter and their research is to shift focus accordingly.

"In light of recent events, Chapter XI is commandeering the expertise of all active xenoscientists in the world, including our program. Miss Crow, your new goal is to analyze the Darkhumanoid's power blast and produce a device that will nullify it or produce a counterattack—Mr. Ho, I believe the design of a nova-cannon you were working on last year will do nicely. Mr. Matthei, Miss Kaur, the Chapter was kind enough to provide a genetic sample of the Darkhumanoid, which you will use to further your preexisting research into Darkviruses' and Darkrats' behavioral patterns respectively, with a new focus on bioweapons. Mr. Jacobs, Miss Petrou, you will now focus on exploring the potential to subdue and trap Darkcreatures in a secure environment—the Chapter is particularly interested in utilizing the nova-light panels of your moth garden." Carr folds his hands over his lap. "I have been asked to urgently resume my own research on controlling the entry and exit of creatures through Darkholes. I will be heading to my facilities upstate tomorrow, but I expect daily reports on your progress from all of you."

The silence in the meeting room is frosted with dread.

Sascia looks at Danny, finding her own rising panic in his wide eyes. Down the table, Shivani is fidgeting with the sleeve of her costume, while Andres taps his fingernails on the glass table. Tae looks as though he's been run over by a horde of stampeding wildebeest.

When Sascia first signed on, she thought she was on the path to brilliance (and, let's be honest, redemption), but the facts quickly dispelled any naive fantasies about the Umbra. It is a privately funded research program, and as such, beholden to those private funders. The cohort's research has always been geared toward findings that can be translated into revenue for its funders: Nova-Corp, leading producer of nova-light products; Hyanzi, the world's largest energy company; LIHT, manufacturers of electronics.

But even so, their research has always been focused on defense. The protection of the human race. A painful, yet safe, coexistence with the Dark.

These reassignments—they are about attacking. *Destroying*.

It is Crow who finally breaks the silence, her voice breathy against her mic. "These sound quite . . . aggressive, sir."

"Public safety is and has always been the Chapter's priority, Miss Crow," Carr answers.

"They think the Darkhumanoid will come back?" Shivani asks.

"It is a possibility we must be ready for. The Chapter has instructed us to prepare for the worst. New austerity policies will become public in the next few weeks."

"*Prepare for the worst*," Andres muses, "doesn't sound like Director Shen. He was always pro-collaboration with potential Darkhumanoids."

"Shen"—the director is always just Shen to Professor Carr, seeing how they have a decades-long academic rivalry that culminated in the run for director of the Chapter six years ago—"has maintained his peace-advocating stance after the Times Square incident. World governments did not respond well to the idea of peacemaking with what they argue is a violent invader. A sapient creature that can bypass our sensors and counteract our nova-guns is an unparalleled enemy. Chapter XI is currently considering appointing a new director."

That produces a shocked gasp from every member of the Umbra cohort. Director Shen is the hero who discovered nova-light, brought down the Shanghai Darkdragon, and founded Chapter XI. Without him, there would be no humanity left to protect. To replace him would mean bringing an end to any possibility of a peaceful resolution.

Some part of Sascia knows she should be the first in the firing squad, eager to eliminate the prince who vowed to kill her only a week ago. But she couldn't fire the killing shot then, and she can't now. The Dark may be filled with clawed, many-toothed things, but it is not inherently evil. She will not treat it as such.

"The elf prince spoke English," she blurts.

Rather loud and rather forcefully, it seems, because suddenly all heads swivel to look at her. Danny coughs, sliding her a wide-eyed *what-are-you-doing?* look.

Cheeks flushing, Sascia quickly pivots, "I only mean that we could talk to him. We don't know what might have been his motive for attacking. It could all be a misunderstanding that we can solve simply by sitting down with him—"

"The *elf prince*," the professor cuts in before she can make her argument. "What's next, Miss Petrou? Should we wrap it up here and start looking into fairy tales and Irish ballads for clues instead?"

The urge to antagonize him is irresistible—Sascia says, "I think that's a great idea, actually."

The cohort lets out a collective groan.

"Oh, shut up," Sascia tells them. She's willing to take shit from Carr, but she sure as hell isn't taking shit from her friends. "We are all here at the Umbra because we found a way to *understand* the Dark. To communicate with it. Me with my moths, Danny with his Darkplants, Shivani with her Darkrats. Andres with his research on immunology and Tae and Crow with their Dark-controlling technology. Instead of preparing for the worst, I think we should pave the way for something better."

"Of course you do," Tae mutters under his breath.

Oh, little Mr. Kiss-Ass wants a piece of her fury? Sascia will gladly grant it. "Go ahead, Tae," she snaps. "Tell us again your wild theory that the Dark is biomatter nanotechnology far beyond our understanding, because *that* makes more sense than—"

She cuts herself short before she says something unscientific, and thus unforgivable.

But it's too late. Carr leans back in his chair and looks at her dead in the eye. "Please, Miss Petrou, go on. It makes more sense than what?"

Suddenly, there's a knot in her throat, making it hard to swallow. The table is quiet, eyes averted. Even Crow's constant typing has petered out. Danny shakes his head imperceptibly, but Sascia is well past saving now. Should she just say it? She's dug herself this far, might as well go for the full six feet, right?

"Magic," Sascia says, then adds a calm, "sir."

There it is. Out in the open.

Sascia's breathing comes a little too fast, too shallow, but there's an exhilaration coursing through her veins. After two years at the Umbra, two years of withstanding Carr's subtle criticisms on her methodology, she has finally said out loud the thought she's held on to like a prayer, a wish upon a star. *The Dark is magic.*

She is not the only one who thinks so. The Darkdragon was named as such because it so closely resembled the water dragons of Chinese mythology. The Darkgriffin looks just like its counterparts in Greek and Roman frescoes. Even smaller Darkfaunas bear a resemblance to creatures from human myth: Shivani's rodents look like Mushika, the rat mount of the god Ganesha, and one of Andres's studies is on a Darkbird that looks like the Alicanto of Chilean mythology. There's a rare type of root Darkplant that squeals when removed from the ground, just like the myth of the mandrake.

The leading theory is that the Dark has touched the human world before, millennia ago, giving seed to the legends that later became human mythologies, but there's no hard evidence. (Of course there's not, Sascia thinks—isn't that the very point of magic?)

Tae snorts. Andres busies himself with a paper. Crow switches her mic off. Danny is rubbing his temples. Sascia glances at Shivani, her last hope. Her humanistic, sociological outlook has so often placed her in opposition to Carr's more pragmatic methods—Sascia loves Shivani for it. But this time, even Shivani tucks her chin into her chest, without a single word of support.

Panic trills in Sascia's mind. It has begun to dawn on her: she went too far.

"All I'm saying," she adds quickly, backtracking as best she can, "is that we might benefit from a perspective that is less focused on defending and more on learning. Instead of how to harm him, perhaps we should be thinking of a way to interact with him. A way that's gentler, kinder, more understanding—"

"Gentleness and kindness, Miss Petrou, are as much the stuff of fairy tales as magic." There's a finality in Professor Carr's voice, a resolute end. The fluorescent lights overhead reflect on the lenses of his glasses, concealing his eyes. "I understand your hesitation. We are men of science, not warfare. We value exploration and discovery, not annihilation. But the forces above us have decided the preservation of our kind is more important than research. It pains me, too, but we have to abide."

The mood in the room shifts to grim capitulation. Even Sascia agrees with them: Carr can be a cold, unbendable bastard, but he has integrity. He is loyal—to science, to research, to results. Yet even he has to bow down to what world governments think is right. Just another tool in Chapter XI's arsenal, no better than

Sascia or Danny or any other scholar of the Dark in this room.

Sascia's rib cage corsets her breath, asphyxiatingly tight. This is not research any longer, not science and experiment. They have moved past the hypothetical to the hideously real.

This is war.

10

FAIRY SMUT

In between heatedly dissecting the ugly developments of the meeting and bouts of silent moping, the Umbra cohort find themselves in the crowd gathering at Seventh Avenue to watch the Village Halloween Parade.

Sascia is in a cheap corner-store cat mask, propped on her forehead so she can munch on candy. Already, she's feeling worlds better—nothing quite as soothing as conciliatory chocolate. By some intervention of fate, her friends have secured prime viewing real estate, just behind the metal safety barriers separating the public from the parade.

"It's decided," Danny says as he studies the other spectators. "People have lost all perspective."

"Why?" Tae asks, brows knitted. He's been the gloomiest of the lot, barely touching his Skittles, but he has never failed to jump to the bait of one of Danny's outrageous statements.

"Look at the crowd around us," Danny says. "There are at least five people here dressed in Darkhumanoid costumes."

Andres shakes his head. "How did they even manage to put together a costume? Times Square was *last week*."

"Darkmania has been the most profitable market in the last six years," Tae quotes dutifully. "My uncle in Korea says he's already had clients come in asking for skin treatments to mimic the 'Dark-humanoid gray.'"

"Dear god," Danny says with a side glance at Tae. The look drips with yearning—Sascia half expects his eyes to start pulsing hot-pink hearts like a cartoon. "Which costume's the best, do you think?"

"Not fair," Crow chirps; they have her on speakerphone. "I can't see what you're seeing."

"Here, I'll turn the camera on." Andres points his phone to a woman in an all-leather outfit and a knee-length black wig. "I think that one's the clear winner, right, Crow?"

"No, it's definitely them," Shivani says, nudging her head toward a couple in matching Renaissance fair costumes.

"I like that guy," Danny says. His choice is a six-foot-tall man who has daubed his skin blue-gray and sewn black ribbons on his sleeves—when he moves, the fabric comes alive in a facsimile of the elf's Dark-controlling powers. "Body paint? That's dedication. What's your pick, Tae?"

Tae does not look like he wants to be part of this discussion at all, eyes darting around the crowd as if it's a wild jungle. "That one, I guess? Their Darkprints are the most accurate."

Sascia drags her eyes to the person Tae picked. Their long hair is held away from their delicate face by black flower pins, their acrylic nails are carved like talons. Streaks of blue neon decorate their cheeks, in a pretty good imitation of Darkprint patterns.

Dang it. Even in a game he has no interest in, Tae still chose the clear winner.

"Sascia," Danny calls out. "You're the expert. Which one of us was closer?"

She nails him with a hard look. Does he even realize what he's just said? "How am *I* the expert?"

"Well, you know..." He trails off, as though it only just dawned on him. "Never mind."

"No, no," Sascia says, pulling on a wicked grin. "Please explain. What makes me the expert?"

It's his turn to narrow his eyes at her. The quirk of his lips seems to be saying: *Oh, it's going to be like that?* She can see the gears of his mind working; something juicy is about to come out of his mouth. "Well, all the stuff you've read."

"I read the same stuff the rest of the Umbra reads."

Danny takes a long, smug sip of his drink, holding her gaze over his straw. It's a look that can only mean trouble. He's got the perfect clapback and is just taking his sweet time delivering it.

"Go ahead," she says with a flourish of her hand.

"Well," he says, all mischievous mirth, "I doubt Tae here spends his nights reading *fairy smut* until four in the morn—hey!"

He rubs his shoulder where Sascia's smacked him, but he's already laughing. Soon, the two of them are roughhousing and snickering at each other while the rest of the cohort tries to avoid stray blows.

"Shiv," Andres says, leaning away from Sascia and Danny's tangle of limbs. "What do gender scholars think of the Darkhumanoid? It had a purple Darkprint, but should we really be calling it a him?"

In seconds, Sascia has extricated herself from Danny and is waiting for Shivani's reply, breath held. She's dying to talk about the elf, even in this roundabout way. In a world where you can change your sex and presumably, for sapient creatures, your gender with a mere thought, is one instance of maleness enough to gender the elf as male?

Shivani perks up, always eager to talk about her work. "Our

research has shown that Darkprints are fully controlled by neurological commands, kind of how chameleons and octopi might change their bodies. So yes, we believe that the Darkhumanoid was what *we* consider male during the attack. But that does not necessarily mean they are *always* male or that in their world, such gender binaries even exist."

Sascia notes the pronoun Shivani uses and asks, "You think of the elf as *they*?"

"While we're in their presence, I believe we should call the elf as they've identified themself through their Darkprint," she explains. "But now that they're not here to show their identity with their marks—and until we're told otherwise—I find it more appropriate to use a gender-neutral term."

Sascia nods. Considering what scientists know about the fluidity of sex and gender in the Darkworld, the elf might identify interchangeably as he or she or they, or he/they and she/they and he/she, or something else entirely.

"I can't believe there's a sapient creature in the Dark," Shivani says wistfully. "I have so many questions to ask them."

A murmur of assent comes from the entire cohort, but its hopefulness is short-lived.

"Do you think we'll ever get the chance?" Danny asks. "Considering the Chapter has bombarded every Darkhole with dozens of nova-bombs, likely destroying thousands of miles of Darkflora? Even the public is becoming violent—some of these hotheads are already arranging neighborhood patrols armed with military-grade nova-guns."

"But who benefits from that?" Shivani asks, jaw set. "Not us, and certainly not the Dark. Making ourselves their enemy is only going to get us all killed. We have to figure out what they want. What they can offer in return. There's bound to be something that unites us—that would be the first step in interspecies collaboration." She brandishes her phone. "I just got an alert for a peace rally next Sunday. I, for one, am going."

"What difference will a rally make? Our life's work is being turned into nova-cannons and weaponized viruses and nova-light traps. Our mentor doesn't have the power to stop them." Tae's whisper borders on a hiss. "It is so sad."

"It's not sad," Sascia counters. Her whole body is wound tight with anger. "Sad is for sudden loss, for unavoidable death. This is intentional violence, discussed and decided on. What it is, is *infuriating*. Even after six years, their first instinct is to destroy."

"Can you blame them?" Andres says coolly. "We're all still operating on a trauma response. We never stopped. Every year, there's a new and bigger threat: first the Shanghai Darkdragon, then the New York Darkgriffin, then the Rio Darkbasilisk, the Baltic Sea Darkkraken, every other major Darkhole in the world . . . now this elf prince. We don't know what they are, what they want. All we know is they attacked humans in Times Square with a scythe."

Resting his elbows on the metal safety barrier, he lights a cigarette, rounding his lips to puff out a perfect circle. To Sascia, Andres has always been a bit too cool for the Umbra; he's got the skills, wits, and charm to be in whichever institution he chooses and he hates New York with a passion, so Sascia can't fathom why he would have ended up at the Umbra.

"Look around you," Andres goes on. "These people have dressed like an elf for Halloween, but they also carry a nova-gun somewhere in their costume that they wouldn't hesitate to use. The Chapter knows this, the government knows this. The world can't handle the terror and violence of another Dark Panic. Don't get me wrong—as a xenoscientist, the existence of sapient life in the Dark is thrilling. But as a human living on this planet, I think that, ultimately, preparing for the worst is the only choice our world has."

Something bitter gathers in Sascia's stomach. If the world is eager to pull the trigger, then what is Sascia's place in it, she who had the chance to shoot and didn't? She thinks of her father's words: *a beetle against glass*. Of Carr's retort about being a clever girl: *start acting like it*. Is this her place? A brainless bug that doesn't know when to quit?

She has the sudden, all-consuming want to *be* someone. Someone worthy, someone important, someone with real power, even if that means she's doomed to die at the hands of an elf prince from the Dark for a crime she didn't commit.

In her pocket, a body presses into the grooves of her palm.

Soft wings tickle her skin. Sascia peers into her jacket. An oversized moth dithers its wings at her—the same one that appeared to her the night of the elf attack. How on earth did it find her again, here of all places?

Before she can blink, the moth shoots out of her palm. It buzzes between the costumed legs and shifting feet of the gathered crowd until it lands on the silken strands of a spectator's head.

The girl has long black hair down to her waist, threaded with vines and flowers in neon colors. Skintight leather covers her body, but wafts of the softest taffeta peek through at her high neckline and the cuffs of her long sleeves. Three daggers are strapped to her thigh, their blades gleaming dark as onyx. Her brows are lifted and her violet eyes are wide with wonder. She stares around, as if she finds the noise and squalor of the parade a pure marvel.

On her high cheekbones, swirls and dots of bright cobalt mark her skin. From afar, the markings look like the crystalline angles of a snowflake.

Sascia's breath hitches in her chest. She hisses a curt, "*Danny.*"

"What?" He follows her gaze to the girl. "Oh, yeah, that's a top-notch elf costume. Look at that hair!" He twists in his wheelchair and dons his most charming smile; before she can wrangle his obliviousness to silence, he calls out, "Excuse me, miss!"

The girl locks eyes with them.

"I'm sorry," Danny says, "is it Mx.? Sir?"

"Miss is fine," the girl replies, with a hint of an accent. The current of the crowd shifts, pushing her into their little group, between Shivani and Andres.

"Me and my cousin here," Danny says, "just wanted to tell you your costume is fantastic."

Sascia barely has time to drag her cat mask down over her head before those violet eyes fall on her, landing on her mouth, peeking out beneath the plastic. This close, Sascia can make out the details of the other girl's face. The Darkprints are the blue of a female, her features softer and younger, but Sascia remembers those eyes, those high cheekbones and full lips. Two small blossoms hang from her locks, right over her neck.

Sascia's chest is a stomping ground. Her breaths gallop in and out. Every instinct is screaming *DANGER!*, but her legs are rooted to the spot, her mind fuzzy with panic.

"Well, thank you," the girl says to Danny, voice lilted with embarrassment.

Not girl, Sascia's mind trills. Not human at all.

Elf.

Her elf.

11

ARIADNE

Sascia stands frozen as Danny and the cohort shuffle around to make room for the newcomer. Compliments on costumes are exchanged, candy is handed out, commentary given on the latest parade float—Sascia barely hears half of it.

Not two feet away stands the princess of Itkalin, commander of the Queen's army and lady of the Jagged Blade. The person sent to deliver Sascia's sentence for treason in the Battle of Feathers. She remembers the hatred in the elf's eyes that day, the slice of the scythe, the threat: *You die tonight.*

Gingerly, Sascia slips her phone from her pocket and sends a simple text to Danny: We need to leave. This girl is the elf prince.

The phone buzzes at Danny's lap, but he's too busy praising this part of the parade, where a team of Sailor Moons performs an intricate ribbon dance. Sascia bumps his elbow, motioning silently for him to check his phone.

An amused frown sits on his face as he texts back. She's just a foreign student with a really big Halloween budget. Chill.

Taking advantage of a sudden ruckus of music and cheering, Sascia leans close to Danny's ear and whispers, "I recognize her face. And her Darkprints."

"If she's the humanoid that vowed to kill you a week ago, why is she just chatting with us and applauding the paraders? Shouldn't she be trying to assassinate you?"

"Out in the open?" Sascia counters. "She's just biding her time, trying to trick me into a dark corner so she can finish her task. Or maybe she's here as a spy to, I don't know, infiltrate human society and find our weaknesses."

Danny cranes his neck to look at the elf. "Sure looks like she's on the right track."

The girl has raised a Sour Patch gummy to eye level and is examining the tiny green candy as though it is the strangest thing she has ever seen. To Sascia, that proves the girl is definitely *not* from this world, but at the same time calls into question the theory that she's an undercover agent hell-bent on toppling humanity. (James Bond would never spend *this* long chewing a piece of sour candy, would he?)

"Cuz," Danny says. "Take a deep breath. You're with us. You're safe. Enjoy the parade. Chat with your friends. Take a page from the pretty girl's book and eat some candy."

He really doesn't believe her. It's nothing new; Sascia has learned to deal with this kind of dismissal. To Danny—to everyone, really—she is the girl who spent nearly a decade imagining that a figure in black watched her from afar. But Sascia is not a child drowning in a dark pond any longer. She is not a middle schooler or a young teenager, collecting glimpses of a mysterious figure. Now she is old enough to know artifice from reality, and this person before her, with her flower-strewn hair and onyx-sharp daggers, is *very* real and *very* dangerous.

Just like that, Sascia has made her decision. Maneuvering her backpack to her front, she slips her nova-gun into the pocket of her jacket. She positions herself in the center of the group, with a strategic view of everyone's movements. Danny might be convinced the elf is just a girl in an elaborate costume, but Sascia knows better.

She knows to be afraid.

"Want some?" Shivani opens a bag of assorted chocolate mini candy, offering it first to Sascia, who's closest.

There's a murderous elf just inches away! Sascia screams in her head. *No, I don't want candy!* But she dons a polite smile and goes straight for a mini Twix, her favorite. "Thanks."

The elf studies her golden and white wrapper, then reaches into the bag to pick an identical one. She mimics Sascia's movements, tearing it open and plopping the chocolate bar into her mouth, then pauses midbite. Her face *melts* with pleasure. (A sweet tooth, this elf.)

"So," Shivani asks the elf, "is this your first time at the parade?"

"It is. A friend mentioned I would enjoy it. She said that today the kind souls of the dead walk the streets to return home, and the living dress in costumes and light bonfires to ward off evil spirits." The elf's accent is elegant, lilting the vowels and softening the *r*'s. She's still looking at the empty wrapper, as though it is a relic of a lost god. "I believe in neither kind souls nor evil spirits, but I do enjoy your people's stories."

Your people, Sascia notes. The elf is careful with her words, committed to her charade.

"Are you a student here?" Andres asks.

The elf shakes her head. "Just a visitor."

"And what do you think?" Danny says. "Of our glorious New York?"

A timid smile tugs at the girl's lips. Her eyes tilt to the night sky above. "It is big and loud and so . . . open."

Big and loud, Sascia can agree with, but open? It's a weird word to describe New York, or any metropolitan city, to be honest. The buildings are too tall, the streets too narrow, the space overhead packed with streetlights and signs and ads.

"Are *you* students?" the elf asks cautiously, as though the question might offend.

The cohort nods, but it's Danny who answers. "Yes, all of us. We actually study the Dark. That's why we just had to tell you your costume is amazing. It's so accurate."

At that, he gives Sascia a very pointed glance.

"Why the Dark?" the girl asks. "Out of all the wonders of this world, why that one?"

"I love nature," Danny says with a shrug, "even the dangerous kind."

"Same," says Shivani. "Discovering new creatures, and how we should treat them."

"It's all about genes to me," Andres says. "Those that have never been mapped before."

Tae speaks softly, "I like making tools. To handle the Dark."

A giant float breaks the flow of conversation. It is the usual pomp and circumstance: marching bands, dancing troupes, and stilt walkers in skeleton costumes saunter beneath an enormous puppet of a Darkdragon. Sequined with hundreds of hanging beads in dark colors, the puppet is a reclaimed, whimsical iteration of a Darkbeast. A dozen puppeteers work in unison to coordinate its steps and the soundless roaring of its jaws.

The elf's mouth opens, eyes alight with admiration.

Sascia's fingers tighten around the nova-gun. Could she be wrong? The girl acts just like any other tourist awed by the funfair of New York. A casual stroller who went all out on Halloween, got complimented on her outfit by a group of friends, and decided to hang around a little longer.

But the big moth burst out of the Dark and flew right to her. Sascia hasn't spotted it since it wove itself into the blooms in the girl's hair.

"You didn't answer," the girl says to Sascia. "Why you chose the Dark."

The two of them stand in silence, a small bubble of it, while the crowd chirps and shifts around them. Sascia can feel the girl's dark gaze on her; suddenly, the cat mask seems like a flimsy cover-up, the nova-gun a laughable weapon. If the girl is indeed the elf, she can blast a force of Dark that would annihilate the entire block. Which begs the question: Why doesn't she? Why is she looking at Sascia expectantly instead, as though her answer might be the most interesting thing she's ever heard?

The truth tumbles out of Sascia unbidden—"I love it."

"Why?"

Sascia's cheeks grow scorching hot. The question is intimate, the kind you only ask a friend. "I don't know. I find it interesting, I suppose, like my friends do."

"You want to discover it? Map it out, like your friend said?"

"*No.*" The word comes out hard. But for Sascia, studying the Dark has never been about explaining its mysteries. She merely wants to be part of it, in whatever way she can. "Humans think our lives are straightforward. A paved road from birth to school to jobs to family to death. But the Dark lies beyond that road. A complicated maze of experiences we never thought we'd have. I just want to walk through it. To explore instead of discover."

"Ah," the girl says, slow and nasal. "An Ariadne in love with the Labyrinth itself."

The comment startles Sascia into furious blinking. The Greek myth of Ariadne, the princess of Crete who helped Theseus navigate the Minotaur's perilous Labyrinth, sounds foreign on the elf's lips. Yet the metaphor is apt: a princess in love not with the hero, but with the unsolvable maze around her.

Sascia's mouth hangs open, half a dozen questions squabbling for attention in her mind. "How do *you* know about Ariadne?"

"I told you. I like your stories."

Never one for shyness (or hard logic, really), Sascia bursts out, "Have we met before?"

Dark eyes roam over Sascia's half-masked face. "I don't think so."

"Don't lie," Sascia hisses. "It was you in Times Square a week ago, wasn't it?"

A frown wedges between the elf's brows. "I have never been in this city before today."

There's no lie in her voice, no duplicity on her face: she doesn't know what Sascia is talking about. Sascia's nose starts burning, a warning of tears to come. She's done it again, hasn't she? Let her mind retreat to wild imaginings. Her fingers ease off the nova-gun. Her stomach tightens with shame. She looks at the ground, feeling the salty wetness sting the corners of her eyes.

A chorus of drums pulsates down the parade. As one, the spectators rush forward with claps and cheers.

The girl (just a girl) leans close to Sascia's ear. Wisps of her hair caress Sascia's skin. Her lips smell of chocolate and caramel, sweetness made flesh. She inhales, deeply, devouring Sascia's scent—accidentally, her lips graze the lobe of Sascia's ear.

"If we had met before," the girl whispers, "rest assured, little Ariadne: I would not forget you."

The air hitches in Sascia's throat. Her pulse speeds, spurred by a tremor deep in her belly.

"But let me remedy my misstep. I am Nugau." On the girl's lips, the word sounds like the mating call of a French bird: *Noo-GOH*. "And you are . . ."

"Sascia," she mumbles, a little breathlessly.

"Sascia," the girl repeats. "It is a pleasure to meet you."

As she leans away, her gaze travels over Sascia—until it flickers to something at her ear. Sascia can suddenly sense the tiny legs there, the soft velvet wings.

Nugau breathes a hushed, reverent hiss. *"Itka."*

Her hand reaches out, but Sascia is faster. She cups the moth and steps back, cradling it against her chest protectively.

Nugau's face slackens into confusion. "Why do *you* have one of the itka? How did *you* find a god of Itkalin?"

The word echoes in Sascia's head: *Itkalin, Itkalin, Itkalin.* She was right. It *is* her—the very princess of Itkalin.

"A *what*?" Danny mutters. He spins the wheels of his chair to face them.

("What's happening?" Crow's voice chirps from the phone.)

"Miss, please, stand back," Tae says, placing himself between the girl and Danny. His eyes are fixed on Nugau's extended hand.

Shadows are whirling around her fingers, thick and liquid. She is wielding the Dark. It is one thing to expect it and another to see it happening before you—terror pumps through Sascia, and she fumbles around to drag her friends away.

Cheery dancing music blasts from the parade at their back. Enveloping them, the crowd hops and bops, oblivious to the elf princess standing among them.

Those violet eyes roam over Sascia one last time, uncertain and befuddled—then the world erupts in sparklers and fireworks. Light blossoms, draping a veil of orange and scarlet over the street.

Shadows deepen and elongate, black given essence around Nugau's feet. Her body sinks into the gathering Dark, first her knees and thighs, then her torso and head. In seconds, blink-and-you'll-miss-it fast, she is gone.

All five of the cohort are breathing hard, huddled close together. "What. The hell. Was that," Andres stammers.

The metal shafts of the barrier dig into Sascia's back. The touch is grounding, as is the press of Shivani's body on one side, Tae's on the other, Danny at her front. They *all* saw it. Nugau, princess of Itkalin, disappeared into the Dark.

A flutter of wings draws her attention to her cupped palms. Slow and tender, Sascia opens them. Her friends peer at the big moth, wearing identical expressions of bewilderment. Over their heads, Sascia meets Danny's gaze. Gone is his worrying, gone is his teasing. Muscles flex at his locked jaw.

He answers her silent question with an equally silent nod.

Sascia turns back to the cohort. "I have something to tell you."

12

SYLVAN FOWLS

Sascia is thirteen and none too pleased about it.

She's overplucked her eyebrows, broken out all over her forehead, and is currently being strangulated by her new sports bra—that seventh melomakarono really did her in. Regardless, she licks off the last remnants of syrup from her fingers with a heaving sigh. Next to her, Ksenya is opening her Christmas present to a chorus of *ooh*s and *ahh*s from the rest of their family. It's a hot-pink pair of rollerblades, bedazzled with dozens of rhinestones spelling out her name.

Sascia and Danny exchange a glance. They both recognize the chip in the third wheel of the left rollerblade—it happened when Danny challenged Sascia to jump over a bench two years ago. She got a sprained ankle and a crack on her rollerblade as a reward, as well as a month's supply of favors from Danny. Now, the shoes have been spray-painted and bejeweled, and passed off as brand new to Ksenya.

Danny's gift was his dad's old iPhone, and Sascia's the latest book in her favorite teen detective series (six months after release and used, but who cares? The words are still there). Their baby cousin Martha got handknit mittens. And the adults got nothing.

The market collapsed after the Darkbeasts broke out of Shanghai,

New York, and the Baltic Sea. Sascia learned about it in school: the Great Recession of the 1930s, the financial crisis of 2008, and now, the Dark Panic. She can't remember exactly how Ms. Deluca defined the term, but she knows what it means. It means that Aunt Sophia and baby Martha had to move back home with Sascia's grandpa. It means Athena's Yard had to let staff go and Mama and Baba have to work double shifts seven days a week. It means Danny had to quit swimming and Sascia has to be really careful about turning the AC on in the summer. It means that adults get no presents at Christmas and kids get hand-me-downs.

Sascia takes Ksenya's hand and leads her outside.

It's not snowing, but the cold is crisp and flat in the air. The woods perch around Grandpa's house like a flock of solemn, sylvan fowls. Sascia loves pines; she loves their resinous aroma and their needled foliage, the sound of pine cones crunching beneath her feet. It's the same woods where she almost drowned four winters ago. She drags her gaze away.

In her new (old) rollerblades, Ksenya holds tight on to Sascia and Danny for balance. The three of them run up and down the driveway, where there's no ice. When their noses begin sniffling, Danny and Ksenya retreat inside for warmth, but Sascia stays behind to look for Ksenya's shoes, which were carelessly discarded in favor of the rollerblades. She finds the right one by the thorny carcass of Yaya Athena's rosebushes. Her eyes scan the dropping darkness for the other shoe; they trail past the bushes and the frozen ground, all the way to the woods.

There's a figure standing there, among the pines.

Her heartbeat skids to a stop. Her breath puffs hot steam over her tightly wound scarf.

It always looks the same, this figure. Its face is hidden by the hood of a black cloak that glistens as though made of cut glass.

It watches from a distance, and when Sascia approaches, it disappears.

"Sascia?" her father calls from the front porch.

She startles out of her reverie. She drops the shoe; it barely makes a sound as it hits the frozen asphalt of the driveway.

She could say: *Look, Baba. Right there. It's real. It's watching.*

She could say: *Let me catch it and bring it to you, so you'll know that it really exists.*

Instead, she lets out a panicked, "Sorry! I was looking for Ksenya's shoes."

"The other one's here," he says. "Come, it's getting too cold."

Sascia picks up the right shoe, then fetches the left one from the bush her father pointed to. When she reaches his side, she can see his jaw is jutting out in a scowl. His gaze is trained on the spot she was just staring at, the spot where the figure in black stood.

Sascia doesn't bother looking back.

She knows that the figure won't be there anymore.

13

A HAUNTING

Nugau.
Nugau.
Nugau.

The name is a repeating litany on the margins of Sascia's notebook. Other bits are scribbled, too, like *An Ariadne in love with the Labyrinth itself* and *Let me remedy my misstep* and little sketches of the blooms on their silky long hair. Sascia even tried her hand at their violet eyes, but alas, her skill is too amateur to properly capture Nugau's essence.

"Sascia," Andres says from the desk. "Are you listening?"

"Yes." She looks up from her notebook to find him giving her a flat look. "No," she concedes. "Can you repeat that?"

Her lab has turned into their unofficial war room. A police sketch of the elf princet (the gender-neutral royal term they've decided on) is stuck on the wall over her desk. Papers are strewn around it, reports and xenoscience theories, data analyses and test results, and every single line they spoke to Sascia during their attack. The trash can is piled high with coffee cups and takeout containers. Andres and Tae are hunched over the lab computers, Shivani over the microscope, while Sascia is on the floor amid a sea of papers.

It's all giving very Unhinged Detective, but none of them care. Carr hasn't set foot in the Umbra offices since Halloween, busy with his own research upstate. They send him daily reports on their new projects—Tae and Crow have already finished their design of a nova-cannon, Andres and Shivani are at the first stages of developing a weaponized virus, while Sascia and Danny have recently figured out how to transform the nova-light walls of their garden into an anti-Dark shield—but the rest of the day they spend in Sascia's lab. It's been three weeks since she told her friends about her first encounter with the princet; after their shock wore off, the cohort did what it does best: research.

"I said, the results are in," Andres repeats. "Crow and I have run your stats through every database accessible to xenoscientists—"

"And some," Crow says from the speaker, "of the less accessible kind."

(For the layperson: classified archives Crow managed to hack into.)

"—and you're right," Andres continues. "Big Boy over there is most definitely an old, *old* ancestor of your other moths."

Sascia follows his gaze to Big Boy. The strange moth is currently pacing atop the glass of her and Danny's map. Even from this distance, its difference from the other Darkmoths is obvious: it's four times their size, roughly the length of Sascia's palm, with feathered antennae and an unusual thick fringe of fur over its eyes. For weeks, Sascia has been collecting data on moth size, shape, and genetic code, arriving at the theory Andres just confirmed: that this moth is far older than any other she's come across.

"But how is that possible?" Shivani asks from the other side of the lab.

"If only we knew." Andres sighs. "It's the great mystery of xenoscience."

"Not all of us are majoring in xenogenetics, Andres," says Tae. "Please explain."

Andres whirls the office chair around and folds his hands in his lap. "Okay, so. As more and more Darkcreatures began making their way into our world, scientists realized that there was an anomaly in their genetic code. The scientific term is *gene paradox*, but everyone calls it the Darknomaly."

He extends a hand toward Sascia's garden. "Take these moths, for example. Xenogeneticists have proven that the DNA of a moth that hops out of the Dark on a Monday is centuries more evolved than the one that hops out on a Tuesday. But on Wednesday, a moth might hop out of the Dark with a DNA that suggests it's millennia behind both of the other two. In human terms, it'd be as if you and your great-great-great-grandchild and your ancestor from five hundred years ago all existed at the same time. Which is of course impossible, unless we assume that Darkcreatures have a much longer lifespan than we do."

"Essentially," Sascia explains, "the hypothesis is that Darkcreatures are immortal."

"And according to our analysis, Big Boy over there," Andres adds, "is the oldest creature that's ever come out of the Dark."

A soft *plop* sounds as Sascia's mouth falls open. "Older than the Darkdragon?"

Andres nods.

"Older than the Darkkraken?" Tae asks.

Andres nods again.

"As old as a god," Sascia whispers.

Her mind flashes back to Nugau, their features sagging with confusion. *Itka*, the princet had said reverently. *Why do you have one of the itka? How did you find a god of Itkalin?*

"Well, that makes sense," Shivani says.

Andres lifts a brow, his piercing glistening in the near-dark of the lab. "It does?"

"I've been studying your moths' interactions. Actually, let me show you."

Shivani skips to the garden, where she props the small hatch open and places the ancient moth inside. At once, the other moths in the garden fly to meet it. Tiny by comparison, but fast, they swarm around it, caressing its wings and body with their little antennae.

"See how they immediately start grooming it?" Shivani asks. "It's what attendants do to a queen bee. I've never seen moths exhibit social behavior like this before, and your Darkmoths certainly don't do it to others in their swarm, Sascia. This so-called *itka* is not just ancient. It's something of a leader. Royalty."

"A royal moth and a royal princet," Crow calls from the speaker. "Both of them obsessed with little old Sascia."

A grunt leaves Sascia's nose as she buries her face in her hands. "I don't understand. The first time I met Nugau, the princet accused me of treason and tried to kill me. The second time, they snacked and chatted with us as if nothing had happened, and when I asked them about the attack, they didn't even remember it. It's like they were two entirely different people—except we've compared notes on our memory of their Darkprints and they were identical. They *were* the same person, they just didn't act in any way that makes sense."

"And while we're trying to solve this unsolvable mystery," Shivani says, reaching out to tap the glass of the garden, "the rest of the world is apparently trying to destroy the Dark inch by inch."

Sascia peeks between her fingers. The garden's normally luminescent surface is marked with dark spots, as though infected with some kind of ugly virus.

The symptom: dead areas of the Dark.

The virus: humanity.

Every day for the last month, since the attack in Times Square, she has arrived at the Umbra to find a new blotch of emptiness on her map. The Darkplants that used to be there are withered, their roots gnarled to stumps. The moths that inhabited that spot have disappeared back into the Dark. All of them victims of the public's rising panic. People have taken it upon themselves to douse pockets of Dark around their homes with fire, or, if excessively rich, explode it with nova-bombs. The cohort did end up attending the peace rally that Sunday and every Sunday since, but their voices are getting hard to hear above the growing paranoia.

"And Chapter XI is doing jack shit," Andres says. Elbows on his knees, he's studying her garden too. "They typically condemn such acts of destruction, but my sources are saying they're currently preoccupied with reassuring world governments. Apparently, they're under pressure from the United Nations to appoint a new director with a military background."

Shivani's hands fly to her cheeks. "That would be a disaster. The Chapter is supposed to be independent of governments and militaries. Its directive is the management of the Dark, not inciting violence. We've always used nova-lights to keep the Dark at bay, but now that they're attacking it unprovoked . . . How long until the Dark decides to fight back?"

A gloomy silence unfolds.

But Tae cuts their pity party short with a slap of his hand on the desk. The sound is startling, the movement so unlike Tae that they all turn to gape at him. "Despair has no place in a science lab," he tells them. "We work with hypotheses and conclusions. With trial and error. If we figure out how the Darkmoth is connected to Nugau and why Nugau behaved like that, then we will have an idea of what they want. And if we know what they want, then we might begin to negotiate with them. We need a hypothesis that we can bring to the powers that be. We might not have arrived at the conclusion yet, but we're close. I can feel it."

All right, Sascia will admit that Tae's genius can occasionally be comforting. If *he* believes they're close, then they must be. An ancient royal moth alerted Sascia to Nugau's presence on Halloween. If it happens again, the cohort can all follow it and find Nugau before anyone else can. They can have a proper conversation. Negotiate terms of reconciliation or advocate for peace or whatever it is proper ambassadors do.

On that note of (perhaps illusional) hope, their war meeting comes to a close. "It's getting late," Andres announces. "We need to go home and pack. It's my and Tae's week on campus starting tomorrow."

The two of them and Shivani share an apartment in a building complex just a few blocks east, a lavish rental that is included in their Umbra scholarships. By special arrangement, Tae, Andres, and Danny split their time between remote and in-person learning at their universities.

The lab fills with the sounds of paper rustling and bags being zipped up. Shivani looks down at Sascia on the floor apologetically. "Sorry for the mess."

"Don't worry about it," Sascia says. "Go home, guys. I can clean up here."

When they trickle out, Sascia mechanically pulls out her phone and calls Ksenya—always good to have company while cleaning.

Her sister answers on the first ring with a drowsy "Heeey."

"Oh, god, I forgot how late it is there." Seven hours ahead to be exact, so around 2:00 a.m. in Greece. "I can call back tomorrow."

"It's fine. I'm just doomscrolling."

"How have you been?"

Sascia begins tidying up as her sister rambles about her weekend: a walk around town on Saturday, complete with food-tasting and flea-market shopping, then a long night out dancing with her friends. Then, on Sunday, lunch with their grandparents, uncles, and cousins, and an afternoon of homework.

In typical Ksenya fashion, she leaves out the juicy parts, which won't do. "Did Alex text back?" Sascia asks.

Even through the phone, Sascia can hear Ksenya's blush. "He did."

"*Ooh!* Tell me everything."

Ksenya does, reciting their texts word for word. To Sascia, it is glaringly obvious the boy likes her, but Ksenya is filled with that all-consuming first-school-crush anxiety. Sascia asks questions and offers advice, doing her best to prod Ksenya into making a move.

At last, Sascia stops to survey the scene. In under fifteen minutes, she has managed to restore the lab room to a near habitable condition. Three bags of trash are piled by the door and a stack of papers sits on the desk, but that's a problem for tomorrow. Letting her shoulders relax, she opens the hatch to her garden and deposits a pile of treats for her moths: raisins and peanuts and roasted almonds.

"How are *you*?" Ksenya asks.

"Oh, you know. Busy with classes and papers and the bookstore job."

"Carr giving you trouble?"

"No more than usual. This elf princet has thrown the whole lot of us in disarray."

Silence descends on the other end of the line. For a long time, Sascia thought her sister would outgrow her fear of the Dark. It didn't make sense that one sister would love something the other feared. But Ksenya never did. In fact, as the years passed, her childish terror morphed into a well-justified, self-aware dread.

"Hey," Ksenya says finally. "What time is it over there? Shouldn't you be at the party?"

Sascia pulls her phone away to look at the time.

Shit.

Today is her parents' twenty-fifth wedding anniversary party and Sascia is the kind of late that makes you an absolute asshole.

14

NAIVE, UTOPIAN, LAUGHABLE

The candles have been blown out, the cake sliced and served.

Sascia stuffs her mouth as much as she can. An infallible tactic: the fuller your mouth, the less you're expected to participate in conversation. It's an almond cake drizzled with sugar syrup called amygdalopita, a staple of Greek pastry cuisine and Aunt Rania's—Danny's mom's—special.

Sascia hates almonds. No, that's not fair. She can tolerate a roasted and, most importantly, *salted* almond as a snack. But she hates it when nuts are peppered in places they don't belong, like pastries and salads and, god forbid, soups. It feels like you're casually enjoying your lunch, then suddenly, you're biting into a piece of tree bark.

And so she has collected a small mountain of almonds on her napkin. It's getting hard to spit them out discreetly, to be honest, which is why she extracts herself from where she's been sandwiched between her godmother and great-uncle in the back corner of the restaurant and sneaks off to the bathroom.

She stuffs her napkin and paper plate in the bin and sits on the toilet seat. Across from her, the mirror reflects a wraith of a girl with her nose scrunched up like a mouse. She smooths her expression and tucks her hair behind her ears. It's freshly cut, barely to her chin, a soft sandy brown.

Her fingers trace a line from her jaw to her ear. *If we had met before*, Nugau said, lips grazing Sascia's ear, *rest assured, little Ariadne: I would not forget you.*

Afterward, Sascia looked up the myth of Ariadne, just to make sure she remembered it right. Every year, King Minos of Crete demanded a host of fourteen Athenians to enter his Labyrinth in sacrifice to the beastly Minotaur. Until his daughter Ariadne fell in love with one of the sacrifices, a young prince of Athens, and decided to help him survive the Labyrinth. She gifted him a coil of red thread and instructed him to unspool it while he walked the cavernous pathways, so that he might retrace his way out. They eloped, but in true Greek myth fashion, Prince Theseus abandoned her on an island and Ariadne ended up marrying the god Dionysus instead.

An Ariadne in love with the Labyrinth itself.

A girl in love with the dark and twisted, the inescapable, the forbidden. Sascia likes how the phrase fits her—dark and twisted things deserve to be loved too, and who better to love them than a girl deemed a little twisted herself? It's strange that she should feel so seen, so understood, by a creature from another world who doesn't even know her.

A knock comes on the door. "Cuz?"

Sascia leans over to pop it open.

Danny wheels himself to the threshold then proceeds to gyrate his wrists and massage the soft flesh around his thumbs. He gets cramps sometimes when he wheels too long. He makes a sympathetic noise at Sascia's glum face. "They're giving you the silent treatment?"

"Worse. They're being nice. All smiles and hugs and clapping me on the shoulder while they talk me up to their friends."

"Arg!" he fake-shrieks. "Forgiving parents—the horror!"

Sascia chortles, entirely involuntarily. She steps around his wheelchair and takes the handgrips, bringing him past the dining space where guests are singing NSYNC and into the quiet solitude of the kitchen. Wine bottles and pizza boxes are piled on the counter like the spoils of war. Sascia goes straight for the medicine drawer and the half-finished tube of pain relief cream. Dropping onto a stool across from Danny's wheelchair, she squirts some in her palm and begins to massage her cousin's wrists.

His head drops back. A pleased hum vibrates from his nose. "So what's the latest on the elf? That's why you were late, isn't it? I knew you'd lose track of time. I should have dragged you away early with me."

Sascia presses her lips together. She and Danny don't keep secrets from each other, ever. He knows every shitty thing she's done, every regret and bad thought—and she knows his. But he's too gentle. Too respectful to actually say what he thinks, that she's turning this elf, this moth, into her latest fixation. Her point being: Danny knows all her secrets, but he doesn't always understand them.

The silence must have stretched too long—he opens one eye and drawls, "What?"

"The cohort thinks the moth is some kind of ancient leader. But we still don't know why it appeared to me, or how it relates to the elf. If we could talk to Nugau—"

"*Sascia*. You are *not* going to try to pull out the elf from the Dark again."

His tone grates against Sascia's ears, the whine of a parent about to tell off their kid. What is it about her that makes everyone want to set her straight?

"Oh, come on, Danny," she says, half-pleading, half-snappy.

"I've met them twice now. The first time, they tried to kill me. The second they didn't even recognize me. The entire world is looking for them and yet *I* keep stumbling onto them. Don't pretend I have any other choice but to get . . . involved. You would, too, if you were in my place."

"No, I wouldn't. That's the difference between you and me, between you and the rest of the world, really. If I was convinced a dangerous elf princet from another world wanted to kill me, I would stay far, far away from them."

"Stay away from who?" Aunt Rania asks, barging into the kitchen with the amygdalopita tray. Only clumps of syruped crumbs are left on the wrinkled foil.

Danny immediately goes beet red, but Sascia is a practiced liar. "I was thinking of taking a new class next semester, but Danny tells me not to. The professor has a reputation for failing freshmen."

"Could he really fail you?" Aunt Rania says, her back to them as she wrestles to fit the tray in the overladen sink. "Since you're only auditing?"

"She's not auditing, Mom," Danny says. "She's taking remedial courses to boost her GPA. She has just as much homework and exams as I do."

Aunt Rania makes a scoffing noise. "Well, not the same as you exactly if she's contemplating skipping a class because she's afraid of a strict professor."

"Gee, thanks, Aunt Rania," Sascia says drily, lifting herself from the stool. She's had more than enough family time tonight. "Your support really means the world."

Her aunt nails Sascia with one of her scathing looks. She is a tall, imposing figure in her rib-knit dress and white-blond pixie cut. She shares a long nose and strong jaw with Sascia's mother, but the two women couldn't be more different: where Mom is gentle and quick to laugh, Rania is closed-off and bitter. After years of observation, Sascia has concluded that Aunt Rania *can* feel love, and does so acutely for Danny and her best friend and her sister. Sascia is just not on that very exclusive list.

"My support," her aunt deadtones. "You had my support. Until I had to sit through a ten-hour surgery wondering if my son would live, because *you* were foolish enough to drag him into the known hunting grounds of a Darktiger."

"Mom," Danny snaps. "For the last time, I knew full well what I was getting into. It's not Sascia's fault."

Sascia barely registers his words. Her chest is heaving with stabbing breaths, with memories heavy with guilt. "I have apologized a hundred times, to Danny, to you—"

"And it's still a hundred times too few," her aunt barks. "You don't get to stand there and use sarcasm with me when you make one bad decision after another. You want my support? *Earn it.*"

Oh, this is too much. "I'm *trying*!"

"Are you?" her aunt asks, with a sincerity that's altogether too uncomfortable. "You got the opportunity of a lifetime of a free Ivy League education and you squandered it. You lied about your grades instead of asking for help. You're gone all day every day, supposedly working on your research, but I have seen that fishing rod sticking out of your backpack, girl. Wherever you might be spending your time, it sure as hell isn't a lab or a bookstore. And you're an hour and a half late to your own parents' twenty-fifth anniversary party."

Sascia presses her lips together.

"Mom," Danny pleads, "stop."

"What's going on?" Sascia's father says from the doorway.

Her mother is peeking over his shoulder. She wears a look of worry, but her father's face is carved with austere lines: a frown on his brow, a pinch to his mouth. He takes a look around the room—at Sascia's arms wrapped around herself, Danny glaring daggers at his mom, Aunt Rania fuming—and then asks a level: "Rania, are you fighting with my daughter again?"

The silence is a heated pressure, pulsing loud at Sascia's ears. Her nose stings. Wetness beads at her eyelashes. She knows the best course is to apologize. To defuse the tension and make it up to them all. But as Aunt Rania just pointed out, Sascia has never been good at making the right choice.

"You know what?" she tells Aunt Rania. "You're right."

Four pairs of eyes land on her.

"I did squander my golden opportunity. I did lie about my grades. I was late to my parents' silver anniversary party and yes, I do know I can never atone for risking Danny's life in that tunnel. But none of this matters. Because no matter what I do, no matter what I say, you've already decided: I'm a screw-up. I'll always *be* a screw-up. So no, Aunt Rania, I'm not going to try to earn your support any longer. You and I both know you were never going to give it to me, anyway."

You, she says, but she means all of them, her parents especially. They're kind and gentle and forgiving, but they're also the people who sat her down for that damned intervention seven months ago and opened her eyes to a painful truth: she's not special. She is made of mistakes and fixations and brazen impulsivity, and she doesn't have her life together and is probably never going to, because the life she wants for herself, a life with the Dark, is naive, utopian, laughable.

Her mother speaks gently. "Sascia—"

"May I be excused?" Sascia interrupts.

She doesn't want her mother's comfort right now. She's angry and she wants to stay angry because anger is better than grief, better than having to confront her own mundanity.

"Sure, honey," her mother says at last. "We can talk about this later."

Sascia slips between her parents and out of the kitchen, hurrying up the stairs to their apartment. When she's safely inside her room, she locks the door and stays there for a moment, letting her forehead rest against the wood. She's not crying, but she has that horrible feeling in her throat, like her flesh is pressing in to strangle her from within.

A loud *thump* reverberates through the floor of her bedroom. The door of her closet rattles against its hinges. Muffled sounds echo and then the knob of her closet is turning. The door slips open and Darkmoths burst out—dozens, hundreds of them, a torrent of black and iridescent neon.

"What—" Sascia chokes out.

Through the onslaught of moths, a body appears. Shoulders clad in armor, long legs in scaled leather, hair tangled and matted to their face. It's *their* face, their violet eyes and arched brows and their wintry Darkprint, blazing a bright white.

The name whooshes out of Sascia in a terrified breath. *"Nugau."*

The elf slips, crashing to their knees. Dark blue blood oozes from a gash on their forehead. Their lips are stained a dangerous kind of black that veins down their chin to disappear in the high collar of their armor.

"Little gnat," Nugau rasps. "Help me."

Then their eyes roll back into their head and they collapse in Sascia's arms.

15

IF I BEGGED

Of all the places life could take her, Sascia has never imagined she'd be sprawled on her bedroom floor cradling a princet from the Dark. The impossibility of it strikes her like a sucker punch, pumping panic into her veins.

Help me, Nugau rasped.

She glances around: The door is locked, thank god, and the nova-lights in her room are turned to low. Her phone is in her pocket, but who would she call? Danny is downstairs, and the rest of the cohort is a train-ride away. They would rush over if Sascia asked, but what if Nugau became violent? Sascia's not risking anyone's life again, not after the rightful wrath Aunt Rania just unleashed on her.

Moths swirl in a tempest around the room. Shadows have taken on new form. Dark pools in the pockets of black beneath the furniture and in the corners of the ceiling. It drips down the walls, a thick tar that fizzes and boils. Bubbles pop in sickening, wet spatters. She has never seen the Dark behave like this before.

"What happened?" she whispers to the elf. "What am I supposed to do?"

At once, the moths surge in a whirlwind above her head and begin pelting Nugau's body like pattering rain. Sascia yelps and covers Nugau's torso with her own. But the moths aren't attacking—from her new vantage point inches away from Nugau's face, Sascia can see they are landing on the elf's lips, on the black veins that trace down their chin and neck, then bouncing off again.

The moths are *showing* her.

With trembling fingers, she pushes Nugau's silken hair away. Her thumb skims over the bow of Nugau's lower lip—the soft skin is slick with a black liquid that sticks to Sascia's fingertip. Its smell is putrid, as though Nugau is already a half-rotten thing. Down their neck, veins protrude in stark black against their porcelain gray-blue skin. Sascia lowers her ear to their mouth; their breaths are a rasp, slow and loud.

"You are poisoned," Sascia realizes.

A clawed hand fastens on her wrist. She jolts but doesn't try to pry her arm away; Nugau's eyes are open. The white around their irises is marbled by blue, crisscrossing outward like burst blood vessels. For a moment, the two of them share the same air, exchanged in short, stabbing bursts, like shrapnel breaking the skin.

"Who did this to you?" Sascia asks.

The elf has to force a swallow before rasping, "We were betrayed."

We, Sascia wonders. Other elves?

"I was trying to find you," Nugau mutters. "But they found me instead. With their light-woven chains. Their ray-sharp arrows. Their mortars of white ash."

Dry coughs rake their body. Spots of black stain Sascia's T-shirt. When Nugau's head lolls back, thick black tar is dripping from their lips. Their hand drops from her wrist, landing limp on the carpet.

They're dying. Sascia could let death claim them and be rid of this threat once and for all. But then what of *I would not forget you*? What of *An Ariadne in love with the Labyrinth itself*? Of the two Nugaus she has met, the vengeful killer and the wide-eyed visitor, which one is this? Which one would Sascia be saving?

The pressure in her chest eases. It doesn't matter. Sascia can make no other choice than the one she's been making all her life: she will love and protect, even if it dooms her.

Overhead, the moths are in a frenzy. The feverish beat of their wings hazes Sascia's hearing. They land on Nugau's body, on Sascia's, on the carpet, then fly off again, agitation bouncing through their every move.

"Calm down," she whispers to them, but for the first time, the moths don't heed her orders. The swarm flurries around the room, making it hard to focus.

Hoisting with all her strength, Sascia manages to lay Nugau on her bed. They are ridiculously tall—their feet stick off the end and their arms hang from the sides. She crouches over them, her mind spinning. She's watched enough medical dramas with her sister to know the first order of business is to check the injured person's vitals. A clear airway is the priority. Sascia begins pulling armor pieces off, stripping the elf down to a silk chemise that sticks to their chest and arms. She turns them on their side; in seconds, their breathing eases.

Next up, diagnostics. Brushing away moths, Sascia inspects Nugau's body, where she locates several open wounds: a deep gash at their temple, a cut on their right arm, and four round wounds at their back. Dark blue blood is oozing from those, but the ones on their head and arm seem to be clotting, which feels like a step in the right direction.

But none of these wounds appear to be the source of the poisoning. No, the dark ooze and bulging veins originate at their mouth.

Nugau *swallowed* something.

Kneeling before the bed, Sascia pries the elf's lips open. Their teeth and gums are entirely black. All around the room, the Dark swells into bulging orbs of black, some of them so enormous they swallow her furniture and knickknacks. Their surface is a thin layer of sleek tar; Sascia fears that when they burst, something terrible will happen. The moths go absolutely berserk, a tempest of black wings over her head. Her heartbeat spikes—are they warning her or trying to stop her? There is no way to know, no time to decide.

She eases Nugau's jaw open and shoves her fingers into their mouth, feeling around: there's their tongue, coated with the sticky tar, there's the roof of their mouth, there's—

Something is lodged at the back of Nugau's mouth.

At her touch, the *something* squirms. Sascia freezes.

As one, the moths assault Sascia with their small bodies, their wings transfigured from crushed velvet into sharp gemstone. Like all Darkcreatures do when met with a threat, the moths have gone into defense mode, hardening their skin to dispel predators. Nicks and cuts jewel Sascia's hands where she's holding the elf, but she doesn't stop.

There's something in there. It needs to come out.

Nugau convulses, but Sascia takes hold of the back of their head, keeping them still. The bulbous masses of Dark on the walls swell even bigger. Black oozes over Sascia's fingers, down the elf's jaw. Her fingertips close around the body lodged in Nugau's throat.

With a quick, decisive movement, Sascia pulls it out. At first, a clump of black sits on her palm. Then the liquid begins to melt and its form becomes clear—it's a moth. *The* moth.

Its wings are tucked in, slick with tar, but its body shivers in short bursts. The other moths have formed a cloud around her hand, pressing against Sascia's fingers with their whetted forewings. She reaches for an abandoned hoodie and carefully places the moth on top. The others follow, swooping to land protectively around their injured leader.

Nugau's mouth is still open. Liquid shadow drips from their lips onto the pillow.

"I'm sorry," she whispers to the elf as she grabs her trash can. "But it needs to come out—all of it."

Then she sticks a finger down Nugau's throat.

Their torso seizes as they retch into the wastebasket. With a sickening *quelch* every bubble of Dark in the room pops, splattering its foul-smelling innards onto Sascia's room. Putrid Dark coats her skin, her bedding and carpet, her walls. Nugau heaves while Sascia holds them and rubs their back and says inane things like *there, there*.

When it's over, Sascia doesn't realize straightaway. Her shoulders are hunched to her ears with tension, her mind fogged with adrenaline. The floor looks like the scene of some vile, black-blooded massacre. It's the elf who signals it's over. They roll to their back, going liquid-soft. Their swollen veins have smoothed to a dull gray.

Sascia glances around and spots her water bottle stuffed in the side pocket of her backpack. Hydration—that sounds like the easiest task right now. Her hand trembles with the aftershocks of panic as she tips the bottle over Nugau's lips.

The first drip goes straight to the pillow, but on the second, the elf parts their lips and swallows a good mouthful, then another.

When Sascia lowers the bottle, Nugau tangles their hand in her hair.

Their violet eyes pin her to the spot.

A drum of fear builds in Sascia's ears. She remembers their scythe posed inches from her neck. She remembers their menace, their fury. *You die tonight.*

The princet's fingers knot into the short strands at the back of her neck. Their thumb nestles in the corner of her jaw, just below her ear. With their other hand, they take the bottle from her, swirling clear water into their mouth, and wiping their lips clean. Their gaze is heavy-lidded, but it is on her, burning with intensity.

Their grip tugs Sascia closer. Their nostrils flare against the column of Sascia's neck.

"Sweet," Nugau whispers. "You always smell sweet."

Their eyes fall on Sascia's lips.

"You always taste sweet."

Sascia's mind just . . . *flees*. She has no thoughts, no reflexes, no feelings. She is a body curved over another, and every inch where her flesh meets theirs is seared with heat.

"Little gnat," the elf whispers. "If I begged, would you kiss me? One last time?"

Before Sascia can answer one way or another, their hand drops and they slip into the dreamless black.

16

A YEARNING KIND OF SORROW

Sascia sits back. Her chest heaves obnoxiously, as though she's run a marathon.

If I begged, would you kiss me? One last time?

She wants to wrench her hair out and scream at the ceiling like a cartoon character: *What! The hell! Is going! On!* The Dark has always been a mystery, but one with rules and boundaries. *This*—a princet popping out of the Dark hell-bent on killing her, then bursting out of her closet in need of rescue, *then* smelling her neck and asking her to kiss them—is more than a mystery. This is a goddamn paradox, an absurdity, an illogicality.

She drags her fingers over her face, but her tar-coated hands leave long foul-smelling smears on her cheeks. On the bed, the princet breathes slow and raspy, unconscious. She flees to the bathroom, locking her bedroom door after her. She lets the water run until it's scalding hot, then steps in, clothes and all. Black swirls around the drain. When she's done scrubbing, she grabs the whole stack of fresh towels and runs back to her room. Nose buried in the soft, lavender-scented towels, she surveys the scene.

It's a bloodbath in a black-and-white filter. Tarry liquid has stained her entire carpet and bedsheets. Imprints of moth wings are splattered on the walls and windows. The little menaces have calmed down now, gathered in a heap over the injured moth's body.

A knock sounds on the door and a timid, "Sascia?"

Oh god, what now?

She flattens herself against the door. "Don't come in! Now's not a good time!"

"Listen, kardia mou. I had a chat with your aunt. She says she's going to call you tomorrow—"

"Baba, can we not talk about this right now? I'm kind of busy."

"Yeah . . . yeah, sure." Sascia can almost picture him, looking at the ground and ruffling his graying hair. He switches to Greek, always more comfortable in it when he has to pick his words with care. "I just want you to know, nothing is already decided. You can be whatever you want to be. You can do whatever you want to do. It matters—to me and to all of us down there."

Wood presses against her forehead. She wants to believe him. She wants to open the door and tell him she's going to be a bowling shoes influencer, then, or a lion tamer, something wild and ridiculous. She wants to see him throw his head back and hear his roar of laughter, have him fold her into his arms and tell her she really can be anything she likes.

But it's not true. *He* is not being true.

She can't be the girl obsessed with the Dark. She can't be the girl who hallucinates a figure in black. She can't be the student who messed up her opportunity at an Ivy League education. And it's not his fault, not really. He's just a dad—an immigrant, working-class dad at that. What he wants is to give her more than he had, to watch her live better than he does, to not worry—and what has Sascia ever been besides a boundless source of worry?

Through the wood, Sascia whispers, "Thanks, Baba. That means a lot."

His feet susurrate on the wooden boards of the corridor, then, with a soft "Love you," his steps recede out of the apartment.

Sascia is alone again, with the unconscious elf and the livid moths and the murder scene of a bedroom. She slips into an oversized T-shirt and proceeds to roll the stained carpet out of the way. Fetching a bucket of room-temperature water, she kneels on the floor and reaches for the big moth.

Its comrades don't like that at all. Their bodies transform to hard onyx again, their wings buzzing furiously.

"Please," she whispers. "Let me help."

Begrudgingly, they begin peeling off the injured moth's body. Sascia wipes its wings with the corner of a towel dipped in water. After a few careful strokes, the black tar recedes. She smooths out its wings with a fingernail and sets it on its legs, but the poor thing must be exhausted; it only manages to crawl in a half-drunk zigzag.

An old, old *ancestor of your other moths*, Andres said. *See how they immediately start grooming it?* Shivani had asked. *It's what attendants do to a queen bee. This so-called* itka *is not just ancient. It's something of a leader. Royalty.*

Her mind flashes to the Darknomaly theory. Glancing around, she takes note of the moths' differences in size, wings, and antennae. If she took a sample from each moth in this group and ran it through the gene analysis equipment in Andres's lab at the Umbra, no two moths would belong to the same era. As though time is a cracked mirror; some pieces reflect an ancient beginning, others the shiny, modern now.

A story told in fragments of past, present, and future.

Sascia's gaze cuts to Nugau. The elf is sprawled on her bed, their chest rising and falling in even, drowsy breaths.

If I begged, would you kiss me? One last time?

One last time, as though Sascia has kissed them before. One last time, as though they want to be kissed. As though they *care* about her.

Three Nugaus exist at the same time. The Nugau who recognized her in that alley on 53rd Street, who accused her of treason and tried to kill her. The Nugau who approached her on Halloween, friendly and full of wonder, with no recollection of the attack or having been in New York before. And this third Nugau who burst out of the Dark in need of help, who showed no sign of hatred and instead . . . *You always smell sweet. You always taste sweet.*

But all three Nugaus are the same person, Sascia is sure of it. Like her moths and every creature of the Dark, Nugau's story is also told in fragments. Past, present, and—

She sits back on her haunches, hands going rigid around the big moth. Her thoughts race, fitting the shards of the fractured mirror back together. The Darknomaly has confounded xenoscientists for six years: How can creatures of different eras exist at the same time? But what if it's not an issue with the creatures but with time itself?

What if the human world and the Darkworld don't run in parallel timelines?

Sascia thinks back to Halloween, the smooth, scarless planes of Nugau's face. They had looked younger, still uncomfortable in their body, lanky and tall and wide-eyed. In Times Square, their face was slimmed down by age and an old scar curved around their neck. When Sascia shot them with nova-light, the skin of their hand had charred.

She reaches for Nugau's left hand, turns it over. On their wrist, the flesh is raised and twisted, exactly where Sascia wounded them a month ago. But this is not the red of a month-old, still-healing burn. This scar is fading, as though it has been healing for a long while.

The truth slots itself into place, impossible as it may seem. Nugau is different whenever they come out of the Dark, because they come from different *times*.

The Nugau of Halloween was from the deep past. They didn't recognize Sascia because they hadn't met her yet, much less attacked her. The Nugau of Times Square was from the future. They *had* met Sascia before. Enough events had transpired that Sascia was now a traitor worthy of a death sentence. And the Nugau of today was from an even more distant future. They carried the scars of Sascia's gun, and yet they trusted Sascia enough to come to her for help.

Sascia's face slackens with shock. Sometime in the future, she will commit treason in the Battle of Feathers. She will spend time with Nugau. She will . . . kiss them.

"Ah. So this is the moment."

Nugau studies her with a lucid, piercing gaze. Their hand stays between Sascia's fingers, as though welcoming the touch. But the intimacy jostles Sascia—she snaps her arm away and breathes, "You know?"

"I have been in your world before. I have seen evidence of your kind felling creatures that were still alive and well in my world. I believe it is a consequence of traveling from our world to yours. We have a word for it: *ymneen*. Knotted time."

"So you—" (God, is she really going to say this aloud?) "You're from the future?"

"In a way, I suppose. It is the future for you, but the past for me."

"From when?" And then, because she can't help it, "What happens in the future?"

Nugau holds Sascia's eyes. "War," they breathe. "A war that neither side can win."

Sascia's mouth goes dry with dread. War, just as the Umbra cohort feared. As the rest of the world is preparing for. "The war hasn't happened here yet. If you tell me how it starts, I can stop it before it even begins. I can help you—"

They reach to cup Sascia's cheek; startled, Sascia lets them. "Oh, but you do, little gnat. Or you try to. You almost die for it. A brave Ariadne in a labyrinth of terrors, clever and strong. But war is cleverer still. Violence is stronger still. You fail. We all fail."

Their touch trails up Sascia's jaw, hitching at the silver hoops lining her ear. Sascia's breath is a captive in her lungs, locked in a rib cage of fear and anticipation. Fear, because this is the very same creature who wanted to kill her. Anticipation, because they now want to kiss her. And threaded between dread and excitement is that old longing, the one she has never quite been able to quench: *magic, magic, let me be a part of magic.*

"My only regret," Nugau whispers, "is that we never found it. The soron mola, the true purpose behind the ymneen. That alone could have saved us." Unhappiness claims the rough edges of their voice. "But we are far past saving now. This, right here, is the best we'll ever have at farewell."

The gravity of that last word pulls on Sascia like an anchor chained to her ankles, dragging her into the deep. Is this what *kiss me one last time* means?

"Why is this farewell?" she whispers.

"It has to be." Their eyes flutter closed. It takes them a long, shaky breath to add, "Separation is the only way to keep our people safe. I understand that now."

Sascia doesn't. She understands very little, except that she stands on the precipice of past and future with no choice to make. Every decision has been made already, for her or perhaps by her, and it is unfair, unbearably and heartbreakingly unfair, to be told that she can do anything, be anything she likes, only to be deprived of the choice by time itself.

On impulse, she blurts, "You asked me to kiss you."

"No. I *begged* you."

Their eyes grow wide and bright, watching her, as though her reaction might be the most important thing in the whole world. Sascia wills herself into stillness, refusing to give away the wild rattle of her heart against her ribs, the purring sensation of heat at her core.

"I am begging you still," they breathe. "Will you kiss me? A parting gift to a lover you have yet to meet?"

"I—" Sascia swallows. "I don't know you."

"Know me, then," the elf whispers.

Their fingers weave once more into the short hairs at her nape. Sascia feels the tug, the pull, the *invitation*, gentle and attentive, expecting nothing in return.

Know me, Nugau pleads, as if lips are the gate to understanding, as if touch is the bridge, and a kiss is a laurel wreath of peace. *Know me*, as if it is that simple—but isn't it, for Sascia, the girl who has longed for the unknown all her life? If the timelines of their worlds are knotted together, if the future has already transpired, then this, here, will be *her* choice, hers alone. Sascia makes it easily, succumbing to the melancholy yearning for a life she has not yet lived and a love she has not yet felt, to hoping and wishing and longing.

She closes the gap between them.

Their mouths meet.

It is a small kiss, a shy greeting of lips, soft and warm and tender, then gone.

Nugau leans back. Their irises reflect swirling spots of bright color. Behind Sascia, the moths have taken flight, illuminating the room with the stark neon of their Darkprints, white and blue and purple. Every sputter of black suctions off the walls and floor to coalesce at the bed, leaving only clean surfaces behind. The Dark breathes and pulses, rushing to Nugau as veins return to a heart.

Don't go, Sascia thinks.

But instead, another question tumbles from her lips, "When? When do I love you back?"

"Oh, little gnat." Nugau's face is whittled with a yearning kind of sorrow. "I don't know that you ever do."

And then, in a whirlwind of darkness and stars, they're gone.

17

THE WELCOME OF A KITTEN

Sascia is almost done with fourteen and glad about it.

The year has dragged by like a plow turning over the soil for a new seeding. It all feels like preparation: first year of high school, new teachers, new classmates, new friends. The field of Sascia's life is all furrows and fresh soil, but nothing has bloomed yet.

Her birthday is on Monday, but her parents insisted on a Saturday night party, for maximum attendance. They went all out: sectioned off the best tables in Athena's Yard and ordered decorations, made her a four-tiered chocolate cake. Sascia decided to match their energy by inviting every kid she even remotely likes, from her class, track team, and drama club. Amazingly, they've all shown up.

A *Happy Birthday* sign hangs on the wall and balloons are sprawled all over the floor. The candles have been blown out, the cake scarfed down, and the space has been cleared of tables and chairs. Danny is DJing to an audience of almost sixty elated freshmen. But Sascia is happiest for her parents, swaying to the music in a corner of the dance floor, bodies close, eyes only for each other. She knew they'd like the nineties theme. They've been trying so hard to make up for last year; she thought she'd return the favor.

Last year, on the twelfth of April, the eve of her birthday, the entire tristate area went on a six-hour blackout. A little after midnight, every power plant around the city just went *boom*. The sky was moonless, overcast—the darkness was absolute. In mere minutes, the streets were crawling with Darkcreatures big and small. Sirens rang over Astoria. Her father had burst into the room and whisked them away to the only safe place in the neighborhood, the New York Presbyterian Hospital in Queens, whose backup generators had quickly kicked into gear.

It had been a terrifying night of wolfish howls and crowing screeches, of police cars and army vehicles zooming past, of nova-gun blasts painting the sky white. Sascia had huddled between Danny and Ksenya in a crowded hospital corridor, watching the adults exchange furious whispers. She'd drifted to sleep sometime before dawn and had woken up fourteen years old, in a city in ruins.

Now, over the music, Danny motions that they're out of cups and Sascia, putting on her best hostess hat, hurries to get new ones. The supply closet is crammed with stacks of napkins, surplus silverware, and a half-dry mop that smells like vinegar. She's skimming the shelves for cups when a high-pitched squeak startles her nearly out of her clothes.

She follows the sound to the very bottom of the shelves, where a Darkrat squirms in its trap. It's a hideous contraption that Nova-Corp launched a year or two ago: when the bait lures the pest onto the flat surface of the trap, a dozen thin strips of nova-light burst out, spearing the poor creature. Dark blue blood oozes from where the light impales the rat's spiky fur.

"Hold on, little guy," Sascia coos. "I'll get this off you."

She yanks the plug from the outlet first, then turns the lights off. Darkness envelops her, soundless and sightless and odorless, an absence of space and yet substantial in all the ways that matter. The kind of darkness that things crawl out of, creatures made of onyx stone and violence. She should turn the light back on.

She doesn't. She crouches and feels around for the trapped rat. "Little guy?"

Small reverberations slit the air: a nose sniffing or claws screeching through. Something touches the back of her hand, wet and warm and alive. She knows it's likely the Darkrat, but her mind imagines elsehow: the muzzle of a unicorn; the webbed hands of a gorgon. They won't look like the illustrations in books, she knows. They will have skin made of black gemstone and razor-sharp scales and rows upon rows of pointed teeth. But they will still be beautiful. They'll still be magic.

"Take me with you," Sascia whispers. "Please, can I come with you?"

For a moment, she thinks the Darkrat pauses. She thinks its head strokes the knuckles of her hand, like the welcome of a kitten after a long time away. It has heard her, she thinks. It has understood. It will take her away and all will be good.

Then fangs are raking through her flesh. Sascia screams.

HALF AN HOUR LATER, her hand is disinfected and bandaged, her sobs have settled down to sniffles, and the entire party is crowded around her, wanting to hear the whole story.

Sascia lies, a skill she's been honing over the years. The light just went out. In seconds, the Darkrat had crawled out of the trap. It bit her before she could throw the door open and let the light of the hallway sizzle it to bits.

Ksenya is hovering at the edge of the crowd, lips pressed together; she ran away when Sascia stumbled bleeding out of the closet. Their parents are whispering worriedly over the first aid kit. The kids are ecstatic—hanging out with sophomore Danny Jacobs *and* an encounter with a Darkcreature? This is the best party ever.

Only Danny knows. He sits with an arm around Sascia through the rest of the night, his gaze locked on the red spots blooming on her bandage. When the kids are gone and the decorations put away and it's just the two of them in their pajamas in Sascia's bedroom, he says, ever so gently, "Sascia, what happened, really? The light was working fine when I checked. But I found the nova-trap unplugged."

Sascia flexes her fingers. Her palm feels sore, but there's no sign of poison or infection. It was harmless, her poor Darkrat, just scared and in pain.

"I'm sorry," she whispers.

She doesn't cry, but burrows deeper into her cousin's shoulder. Danny lets her rest there for a long, long time.

18

ONE THOUGHT

Sascia lies on her bare mattress with her fingers interlocked over her belly, staring up at the ceiling. Her room is now free of black gore, courtesy of whatever suctioning magic Nugau performed during their exit. Her parents have made their drunken return from their anniversary party downstairs, but dawn is still hours away.

Her mind is a minefield. Every step might blow her to smithereens: *We were betrayed*—boom. *A war that neither side can win*—boom. *I am begging you still. Will you kiss me?*—boom. And that kiss, that gentle caress, that amaranthine farewell. It is nuclear, annihilating.

Ymneen, Nugau called it. Knotted time.

The timeline of the human world and that of the Dark are not linear. If you travel from one to the other, you might end up in the future or the past or somewhere else entirely. Earthly creatures can't travel through the Dark—technically, they can *go in*, but the temperature drops so low that all animal-manned expeditions have immediately lost contact. Darkcreatures can come and go as they please, and for six years, millions of them have been arriving from their world, separate from our own, with DNA so vastly different that scientists have been baffled. But Sascia has figured out the truth behind the Darknomaly.

Darkcreatures are not immortal. They can just, well, time travel.

Sometime in the future, Sascia will meet Nugau again. War will break out. Sascia will try to stop it, but she will fail. In the Battle of Feathers, she will commit treason. Nugau will end up poisoned and dying in Sascia's closet. *My only regret is that we never found it. The soron mola, the true purpose behind the ymneen. That alone could have saved us.* Nugau was convinced their meeting tonight was the end, a farewell. But what they don't realize is that their farewell might have changed everything.

Sascia is right here, in the before. She can alter what's to come. Not because she's some grand genius who will unlock the mysteries of space-time, but because she is armed with the knowledge of knotted time and all the crumbs of information Nugau unwittingly left behind.

There will be a labyrinth of terrors—Sascia vows now: she will make it out. There will be a betrayal—she will stop it. There will be a great battle—she won't commit treason.

A screw-up she may be, but no one can deny she *learns* from her mistakes.

This time, she will make all the right choices.

Beyond her curtains, the sky is threaded with predawn turquoises and purples. Sascia's eyes ache from lack of sleep. Her jaw hurts from clenching. She gets up and rolls her shoulders, then scans the room.

"Are you here?" she whispers. "Come out."

For a moment, there is only the pink-hued light of dawn.

Then comes the fluttering of wings. A small body lands on Sascia's bare knee. The ancient moth looks far less beaten up than last night. Its antennae brush vividly against her skin. Its Darkprint pulses a brilliant white.

The moth begins pecking at her skin until Sascia realizes what it wants: she gets up to fetch it a treat from the kitchen. As she watches it devour the raisins, she decides it can be "it" no longer. It deserves a proper name.

Mooch, she decides.

"THIS IS WILD," DANNY says as he steers the wheel right. "Wild, life-changing, Nobel Prize–winning stuff. You just solved the Darknomaly, cuz."

"I did, didn't I?"

"With Nugau's clues, we can figure out how to stop this war before it even begins—and when we do, we can take the information to Chapter XI." He chortles a near-hysterical laugh. "Imagine their faces when a group of students tells them they've spoken to an elf princet from the *future*."

His good mood is infectious. "Imagine their faces," she counters, "when we tell them the elf princet *kissed* me."

Danny lets out a proper holler. "I'd skip that part, if I were you. *It was barely a peck, anyway. It didn't mean anything.* Isn't that what you said?"

"Yes, but—" She must really be losing her mind, because her thoughts keep returning to it, to that touch, as though afraid the memory will fade. "It's just that Nugau looked so . . ."

"In love?"

Sascia closes her eyes. Love, yes, that's the word. She hasn't dared think it, much less speak it out loud. She won't now, either, because she vowed to make the right choices, and fixating on the sentimentalities of a time-traveling princet doesn't sound like a good one.

As though it can sense the sudden jump of her heart rate, Mooch gives her a little nibble at her ear. She had assumed the moth would stay in the thick shadows of her room, safe from the daylight, but when she slipped into the passenger seat of Danny's car, Mooch had burst out of the Dark beneath her seat and burrowed into the folds of her burgundy hoodie.

"Don't tease," she tells Danny.

"Please, just a little?" They're stuck in traffic on Broadway and Danny's cheerily drumming his fingers on the steering wheel. "Just until we get to the Umbra? Then I promise I won't bring it up again."

"Fine," Sascia grumbles.

"Okay, so when you guys had your meaningless peck, was there tongue involved—"

Mercifully, that's when Crow's number pops up on Sascia's phone. She accepts the call lightning-fast, putting their friend on speakerphone. "Tae and Shivani are already at the Umbra," Crow informs them without preamble. "Andres just landed and is rushing to his hotel. I've sent you all the link to an encrypted meeting room. Now, please, for the love of all that is holy, can you tell me what this is about? You can't just drop *URGENT SOS WE NEED TO MEET ASAP* in the group chat and expect us to be calm."

Sascia had waited until a reasonable hour (8:00 a.m.—Danny is, unsurprisingly, a morning person) before knocking on his door. The moment she had finished narrating the events of last night, he had made her send the aforementioned text to the cohort. Tae had been able to postpone his trip to Cambridge, but Andres was already in the air.

"Now, now, Crow," Sascia says. "That wouldn't be fair, would it?"

"*Come on,*" Crow moans. "We all know I'm your favorite—"

Her voice cuts off because several things happen at once.

Mooch explodes out of Sascia's hair and starts flying around, knocking into her and Danny, the windshield, the roof of the car, the windows. Startled, Danny swerves the wheel. All around them, cars honk and drivers bark insults.

"What is wrong with it?" Danny yells from where he's bending low in his seat, trying to avoid Mooch's barrage against the windows.

"I don't know—"

But her eyes latch on to the stretch of asphalt and cement beyond the window. They're coming down Broadway right past 23rd Street; in the distance, she can see the concrete barrier that surrounds the Maw.

All the nova-lights around it are at maximum lumen.

Even in the daylight, the sight is blinding. Artificial light congregates into a blaze of white, what New Yorkers call a Flare. It only happens when something big and dangerous is detected inside the Maw. Sascia hasn't seen a Flare for years and never from this close up.

Cars are coming to a stop. Drivers are climbing out. Pedestrians stand frozen on the sidewalk. Sirens approach; overhead, a pair of helicopters rush to the scene.

Sascia turns to Danny—she needs to help him into his wheelchair and get the hell out of here—but before she can get a word out, Mooch *launches* itself at the window. The glass shatters on impact, shards raining into Sascia's lap. Her arms come up to shield her face, her heart gallops at her neck, and Danny cries, "It's going straight to the Maw! Those lights will fry it!"

Her fingers get the seat belt off and the door open before she's even realized what she's doing. Danny grabs her wrist, but before she can say *I have to*, before she can plead *Please, don't try to stop me*, Danny shoves a short metal rod in her hand, shaped like a hilt that's missing the blade.

"It's a nova-sword," her cousin says in a rush. "Tae made it for me. When you tap the pommel, the nova-light blade comes out. Go!"

For a moment, Sascia is struck; here Danny is, her best friend, her greatest ally, offering a weapon and telling her to go, understanding, in that way only Danny can, that Sascia *has* to save Mooch.

She turns and breaks into a run.

Her lungs heave, her legs burn, her shoulders bump into startled onlookers. Her only thought is the nova-lights—if Mooch flies into their beams, they'll vaporize it instantly.

But Mooch has stopped, hovering in midair before the eastern entrance of the observation deck. When Sascia reaches it, panicked and out of breath, it doesn't let her stop. It grabs one side of her hood and drags her, with impossible strength, up the stairs.

The deck is in pandemonium. Security guards usher people away, tourists scream, selfie sticks and tour-guide flags flap around. Mooch is pulling her against the flow of the panicking crowd. Sascia's mind empties. She becomes instinct and dread, fighting her way across a sea of bodies, swallowed and resurfacing and swallowed again.

And then, finally, she's standing before the windows.

Her muscles are clenched with tension. Her knees shake from the run and the climb and the near stampede, and her phone is buzzing in the back pocket of her jeans, no doubt Crow or Shivani panicking over the Flare. But Sascia ignores it all because the Maw is *moving*.

Ripples shatter its smooth black surface. At the very center, a bulge is growing, as though something is pushing it from the inside. An arm breaks through the liquid dark. A figure pulls itself out, then two more. Three elves climb out, nova-light bouncing off their onyx armor and long crystalline swords. One has long white hair, the other gnarled horns, and leading them is Nugau, with his purple snowflake Darkprint and angular features and intelligent violet eyes.

Soldiers rush down the walkway at the top of the concrete barrier. Assault rifles glisten beneath the glow of the nova-lights. A teeth-rattling sound echoes across the barrier as a giant cannon begins whirring into position. Sascia recognizes it instantly: Tae's cannon. He and Crow completed the designs just last week and already the Chapter has forged it in metal and plastic. In the ten-foot-wide barrel, a beam of light has started to form, larger and stronger than from any nova-weapon previously in existence.

At the center of the Maw, Nugau and the elves shield their eyes from the blinding force of the nova-light panels of the barrier. They don't see the cannon aimed directly at them. They don't realize they're only seconds away from instant death.

Sascia's legs react on their own, breaking into a sprint. Tucked into the side of the observation deck, there's a nondescript restricted-access door that leads to the barrier. It's propped open by a security guard while he fumbles with his nova-gun. Sascia slips right past him, ignoring his shouts. Up the stairs she goes, past a team of soldiers, out another door, then—

She's standing before the Maw. Mooch twirls around her head in a frenzy. On her left and right, soldiers and Chapter XI agents stomp down the walkway. Orders are being barked. Guns are being cocked. Cheeks flattened against rifles, fingers on triggers.

Straight across from her, the nova-cannon has loaded up to full capacity.

In Sascia's mind, there's only room for one thought: *Nugau will die.*

Only: *I can't let Nugau die.*

She puts a foot on the metal fence of the walkway, heaves all her strength behind her legs, and jumps.

PART II

Thistha Ren (theesh·thuh ren) *compound noun*

a Heart Claim; when a desire is asserted and proven through a test of the claimant's intentions, typically endorsed by a group beating their fists against their chests.

Technical; while its origins are unknown, it is widely accepted as the oldest and most fundamental law of Itkalin. The practice of mimicking the heartbeat against the chest emerged during the Reign of the Hundred Monarchs, where at least five new challengers to the throne demanded a Thistha Ren per day and endorsement by ballot became tedious to the voters.

19

PRETTY FEAR, PRETTY TERROR

It is nothing like falling. There's no air whooshing past, no drop in her stomach, no rampant flailing of the arms.

The Maw simply *swallows* her.

Her arm is around Nugau's waist, where she grabbed him to save him from the cannon. Her other arm is around the second elf's, with the third elf trapped between them, all four of them a tangle of limbs and strained squeaks of alarm.

Darkness presses in around them, tight and heavy and *cold*. Mere seconds have passed and yet Sascia is already struggling to draw a breath. Her skin stings. Her arms are going numb; consciousness threatens to abandon her. In the moments between panic, she thinks: What a fitting death for a girl in love with the Dark. An endless fall into the bottomless black.

But then, Mooch flutters across her vision. In the pitch dark, its Darkprint is doubly vibrant, a kaleidoscopic gleam of light with every snap of its wings. It soars in a circle around the four bodies. At every fall of its wings, the Dark *splits*. A rip of light cuts through the black right beneath their feet, and between one moment and the next, the Maw disappears.

Sascia drops like a sack of potatoes onto smooth concrete. Stabs of pain splinter down her left hip. She rolls to her back and rubs her thigh, gritting her jaw to keep her cry in. She is aware of movements around her, words spoken in a strange language, angry questions from the three elves.

Reality comes crashing down: she just jumped into the Maw. To save three elves clad in armor and carrying weapons and looking all-around very hostile. What the absolute hell was she thinking—except she wasn't thinking, as per usual, and now she has to face the consequences.

Hastily, she fumbles for the nova-sword Danny gave her and points it away from the Darkhumanoids, so as not to hurt them. It flicks on with a lightsaber type of *whoosh*. A needle of a blade emerges from the hilt, dotted with hundreds of tiny nova fairy lights. They coalesce into a long, thick beam of solid light, which casts a bright glow on her surroundings.

It's a subway station. The vibrant white of the sword reflects on the turnstiles a few feet away. Posters peel off the walls and glass shards dust the floor, as though the station is some great serpent, shedding its human skin to welcome the onyx scales of the Dark. The walls have surrendered to a mural of ivy. Moss coats the tiles, weaving the cold concrete into a tapestry of black stitched with the neon colors of the Darkworld.

A blue-and-green tile names the station: 23RD STREET. After the Darkgriffin tore a hole into Manhattan, the city discontinued this section of the subway, redirecting lines to run around the Maw. But deep in the bowels of Manhattan, the abandoned stations still stand. In the absence of light, the Dark has overrun the place, claiming it as its own.

She sweeps the blade to her left—

A stunned scream rips through her throat.

The face of an elf hovers inches away from her own. It's the scariest of the three she just saved. Two thick ramming horns, like those of a buffalo, carve their temples and frame their cheeks in a crown of ivory. Yellow eyes flicker beneath menacing brows. Their mouth is open; a long tongue swings from side to side, so fast it becomes a blur.

In an instant, Mooch is on Sascia. It batters its body against her chest, pushing her back with its impossible strength. She knows what this means, she knows what it's trying to tell her: *Run.*

The elf bares their fanged teeth. A snarl splits their mouth, echoing down the walls of the station.

Sascia's knees buckle. Rational thoughts scatter—she is only instinct, only flight, only terror. She scrambles up and runs, but her limbs are not responding fast enough. She stumbles on the jagged cement and drops to her hands and knees. Her sword skids across the tiles, landing on a thicket of Darkmoss.

The echo of feet pounding sends her heart hammering. The elf is scampering after her. She twists and aims a kick at their head, but the elf easily sidesteps it and, within seconds, scrambles over her fallen body, pinning both her wrists to the ground.

"Pretty fear, pretty terror!" the elf screeches. "Too bad it has to die."

Their face leers inches above her own, yellow-eyed and barefanged. Saliva drips from their mouth to her cheek.

Frenzied whimpers torrent out of Sascia's mouth. "Get off, get off, get off!"

Then their weight on her eases. She scrambles back until she hits a wall and lunges for the nova-sword—an elegant leather boot lands on its hilt.

Nugau stands above her.

On his cheeks, the swirls of his Darkprint glow a deep purple, as they did in Times Square. His tall frame imposes against the backdrop of shifting shadows; he's dressed in a breastplate inlaid with floral designs over a tight jacket and pants. His hair is in the careless shag she first saw in Times Square, yet his neck is bare of the scar he had when he attacked her then. There is no gash on his forehead like when he arrived poisoned in her bedroom. This is a Nugau before the attack, before the poisoning. But is it a Nugau who knows her? Who trusts her? (Who cares for her?)

He holds the horned elf suspended in the air by the back of their collar. Behind him stands the third elf, short and slender with long white-blond hair and a metal mask over the lower part of their face. Nugau and the horned elf are going back and forth in low, hissing tones.

The horned elf bursts out in English, "Spy! Assassin!"

Nugau answers in rapid words, of which Sascia only catches one: *itka*. His hand flourishes in the direction of Mooch.

All three elves study the moth now sitting on Sascia's chest.

Itka, Sascia thinks. An ancient leader to the other moths. A god to the Darkworld. She doesn't need to know the language to realize Mooch's affection for her just saved her life.

"Human," Nugau says. "Who are you? Why did you push us back in?"

His eyes slide to the ceiling. The concrete is smooth now, no evidence of the rip Mooch created or the searing black of the Maw beyond.

Human. Not *Sascia*. Not *little gnat*. Nugau doesn't know her yet.

Stricken and befuddled by her own thoughts, Sascia takes too long to answer.

Nugau releases the horned elf. In a flash of movement, they have pinned Sascia's arms to the wall and dug their knee into her chest. "Answer, pretty," they hiss. "But no lies. The prince of Itkalin does not like lies."

Pain is crushing into her torso. Her lungs struggle; her mind fills with terror. "I was trying to protect you! They would have struck you with the nova-cannon—it would have killed you!"

Nugau cocks his head. "And what interest do you have in our well-being, human?"

The horned elf's knee rams into Sascia's rib cage—

"I know about ymneen! About knotted time!" Sascia shouts. "I have met you before. A version of you from the future. You told me a war is coming that neither my species nor yours can survive. I am not a spy or an assassin. I'm just a student who works with Darkmoths—what you call *itka*."

Her revelations ring around the empty station. The pressure on Sascia's chest eases as the horned elf glances at Nugau over their shoulder.

"You know the human?" the elf spits at Nugau.

Their tone is accusatory; in response, a frigid mask slides over Nugau's features. He replies in their language with well-measured, confident words, but the horned elf still looks suspicious. Sascia's senses are alert, all too aware of the threat closing in around her. Is it a crime to know her? Do these elves hate humans?

"The itka," Nugau says. "When we were traveling between our two worlds just now, you were freezing. You would have died. But the itka protected you. It brought us back here to the tunnels. Why?"

"I don't know. I have always had an affinity to its kind. This one just appeared one day—" Sascia stops. If knowing her is a reason to suspect Nugau, perhaps she shouldn't reveal exactly how Mooch came to her, at least not in the presence of the horned elf. "I protect it," she says instead. "And it protects me."

The statement must carry some gravity in their world. Matching expressions of disbelief draw on the faces of the three elves.

Then, without warning, the horned elf slaps her. *"Liar!"*

Sascia's head flattens against the wall. Her skull rings with the force of the strike; she can taste blood in her mouth. Slowly, her senses recover—when she opens her eyes, the horned elf is sprawled on the floor halfway across the room. Their arms are up, and they are squeaking and cursing against a battering of blows from Mooch.

Nugau stands before Sascia, his back to her, legs splayed and chest heaving, as though he's the one who just tossed the other elf across the room.

The tension is broken only by the white-haired elf, who is chuckling at their comrade's squeaks against Mooch's assault. Leisurely, they nudge their head in Sascia's direction. "We cannot leave the human here," they tell Nugau. "We will bring them to the Queen. Let her decide their fate."

Nugau gives an almost reluctant nod. "Stand, human. You're coming with us."

Sascia gathers herself up as best she can. Her cheek blazes hot with stinging and shame. Her jeans are wet and her Doc Martens caked with black mud. A patch of moss has attached to her elbow; she flicks it off and tugs her hair behind her ears. That slap has morphed all her terror into anger.

When Nugau makes to take her by the elbow, Sascia snaps her arm away.

"Walk, human—"

"Sascia," she cuts him off. "My name is Sascia."

If he recognizes the name, he doesn't show it.

20

MAKE THE CLAIM

Sascia can tell they're nearing their destination when the air begins to vibrate with the collective buzz of a big crowd. For the past hour, the elves have been leading her through a maze of abandoned tunnels. Behind her, Nugau is a solemn presence. He hasn't spoken another word to her during the trek, but she has caught his eyes on her, there and gone the instant she looks back, as though he is studying her just as intently as she studies him.

They come to a stop before a double door. The horned elf (Ktren, Sascia has learned) slips past the rest of them and disappears through it, leaving a husky laugh in their wake. Without speaking, the white-haired elf (Lady Thalla, she introduced herself as) falls behind Sascia, and Nugau steps forward to take the lead. Before stepping through, he takes a moment to gather himself, schooling his features into a frigid indifference.

Soft blue light casts silken shadows on the crumbling subway station that opens before them. Rungs of twisted metal support a collapsed ceiling fifty feet high. Rusty skeletons of subway cars lie on their sides around the perimeter of the vast cavern. Rubble has been piled in the corners, creating an open floor at the center.

There are elves everywhere.

Lounging on the overturned cars, perched on benches and dismantled seats, hanging from swings made of vines. They number in the thousands, of different skin tones and facial features and body types, but all dressed in onyx leathers and carrying blades on their hips, backs, or arms. Some have horns that slope between serpentine locks. Others sport tails or extra-long limbs or scales that cover them from head to toe. A few have the velvet-smooth wings of a bat.

At the far end of the cavern, a majestic elf is sitting on a throne of interlocked roots and vines. A flowing black gown falls over their shoulders, accentuating their narrow waist and drifting into puffs of smoke around their ankles. Their angular face seems chiseled out of pale porcelain to show off a pair of striking violet eyes. A crown of onyx shards laced with silver crests the curls that drape over their chest and spill onto the ground at their feet. The Darkprints on their cheeks are a feminine blue. Sascia knows who stands before her: the Queen.

On the Queen's left stands Ktren, bent at the waist and whispering furiously into their regent's ear. As Nugau leads their small procession down the clear space of the cavern, the Queen's eyes cut to them. When Ktren has finished talking, she twirls a hand at a guard, who draws an elegant crystal sword from its scabbard.

Sascia stops walking. That sword—it's for her, isn't it? Without a word spoken, without a single chance given, they're going to kill her. Her feet shuffle back, but Thalla is already there, her small frame a wall of armor.

Sensing danger, Mooch drifts out of her hood. Sascia quickly tucks it back against her chest, but the crowd has noticed.

A chorus of hisses rushes through the room. It does not quite sound like human hatred, but there's no other way to describe it;

all around her, the crowd has gone wild and furious. They bare their teeth and flare their wings and spew a single word in their language—then, from one of them, in English:

"Thief!"

The Queen's attention has shifted to Mooch. She leans eagerly forward and speaks a soft command, at which Nugau obediently approaches Sascia. Her hands come up on instinct, flat against Nugau's breastplate. Over his shoulder, she can see the Queen's soldier advance toward her. Their sword is drawn, glimmering where it catches the light.

Palpitations choke Sascia's throat. "What—"

"The itka are sacred to us." Nugau is so close his whisper shifts her hair. "My kin don't believe it came to you willingly. They believe you stole it and trapped it. The Queen is ordering you to release the itka to her. If you don't, she will not hesitate to use violence."

"I didn't steal it or trap it," Sascia breathes. "Mooch comes and goes as it pleases—"

"Prove it, then. Release the itka to the Queen."

Sascia looks down at where she's holding Mooch against her chest. The Queen won't harm it, not if the itka are considered gods, but it still takes a lot of willpower to pry her fingers open. Liberated, Mooch instantly drifts into the air. Across the cave, the Queen stands and unfolds her palm. But Mooch doesn't fly to her; instead, it leisurely twirls about and lands back on Sascia's hands.

"Now's not the time to play favorites," Sascia whispers. *"Go."*

As if to spite her, Mooch settles deeper into her palm and begins pulsing contently, like a purring cat.

The Queen lowers her hand, her ire betrayed only in the sneering reaction of a select group of elves gathered around her dais.

Her councilors, perhaps; they're all strapped with jeweled scabbards and fancier armor. The guard begins to advance once more.

It can't end like this. Sascia was supposed to have another chance. To make the right choices this time. To stop the war. She jumped into the goddamn Maw—for what? A swift death in the bowels of the city, unseen and unremarkable?

The guard is almost there, their arms swinging back to land the blow.

A sound echoes through the cave, flesh against metal. *Thump, thump, thump.*

Nugau stands tall at Sascia's side, his fist thumping his breastplate. He shifts his chin and whispers, for her ears alone, "This is the only thing I'll ever do for you, human. Try not to waste it."

"*Nugau,*" Thalla hisses behind Sascia's shoulder.

But the prince does not heed his friend's unspoken objection. He steps forward, placing himself between the guard and Sascia, and begins speaking in the language of the elves.

"What is happening?" Sascia whispers. "What is he doing?"

For a few seconds, it seems as if Thalla will not reply. Then, when Nugau is done, Thalla explains, quiet and hurried and filled with dread. "He is making a Thistha Ren. A Heart Claim. Under our law, it is the highest form of judgment—and the only thing that can save your life. When a Claim is made, it has to be proven through a trial. Right now, he is making a Claim on your behalf: That the itka protects you and you protect it. That it showed you the way out of our darkness. The Queen has no choice but to test the truth of your Claim."

A despotic silence falls upon the room, heavy and absolute. The violet beads of the Queen's eyes are locked on Sascia and Nugau. Slowly, deliberately, her lips split back to reveal long, blackened fangs. A hiss echoes down the chamber, raising the hairs on Sascia's arms. Black gathers at the fingertips of the Queen's left hand, like the crackling of electricity before the inevitable lightning strike.

Her arm shoots out. Tendrils of Dark explode from her clawed fingers.

Sascia braces herself—but she is not the target.

Nugau drops to his knees, held there by a grip of darkness around his nape. His eyes are wide, his arms braced against the marble. Horrible, strangled gasps sputter from his mouth.

Sascia has little time to react—the Queen is addressing her, which Thalla translates in swift, panicked bursts. "Under our law and tradition, a Heart Claim must be tested in a Heart Trial. If you pass the Trial, you will have proven your Claim true. If you fail, you and the prince will suffer whatever sentence I see fit."

Sharp murmurs flow through the cavern, the elves sharing in their queen's displeasure.

Through trembling lips, Nugau whispers, "Thalla. Orran. Help the human."

As though summoned out of thin air, a new elf, big and winged, steps out of the shadows on Sascia's left. With practiced speed, Thalla removes her breastplate and chain mail and the other elf, Orran, places them over Sascia's head, strapping her in tight. Then, just as quickly, they both fold back into the shadows.

The gravity of the situation suddenly crushes into Sascia, as terrifying and unwelcome as the black metal on her shoulders. They have armed her for *battle*.

Around her, thousands of elves perch at the edge of their seats, brimming with bloodthirst and anticipation. With a flick of the Queen's free hand, a curtain of darkness rushes over the grooves of the stone floor and coalesces in the middle of the cavern.

The dais and the elves' resting spots catapult to a staggering height, while the floor of the cavern plummets. Behind Sascia, concrete ripples and Darkflora shudders. The earth splits and morphs into a tangle of sharp turns, dead ends, and convoluted passageways that stretch to the other end of the cave.

A labyrinth.

Sascia's mind flashes back to last night in her bedroom. *I can help you*, she had told Nugau. *Oh, but you do, little gnat*, Nugau had said. *Or you try to. A brave Ariadne in a labyrinth of terrors, clever and strong. But war is cleverer still. Violence is stronger still. You fail. We all fail.*

Sascia refuses to fail. Her eyes skid over the alleyways, trying to memorize some course to the single opening across the room, but the thunderous strike of a gong chimes through the air, drawing her attention back to the dais, now perched twenty feet above her.

The Queen is gazing down at her and Nugau, the two of them separated from the rest, like sheep headed to the slaughter. Her grip of darkness still holds the prince bent over the ground. Strain and ache groove his face in deep lines. Yet when she speaks, he is obliged to translate.

"My son Claims you are a friend of the itka," Nugau breathes. "That the itka guided your way out of the Dark. So here is your Trial, human: a labyrinth. You have until the third strike of the gong to prove my son's Claim and find your way out."

Then, without warning or preamble, the Queen swats the air.

A beam of Dark shoots across the arena.

It knocks Sascia straight in the chest—she goes flying over the edge and into the Labyrinth.

21

GNARLED ANTLERS

She lands on her side, the rough-hewn onyx of the breastplate digging into her rib cage. The walls of the Labyrinth are twice her height, slick and lustrous as though cut from the earth with a heated blade. The passageways are narrow; now standing, she can touch each wall if she spreads her arms. Above the Labyrinth, she can make out the elves. They're hollering at her, heedless of the fact that she can't understand a word. Yet the Queen is serene. At the foot of her dais, Nugau is slumped on his hands and knees, the black grip of the Queen's power around his neck.

This is the only thing I'll ever do for you, human. Try not to waste it. Nugau risked this anger, this punishment, for Sascia. He made the Thistha Ren, the Heart Claim, to save her life. He asked his friends to help her. Sascia can't fail him, or fail this Trial.

The two sides of the passageway look identical, but she needs to be careful with her choices. In the corn maze she and Danny once visited while their aunt Sophia lived in Vermont, they had been advised to keep their right hand against the wall of cornstalks and follow it out. In the myth of Ariadne, the princess gave Theseus a thread to unspool to find his way out. But Sascia has no thread and no time to waste.

What she has, the whole point of this damned kerfuffle, is Mooch.

"Little guy? Are you here?"

Wings caress the soft skin of her neck. The moth nibbles at her earlobe. *A friend,* Nugau said. Sascia feels it now, as she always has: Mooch protects her and she protects it. Nugau has not made a false Claim—she is a friend, not a foe.

"Can you help me get out of here?" she asks. "Please?"

In response, Mooch launches down the left end of the passageway. Indignant sighs carry down from the elves on the perimeter of the cavern. Sascia smothers her smile—take that, you disbelieving gremlins!—and follows Mooch, picking up speed. Sharp turns and endless black walls fly past for several minutes.

Then, just as Mooch dives low down the path, the wall *shifts*.

Stone whooshes past to bridge the opening that had been there before. Her mind registers the change too late—she smacks face first into the wall. Above, the elves burst into a wave of snickers.

Sascia won't give them the satisfaction of her anger. With a step back, she surveys the new obstacle. The edges of the wall have smoothed over, swallowed into the rest of the rock. Sascia pokes at it with the reliable sturdiness of her Doc Martens; the wall is hard stone, but its foundation is a liquid kind of black, the tip of her boot sucked into its depths.

The Labyrinth is made of Dark.

She snaps her foot back with a sharp inhale. If the maze is constructed of the eerie void that makes up the Dark, then the Queen can command its essence with a mere flick of her wrist. She can change its pathways and turns, sending Sascia on a wild goose chase through its walls.

This game has been rigged from the beginning. The Queen only accepted this Heart Claim because she knows a human girl has no chance of winning this Trial.

Blood and fright pulse vivid at Sascia's neck. "Mooch?"

The moth had been on the other side when the opening closed. At her call, it emerges, squeezing through the Dark at the base of the wall.

"How am I supposed to do this?" she mutters. "If the Queen can control everything?"

Mooch twists around and swoops in the air, diving low before it disappears into the wall. Then it reappears to hover in the air on the level of Sascia's eyes. It looks at her; she looks at it.

"*Oh*," Sascia says. "You knew it was going to do that. You were telling me to go low."

In reply, the moth surges forward to boop her on the nose. Silly, wonderful creature.

"We move fast," she tells Mooch. "We stop at nothing. Straight to the exit, before she realizes you know how she will manipulate the Labyrinth. Yes?"

The moth boops her again.

Sascia rubs the tip of her nose. "I'm not too sure I like this new means of communication. Ready?"

Evidently, Mooch is one hundred percent ready, because it launches in the air, faster than Sascia can follow. She breaks into a run after the moth, turning when it twists, jumping when it flies high, crouching when it dives. The Labyrinth becomes a blur; she senses the whoosh of air when a wall comes down to block her path—but Mooch has already instructed her to slide beneath the dropping stone. She stumbles when a wall sprouts from the ground to cage her in a dead end—but Mooch warned her to jump over it. She edges sideways and scurries through when the walls narrow in on her.

Somewhere above, the gong echoes with two strikes. God, she didn't even hear the first one. How long before the next and final strike?

"How far away are we?" she calls up ahead to Mooch.

In response, the moth doubles its speed, soaring in an arc to let her know she needs to jump over an obstacle.

As a wall of cut stone surges from the ground, Sascia makes a split-second decision (arguably, her forte). Instead of over it, she jumps on it. Her arms flail, desperately trying to balance as the wall grows to its full height. Sascia is suddenly standing on top of the Labyrinth, a view of mazework and elves stretching all around her.

Her trick is met with equal parts excitement and fury. Howls and whistles echo down to her, far louder here than in the passageways of the maze. Up ahead, the way out is marked by a simple absence of wall at the end of a path, barely as wide as a door. Sascia takes stock of the space that separates them: if she uses her good balance and light steps, she can make it to the exit *on top* of the Labyrinth.

But that's not happening if she's being weighed down by what feels like twenty pounds of metal. Steeling her legs, she begins stripping. Down clatters the breastplate. She's tugging the chain mail over her chest when the wall beneath her quakes.

Shit. The Queen is onto her.

The royal elf stands at the edge of the dais. Her fingers rotate—on her end of the Labyrinth, its entrance, the passageways begin to crumble. Puffs of black dust rise from their collapsing forms, rousing a cheer from the elves.

Time to skedaddle. Sascia lets the chain mail fall back on her torso, crouches down, and jumps. Mooch is right there with her, fleeting in and out of her vision as she lands smoothly on the opposite wall and keeps going.

Behind her, the roar of crumbling stones is growing closer.

Ahead, the way out is only fifty feet away.

Then, from the corner of her eye, she sees it.

For the first few seconds, it is nothing but a shadow scurrying down a passageway. Then its body comes together out of the Dark: abnormally long limbs, a curved spine and skeletal torso, a head topped with twisted, menacing antlers. It looks like a werecreature, half man, half deer, except it has no eyes and no fur—its body is coated with a liquid darkness that splatters the walls with blotches of tar.

It's the most terrifying Darkcreature she's ever seen.

With increasing speed, it propels itself off the opposite wall and launches into the air. The impact of its landing sets the wall trembling. Sascia slows to a stop, crouching low. The creature is blocking her path. It stands on all fours, its taloned feet scraping against the stone, a horrible, grisly sound. Its nostrils flare. Its sightless head snaps to her.

It moves like a half-dead thing, joints creaking and bending in unnatural ways, steps wild and erratic, skin dripping that black, rotten pus onto the wall.

Sascia's legs have gone weak. If it lunges—*when* it lunges—there's nothing she can do to stop it. Its fangs are a row of jagged, broken teeth, its lips so wide they reach up to its antlers; in some twisted, horrid way, it looks like it's smiling. One swing, and those fangs will sink deep into her flesh. Even with the stupid chain mail, she doesn't stand a chance—

The chain mail. It's little protection against the creature's long, thin teeth, but it doesn't have to be *protection*. It can be a weapon, instead.

Slowly, Sascia begins backtracking, staying low as she slips her arms out of the sleeves of the chain mail. The Darkcreature follows, its movements shifting between cautious and jerky. Sascia tugs the chain mail over her head. She'll have to be fast now, and attack first—

"*Mooch!*" she screams.

The moth has been cutting frantic circles over their heads, but in a lightning-fast move, the Darkcreature straightens to its full height, opens its snout so wide that its lower jaw touches its chest, and closes it around Mooch.

Oh hell no.

Fury pumps into Sascia like a shot of adrenaline. She lets impulse take the wheel: she holds the chain mail like a net between her arms and jumps at the Darkcreature. The wetness of its skeletal body smears her skin as she wrestles the net around the creature's head. It thrashes about, trying to dislodge her—gravity takes over.

They drop like a stone back into the Labyrinth. Pain shoots up her leg where her ankle twists at the landing, but she wiggles herself over the creature's back. Its long limbs are spread out, talons scraping grooves into the stone. It tosses its head this way and that, but the chain mail is twined firmly into its antlers.

Sascia smacks its snout as hard as she can. Her fingers come away coated in black tar, but she doesn't care. The maze echoes with elven shouts. She punches the creature again and again, her whole body aching with the effort of holding its body down, until finally, on the sixth strike, the Darkcreature opens its jaws. A terrifying screech grates out of its throat—

And so does a small patch of luminescent white.

In its hurry to escape, Mooch bangs into a wall and collapses on the ground. Sascia disentangles herself from the creature and scurries over. "I got you," she stammers, picking Mooch up. "You're safe."

The Darkcreature is dazed, writhing flaccidly against the chain mail. Sascia grabs hold of one of its antlers and drags it down the passageway as it tosses and thrusts behind her. Snot is dripping down her nose (is she crying?), something hot is leaking out of a gash on her arm, and her twisted ankle throbs with every step, but she keeps going, because that's all she knows how to do.

She's moving fast, spurred by adrenaline, leaving no room for the Queen to stop her. The long corridor opens before her—she makes it through the final opening mere seconds before the third gong sounds.

The room explodes with sound, cheers and hisses and, above it all, gradually building, the sound of fists against breasts, the thudding of a heart. It carries meaning, this inhumanly slow heartbeat, as though it is a vote cast from the chest, because Sascia *is* special after all, chosen by their precious god, gifted with the kind of magic that can carry you through a deadly Labyrinth. In the triumph of noise, Sascia throws her head back and gulps hungry breaths.

She did it. She *won*.

Tendrils of hair waft in her face as the Labyrinth fades away. Once again, Sascia stands in the middle of the throne room, a bleeding, sweating speck on the expanse of hard stone. In the distance, the Queen sits back on her dais. The heartbeat of the elves' support dies off.

Footsteps prowl behind Sascia. Hands lock around her arms.

The Queen's guard is a hulking mass of armor and hard serpentine skin. In her palm, Mooch's wings are slick with the creature's black saliva. They need to be cleaned, as quickly as possible. But when she tries to inform the elves, the guard silences her with a taloned grip at her nape. The precious glow of her victory fades away, draining the drum of *special, chosen, magic* that beat through her veins only a minute ago.

Reality comes crashing back down. She won her Trial, proved her Claim, but that doesn't mean they will release her. They're going to toss her in a dungeon to rot for the rest of her short, miserable existence, because she already *knows too much*—that there are thousands of elves gathered in the discontinued train tunnels beneath Manhattan, armed and hateful.

Her neck strains against the soldier's grip to glance at Nugau. He lies at the foot of the dais, still yoked by the Queen's plume of Dark.

The threat of tears prickles at her nose. She did what he told her. She did not waste the chance he gave her. She crossed a moving, shifting labyrinth and fought the scariest Darkcreature she's ever encountered and saved Mooch from its jaws. After what they just saw, surely no one can doubt she is protected by the itka, a lover of the Dark, an ally who only came here to stop a war—

The thought strikes deep, echoing up from the well of her heart. *Special, chosen, magic* is her oldest, truest longing, yes, but that is not why she jumped into the Maw, why she saved a poisoned Nugau, why she lowered her nova-gun in Times Square. This morning, as she lay in bed puzzling out the intricacies of knotted time, the mistakes she has not yet made, she had decided: What she wanted was another chance. A different choice. *Peace*.

When a Claim is made, it has to be proven through a Trial, Thalla said. *The Queen has no choice but to test the truth of your Claim.*

As she's shoved and manhandled down the throne room, Sascia brings her fist to her chest. The sound is soft at first, then, as the elves notice and fall quiet, it rings clear.

Thump. Thump. Thump.

"I make the Thistha Ren," Sascia cries out. "I make a new Heart Claim. You saw it just now. I protect the itka and the itka protects me. But I'm not just a friend or ally. I make my Claim now and demand a new Trial, to prove what I really am—your ambassador to humans, a messenger of peace!"

22

THEN DON'T

Sascia and Danny are both fifteen, that strange liminal space between her birthday in April and his in June where he'll jump a year ahead again.

Their parents and the restaurant staff have come down with a nasty flu. Athena's Yard has been closed for the week and the three kids have been shipped off to Sascia's godmother's place down the street. Noná Beth is a single woman in her mid-forties with a lucrative banker salary; her house contains a pristine assortment of minimalist furniture and abstract paintings. On the days Beth works from home, there is a strict no-noise rule. Ksenya has taken to long history podcasts; Sascia and Danny have taken to sneaking out.

Beth is getting a pool installed in her backyard. The earth has been carved open and the piping laid down. Sascia and Danny like to climb into the hole and poke at the mounds of dark dirt, while gossiping about the kids at school. One day, Danny kicks a canvas-covered object that rings hollow and metallic.

It's a manhole of some kind. The builders must have discovered it while digging. Sascia and Danny glance at each other, retreat into the house, and return with flashlights. The bottom of the manhole opens up to a concrete tunnel about seven feet wide. Soon, the metallic chime of their footfalls is replaced by soft susurrations.

Thick Darklichen covers the tunnel floor.

"*Ooh,*" Danny coos. "It's so beautiful."

It is, frankly, stunning. A microcosm of delicate tendrils sprouts from the moist earth, drawing a vivid mosaic of greens and pinks and oranges. The leaves seem to breathe, rising and falling like a single, shared lung.

Danny has always loved plants. Lately, with college applications looming on the horizon, he's taken an interest in botany. He wants to come back with tweezers and a light-proof box to gather samples—Sascia is elated to oblige.

The next day, they venture a little farther. On the third, they find another manhole that comes out on Beth's grumpy neighbor Joe's backyard, behind his shed. By the seventh day, they have a tiny colony of lichen growing in two Nike shoeboxes.

By the end of the month, their parents are healthy again and the two shoeboxes have become a whole abandoned utility closet at the very back of their building's basement. The lichen has become a proper garden, blooming with what Danny believes to be Darkirises, Darkhydrangeas, and Darkfoxgloves and crawling with Darkants, Darkcentipedes, and little buzzing Darkbees. (Sascia likes those best, the insects, their wings and antennae and too many legs, and the symbiotic relationship they develop with the plants they feed on.)

By midsummer, three months later, they discover a nest in the tunnel system. At first, they can't understand what they're seeing. It looks like a cocoon spun from moonlight itself, attached to the walls of the tunnel by a dozen silken webs. But when they flash their light on it (turned extra low, to cause no damage), they can see tiny larvae holed into cocoons—*pupas*, as they're called at this stage. They don't touch the nest, but they come back every day to check on it.

A few weeks later, they visit the manhole behind Joe's to find it hammered closed. DISINFECTION IN PROCESS, the sign on top reads. DO NOT ENTER.

Danny starts panting with the same panic Sascia feels galloping through her chest. Disinfection means men with nova-blasters and flamethrowers razing everything in sight. All those blooms and bushes, all those insects and rodents—gone. It takes long, agonizing minutes for Sascia to wrench the cover off with a crowbar. She and Danny run through the tunnels, flickering their flashlights on and off at full lumen. It's a trick they've learned from other Dark aficionados on the internet. The quick bursts of nova-light don't harm the Darkflora and fauna, but scare them enough to force them to retreat back into the Darkworld.

But the cocoon doesn't react to their warning. The larvae inside are too young, too brainless to realize what the blaring alarm of Sascia's flashlight means.

"They're here," Danny warns.

The furnace of the exterminators' flamethrowers reflects on the walls at the end of the tunnel. Orange grooves into the concrete. The air distorts with waves of heat.

"We need to get out before they see us," Danny warns. What they're doing is not exactly legal.

"I can't leave them here to die."

His gaze holds on to hers, like a secret agreement. "Then don't."

Sascia takes off her coat, pulls the cocoon into it, and runs.

THEY HATCH IN EARLY September.

Now that they're busy with schoolwork again, Danny and Sascia take turns sneaking down to the basement and caring for their little garden. On a random Tuesday, Sascia finds the cocoon split open. Empty gray pupal cases are scattered everywhere. Tiny bodies try to unfold their delicate, crumpled wings. Those with expanded wings crawl on the sides of the closet, while others fluff about, trying to fly.

Moths, all of them, the prettiest creatures Sascia has ever seen.

23

LITTLE GNAT

Sascia wakes to a bowl of soup.

It's placed on the sofa inches from her face. It smells briny, like ramen; some kind of baked good is balanced on the rim of the bowl. Sascia is suddenly aware of how empty her stomach feels, how slow and weak her limbs.

Last night, after making her Heart Claim, she was escorted to what must once have been a staff break room, with two beaten-up sofas facing each other, a row of mass-market paperbacks abandoned on a side table, and a water cooler growing a whole colony of fungi in the corner. She tended Mooch back to health and cleaned her own wounds as best she could, then sat on one of the sofas, her arms wrapped tight around her knees. She doesn't remember falling asleep, but now, as she begins to stir, her body creaks and groans all over. Nearly a day must have passed since she jumped into the Maw—she imagines Danny and the cohort, her parents, huddled together, worry lining their sleepless eyes.

Yet *she* slept. She, who found herself among thousands of elves, narrowly survived their Trial, and volunteered for a second one. Guilt straps tight around her chest—her choices, however noble, mean that somewhere above these tunnels, her loved ones are hurting.

A knot of cerulean flames twines in midair over Nugau's hand.

He is watching her from the sofa opposite hers, elbows resting on his knees. Thalla is perched on the arm of the sofa behind him and the large, winged elf, Orran, leans against the door.

She didn't get a good look at Nugau's friends yesterday, but today, Sascia lets herself study them. Lady Thalla's Darkprint pulses a soft blue on her cheeks, just as it did yesterday. She is small and lithe, with long legs that curve back like a deer's. Her eyes are far apart; no discernible eyebrows frame them. The lower half of her face is covered with black chiffon.

Orran, on the other hand, takes up nearly half the room: shoulders so broad they pull at the seams of their scaled jacket, thighs so thick they could crush a tree like a woodchipper. Their skin is dark, a russet hue compared to Nugau's gray-blue and Thalla's light turquoise. Enormous iridescent wings sprout from their back, so large that the tips drag on the floor. The Darkprint on their cheeks is a mix of purple and white, one of the elusive genders that human scientists haven't been able to decipher yet.

"Eat," Nugau says, gaze dropping to the bowl.

Sascia drags herself into a sitting position and takes an experimental spoonful. It's rich and salty, like all the best foods. Under Nugau's stare, the working of her jaw feels too mechanical, her bites too loud.

After what feels like an unnecessarily long time, Nugau looks away and speaks, tonelessly, as though he's not addressing her at all. "That is Orran. In the terms of your language, you will address Orran as both he and they. Lady Thalla, you can address as she, but she has also been known to be she-and-they."

"And you signal this change through the marks on your cheeks?" Sascia asks.

He nods once. "All aesin can shift among genders, but not all choose to. Thalla and I prefer to change; Orran and the Queen, among others, prefer to stay in their chosen gender. Blue is female, purple is male, and white is closest to what your people call nonbinary. Two or more colors signify an open fluidity among those genders. How do we address you?"

Sascia holds his gaze. "I prefer she. And you?"

"Me," Nugau drawls, "you claim to know."

"I know only your name. Your pronouns seem to change."

"In Itkalin, I am *siff*. Your language has no direct translation. The closest word is *all*, all genders and all colors, but in terms of pronouns, your gender-neutral *they* will suffice. In fact, it will suffice in any situation when you are unsure. If I am before you, you will address me as what I prefer in the moment." He taps at his purple Darkprint. "Right now, I am he."

It's gratifying to hear Shivani's theory on the many facets of gender in the Dark confirmed, but this is more than an introduction. This feels like instructions. On how to address his friends, but also the rest of the elves—the *aesin*, as he called them. There is no purpose to such directives unless he expects Sascia to be here for a long time.

"Am I to stay, then?" she asks.

"You gave the Queen no other choice. She will set a new Trial for you when she returns from her duties."

At her nape, Sascia senses Mooch's wingbeats. The moth emerges from the tiny pocket of Dark between her hair and goes to perch on its new favorite spot: atop her left ear. Nugau and Thalla pretend not to notice it, but a string of hushed words slips out of Orran's mouth. They place the knuckles of their index and middle fingers against their lips, in a gesture that looks—and sounds—like reverence.

The slow drumbeat of thousands of fists against thousands of breasts echoes in Sascia's mind. Last night, for those brief moments when the aesin cast their vote, she had felt aglow with essence, incandescent with purpose: out of everyone up in the city, out of everyone down here, Mooch chose *her*. In the human world, Sascia's affinity with the moths was just one of the many abnormalities of the Dark, but here, it is *power*, a skill she can wield to her advantage, the kind of magic she has longed for all her life.

"What happens now?" she asks.

Over her covering, Thalla's cheekbones rise as though she is smiling—or smirking. "A bit late to regret your Claim now, human."

"I don't," she says resolutely. She has proven herself; perhaps it's success, perhaps it's the itka's favor, but she feels like she can do so much *more*. "A version of you from the future came to me for help," she tells Nugau. "You were poisoned and dying. You told me a war is coming that neither my kind nor yours can survive. That we'll try to stop it—and fail. That I would face a labyrinth of terrors and nearly die in it. But yesterday, I did not come close to dying. I *won*. I changed how things came to pass. I plan to change the rest of it too."

Nugau looks at her impassively, but behind his back, Thalla and Orran share a glance. They speak to the prince in the tongue of the aesin, wearing matching frowns.

"I didn't know," Nugau replies. (Is the English for Sascia's benefit?) "In the tunnel, she only said she has met me. Who poisons me, human?"

"You are betrayed. That's all you said."

That sparks a long back-and-forth among the three aesin. Sascia can't understand a word, but a lifetime in a dual-language household comes in handy. She watches their gestures as they speak, notes the changes in tone and emotion, marks repeated and emphasized words. They are disagreeing over *ymneen*. Knotted time.

"I can tell you everything," she offers, cutting through their conversation. "We can work together to stop it—"

"No." Nugau punctures the word with a slice of his hand through the air. "Ymneen is a curse. I have no interest in engaging with it, with the decisions of a self that will never be. The future you glimpsed will never come to pass. I will make sure that I am never betrayed, and that I never have to stoop so low as to be at *your* mercy."

"Believe me, I don't want that future either," Sascia bites out. "Together, we can ensure it never happens. You can help me prove myself as a messenger of peace. We can convince your kind that war is not the answer. I want to *help* you."

"And what gives you the right to want, human?"

Nugau's outburst is quiet yet sharp, carving Sascia open to expose all the tender parts underneath. She has kept that question sheathed all her life, terrified of its cutting edges. Who is she to long for more, long to be special, to be magic herself? She is no better than anyone else, after all; hasn't life proven that already?

She has no answer to give him, only irritation. She jumped into the damned Maw to save him, she went through the harrowing Trial he volunteered her for, she signed up for a second one to try to make peace between their worlds, and here Nugau is, *mocking* her.

She lets herself just say it. "Why do you hate me?"

The question takes Nugau aback. His pointed ears flatten against his head, yet his voice seethes with revulsion. "You do not know me. You do not know the chaos your kin have brought unto my world. You don't know what war means. What peace costs. Hatred is too small a word for what I feel."

Her stomach twists into knots. She can understand his anger, his fear and confusion; she feels those too, a jumble of emotions ramming between her ribs, but hatred? No, Sascia doesn't understand hatred. From the moment the unknown burst into her life, all she has ever wanted was the freedom to *love* it.

"I am not your enemy," she hisses around the thickness forming at her throat.

"You are human. To the aesin, you'll always be an enemy."

To the aesin. It's an odd way to phrase it. It feels like a choice, not to say *us*.

"And to you?" she asks.

"To me, you are nothing." His features marble into the crystalline indifference he donned while facing the Queen. "An enemy is dangerous because they are an equal. But you, you are just a girl starved. The itka might have led you to us, but it was your hunger that made you follow. It was your greed that made you Claim to be more than you are. And what you are is a little gnat. Vexing but ultimately too ephemeral to be of any consequence."

She should be offended. She should snap back a string of insults. But instead, her mind snags on two words, spat like a curse between clenched teeth: *little gnat*. Nugau has called her that before, when he begged her to kiss him.

The complicated knot of their lives snatches tight around her. Is this the birth of an insult that will turn into a tender nickname? Or has Sascia altered the events of the future enough to erase all potential tenderness from those two words?

A strange kind of confidence pumps through her veins. She leans forward, mimicking his casual stance, and says, "I don't think that's true. I don't think I am nothing to you."

"Oh?" he breathes, as quick to rise to her challenge as she was to set it.

"You made the Heart Claim for me. You told your friends to arm me with protection. You wanted me to live. All of that for an inconsequential gnat?"

Nugau's eyes never leave her face, his features don't shift, not an inch of his body moves, but Sascia *knows*. He is keeping himself still. In this sparring of insults, she has struck the winning blow. A smile steals into the corners of her lips. Abruptly, Nugau unfolds and turns away, a deep mauve dotting his cheeks. It looks almost like Sascia ... *embarrassed* him.

"The Queen has made me responsible for your well-being," Nugau says. "You will stay in this room today to heal and rest, but tomorrow, you will start earning your keep like the rest of us, until the Queen returns to set your Trial. Is that understood?"

His discomfiture is a contagion; her own cheeks heat and her chest feels crammed with the beating of a too-wild heart. She gives Nugau a hurried nod, eyes averted.

"Show her how to use the medicine," Nugau tells his friends. In a few strides, he is at the door, but before he steps out, Sascia catches a glimpse of his neck, just above his high collar. A necklace of bruises marks his skin, deep blue against the smooth porcelain.

Around her, the two aesin spring into action. A tray of pots and vials is placed on the ground before her. Orran instructs Sascia to slather a thick layer of paste on her sprained ankle. He is speaking, but Sascia's mind has glitched: Nugau on his hands and knees, Nugau gripped by a claw of black, Nugau in pain.

"Your queen," Sascia cuts in. "She hurt him. For helping me?"

Orran nods. "The prince and the Queen—"

"Orran," Thalla interrupts. "Don't. Nugau won't like it."

"If she's to survive here," Orran replies quietly, "she has to understand."

"And are we so sure we want her to survive?" Thalla says brazenly.

"We are." With their chin, Orran points to Mooch, now hanging off a strand of Sascia's hair.

Whatever power the itka holds, it certainly shuts Thalla right up.

"The prince was right," Orran tells Sascia. "Your kind has wrought unspeakable damage on our world. The Queen wishes for the destruction to stop, for our lost to be avenged and humans punished. She brought the Jagged Blade, her army, here with that goal in mind. But in your world, the Dark does not obey us as it does in ours. We cannot find a way into your city. We have been stuck here, in these tunnels, for months."

Stuck in an underground station that humans have sealed off and the Maw presses down on—no wonder they can't find their way out. All this time, there has been an entire army less than a mile beneath New York. War was far closer than Sascia had thought.

"But yesterday, you found a way out," Sascia says to Thalla. "Does the Queen know?"

The lady's gaze narrows. "She does. Ktren, the horned aesin, is one of her spies, a part of her trusted council. She assigned them to our scouting party to keep an eye on Nugau. It is the first time we have managed to find an opening to your world. But you stopped us—the Queen knows that, too, human."

"That's where she has gone now, with most of her battalion," Orran says. "To try to find the way out again."

Sudden dread knocks the breath out of Sascia. She's trapped here while a whole battalion pokes at the fabric of the world, trying to fight a path into her city, her family, her friends. "Why would the Queen spy on Nugau?"

Orran opens their mouth, but Thalla cuts them off. "That part is definitely not your story to tell, Orran."

They agree with a grunt and say instead, "The prince has been trying to change the Queen's mind. He argues for a retreat of the army. He wants to seal off the entrances to your world and separate our kind from yours forever. No war, no bloodshed. No more death."

But if Nugau doesn't want war either, why refuse to help Sascia? She thinks of her accusation: *All of that for an inconsequential gnat?* She thinks of his blushing cheeks, his avoidant eyes. Is his objection not to peace, but to Sascia herself?

"The prince does not hate you," Orran says, as though he senses the pathways of her thoughts. "But he is not pleased. He plays a dangerous game: he cannot outright challenge the Queen, but only discuss and debate as respectfully as befits her only living child. Making the Claim on your behalf forced him to show his hand. That he wants neither aesin nor humans to die. And your own Claim has only made things worse. The council now believes he plots against his mother, using you as a pawn to convince the aesin to trust humans and abandon the war. The Queen believes he aims to make himself king."

In a flash of movement, Thalla jumps from the sofa and lunges at Sascia, bringing her face inches away from Sascia's own—terrified, Sascia flattens herself into the sofa. The coppery smell of fresh blood emanates from the elf's concealed mouth.

"And *that's* why she punished him yesterday," Thalla says. "That's why she humiliates him now by making you his ward."

"Thalla," Orran is saying, reaching for the other aesin's arm. "You're scaring her—"

"She *should* be scared." The hiss comes low and guttural, grazing against Sascia's ear. "You only won Nugau's Claim because of the itka. But your kind has destroyed our homes and killed our loved ones for generations. To win your own Claim, to become our ambassador, you will need the favor of the aesin—and unlike our prince, *they* do hate you, human."

24

THE BLUE OF BLOOD

Nugau arrives the next morning dressed in tight black leathers made of thousands of small iridescent scales. Green drops hang from his ears and a belt with three daggers is strapped on his thigh, the same one he wore on Halloween. His hair, usually a shaggy mess framing his face, is pulled back in a low ponytail.

He stands at the threshold for a long moment and draws in a deep breath. "Let's go."

As he turns sharply on his heel, Sascia scrambles to follow, with an overeager Mooch in tow. In the months the aesin have been trapped here, they have converted the abandoned station to a military compound. Sascia and Nugau pass storage rooms packed with weapons and corridors of archery training. From the floor below echo sounds of metal clashing against metal. Aesin cross their path, first gawking at Mooch, then throwing a mistrusting glare at Sascia, then lowering their gaze at their prince before scurrying away.

Nugau opens a door to what used to be a staff locker room. A shower is tucked in the corner, narrow and curtainless. Without speaking, Nugau points to it.

That long, deep breath in the break room—god, she must really stink. Once he's stepped out of the room, Sascia wiggles out of her torn hoodie and muddied pants and steps into the water. (Freezing, of course, but she won't complain; water alone is a luxury in a station sealed off from the rest of the world.) As she scrubs herself clean with the bar of green soap at the holder, she buries her feet deep into the thick layer of Darkmoss on the shower tiles. Moss is one of the gentlest, most benevolent kinds of Darkflora, according to Danny.

Her muscles clench at the thought of him up there, very likely cursing the moment he stuck Tae's nova-sword in her hand and told her to go. News of her jump into the Maw must have trickled through to the rest of the world by now. She can almost picture Aunt Rania's satisfied *I-told-you-so* smile. But Sascia is determined: she'll prove her aunt wrong, prove all of them wrong. She has altered the very first part of what Nugau-from-the-future told her would come to pass. She will complete the Queen's new Trial and emerge from the Dark victorious, with her moth god and an army of allies.

A pile of clean clothes has been left for her by the door, one of the uniforms the aesin wear: a matching set of jacket and trousers made of that glistening scaled fabric, cinched with tight strings at her waist and hips. She takes a moment to scrape the dirt off her Doc Martens and run her hands through her wet hair, combing it back behind her hoop-strewn ears.

She's feeling quite pleased with her black-lizard look until she opens the door—Nugau sets off at once, without a single look at her. "You will be shadowing me today," he says over his shoulder. "Cooking, cleaning, maintenance duties, training. We do things communally, in the army and in our world in general. If you don't help cook, you don't eat. If you don't help clean, you won't get a sleeping cot."

"If I don't do the laundry, I don't get another bomb-ass outfit?"

His head swivels to her, deliberately slow. "Was that a joke?"

Yes, but *that* was certainly not the reaction she was hoping for. "How do you speak my language so well?" she deflects.

"I learned it."

"In *my* world."

"In *your* world," he repeats, mimicking her tone.

She waits, but he doesn't expand. "How about Thalla and Orran? Did they learn it in my world too?"

"No. I taught it to them and anyone else that wanted to learn. We pick up languages with ease, but only a quarter of the army speaks yours. Most aesin will not understand you."

Nugau brings them to a stop at the top of a staircase. From the bottom comes a ruckus of voices and clanging of pots and pans. They seem to be tackling the first item: cooking.

"Do not draw attention to yourself," he commands. "Be quiet, invisible, and respectful. The aesin do not trust you. They will not hesitate to hurt you."

"But why? Why do they hate humans?"

"There is not one aesin in this army that hasn't lost a loved one because of your kin."

Thalla's slithering voice rings in Sascia's ears. *Your kind has destroyed our homes, killed our loved ones for generations.* But humans only learned of the existence of Darkhumanoids a month ago—and had only known of the Dark for six years before that.

"Come," Nugau commands. "We're already late."

The tunnel at the bottom of the stairs is indeed a dining area. Dual tracks line the floor, separated by a row of vine-wrapped columns. In the far left corner, fires burn beneath oddly shaped pots. About a dozen soldiers move purposefully, stirring and chopping and washing, while the rest sit in small clusters around dining tables fashioned out of slabs of metal, torn boards, and decrepit benches.

Hundreds of eyes track Sascia and Nugau as they weave between the tables. Sascia draws herself up to look as casual and indifferent as the prince, but her bravery is only surface level—her heart pulses a thousand beats per second. Thankfully, the soldiers direct her and Nugau to prepping duty the moment they arrive in the kitchen: Sascia is instructed to wash a pile of Darkvegetables while next to her, Nugau skillfully chops them into thin slices.

The repetitiveness of the motion is a balm, familiar from Athena's Yard. For a while, she is only the shift of her fingers, the rough-hewn skin of Darkmushrooms, the soft fluttering of a curious Mooch. She's only distantly aware of aesin coming and going as each battalion wolfs down its food, then sets off again.

Minutes pass, or perhaps hours, before Nugau reappears with two bowls of some kind of orange-tinged gruel. "Come. It's our turn to eat."

Sascia follows him through the sea of tables to where Orran sits. While Nugau falls easily into the aesin's conversation, Sascia spoons her food with one hand and uses the other to offer small bites to Mooch, who devours them in seconds, the little glutton.

"Can I?" Orran says, face shimmering with admiration.

"Of course."

Orran scoots down the bench, dragging his bowl with him. When the moth nibbles at his offered bite, Orran lets out a cooing giggle. "I never thought I'd actually see one."

"Really?" Sascia breathes. "Why?"

"There hasn't been a sighting for nearly a century. We call, but the itka don't come."

Sascia is enraptured again, throat parched for wonder, for veneration, for the magic reflected in someone else's eyes. She recalls that day in the drainage system in Astoria, the moth cocoon wrapped in her jacket as flames consumed the tunnel. She thinks of Mooch, the otherworldly way it seems to understand her. The old yearning thrums through her: *magic, magic, magic.*

"Does it have a name?" Orran asks.

"I call it Mooch. Because it mooches any food it'll find, don't you, little guy?" Her tone goes embarrassingly baby-voicey at the end there, and she quickly glances up, afraid she has somehow offended the aesin's god.

But instead, a smile curves Orran's mouth. "It certainly looks like it—"

A shadow lands on the table and lunges for Mooch.

Bowls rattle, gruel spills, benches are thrown back. The front of a Darkcreature's long body dangles in the air, while the back is hidden among the swirls of Dark between the vines on the ceiling. Three tongues leap out of a horrifyingly humanlike head. Sascia sucks in a breath; she's never seen a Darknaga up close before, one of the serpent creatures that resemble the nagas of Asian mythology. Mooch evades it with ease, burrowing into Sascia's hair, but the damage has been done.

A series of sharp, electrical beeps is the only warning. Sascia knows what will follow—her arms come up, shielding both her eyes and Mooch from the coming light. Nugau barks an order. Chair and table legs screech against the floor. A blast of novalights sears white against Sascia's lids. Then come the hisses, the curses, the cries of pain.

Nova-panels are so common, such a part of her world, that Sascia didn't even notice them mounted on the walls. This tunnel must have been one of the few the city tried to reclaim from the Dark. For a while, after nova-lights were installed, train tracks around the Maw ran smoothly—until the Blackout, when they were surrendered back to the Dark with no hope of return. Activated by movement sensors, wards like these are meant to prevent potential Darkcreature emergence. Subway panels are particularly powerful, more than a hundred thousand lumen, and extremely durable—Sascia can see where the aesin have attempted to smash them and were unsuccessful.

On the table before her, the Darknaga is now a mass of amorphous charred flesh. The aesin begin to peek out from under tables and behind chairs. Angry welts shimmer on their skin where the nova-light struck them before they could take cover. Sascia is the only one still sitting at the table, unhurt.

An aesin, one of the councilors who stood closest to the Queen the day of Sascia's Trial, points their clawed finger at her. They scream in their own language, spittle flying from the jaw, and others quickly join in, in English, "Traitor! Traitor! Traitor!"

The aesin shuffle toward her, furious and hateful, and within moments, Sascia is being mobbed, elbows in her ribs, nails on her arms, a boot at her back.

It starts fast and ends fast—a blast of pure Dark throws everyone off their feet, Sascia included. From the floor, she gawks at Nugau. His fingers are splayed, shadows curling at their tips. With a last, murderous look at the aesin who attacked Sascia, he grabs the back of her collar, lifts her off the ground, and unceremoniously marches her out of the dining area.

With every step, shock settles into terror. His grip is iron-made, his fury swathed in blood. "I didn't do anything!" Sascia shouts. "I was respectful, just as you told me—"

"And it made no difference. They think you triggered the lights to escape. Do you understand now, why your Claim is futile?"

"I'm not a traitor or a thief or a liar, I am here to convince you that our worlds can be allies instead of enemies, and I won't stop until—"

"Until you're dead. Which you will be, soon from the looks of it."

"Why didn't you just let them stomp me to death, then? Why protect me?"

"Because my *queen* ordered me to."

He brings her to a stop at the end of a corridor, where he drags a sliding door open with one hand and shoves Sascia forward with the other. She throws her arms out for balance—before her is a plunging drop. An elevator shaft stretches above and below, snapped cables hanging in midair like torn ligaments. Neon ink shimmers on the walls; the whole shaft has been painted from top to bottom with scenes depicting aesin life, aesin love, aesin *death*.

"Our sun," Nugau snaps, pointing to a black sphere in the middle of one drawing, "is much weaker than yours. Our world is ruled by darkness. To us, light is painful."

He gestures to another mural: orbs of white strike a valley, leaving rubble and corpses behind. "We did not understand at first, when your bombs dropped from the sky. They looked like comet showers. But when they crashed into land, their explosion was unnatural. A burst of light, as wide as a city. Your bombs destroyed miles of rare forests, hurt our livestock, tore holes into our underground cities. And they woke the Ul'amoon. The Old Ones."

He rotates her to another mural that depicts a host of giant creatures tearing through a city, creatures that Sascia recognizes, either from the news or from myths: a dragon, a hydra, an ogre. Destruction and waste lie in their wake. Blue dominates the other colors, not the blue of the sky or the sea, Sascia realizes, but the blue of aesin blood.

"You call them Darkbeasts," Nugau says. "You give them names from your own stories: dragon, griffin, basilisk, kraken. But they are not fairy tales to us. They are our oldest enemies. We have been fighting them for centuries, and struggled to trap them in cages beneath the earth. When your bombs struck, the strongest of the Ul'amoon tore free. Your light drove them into a violent frenzy. Entire cities were destroyed. Thousands died. My other parent, Kilorn, the Queen's consort, was one of them."

But that isn't right. In human history, the Shanghai Darkdragon, the Rio Darkbasilisk, the Manhattan Darkgriffin, the Darkkraken of the Baltic Sea, they arrived *first* in the human world, unwelcome and destructive. Director Shen helped NovaCorp create the nova-light weapons that brought down the Darkdragon and every Darkbeast thereafter. Ever since, nova-bombs have been routinely thrown into Darkholes to keep them dormant. Nobody really knows where these bombs go. They just disappear into the Dark.

But now—now, Sascia knows. Those nova-bombs traveled far, through not just space, but time too. They ended up in Itkalin, in a timeline before the aesin even knew about the existence of the human world. Before the Darkbeasts had ever emerged into human cities.

Because of ymneen, because of knotted time, the very weapons that were meant to kill the Darkbeasts ended up *waking* them in the first place.

Sascia had thought ymneen was a tool she could use to change the future, but maybe Nugau is right—it is a curse. If the universe is a quilt, then her world and Nugau's are a knot in the threads. Time loops and folds, creating endless tangles. Any action she takes might implode the world, just like Chapter XI's nova-bombs.

"But *you* know that wasn't our intention," Sascia rasps, and suddenly she's angry, at the knotted time, at the Darkbeasts, at the aesin, at *him*. "You told me so. You said you've seen evidence of humans felling creatures that were still alive and well in your world. You know we didn't send the nova-bombs to cause destruction. We only sought to protect ourselves against the very enemy you hate. So why won't you tell the rest of the aesin? Why won't you convince the Queen that we're not the villains she thinks we are?"

"*They don't believe me*," Nugau snaps. "I'm the only one who has traveled to your world and seen the Ul'amoon fall. The aesin who attacked you back there, the Queen's closest confidants—they look at you and see the cause of all this destruction." He flourishes a hand at the mural of blue blood. "Intentions don't matter. Our worlds are doomed to the whims of the ymneen. An endless circle of violence, loss, and violence again. We aesin have a saying: *Harin ye o' skish, o' skish thi haro*. When met with a blade, with a blade you'll meet."

It has a sense of despair, this saying, spilling from his lips like the final notes of a swan song. His chest rises and falls, and he snaps, "Do you understand now, human?"

She doesn't and it's plain on her face—Nugau's lip snarls.

"It doesn't matter," he bites out. "I understand enough for the both of us. The aesin have suffered too much to forgive. They will never accept peace. Your Claim is futile."

"I still need to *try*!"

It bursts out of her, surprising them both. He just stands there, and she stands there, the two of them pillars of obstinacy, and Sascia thinks she'll find her own anger reflected in his face, except what she sees is not anger, not really. The shape is similar, the outline just as knife-sharp, but instead of all-devouring black, it is hued in bright crimson and blue, the colors of human and aesin blood, shed senselessly by blades that neither meant to raise.

Nugau is *desperate*, and so is she, and while he may be satisfied to lick his wounds and let them scab over, Sascia never learned how to sit still long enough to heal—she can only march forward, even with bright crimson gushing out, even with an army closing in, even with time itself standing against her.

I will try, she vows, and in that quiet comfort of her own resolve, she finds it: the first inkling of how she's going to prove herself.

25

A MIDNIGHT SNACK

Sascia lies on the beaten-up sofa, staring at the shifting leaves of the Darkflora overhead. Mooch swings in lazy, happy circles after yet another gluttonous meal, courtesy of Orran, Thalla, and other reverent aesin.

Nugau didn't speak to her the rest of that third day, nor the six days since, except to give her emotionless instructions on their current task. They always start with chores—cooking or washing or cleaning—then move on to training. Sascia is not allowed near weapons; she has to watch as Nugau practices with their unit. Evenings are spent doing maintenance work, the most physically draining part of the day: they clear debris from tunnels, fashion furniture out of abandoned materials, poke at ventilation shafts.

There are other tasks, things she's not allowed to see. Sometimes, Orran, Thalla, and the rest of Nugau's friend group arrive at dinner drenched in gore and sporting shallow wounds. Patrols, if Sascia had to guess, or exploration of the tunnels. At random intervals, she is startled by animal screeches, short and sharp and violent, like an eagle's caw.

But at night, she is blessedly alone, to think and analyze and *plan*.

She had gone about this the wrong way, misjudged her opponents. She'd thought winning her Claim meant winning over the aesin, but it quickly became clear that the aesin value her as little as a bug beneath their boots. It took her some time to find the right way to go about it. Tae helped, the bastard. *Despair has no place in a science lab*, he had said the day before she jumped into the Maw. *We work with hypotheses and conclusions. With trial and error. If we figure out how the Darkmoth is connected to Nugau and why Nugau behaved like that, then we will have an idea of what they want. And if we know what they want, then we might begin to negotiate with them.*

Sascia, surprisingly, now knows the answers to nearly all the questions the cohort had come up with that day, starting with what aesin want: revenge on humans, yes, but also, and more importantly, *safety*.

The aesin have fought the Ul'amoon for centuries. Humans have fought them for only a fraction of that, but no less fiercely. Both worlds have suffered under the beasts; both would benefit from their eradication. Together, aesin magic and human technology might achieve what each alone could not.

Her immediate problem is how to get both parties to sit at the same table. She might know what the aesin want, might even have an idea of how to get it to them, but if they don't trust her, they'll never stop to *listen*. She simply has to find a way to earn their trust.

The answer came to her just a few hours ago, as she watched Orran, Thalla, and three other aesin sneak bites to Mooch. The moth had grown bold, or perhaps a little careless, and flew right into one of the nova-panel sensors. In seconds, the dining area was yet again blasted with light, leaving the aesin nursing their burns and casting hateful looks in Sascia's direction. Mooch, of course, had slipped into a corner of Dark while all that was going on, and popped out only when Sascia was alone back in her room. But this time, the blast of the nova-panels had sparked a theory.

Her hypothesis: human light is the source of the aesin's hatred.

Her conclusion: light has to go.

Stealthily, Sascia unfolds from the sofa and eases an ear against the door. Sometimes, deep in the night, she'll wake to shuffling sounds outside her room, followed by hisses. Tonight, however, it has been quiet; Sascia dares to peek out.

Nugau sits against the wall across the corridor, arms propped on his knees. His scythe rests at his side, which sends a quiet wave of terror down Sascia's spine; she hasn't seen him carrying it since he attacked her in Times Square. He makes no move—merely looks at her beneath his fringe of hair as she opens the door the rest of the way, spilling light onto him. Sascia doesn't want to ponder what he's doing outside her door this late into the night, when, supposedly, *hatred is too small a word for what he feels*, so she reaches for the irritation produced by his cold-shouldering this entire week.

"Can a girl not get a midnight snack, then?" she snaps.

"By all means," he drawls from the floor, "have a snack. It's not as if there's an entire army in these tunnels that would rip your throat out with their teeth."

Yes, she's considered that possibility. Which is why she's not going alone. Mooch, her one and only ancient god, is right there, cozy on her ear. "Wonderful, thanks," she mutters, and, before she can lose her courage, closes the door behind her and heads down the corridor.

At her back, Nugau groans and drags himself upright. He trails behind her wordlessly for a long time as Sascia tries to get her bearings, fails, retraces her steps, and starts again. Finally, she finds the tunnel that hosts the dining area and kitchen, where she sinks her teeth into one of the black plums the aesin so enjoy.

As she chews, her eyes trace the cables above the nova-light panels and follow them to a fuse box mounted on a wall. Good, that should do. She could cut the power off right now—and she does consider it, just walking over, prying the box open and flipping the switch—but then, no one would know it was her besides Nugau, and she doubts he'd do her the courtesy of praising her selflessness for all to hear. (Because it is, or rather will be, selflessness: nova-light hurts the aesin, but it spares *her*.)

She exits the dining area instead, and walks leisurely through the tunnels, following the wires—a good thing, too, because there is another set of nova-panels in the sleeping quarters and a third in the armory. Nugau lays a hand on her arm when she tries to enter into that and, after a moment, she realizes why: there are aesin in there, whetting their blades from the sound of it.

The black plum is consumed almost to its hard gemstone pit. Sascia pockets that, for Danny, if—*when*—she sees him again, and lets her feet carry her farther into the underground station, an aimless walk that turns out not to be so aimless after all. There, a few turns before the big cavern, she spots the station's control room. She has found what she set out for, but a new idea pops into her mind.

"What are you doing?" Nugau whispers when Sascia wrestles the door open.

A waft of dust and moisture rises to meet them. A cluster of Darkspiders the size of Sascia's fist flee to their webs on the ceiling. The computers are all dead—there's some electricity in the tunnels, the nova-wards are proof of that, but not in here. She finds a cell phone abandoned on a desk, equally dead, and every book on the shelves is either a manual or a useless gossip magazine from six years ago. She's almost done rummaging through a cabinet when

Nugau pulls her away. His fingers are soft around the crook of her elbow.

"Human," he snaps, low and irritated. "What are you looking for?"

"Would they believe you?" Sascia asks. "If you had proof, video or photographs of the attacks and the fallen Ul'amoon, could you convince them?"

His stillness is loaded with a dozen feelings, too fleeting for Sascia to decipher. The curve of his cheekbones becomes alight, purple to white to blue, then all three together, framing their face in a phantasmagoria of color. Is this what siff, *all*, looks like? But before that question can be answered, the shift is over. Nugau blinks their wide eyes and looks away from Sascia, their Darkprint settling into white.

Sascia wants to say something, *that was beautiful* or *you are beautiful*, or an equally soppy compliment, but she doesn't get a chance. Perhaps Nugau notices the mellowness of her gaze, perhaps they remember where their skin is touching—they drop their hand from her arm and slide out of the room with a snappy, "Find your own way back," thrown over their shoulder.

ON THE TENTH DAY in the tunnels (if her calculations are right), Sascia is sitting at dinner, narrating Nugau's latest kerfuffle to Orran and Thalla. The princet is terrible at maintenance work, constantly at risk of hammering their own fingers or tearing out an eye. Their friends have taken to asking Sascia what happened, partly because Nugau refuses to explain but mostly because Sascia performs an Oscar-worthy impersonation of them that leaves their friends in hysterics.

By her side, Nugau is wearing a barely-there smile. They did not enjoy her very first story; at Orran's and Thalla's snickers, they got up and left. But their friends must have teased them about that, too, because the next day, they stayed. The one after that, they interrupted with a long explanation. On the fourth, they began to chip in corrections that made the tale even funnier. They still largely ignore her for most of the day, but during dinner with Orran and Thalla, they seem to endure her presence just a little bit better.

Today's tale is one of straightforward but hilarious minor electrocution. Sascia concludes it to heady chuckling from Orran and Thalla, then, just as she picks up her spoon to resume eating, a scream cuts through the tunnel.

Another Darknaga has swooped down from the ceiling in search of food. Two aesin are trying to wrangle it to the table, while a third is rescuing bowls left and right.

The wards begin to beep.

As one, the aesin scramble for cover, the poor Darknaga abandoned, flopping on its back. Sascia moves fast: she climbs on the table and jumps from surface to surface. Her spoon is still in her hand—when she reaches the fuse box, mounted at the top of the wall near the stairs, she uses it to wrench the box open, switches the fuses off, and proceeds to pull out any cable that she can see.

The wards stutter dead, their light fizzling out entirely.

Sascia lowers her hands from the fuse box, all too aware that hundreds of eyes are tracking her. She jumps down from the table and makes her way back to her seat. Around her, the aesin are straightening from their crouches, unharmed and utterly shocked. Even the Darknaga has survived; it snacks on the contents of an overturned bowl, oblivious.

As she slumps into her seat, a feathered aesin from the end of the table calls out, "Thank you, human."

Sascia merely nods. She spoons a bite into her mouth and chews.

Slowly, conversation resumes. Glances are thrown her way and whispers rise around her, but at least the aesin are no longer blatantly sneering.

Sascia can feel Nugau watching her. Their elbows rest on the table and their cheek is tucked into their palm. Casual, observing, perhaps even interested. In a whisper laced with bemusement, they ask, "A midnight snack, huh?"

A smile tucks onto her lips. Vexing she may be, but she is not inconsequential.

"You said they don't trust me," Sascia replies. "Now they might begin to."

26

A COWARD

The door creaks, deep in the night.

Sascia is awake (it has been hard to fall asleep when there is no sun to mark the days). She lies motionless on the sofa, watching Mooch's flight, waiting for exhaustion to steal her away from consciousness. At the sound, she jumps upright and grabs the first thing she can find: a beat-up magazine.

A baffled smile crosses Nugau's face. The Darkprints blaze blue on her cheeks, but otherwise there is no physical marker of her shift: the same lovely violet eyes and cutting jawline and lithe limbs. She closes the door and leans against it.

"I could," she announces.

Be my ally? Sascia wants to ask, but she knows that's not the right question. Still, ever since her stint with the nova-wards two days ago, things have been different. Cold disregard has settled into something watchful—curiosity, perhaps.

"Do not mistake me," Nugau says. "I still believe your naive notion of peace is not an option. My people are born and raised on war. That's how we deal with threats. But with proof that your bombs were not an attack, and that they will not continue to destroy our world, I could persuade the aesin to return to Itkalin.

Separate my world from yours forever. We could avoid mutual annihilation."

The idea of separation sends a trickle of dread down Sascia's back. How can she ever return to her dreary life of classes and papers and SATs after living among magic and being favored by a god? But Nugau is here, she is willing, she used *we*; it's a start.

"If we find one of your devices, your screens, can you get it to work?" Nugau asks, studying Sascia with a kind of caution that betrays a secret.

The subtext is obvious. "You know where to find one."

"No one can see us," Nugau warns. "If they find us sneaking out, they will accuse you of trying to escape."

"They will accuse you of helping me escape," she counters. But she's already pulling her boots on.

As she stands, they regard each other across the room. A thread of understanding snaps taut between them: they are something of a team now.

When Nugau slips into the corridor, Sascia follows.

With every step they take, it becomes more evident that this is not the first time Nugau has snuck out of the army compound. As the princess leads Sascia through a convoluted maze of tunnels, stairs, and exit doors, she knows just where to hide to avoid a patrol, where to place her hands on half-demolished ladders, where to go slow and quiet beneath a colony of Darkbats. Her attention is never long away from Sascia; she will look over a shoulder to make sure Sascia's keeping close or offer a hand on a steep climb or cast an orb of her cerulean fire when the darkness becomes too thick.

But Sascia does not mistake the princess's care for affection. She remembers her words twelve days ago all too clearly: *I have no interest in the decisions of a self that will never be. The future you glimpsed will never come to pass. I will make sure that I am never betrayed, and that I never have to stoop so low as to be at your mercy.* They might be a team now, on this, but they are not friends.

Yet she still finds herself noticing Nugau. The way the princess moves through the world, with the cutting ease of a freshly sharpened blade. Her long, slim legs, the small twitches of her pointed ears, those full lips and the sharp incisors beneath them. Sascia's first impression of a beautiful killer was entirely wrong. The aesin is dangerous, yes, but in the manner of the endless ocean or the roll of thunder before a storm. Wild but not vindictive.

"How old are you?" Sascia asks as they cross a tunnel of overgrown Darkferns.

"Four."

A startled laugh bursts out of Sascia.

"Our years are much longer than yours, because our world revolves very slowly around our sun," Nugau explains. "But to give you an idea, in my culture, four is considered just on the cusp of adulthood. How old are you?"

"Eighteen."

"An old, old lady."

"I'll have you know I'm on the cusp of adulthood in *my* culture too."

"You are a student." It's not a question. With a furtive glance at Sascia, Nugau adds, "I remembered you. I couldn't at first, because you had been wearing that cat mask. But working so close to you, I recognized—" Nugau cuts herself off.

Her *smell*, Sascia realizes. Nugau recognized her smell. That night on Halloween, the princess had leaned into her neck and breathed in deep. And on her parents' anniversary, Nugau had whispered, *You always smell sweet.* A shiver crawls over Sascia's skin, gathering at the tender flesh of her throat. Her heart pounds there, flustered by the thrilling possibility that she smells just as sweet now, to Nugau.

"You were with your friends." The princess holds a hanging Darkvine aside for Sascia. "They smiled a lot. They gave me candy. It surprised me that you were all studying the Dark. Until then, I had thought humans typically fear it."

Ah, yes. Nugau's mysterious past. The story that Thalla warned Orran was not theirs to share. Sascia wants to pry, to ask a million questions, but instead, she says, "Not everyone does. There are many of us, like my friends and other scientists and even lots of regular people, who actually admire the Dark."

"But not you. You love it."

"I—" But how can Sascia put her love of the Dark into words? She has never tried before; it feels unfathomable. "You called me an Ariadne in love with the Labyrinth itself."

If the naming holds significance, Nugau doesn't show it. Her eyes land on Mooch, who flutters leisurely ahead. "And *them*, you love the most."

"The moths? Of course I do. What is there not to love?" *They brought me here,* she doesn't say. *To this.* Her fingers splay as Mooch twirls around them. "Would you tell me about them? Are they really gods?"

The outline of Nugau's face is drawn in the soft blues of the orb of flame that lights their way. "Both our priests and our scholars agree that moths like this one, what we call the itka, are as old as our world itself. Across the millennia, it has been documented that they disappear suddenly, for decades or even centuries, then reappear."

The princess's voice has taken on the lilt of storytelling.

"That is where the priests and the scholars deviate. Science hypothesizes that the itka simply migrate to some unknown part of our world. But the old lore tells a different story. That the itka are saviors. That they hear the call of worlds in need and split the fabric of time and space to bring them together so that they may help each other. According to these legends, the itka led the Ul'amoon from their dying world to Itkalin, where they could live in safety. And the Ul'amoon saved Itkalin, in turn. A centuries-long winter had stricken our lands. We would have died if our ancestors hadn't discovered that the Ul'amoon radiate heat and that trapping them beneath the earth would save our civilization."

"When I jumped into the Maw," Sascia whispers, "we were falling through the Dark. We would have ended up in Itkalin, wouldn't we? But the cold was killing me. And so Mooch did something. A slit appeared, cut into the Dark itself, and we fell back into these tunnels." Her eyes are wide as they track Mooch's zigzags overhead. "It's not just *old lore*."

"No," Nugau agrees. "I don't believe it is. When I first came into your world as a child . . . it was because I was in danger. One of the itka split the world for me and brought me here, to the human world. I'm confident it was this same itka. Your Mooch."

Her Mooch. Sascia holds no delusions about owning the moth—the very notion of ownership goes against everything she believes in—but she feels the depth of its significance, pride and gratification and *validation*. The directive of the itka is to save, creatures and people and entire worlds, and out of all of them, Mooch chose *her*. Four times now, it brought her and Nugau together. She doesn't understand why, but maybe it's for this—for peace. Her vow drums through her: she will try, and she will not fail.

"The Ul'amoon," Sascia says, "they look like creatures from our oldest myths. And you, the aesin, bear similarities to anthropomorphic beings from our myths: the fair folk, the angels, were-creatures. Could the itka have led you to our world once, a long time ago?"

"We have stories like that, too, of long-necked giraffes and colorful schools of fish and round-eared demons." The princess pauses to study Sascia's ears. "It seems that our worlds have been catching glimpses of each other for a long time, through the knots of the ymneen."

"But shouldn't that mean something?" Sascia asks. "If the itka open the door between worlds so that they can save each other, shouldn't it mean something that the itka brought you and us together? That they chose to save *you* by bringing you to the human world?"

"It does, to some. To the faithful like Orran. To those who trust me, like Thalla and my battalion. But the others—what they've seen with their own two eyes, what they believe in, is that an open door lets through *threats*: The vicious Ul'amoon. Your novabombs. And sooner or later, *you*. The rest is fiction concocted by their coward princess."

Nugau's jaw clenches tight. Gently, Sascia says, "You don't strike me as a coward."

"I am. A coward through and through." Her voice has taken a sharp edge. "Let's pick up speed. We're close."

The tender openness of the conversation snaps shut. Nugau cuts through the Darkferns with sudden ferocity and Sascia follows, submerged in her own thoughts, wondering why the princess calls herself a coward when Sascia has only seen bravery.

"We're here."

Ahead of them, the tunnel opens to a vast space. Below, corridors and aisles spread between half-demolished shops. An entire forest of Darktrees has risen from the broken tiles, branches growing through windows and twisting around signs. The whole thing looks as though an architectural model was dropped from some great height—oh.

This is Penn Station, Sascia realizes. When the Darkgriffin was felled by the Chapter's air strikes, the impact of its enormous body created a massive earthquake. Several structures in the area toppled or were severely damaged, and the underground part of Penn Station was swallowed whole. Apparently, the shops and food stalls of the station remain intact, deep beneath the ground.

In a daze, Sascia climbs down to the cracked tiles. Produce has shriveled into black lumps on food carts. Dust blankets the racks inside the abandoned stores. A stroller lies on its side, and at the end of an aisle, two legs peek out.

Men's work boots, lying at an unnatural angle.

"Are you all right?" Nugau says. She stands shoulder to shoulder with Sascia, peering down at her beneath furrowed brows.

"And they don't believe you," Sascia snaps. Is she angry? *Yes.* She's so, so angry. "The aesin live in our abandoned tunnels, using our lost items and forgotten furniture—but they refuse to see *we* have gone through as much pain as *they* have. Were there bodies in the tunnels you now sleep and cook and train in? Did you all just remove and repurpose them like you've been doing with the rest of our things?"

Nugau steps before her, blocking her view. She speaks fast, voice tinged with worry. "I shouldn't have brought you here. I didn't think—I didn't realize how much it would hurt you. Forgive me. Let's leave. We can look elsewhere."

Impulsively, Sascia drops her hands onto Nugau's shoulders, like she'd do with Danny or Ksenya or the cohort. The princess startles and goes utterly still, but Sascia's fury is coming to a boil. "No. You were right to bring me here. It's the best place to find a working phone. I can soldier on—god knows, we've all grown skilled at soldiering on."

"But you're angry."

There's a shrill disquiet in Nugau's voice that makes Sascia pause. Why is the princess panicking? Yes, Sascia is angry, but her anger is not dangerous. Except—perhaps for Nugau, anger does mean danger. And pain, that of the Queen's grip of Dark around her neck.

With care, Sascia smooths her face and calms her voice. "I'm not angry at *you*. I don't blame *you*. I am angry at all this violence. All this death—ours, and yours too. So let's get you your goddamn proof, princess."

When she takes Nugau's hand and tugs, the aesin comes, with no resistance at all.

NUGAU TAKES THE LEAD in the search, shielding Sascia from the sight of any other bodies, while Sascia looks for dropped electronics. They discover plenty of cell phones, tablets, and laptops that first day and, on the next three, they amass a veritable pile of chargers. Every night since, they spend near the turnstiles where they first landed, which host the only working socket in the tunnels. Device after device they charge and scour through, hoping it belongs to an utter weirdo who would want to hold on to photos or videos of humanity's greatest disasters. (There's no internet beneath the Maw and as such, no way to download them anew.)

They find none.

Yet it is not time wasted; they find other things.

Sascia learns that Nugau loves art, aesin and human alike. She learns how she and Orran and Thalla met: in the military academy as children. Nugau was instructed to associate with the council members' children, but she found them prideful and selfish; she much preferred the company of those who knew the cost of battle and war-making. She learns Thalla and Orran come from rival clans in Itkalin. Orran's are winged do-gooders, while Thalla's are ruthless blood-drinkers, but they fell in love anyway. She learns Nugau's parent Kilorn was her favorite person in the world. When the subject turns to them, grief still cuts deeply on the princess's features, so Sascia doesn't prod further.

Nugau learns too. The princess is a collector of stories: as they work, she pries them out of Sascia. The story of the moth map, of Danny and Ksenya and the cohort, of her turbulent tenure at the Umbra. Sascia discovers she enjoys the telling; the page is blank, the ink fresh, and here, she is not the sum of her failures but a collection of choices, good and bad, and—to Nugau, at least—always, always interesting.

They're sitting close now, shoulder to shoulder, as Sascia scrolls through another phone. Personal photos she barely glances at, grief gripping her rib cage, but screenshots she reads through: memes and funny tweets and the occasional bit of news.

"What is this anyway?" Nugau asks, rapping her knuckles against the vending machine they had to unplug to use the socket.

"It's a vending machine. You put money inside and it gives you drinks and snacks."

Very carefully, as though in a trance, Nugau leans forward to peer at the contents. Her hair is pulled back in a ponytail; Sascia's gaze snaps to the long column of her neck.

Her mind travels unbidden to memories of other necks, of kisses dusted with Greek sand and furious make-out sessions on school bleachers. Kissing has always come easy to her, but the rest, dates and relationships and proclamations of love, feel awkward on her, draped loose and unflattering like a dress two sizes too big. Sascia has never particularly worried about it, because she was raised by two people incandescently in love. *When the right person comes along, everything will feel easy*, her parents like to say, and even though things haven't felt easy Sascia still finds herself returning to these impossible, heart-stopping thoughts: *If I begged, would you kiss me?*

"What kind of snacks?" Nugau asks, standing to take a proper look. "Candy?"

"Yes, among other things," Sascia says around a smile. She has forgotten: Nugau has something of a sweet tooth. "Try shaking it. Something might pop out."

The princess gives the vending machine an enthusiastic rattle, which results in two plain granola bars and a packet of chips, empty courtesy of a small army of Darkants.

Nugau's mouth tugs downward and, in her bitter disappointment, Sascia finds the truth that has been slowly unveiling itself this entire week: Nugau loves the human world, just as much as Sascia loves the Dark.

"I'm sure we can find some other snacks around," Sascia says quickly, before she can burst out laughing. "We need to pick up more phones, anyway. This is the last and it's not showing any promise—"

She cuts off mid-sentence, because she has glanced back down to the screen, where she had scrolled to a new photo before Nugau started terrorizing the vending machine. She looks at it properly now: not a photo, but a video, from a street-level point of view, of the Darkgriffin tearing through the skyscrapers of Manhattan.

27

A COURAGE THAT SHEDS NO BLOOD

"What's wrong?" Nugau asks. "You smell different."

Sascia looks miserably down at herself, the pillow on her abdomen, her hands plastered on top for maximum warmth. "It's a, um, part of the human reproduction cycle." (What she means is she got her period, but she isn't sure Nugau will understand that. Reproduction among the aesin is not a subject they've had reason to broach.) "Perhaps we can stay here tonight?"

"Of course." Nugau closes the door behind them, their brow grooved by a worry line. For the past few days, their Darkprint has beamed white and purple. A multigender identity, Nugau explained, they and he both, in human pronouns. After weeks with Nugau, with hundreds of aesin and their shifting Darkprints, Sascia has gotten good at recognizing how they identify. It is a learning process, but it never ceases to fill her with wonder: a world of openness and inclusion, of shaping yourself however you wish.

Nugau slips onto the sofa opposite Sascia's and looks almost miserably at the various items on the coffee table: the phone with the Darkgriffin video and various newspaper clippings about the Darkdragon attack. In the past two weeks, they have been collecting their proof and formulating their plan: when the Queen returns, Nugau and Sascia will present their evidence and convince the aesin that attacking the humans will only bring on more destruction. Sascia will lead a group of delegates through the tunnels (with Mooch's help) and to Chapter XI, where they can begin to figure out how to separate their worlds forever. Sealing the doorways is the only thing that will work, Nugau is adamant about that. No matter the terms, the Queen will not accept promises of peace.

"And the human reproduction makes you sad?" Nugau asks.

"No—well, I mean, yes, generally, it can—but right now, it just makes me hurt." By some divine miracle, she was able to find a full pack of pads in one of the lockers in the staff room, along with a bottle of ibuprofen only a few months past its expiration date. "I'm sad because this means I've been here for almost a month."

Her last period was two days before her parents' anniversary, three days before she jumped into the Maw, which means she has been down here for four weeks. Danny, the cohort, her parents, and Ksenya have spent *four weeks* wondering whether she is alive, and the rest of the world . . . Who knows how badly things have escalated since three Darkhumanoids peeked out of the Maw and were promptly shoved back inside by a human girl?

"We don't have to wait. Mooch can find you a way out now." Nugau's voice is quiet. "I can handle the Queen on my own. Even if she doesn't believe me, the rest of the aesin will not pass up the opportunity to rid Itkalin of your light bombs."

"We can't risk it. Without Mooch, it might take you months or years to find a way out of these tunnels." Sascia lets her head drop back to the swell of the sofa. "I have to be the one that leads the delegation out. When they see me, a human, our soldiers will pause long enough for me to explain. If I go now, I'll be just what the aesin accuse me of: a traitor."

"I don't think they believe that any longer. There have barely been any assassination attempts lately."

Sascia bolts upright. *"What?"*

Nugau scrunches his mouth as though caught in a blunder, the most human gesture Sascia has ever seen on him. "Did you think spending my nights sitting on the floor outside your door is my idea of fun? Ever since you arrived, someone has tried to enter this room while you slept. Ktren, a couple of times, and a few others sent by my mother's council. Orran, Thalla, and I have been taking turns standing guard, but in the past few days, there have been no unwelcome visitors."

Sascia doesn't know what to do with this information. Thank Nugau, Orran, and Thalla for their efforts? Pee herself from fear? Dazed, she mutters, "Were you not going to tell me?"

"No." It comes out firm. "You barely sleep as it is."

That shuts Sascia right up—it had never occurred to her that the princet would notice. Between her anxiety-induced insomnia and their late-night explorations, she has been sleeping at most four hours each night. (Perhaps that's why she feels like an utter blob of flesh today. She's always triply exhausted when she's on her period.)

She drops back down. She would kill for a snack right now, something sweet to ease her nerves. "When will the Queen return?"

"It is unclear. The passage we first came through has collapsed and the rift Mooch created is long gone, but the Queen has been trying to rip it open with her powers."

"Do all aesin have powers like hers?"

"Some. Thalla has control over vapors and liquids, and Orran can produce a strike of lightning. Only the most powerful can wield the Dark. That's how my mother rose in the ranks; her power was devastating on the battlefield. But what she can do now, as Queen, is a hundred times stronger than any other aesin. We use the word *queen* with you because that's the closest thing your language has. But leadership is not hereditary in Itkalin. You have to Claim it and prove it in a Trial that Itkalin itself sets for you: for my mother, it was the capture of one of the strongest Ul'amoon, what you call the Darkdragon. She subdued it single-handedly. If the aesin thump their chests for you when you complete your Royal Claim, you become our leader, but not just in terms of authority. The Thistha Ren is old magic, as old as the itka themselves. It recognizes the courage of making the Claim, the strength of proving it, and it rewards you with a gift. To those who prove the Royal Claim, it grants an amplification of your power a hundredfold, so that you may protect your subjects and defeat your foes."

Nugau blurts all that out in a squeaky outpour, studying their fingers intently, and Sascia gets the very clear idea that they hurried through because they don't want Sascia to notice what they've left out: their own part in it. Sascia remembers Orran's whispered revelation, that the Queen believes the princet plots against her to steal the throne. She remembers Nugau thumping his chest, making the Thistha Ren to save Sascia's life, and the Queen's violent punishment. She remembers Nugau's hissed confession: *a coward through and through*. It all slots into place; Nugau could make the Royal Claim. But he hasn't.

"Why not . . . ?" Sascia asks, and the rest of the question must be obvious, because Nugau shrinks into the sofa.

In a hushed voice, he whispers, "She is my mother. I admire all that she has achieved. I respect the sacrifices she has made. I love her, for who she used to be, who she can be again. And yet—I have taken so much from her. I won't take this too." The princet casts Sascia a pitiful smile. "See? A coward."

But Nugau isn't a coward, and Sascia desperately needs to tell them, to show them, to make them understand, because she is that person too, who refuses to hurt even when hurt is the easiest solution.

"Not all bravery is loud," she tells them. "Not all defiance is violent. What you're trying to achieve with words is powerful and courageous *because* it sheds no blood."

Nugau ducks his head again, in embarrassment or perhaps in thanks, and lets Sascia's words linger between them. Silence follows, but it is not uncomfortable. Sascia rubs her belly; the princet kicks off their boots and lies on the sofa. Overhead, glossy Darkvines coil and uncoil, in constant exploration of their surroundings, small, curious Ariadnes.

"Beautiful, aren't they?" Nugau mutters. "Our world is colder than yours, though not by much. But it is much tougher, less humid. In Itkalin, vines only grow to short, stubby saplings. Here, where there's more heat and humidity and rich earth, they *flourish*."

"My cousin loves your plants," Sascia whispers. "His dream is to create an entire botanic garden of them, full of greenhouses that people can visit and explore."

His voice mellows to something wistful. "I'd have liked to see that."

You could, she thinks, and then she says it out loud. "If you stayed, you could."

She means the plural *you*, the aesin race, but Nugau understands the singular. "Don't ask me that," they whisper. "I won't abandon them again."

At that precise, preciously tender moment, Mooch decides to burst out of the Dark. A slit of black tears across the ceiling and a flurry of objects rains on the coffee table, bouncing off and scattering on the floor. They're snacks from the vending machine at Penn

Station, bags of chips and packets of cookies, brightly colored drinks and heaps upon heaps of candy. Smugly, the moth comes to perch on Sascia's knee.

"Well, isn't that a neat new trick? This is exactly what I was craving," she coos at the moth, "but are these for my benefit or for yours, you ravenous little beast?"

Mooch responds by climbing on her knuckles as she tears one of the bags open, and diving inside before she can even pull the first chip out. (An ancient god, traveler of time and space, yet susceptible to the worst munchies.) The moth resurfaces dotted all over with paprika powder, then shoots right off into the Dark, no doubt to fetch even more.

"Little gnat." The words tumble carelessly out of Nugau's lips, but Sascia is enraptured. For the first time, it sounds like a nickname, like *endearment*. Raised on an elbow, Nugau is gawking with eyes wide as saucers—at the slit on the ceiling, slowly stitching itself together, at Sascia. "Did you ask Mooch to do that for you?"

"No, it's just generous that way."

"But during the Heart Trial, you did ask it to help. I heard you speak to it. And just now, before it appeared, I could feel you . . . *calling* it. Like we aesin call our powers."

"But I'm not aesin." *And*, she doesn't add, *I'm not magic either*.

"Humor me." Nugau shifts to a cross-legged position. "Close your eyes."

Sascia doesn't—but only because she's too curious to see what Nugau will do next. Their eyes are closed. Soft tendrils of black curl around their long fingers.

"Spread your awareness," the princet continues. "Think of the Dark, all around us, vast and powerful. Of how it stretches and narrows and shifts. A place of infinite change. Reach into it and send out your command."

At that last word, the Dark tucked in the corners of the room, the vines of the ceiling, and the moss on the floor all shoots to Nugau's palm and crystallizes into a long shaft with a curved blade. His scythe, Sascia realizes. He fashions it out of Dark itself.

Sascia looks down at her own fingers, spreading them into an open palm. "It doesn't feel like a command. All the interactions I've had with Mooch and my other moths, they feel like a conversation. Equal parts giving and taking."

Nugau slips off the sofa and comes to their knees in front of Sascia. Their voice is soft when they ask, "Show me."

Heat creeps up Sascia's neck. Beneath the full force of Nugau's focus, she feels choked and just a little bit light-headed. She shuts her eyes and spreads her awareness, just as she's been instructed to, but its range is small. She can only sense the heat of the leather beneath her bottom, the undercurrent of pain in her abdomen, the princet's breath against her skin, the eerie absence of matter in the pockets of Dark around the room, the—

Oh. There it is.

Now that she's been forced to pay attention, it is all around her, like Nugau said. Not absence of matter, but an essence in constant flux, shaping and reshaping itself. Sascia cannot sense it exactly, not with any physical receptor of her neurological system, but rather with a vague perception of elsewhere, elsewhen—like those few seconds of lucid dreaming before you jolt truly awake. Grabbing for it feels like a violation; instead Sascia reaches out with a question, a silent, unshaped wish: *come.*

Tiny feet land on her palm.

Across from her, Nugau is breathing hard. His long bangs drape over his face, framing his dark eyes with strands of black silk. His hands hover on each side of Sascia's palm, as though protecting a flame from the wind.

"What's wrong?" Sascia asks.

"I have never felt anything like this. You didn't send out an order. You sent a—I'm not sure what the right word is. It kept changing shape, like the Dark itself does, at times a plea, at times a claim, at times something else entirely."

(Sascia knows the right word, but dares not say it, not out loud, not to Nugau: *a longing*.)

"I wonder . . ." Nugau whispers.

Squatting before Sascia, their height puts them at eye level with her. Their hands have come to rest on each side of her thighs. The distance between them is so narrow; if Sascia leaned in, she would touch them, just as Nugau begged for all those weeks ago—just as her own body begs. But she can't. Sascia doesn't think Nugau finds her vexing anymore, but the doubt still remains. If she touches them, will she be making the wrong choice, the one that leads to Nugau on the brink of death, Nugau despairing, Nugau kissing her farewell? Will she be sealing their mutual destruction with the touch of their lips?

"All aesin are warriors first, but my parent Kilorn was also a scholar," Nugau says. "When the first doorways opened, raining your bombs on our land, Kilorn looked for answers in the old lore: why the itka brought our worlds together, how we were meant to save each other. They found none and, eventually, their research cost their life. Upon their death, the Queen forbade further study and set out to rid us of the threat of humans the only way she knows how. She and the rest of the aesin believe Kilorn was enamored with a fairy tale. That the itka are just rare creatures with strange abilities and not benevolent gods who wish to save us."

His gaze bores into Sascia. "But if they felt what I just felt, if they saw Mooch bring you exactly what you need . . ."

"They would understand that the itka are trying to help. That there is a *purpose* behind all of this—" Sascia pauses, her mind slipping back to the Nugau of the future bidding her farewell. *My only regret is that we never found it. The soron mola, the true purpose behind the ymneen. That alone could have saved us.* "We were looking for it. The soron mola."

The princet's gaze becomes ravenous, as though they can drink Sascia up with their eyes alone. "How do you know that term?"

"You mentioned it to me. When I met the version of you from the future, you said we were trying to find it. You believed it could save us."

"These two words were scribbled over and over in my parent's notes. It's an archaic term that can mean both *purposeful truth* and *true purpose*. Kilorn believed that it signifies the true reason why the itka open the doors between worlds. That if we understood it, we would know how we're meant to save each other." The princet pauses to take a long, steadying breath. "With the soron mola, we could convince them all—aesin and humans alike. We could be allies instead of enemies."

Sascia's heart hammers in her chest. *Allies*: Nugau is talking about peace. Not retreat, not separation, but coexistence. She leans close to Mooch where it's rifling around the chips bag. "What is the purpose, little guy? Why did you open the door?"

At the sound of her voice, Mooch peeks out of the bag, depthless black eyes peering up, antennae standing ramrod still. For a long moment she is sure it will answer, give her one of its wordless clues, but the moth just flutters its wings at her and returns to munching.

On their knees before her, Nugau wears a faraway look. "We

can't convince the aesin your kind is innocent, because you're not. You threw those bombs into the Dark with no knowledge of where they would end up or who they would hurt. You didn't *care* who got hurt—the Queen's council will use that to their advantage. But we can convince them that there is a reason the itka answer your call. That they opened the door because our two worlds can help each other in the future."

"The Ul'amoon," Sascia says breathlessly. "They have caused havoc in both our worlds. What if the itka brought us together to defeat them? What if, when we present our evidence to the Queen, I show them how I call Mooch? They will feel what you felt, and see it rip open the fabric of time and space to bring me what I need, and they will realize that it did the same for them. That it brought us together because we need to unite against an enemy neither of us can face alone."

"Screw the Queen," Nugau says, quiet and rough. "You're right—there is *no time* to wait for her. And we don't have to. It is traditional for the sovereign to set the Heart Trial, but we don't really need her. As long as you prove your Claim before the aesin and they beat their chests for you, the magic of the Thistha Ren is complete."

"What are you proposing exactly?" Because there *is* a proposition here, and judging from Nugau's cautious tone, Sascia is not going to like it one bit.

"Let's set our own Trial. A grand performance before the whole army, where they can see how humans and aesin can be useful to each other against our shared enemy. My mother is not a fool. If the army is on our side when she returns, she will have to try things our way."

Our way. Hope unfurls in Sascia's chest.

"It's going to be dangerous—it has to be if we want the aesin to truly believe—but, please, little gnat," the princet whispers, "will you try?"

"I will," she whispers back, "you know I will," and this precious tender thing between them becomes an oath, a promise: she will try and Nugau will try, their only weapon a courage that sheds no blood.

28

A CALL AND A WANT AND A PLEA

The throne room is packed with spectators. Almost the entire army of the Jagged Blade—eight thousand, according to Nugau—have come to watch. The space is thick with their heat, loud with their voices, luminescent with the shimmering colors on their cheeks.

Sascia stands in front of Orran, who's strapping her into armor. She's been allowed to carry weapons for this exercise: a bow and quiver. Orran moves in jerks and jolts; in the past six days while he's been training her, Sascia has learned Orran can get very jittery when he's nervous, a fact Thalla endlessly teases him for.

"Remember," they say, low and comforting. "You're smart. You're fast. Think before you move, decide what's best. Do *not* take risks."

"Orran," Sascia says, "that's like telling a rooster not to crow at dawn."

Their frown is epic. "What is a rooster?"

Sascia huffs, her perfectly good joke ruined by Orran's cluelessness.

Armor straps secured, Orran rotates her by the shoulders to face the arena. On the other side sits a simple bell, positioned on the bare floor. Her task is simple: cross the arena and ring the bell before Nugau's shadow magic can stop her.

She throws her shoulders back and begins jogging in place. Muscles need to be warm, Orran warns before every training session, and the mind needs to be sharp. Slipping an arrow from the quiver at her hip, she notches it into the bow and pulls it back in a practice draw.

The crowd in the cavern explodes with hoots and howlers.

"We'll see who has the last laugh!" Sascia says, obnoxiously loud.

One of the aesin translates and a moment later the rest of them are hissing jeers. On a jut of rock above Sascia's head sit Ktren and the rest of the Queen's loyalists—the anti-Sascia faction of the aesin.

"It will not be you, my pretty. Our queen returns soon," Ktren calls down. They toss an onyx bead to a short-haired aesin rushing through the crowd below. "My money is on you lasting less than a minute."

With a timid glance at Sascia, the bookie pockets the bead and scurries away.

Six days ago, on the morning after their conversation about the itka's purpose, Nugau stood in the dining area and announced, loudly and authoritatively, that Sascia would begin training. *I am tired of saving her weak ass from every creature she happens upon*, Nugau had said in the aesin tongue, according to Thalla. *Besides, if she claims to be an ambassador to Itkalin, she should know the worst we have to offer: serving in the military.*

The soldiers around them had snickered. That same afternoon, almost a hundred of them had come to watch Orran train her. Footwork, sword fighting, shielding, archery—day after day,

Orran drove her until she lay in a puddle of her own sweat. Then Nugau would take over. Shadows bowed to their magic, creating an obstacle course fashioned out of the Dark that left Sascia with very real scratches and bruises.

Naturally, the aesin had a blast watching Sascia fail. Whether tentative allies or downright enemies, they watched Sascia fall and rise and fall again as though it was the entertainment of the decade. Among that first batch of spectators was an unofficial bookie who saw a golden opportunity to profit from Sascia's failings. Now there are a *dozen* bookies hurrying through the groups of aesin gathered on the sidelines of the arena.

"Ready, human?" Nugau calls from their perch on an overturned train car. Their Darkprint gives a pulsing bloom of white.

"Ready," Sascia says, amazed at how calm and measured her voice comes out.

Before her, the arena bursts with Dark. Sascia is moving before the first obstacle forms fully, swinging her bow to scatter Nugau's dark shadows. The second is just as easy. A swinging rod three times the size of Sascia's body comes for her midriff—Sascia takes advantage of her momentum to drop to her knees and slide beneath it.

The aesin crow their approval and hiss their displeasure.

Sascia's a good third of the way to the bell with minimal damage when Nugau decides to pull out the big guns. Out of the Dark amassing in the corners of the arena steps a pack of Darkhyenas, fashioned from Nugau's shadows. Their torsos are longer than they should be, humanlike in their latticework of stark, starved ribs. Their chins are frothed with hunger, their eyes glowing a brilliant white as they zero in on Sascia.

She nocks arrow after arrow between her knuckles and lets them fly in quick succession, just as Orran taught her. The first smacks uselessly against the floor, but the second and third strike true—two of the shadow-hyenas dissipate into thin air. Two remain, bridging the distance. As the hyenas near, so close now that she can hear their wet breaths, she lunges into a sprint toward one of the gaping holes in the walls where a torn tunnel spits its train tracks into the throne room. The fastest of the hyenas is already at her heels, snapping at her calves. She skids to an abrupt halt before the mouth of the tunnel and brings her bow down in an arc, slicing through the hyena's body. It evaporates into black mist that blooms around her ankles. Only one left now, but where is it?

A roar sounds at her back.

It is not the snarl of a shadow-hyena. It is the bellow of something far bigger and far angrier. A wave of terror rises from the aesin.

Sascia and Nugau planned meticulously for this, counted desperately on it, trained laboriously for it—for Mooch to create a rip between their worlds and lure out a real beast that Sascia can fight and defeat. And yet it still takes every ounce of courage in Sascia's brain to turn and see with her own eyes what awaits her.

Mooch and its rift are not visible from where she stands, their presence swallowed by the pure Dark seeping through the mouth of the tunnel straight ahead of her. A ten-foot-tall body has stepped through it, so large it dwarfs Sascia. Its head resembles a lion, with a lustrous mane of cut onyx and a row of teeth as thick as her wrists. But its body is insectoid: at least eight legs that Sascia can see, two of which end in pincers like a scorpion's, as though it is a twisted version of the mythological manticore. The last shadow-hyena is pressed between one of these pincers, its neck slowly dissolving into black.

The crowd goes wild with panic.

A real, bona fide Darkbeast stands before them.

This was the crux of her and Nugau's plan. For the aesin to accept this grand performance as a Heart Trial, it needed to be truly *dangerous*. Sascia needed to show the army that humans and aesin could work together by showing off how Mooch could help her defeat an actual Darkbeast. The idea sounded better before she found one looming above her.

It lunges without warning.

Six days of Orran's defensive drills have now been instilled in her brain; Sascia pivots out of its way and grabs an arrow from the quiver, jabbing it up into the beast's belly. It roars in fury—one of its pincers is already in front of her, far too close. It rams into her breastplate, knocking her off-kilter. As she falls, the Darkmanticore's jaws snap around the empty space where her head was only a moment ago. On the ground, Sascia stumbles backward frantically. Before her, the beast's limbs susurrate loudly against the rock as it rears for another attack.

"*Fight, you fool!*" Nugau screams from their perch. The desperation in their voice is real, but the timing is carefully chosen.

This is Nugau's signal.

"Mooch!" Sascia calls. "Now!"

Her awareness shoots out, an arrow into the Dark, as Nugau has been instructing her this entire week. Her frantic mind forms a simple message; a call and a want and a plea. *Help*.

Mooch pops out of the Dark directly above her head, and dives toward the ground. With every flap of its luminescent wings, the fabric of the world splits. A nick at first, then a slice, then a rift. Sascia lifts her arm, fingers splayed, and Tae's nova-sword drops straight into her waiting hand.

Bow and arrow she's mastered as well as she can (which is to say, barely adequately), but the sword is different. She's got an eye for it, according to Orran. It feels comfortable in her hand, the movements flowing and natural.

The crowd cries out in surprise at the doorway between worlds in the center of the arena, at the itka coming to the rescue, at the blade of white that bursts from the hilt of the nova-sword. Sascia brings it down in an arc, just in time to slice one of the Darkmanticore's pincers. The beast throws its head back and roars in pain, and Sascia scrambles to her feet, holding the nova-sword between her and the beast with both hands.

She should end it now. She has the advantage while it's distracted, a clear shot at its furry neck. But as it thrusts she hears that sound again, the susurration of flesh against stone, except it is not flesh—it's a chain. A heavy, black gemstone manacle weighs down one of its many hind legs, its chain dragging on the ground to disappear back into the tunnel of Dark. And now that she has noticed it, Sascia looks for other things: the open wound beneath the shackle, the hairless patches on its fur, the ribs pushing against its starved belly.

A centuries-long winter had stricken our lands. We would have died if our ancestors hadn't discovered that the Ul'amoon radiate heat and that trapping them beneath the earth would save our civilization. This is one of those trapped Ul'amoon, doomed to a life as the aesin's radiator.

The aesin are drawing their own blades, scrambling out of their perches. They scream at her in their own language, in hers— "*Kill it!*"

But Sascia can't. Mooch is hovering in the air before her, between her nova-sword and the frenzied monster. But the Darkmanticore is no longer a monster to Sascia. She can see it properly now. It's an animal, a wounded, mistreated animal, doing anything and everything to survive, just like that rat that bit her on her fifteenth birthday. She and Nugau thought their plan was straightforward: an arena of aesin to witness her prove her Claim, an Ul'amoon lured out of the Dark by Mooch to reveal their shared enemy, a nova-sword to demonstrate how humans and aesin could work together to fell the beasts, the very reason the itka brought their worlds together.

But Mooch is standing in her way. Which means slaying the Ul'amoon can't be the soron mola. The itka open the door between worlds so that they can *help* one another, and once upon a time, the itka opened the door between Itkalin and the dying world of the Ul'amoon, which means that the itka want—that Mooch wants—to save these scary, violent creatures too.

Mere seconds have passed while Sascia stands there and thinks, but as soon as she's reached her conclusion, as soon as she's made her decision—*I won't kill it*—Mooch flies at her face, boops her nose, then dashes upward.

It dives in an arc over the Darkmanticore, opening a rift, and between one blink and the next, the Dark has swallowed the Ul'amoon back into Itkalin.

Tension settles on the arena like a breath held. Sascia and Mooch didn't defeat the Ul'amoon, not as she and Nugau planned, not as the aesin usually do, but the threat is no longer here and that—that *is* a victory. The only question is whether the aesin will accept it.

With Mooch fluttering around her head, Sascia walks to the end of the arena, leans down, and rings Nugau's bell.

The room erupts with cheers.

On every bleacher, every hanging balcony, the aesin are throwing back their heads and howling. The bookies are running around like crazy, trying to answer calls. Even the Queen's council members seem impressed, their faces slack with surprise. And across the cavern, Nugau is smiling.

The princet stands on the side of the overturned train car, a lithe presence that demands everyone's attention. They place their hand on their chest and begin: *thump, thump, thump.*

The aesin don't take too long to follow. Sascia's Claim to peace is picture-perfect: here is their victory, here is their time-traveling god, here is a way for their worlds to be *allies*—

Nugau's head snaps to the other end of the throne room. Their lips part. Their hand freezes. The heartbeat of the Claim trails off.

The Queen stands at the entrance, in her massive armor and floor-length furs. She takes in the packed room, the elated aesin, the triumphant princet, the human at the center of it all, and her violet gaze narrows like a viper readying to strike.

29

AS IT SHOULD

There is no blast of Dark, no swing of the blade, no punishment. Instead, Sascia is simply escorted away. Her last glance over her shoulder paints a somber picture. The army shamed into silence. The princet lowering their head. The Queen surveying them all with a clenched jaw.

In Sascia's cell, the Queen's guards strip her of her weapons and armor with swift, methodical movements. The door locks after them, leaving her alone with Mooch and a sense of danger pressed like a blade against her neck. She imagines a hundred scenarios: the Queen punishing Nugau for their insurrection; the terrible, deadly Trial she will concoct for Sascia, since this one came to an abrupt end; the Darkmanticore, chained and starved and frantic with bloodthirst.

"The Ul'amoon are not the reason you brought us together," she whispers to Mooch. "But what is? How are we supposed to help each other?"

The itka reveals none of its plans. It perches on a pillow on the sofa and, after a moment, Sascia goes to sit by its side. Together they wait. No tray of food or medicine arrives. No gentle Orran or snarky Thalla or somber Nugau. When the door finally creaks open, hours later, a box is tossed in, sliding over the floor to land at the feet of the coffee table.

Inside lies a fabric made of starlight. A cerulean cloth, softer and more liquid than the finest organza, draped over a piece of black leather stitched with a hundred thousand tiny gemstones. The leather is form-fitting, the organza is sheer, and the neckline is deeply revealing. Sascia has been sent a ballgown.

THE STARLIGHT DRESS WISPS around her legs as Sascia is shepherded into the throne room a few hours later. She has pulled herself together as best she can, washed the dirt from her face, combed her hair back with her fingers. Mooch sits on the edge of her plunging neckline, like a living, breathing brooch.

Heads crane around at her entrance.

The vast arena of the throne room has transformed. Curling vines and slabs of onyx have been fashioned into tables and stools spread on the floor. From the ceiling hang vines carrying bulbs of flame and crystalline ornaments. Garlands pillar the room, woven with flowers that iridize with every shift of the light. Near the throne, a band plays lively music on long, oddly shaped stringed instruments. There is no dance floor that Sascia can discern, but dancers crowd every open spot, easily weaving between the tables.

Sascia feels like a character in a storybook. She has just stepped into a goddamned *faerie revel*.

The twirling dancers and flushed-cheeked drinkers twist their heads to watch the guards march her through the feast to the dais. The Queen wears a resplendent gown of black velvet and a placid smile. Her long fingers tap the rhythm of the song against the armrest of her throne. When she notices Sascia, she gestures to someone at a nearby table.

Nugau unfolds from her chair and slips through the dancers. Her cheeks now blaze with a soft blue Darkprint. Her hair is pulled back in an intricate braided updo, her lips painted a stark black, the pointed tips of her ears sporting silver flower-patterned cuffs. She wears a see-through shirt with flowing puff sleeves beneath a high-collared leather vest top that cinches her waist like a corset and long, tight trousers. She is a nymph emerging from the ancient woods, a faerie offering a wicked bargain, a goddess made of blooming dark.

She comes to stand next to Sascia, shoulder to shoulder, and when the Queen addresses the room, the princess plants a calm expression on her face. Another mask, but not the cold, dissociating facade she used to wear. This one is distinctively, unapologetically *proud*, even as the aesin snicker at the Queen's statement.

This new, assured Nugau offers Sascia her hand. "The Queen would like us to dance."

Of all the things Sascia thought might happen when she jumped into the Maw, dancing with a princess during a faerie revel certainly wasn't one of them. Nugau's question echoes in her mind, part accusatory, part pleading for release: *What gives you the right to want?* Sascia didn't have an answer then and she doesn't have one now.

But she feels it again, the longing, and lets her hand fold into Nugau's. The princess guides her through the throng of aesin. She closes the gap between their bodies, prompting Mooch to scurry to Sascia's ear, and positions Sascia's palm on her waist. She leans down, placing her cheek against Sascia's. Warmth unfurls in Sascia's core, like flower petals greeting the sun.

"We dance slow and close. Our cheeks should never stop touching. Our eyes should never meet." Nugau's whisper is a tickle on Sascia's skin. "I will guide you."

The music blooms into a soft, sinuous rhythm. Sascia doesn't know what to do at first, but Nugau is a gracious partner. She leads with infinite gentleness, easing Sascia into the steps of the dance. On every swell of the strings, she pulls Sascia closer, until they are flush against each other, their hips so close that Sascia can feel the slightest shift of the princess's muscles. Sascia's nose burrows into Nugau's neck, into the petal-soft smell of her.

"I'm sorry," Sascia whispers. "If I hadn't hesitated, if I had killed the Ul'amoon as we had planned, I would have proven my Claim before the Queen came in. But Mooch got in my way. It didn't want me to kill the beast—"

"I know, little gnat. I saw. The aesin saw that too. They felt your call, they saw Mooch open the doorway, and after you were dragged away I presented our evidence. They believe us now—it might just take them a while to admit it, especially the Queen and her council."

Across the dance floor, the Queen's councilors are deep in conversation at a remote table. Ktren is among them, their eyes fastened on Sascia and Nugau. "Who are they?"

"Some of the most powerful aesin in Itkalin. Weapons makers, Ul'amoon wardens, those who breed our war mounts. They funded this war campaign." Nugau's voice lilts around a blooming smile. "But you did well today, little gnat. So well, in fact, that the Queen can no longer openly target us. She can only resort to this: the humiliation of dancing the tarant under the gaze of thousands."

"It is not humiliating," Sascia breathes. It is a pleasure, as potent as magic itself, the music and the sway and the touch. (Oh, *the touch*.)

"No? Perhaps only for me, then." In a low, husky voice, the princess whispers, "The tarant is a mating dance. You invite your chosen partner to the floor. You dance as close as you can, without looking at each other, without touching . . . lips."

Is Nugau flustered? Sascia can't turn to see for herself, but she feels the lines of Nugau's tension beneath her fingers where they rest on Sascia's body. The princess's soft disquiet tugs at Sascia's own senses with a maddening flame.

"Don't you worry, your ladyship," Sascia teases. "Your lips are safe. Unless . . ."

The *pleasure* Sascia feels when Nugau swallows is mind-numbing. "Unless?"

"Unless you beg me," Sascia challenges. "Unless you say *mata ne, jite ve.*"

The words mean *kiss me, I'm begging*, often spoken by Orran to Thalla.

A choked chortle escapes Nugau's nose. "Where on earth did you pick *that* up?"

"Oh," Sascia croons, "wouldn't you like to know?"

Absurdly, impossibly, delightfully, Nugau bursts into a laugh. It is loud and wild, at odds with the princess's usually put-together demeanor. It vibrates through their joined chests, hums beneath the fingers Sascia has splayed on the princess's back.

Over Nugau's shoulder and across the room, the Queen's head twists toward the two of them. Her perfectly cultured smile vanishes. The atmosphere in the room changes; the cerulean flames flicker and the vines overheard curl in on themselves.

Nugau whispers, "She heard?"

Sascia nods against the princess's cheek. "Why does she hate you?"

"Is hatred what she feels? She is angry, disappointed, grieving—

but not hateful. She grew up on the battlefield, hardened by the horrors of the constant war against the Ul'amoon. Yet she has always loved her family, as best she can. To her, duty is love. Loyalty is love. Our relationship deteriorated because I *broke* that loyalty."

The princess breathes in deep, her chest pressing into Sascia's.

"When I was a young adolescent," she goes on, "the first of your bombs crashed. Back then, we thought it was just another comet. It tore open the cage of one of the oldest Ul'amoon, what you call the Darkbasilisk, which then unleashed its wrath on the surrounding land. My mother, already the Queen by then, set off to recapture it. My parent Kilorn and I accompanied her, tracking the beast. One day, we were underground, scouting the caves, when a flock of bats attacked us. They would have shredded me to pieces if Mooch hadn't been there. The itka split time and space for me and I fell through—to your world.

"It was summer. The air was warm, the sky was cloudless, the sun bathed everything in a golden glow. I stood in a thicket of trees—birches, I later found out—with long, spindly trunks that seemed to lean on each other for company. I stumbled out of them hurt and bleeding, and across from me was a house with a person sitting on the porch, an old lady by your human standards. She saw me, with my gray skin and pointed ears and heavy armor, and she didn't scream. *I* was afraid of *her*, but she wasn't afraid of me. She ushered me inside, tended my wounds, fed me, and made a bed for me. Every day, she taught me a little bit of your language. She bought me whatever book I asked for, about your history, your art, your silly jokes. I called her Nan. That's what her family called her when they chatted on the phone, although she always hid them from me—she even removed all the pictures from her walls when I arrived.

"I stayed with her for a human year, learning everything I could about your world. But I was a kid. I wanted more than books and stories—I wanted the real thing. So one day, I snuck out. I followed the road to the center of a town. People didn't immediately scream when they saw me. But then a dog barked at me. It startled me, scared me, and I reacted: I threw up a shield of Dark that hurt the dog's leg. The owner fetched a gun out of her purse, with bullets of light that scorched my skin off. I called on the Dark to widen my shield, but I must have pulled more than I thought. The Dark cocooned around me and suddenly I was back in Itkalin."

Silence folds over the princess, tempering her limbs to a slow crawl through the steps of the dance. "In Itkalin, the equivalent of five human years had passed. More bombs had devastated our lands. Dozens of Ul'amoon had broken free. Kilorn had seen the itka open the doorway to whisk me away and so they spent all this time researching old lore, trying to find a way to bring me back. In one of those research trips, they got caught in another bombing. The Ul'amoon that you call the Darkgriffin broke free. Kilorn was among its many victims. I came back after a year of lazing about in your warm, sunny world to find mine in ruins."

"But none of that was your fault—"

"You must understand. It was a *choice*. When I returned, I didn't know how long I had been gone or what kind of devastation had come to pass. In my excitement, I told my mother everything, every little detail of my time in your world, every moment of wonder and love. She asked me when I had realized that I could just step into the Dark if I wanted to return to Itkalin. I told her the truth. That I knew all along. That every day for a year, I made the choice to abandon my family and my people to stay in your colorful world with your strange stories and your sugared food. I chose *you*, humans, and my mother will never forgive me for it."

Guilt crawls out from deep inside Sascia's chest, a jagged, sharp-edged thing. Like Aunt Rania in their restaurant's kitchen, listing every bad decision Sascia had ever made, making it abundantly clear that her decisions too will never be forgiven.

"It is not *fair*." The protest shoots out of Sascia, furious and childish.

Nugau's cheek shifts as though she's trying to look at Sascia. "What is not fair, little gnat?"

"I'm sorry. You made me think about my own unforgivable choices."

"Tell me."

"No, this isn't about me—"

"But it is. In the last few weeks, with you, I have felt myself stepping toward another unforgivable choice."

With you: heat sears Sascia's insides.

Unforgivable: her chest clenches like a sucker punch.

"I would like to hear your story," Nugau goes on, "if you want to share it."

Sascia takes deep, steadying breaths. "I told you about Danny. About our garden and our moths. But I didn't tell you about the accident." She has never spoken this story out loud, never needed to, because everyone she had met since already knew. Like a mark, she has carried it, branded deep into her skin.

"Two years ago, we found a new sewer to explore. I was careless. There was an accident. Danny fractured his spine in three places. He can no longer move his legs." Her eyes have closed. Her breathing is hard. She feels that pressure in her nose again, the gathering of sobs. But she has to go on. She has to see the story to the end, even if it damns her. "I made a mistake, I know that, a mistake that changed my cousin's life. Danny has forgiven me. I don't think he ever even blamed me. And I've tried . . . I got into the Umbra to be by his side. I'm trying to get into college to *stay* by his side. But the choice I made that day—I can never forgive myself."

It is a blessing that the tarant forbids them from looking at each other. Sascia can't bear what she might see in Nugau's eyes right now. The disappointment. The blame. The affirmation of what Sascia really is: a screw-up.

"But it was *a* choice." Nugau's voice vibrates through their pressed chests. "It was one choice among the many we have made and will make in the future. Doesn't it count for something? The new, better choices we made after?"

"I chose to jump into the Maw, to make the Heart Claim," Sascia whispers into their shoulder. "These are still dangerous, reckless choices, aren't they? And you just said yourself that these last few weeks seem like another unforgivable choice. You still call yourself a coward. I still call myself a screw-up. How is that any different?"

"It *feels* different," Nugau says, heatedly. "It feels as though they were the choices of curious children that were only labeled bad by people who never tried to understand. But now, perhaps, someone does understand. Someone who refuses to call me a coward and who I refuse to call a screw-up in turn."

Against Sascia's, the princess's chest rises and falls in furious breaths. Their bodies meet through leather and organza, the touch made more intimate still by this confession. And because Sascia *is* curious and fearless, almost to a fault, she pitches her voice low and husky, challenging and teasing, and she asks, "What should we call each other, then?"

Nugau's breath catches. Her body goes still. Sascia can almost feel that icy mask slide back down, tenderness giving way to embarrassment, but instead Nugau whispers, "Do you care about the rules of this dance? Because I would like to look at you."

"Look at me, then."

The princess's gaze, when it lands on her, is a heavy thing, building a pressure of all the things unsaid. The sole point of Nugau's focus is the bow of Sascia's lips. "When I met you in that future," she says. "Did I want to kiss you?"

Sascia is an ocean of rolling waves; Nugau's question is a dam torn down. Yearning torrents out of her, a great saltstorm of desire. "Yes."

"And did I?"

Sascia is strung taut, an exposed nerve of want. "Not as you should."

An eyebrow climbs up. Then Nugau smirks. "Good. I would like our first kiss to be *as it should*, and far, far more."

Sascia is a blazing fire, from her curled toes to the slicked-back waves of her hair. She wants and wants and wants, and in that moment, there is no shame in it, no control. Nugau doesn't need to beg any longer; Sascia is more than willing to do the begging herself.

Nugau's fingers tighten on Sascia's waist. "Little gnat—"

Darkness erupts. In the foliage of blooms overhead, around the dancers' ankles and their clasped palms, the black swells and gorges and explodes. Tendrils coalesce into streams, then into torrents. The Dark snakes around Sascia's feet, creeping up her body. Nugau breathes a hiss and pulls Sascia behind her, but it's already done.

Walls solidify around them, splitting the aesin into small groups. The dais looms above them all, where the Queen leans back in her throne.

She's dropped them all into the Labyrinth, allies and enemies alike.

The true Heart Trial has begun.

30

A SKILLED ESCAPE ARTIST

Sascia's muscles lock up. The Labyrinth stacks its black walls around her, shadows leering in the corners, thick and alive with too-long claws and sightless skulls and gore-dripping fangs. A despairing terror grips her throat; she shouldn't be back here. Not again.

The aesin are panicking, bodies pressed against the narrow passageway. A face appears in her eyeline, but Sascia's mind refuses to bring the world into focus, to accept what is about to happen. Palms cup her cheeks in a feather-light touch.

"Sascia?" Nugau is saying. *"Sascia!"*

In the princess's voice, her name is a foreign incantation, the vowels too melodious, the *s* too thick—that's what pulls her back. Nugau has never called her anything but *human* and *little gnat* before.

"When I met you, the you from the future," Sascia stammers, "you told me I would try to help you. That I would almost die in a labyrinth of terrors. After my first Trial, I thought I had changed that future. I thought I had survived it."

A frown disfigures the planes of Nugau's face. "Nothing will happen to you. I won't allow it. But first, we need to move, little gnat."

In the narrow corridor between the towering walls of the Labyrinth, Orran is shouldering out of his dress jacket and Thalla is hitching her floor-length skirt to her hips, revealing a duo of daggers strapped to her thigh. She hands one to Orran.

"I'll stall them," the lady says.

Before Sascia thinks to ask *who*, Thalla steps into the center of the corridor, palms out. Her eyes mellow into a translucent white, the veins in her neck a stark silver against her skin. Mist beads out of her fingers like vapor steaming off a pot—in seconds, the entire passage is clouded with the haze of her magic.

A howl rips the air. It is the wail of a wolf calling at the moon, but rough around the edges—it's coming from an aesin throat. Sascia has heard this reckless wildness before, in the tunnel after she jumped into the Maw. Ktren, the Queen's spy and leader of Sascia's haters. Footfalls follow, and the sound of open palms slapped on the walls.

Panic seizes Sascia anew, her eyes seeking Nugau's.

"We aren't the only ones the Queen dropped into the Labyrinth," the princess confirms. "Ktren and their friends are going to try to interfere. My mother likes to discipline with lessons. This is ours, for your performance this morning. We chose to involve ourselves with your Claim, and now we will become a part of your Trial in earnest."

"This is why the aesin admire the Queen," Orran says in their low, rough voice. They stand guard at Thalla's back while she maneuvers the fog to shield them. "She is astute and methodical. She aims to solve three problems at once: the human's new skills, the princess's defiance, the crowd's support."

"Only if we fail," Nugau says. "And we won't. Thalla's mist will camouflage us, which will buy us time with both Ktren and the Queen—as long as she can't see us and can't feel us touch the walls, she won't be able to shift the Labyrinth to block our path."

Another howl echoes down the passageways.

"And if they catch up to us? They sound like"—Sascia's chest rattles—"*dozens.*"

"If they catch up to us, we will fight." Nugau's voice softens. "The Queen believes you will cower before her Labyrinth. But she does not know. You are an Ariadne. This is *your* Labyrinth. So find us a way out."

Ariadne: the name blankets Sascia in the warmth of magic, the worn softness of myth. All Labyrinths have a way out and all Ariadnes know how to find it. Sascia is a skilled escape artist, squeezing her way out of dark sewers and failed exams and the black depths of the Maw. She can do it today too, with Nugau holding her hand, with Mooch guiding her steps, with Orran and Thalla surrounding her.

On the long bone of Sascia's clavicle, Mooch gives an encouraging flutter of its wings. It cannot guide them by flying ahead, as Thalla's fog has settled thick and liquid around them, making it impossible to see beyond a few feet. They cannot touch the walls to guide themselves, and they can't make any noise. Sascia will have to improvise.

"Form a line," she says, "and take each other's hand."

The three aesin shuffle into a row behind her: first Nugau, then Orran, and Thalla at the rear so that she can control the mist with her free hand.

"Mooch," Sascia whispers. "Can you guide us by touching me? One tap is right, two is left, three is straight ahead."

The moth nibbles at the base of her neck, then taps two times.

"Left," Sascia instructs.

As one, the four of them move. The mist consumes all sounds: their footsteps, their breaths, the wild beating of their hearts.

Sascia feels as though she's taken a dive in a tranquil pool; the only things she can sense are the swish of her dress around her thighs, the soft taps of Mooch's wings on her collarbone, Nugau's fingers around hers. Minutes pass in absolute silence. The first gong rings. They have woven deep into the heart of the Labyrinth, taking turn after turn, when the ground begins to tremble.

Nugau draws them to the center of the passageway. "Don't touch the walls!"

Distorted shouts reach them from the direction of the spectators. The mist hides the audience from view, but Sascia can hear astonishment in their voices, and then a mix of disapproval and excitement.

Pointed ears perked, Nugau listens. "The Queen has flattened the walls on the first half of the Labyrinth. Ktren and their group can move freely now. They're headed toward where the mist is thickest. Thalla, can you widen the reach of your magic?"

"I can. Orran," Thalla whispers to her partner, "don't let me faint."

Serpentine swirls of white slither to the floor and uncoil up the walls, over them, swallowing as much of the Labyrinth as Thalla can manage. The mist hazes the entire passageway; Sascia can see no farther than the tip of her nose.

"Thalla can only hold this for a few minutes." Nugau's voice comes from someplace behind her. "We need to move faster, Sascia."

At the base of her neck, Mooch taps three times. Picking up the pace, Sascia pulls them straight ahead, then left and left again. They build a frenetic rhythm of running, turning, running again. With the mist so heavy, black walls appear out of nowhere—she has to swerve and snap her limbs close to avoid crashing into them. An adrenaline-fueled drumbeat pounds relentlessly in her chest. They depend on her, Nugau and Orran and Thalla. Above, the second bell reverberates down the Labyrinth.

Mooch taps, two times—

Sascia shifts her body to turn left—

Then feels its third tap. Not left. *Straight.*

She crashes into the wall, shoulder first. The pain is minimal; it's the horror that roots her to the spot. She has touched the wall. The Queen knows where they are now.

She shouts, "*Run—*" but the command is ripped from her mouth.

The Labyrinth ripples like a mirage pulled apart at the seams. Both ends of the passageway are sealed shut. The wall on their left disappears. The four of them frantically reach for each other as the ground beneath them tilts.

Sascia cups a hand protectively over Mooch's body as she tumbles down the slope. The soft fabric of her dress tears, the jagged rock nips at her exposed flesh, and all around her the misty plains of Thalla's power slacken. White gives way to milky gray, then clear air. Realization jolts through Sascia like an electric current: the Queen tipped them back down to the beginning of the Labyrinth, where the arena is flat and mistless.

A command tears through Nugau's lips; in response, he and the other two aesin draw their weapons. The second their feet connect with solid ground, they are running. They fall into formation like a well-oiled machine, Orran in the center, Nugau and Thalla at his sides. Rivulets of Dark warp around Nugau's hand and solidify into her curved scythe. Thalla's thin dagger glimmers with white mist. Orran's wings flick open and he shoots up in the air, soaring over the ground.

Ktren's group bursts into view: two dozen of them, three, four, faces Sascia recognizes as the council's guards. They surge through the vast expanse of the arena, a small army headed their way. Orran swoops down and clashes with four of their enemies, knocking them a dozen feet back.

Sascia is still flat on the ground. She's still panicking. Mooch is safe against her chest, but no one else is and she can't help them—she's too small, too weak, too *human* to be of any use.

"Little gnat!" Nugau calls back from where she holds the line a few feet away. "We are all here with you, but this is *your* Trial. You're the only one who has to make it across the Labyrinth. We're going to hold them off and you—"

"I won't leave you!" Sascia cries.

"Yes, you will!" Nugau snaps. "You cannot fight your way out of this—but you can outsmart it instead. So *move.*"

And Sascia does move. She jumps to her feet and steels her shoulders. Over the stretch of flat ground behind her, she can see the way back into the Labyrinth. But ahead, Orran is snapped from the air by a meaty hand and tossed across the floor like a rag doll. He skids to a stop at Thalla's feet, his shirt torn and hanging in tatters from his back. Blood is running down his temple. A roar tears from Thalla's throat.

Nugau swings her blade over her head. At the lowermost point of its arc, Dark explodes from it, a swooping slash of shadow that zips down the arena. The blast hits the first line of the soldiers square in the chests. They are knocked off their feet, but others are instantly there to replace them, blades drawn, mouths sneering.

"Orran!" Nugau cries. "Can you fly?"

Thalla has wrapped her arms around her partner, pulling them to their feet. Her fingers catch their jaw. "You do not die tonight, Orran S'uravot. You do not die without me." She presses her lips against Orran's, a stab of a kiss, and stands to face Ktren and their soldiers. "Get Sascia out of here."

Orran's feathers ruffle, wings elongating. He breaks into a run. Sascia places Mooch in the hollow beneath her ear, where it's safest, and opens her arms. Orran crashes into her, his arms a cord of muscle around her waist. He struggles under her weight, but his wings beat furiously around them—they shoot into the air. Sascia's stomach plummets. The ground rushes past and, after a few seconds, so does the Labyrinth; Orran means to fly her over the last part of the maze, straight to the exit.

Twin war cries torrent down the arena. Over Orran's shoulder, Sascia spots Nugau and Thalla launch into the battle. The two move faster than her eyes can track, strikes of the blade and grunts of effort the only things she can make out.

Orran swerves a hard left—her body nearly slips out of their grasp. A wall of black has spurted out of nowhere. The Queen is none too pleased about Orran's plan to fly straight out of there. The passageways rush up to meet their height, walls towering taller and taller until they crash into the ceiling. The new architecture plunges them into darkness, making it even harder to spot the sides. Orran veers left and right as best they can, but the way through is too narrow for the span of their wings.

"You'll hurt yourself," Sascia cries over the rushing wind. "Get us to the ground."

The aesin obliges, swooping through the air for a gentle landing. Sascia immediately scans her surroundings, but the towering tunnel of the Labyrinth allows no light but the Darkprints on Mooch's wings and Orran's cheeks. It doesn't matter; if her calculations while they were airborne were right, they're less than five turns from the end of the maze. If they hurry, they can make it out before Nugau or Thalla get hurt.

"Are you good?" she asks Orran. "To keep moving?"

Eyes closed, face tilted up to the ceiling, Orran is taking deep breaths. His face and back are torn with dozens of small scratches; blue blood dots his dark skin. But at her question, he straightens and flashes her a wicked grin. "Always."

They move faster: Mooch leads, Sascia follows, Orran pulls up the rear. Both their breaths are labored, their feet heavy with exhaustion, but they keep walking, counting the turns. Orran has tucked in his wings to avoid touching the walls. The Queen has fallen prey to her own trick by connecting the walls to the ceiling—she can't see them now either.

Time passes like blinks between dreaming and waking—all of a sudden, Sascia takes a turn to find the exit at the very end of the passageway.

"We made it," she whispers.

"We did," Orran says.

She grabs their arm and pulls them along, sprinting the last few feet to the exit—

Something slick swishes through the air.

Orran is ripped out of her grasp.

She turns, breath lodged in her throat. The walls have returned to their normal height. She can see the perimeter of the cavern, laden with aesin—they are unnervingly quiet. The Queen sits as nonchalant as ever on her throne.

And Ktren stands at the other end of the passageway.

Their fingers are extended in her and Orran's direction, but there is no weapon in them.

Orran is looking at her. The white is showing around the pupils of his eyes. His smile has deformed into a look of surprise. A dagger sticks out of his back, right where his wings grow from his spine. His left wing droops, dark blue blood soaking his feathers.

"Go," Orran whispers. "Once the third bell rings, it's against our laws for Ktren to hurt me. I'll hold them off until then. Go!"

At the other side of the passageway, Ktren edges closer, a hand claiming a new dagger.

Orran struggles to stand, but their strength fails them; they collapse on their side.

Sascia casts a glance over her shoulder. The exit is there, a simple, inconspicuous absence of wall between passageways. If she runs, she will be there in less than a minute—if she runs, Orran will take another dagger for her.

She is a skilled escape artist, dodging every obstacle in her path.

But this time, she's not going to run.

She squares her shoulders and turns to face Ktren.

31

THE WHINE OF A CORNERED DOG

"Ah, the pretty human thinks she can fight me," Ktren mocks. "Please, don't stop because of me. Win your Trial. Victory against the mighty Orran is a much bigger prize than you'll ever be. I wish to hear the undefeated warrior of the Jagged Blade beg for mercy."

The aesin spy calls out a question in the elven tongue, loud enough for the audience to hear. Murmurs hiss overhead, muffled agreements. The rules of aesin conduct were never clear to Sascia, but this she can decipher: Ktren just asked permission to kill Orran. On her dais, the Queen dips her head.

"Finally," Ktren breathes around a satisfied sneer, "I can be his ending."

"You aren't going to be *shit*." Fury takes over; Sascia bends down, snatches Orran's dagger from the ground, and steps in front of her friend. There will be no endings today, not on her watch.

Across from her, Ktren throws their head back and lets out one of their wild yowls. It should be intimidating, it should grind her courage to dust, but all Sascia can feel is wrath and justice—before the aesin can collect themself, she lunges.

The dress flings open around her thighs and her Doc Martens pound on the rock as she sprints down the passageway, gaining momentum, and swings her blade in a horizontal slash at the aesin's chest. They slide away, liquid fast, wearing a satisfied smile. Their own dagger flashes out, its polished blade a glint of onyx before it finds purchase in Sascia's flesh.

Heat blooms at her side, where the blade has nicked her. She doesn't stop—she drags her dagger in a low blow, aiming for the aesin's legs, but she's still too slow. Ktren jumps over it with ease, bounces off the wall, and dives for Sascia's face. The punch connects with her cheek, reverberating through her skull and down her body.

Nicks, punches; Ktren is toying with her. They're going to make it hurt and make it slow, a show of power for the aesin gathered in the throne room. Sascia fought to sway the army to her side, to prove herself to them—she can't let Ktren bring it all down. And Orran—she has driven Ktren back down the tunnel where they came from, but at her back, her friend is still lying on his side. How can she ever defeat an enemy who's twice her size, three times her speed, and endlessly stronger?

Sascia raises her dagger and dives into a series of moves that Orran drilled into her muscles. The spy deflects each blow with a mere twist of their wrist, facing her dagger with their own. Soon, Sascia's covered in sweat and blood from the dozen little cuts Ktren inflicts on her flesh. But after every parry, every stab, she picks herself up and launches once more.

Like a beetle, her father had said. *You keep throwing yourself against the glass, again and again, instead of flying out the open window an inch to your right.*

What you are is a little gnat, Nugau had said. *Vexing but ultimately too ephemeral to be of any consequence.*

A beetle and a gnat, bugs the both of them, pests that annoy because they just won't quit. But to Sascia, bugs have always been the most interesting of creatures: glorious in their smallness, resilient in their fleetingness, ingenious in their folly. They are underestimated and swatted at and stomped, but they don't give up. Not beetles, not gnats. And not *moths*.

"Mooch," Sascia whispers as she crouches on the ground after a particularly nasty cut to her midriff. Ktren has turned to face the spectators above, basking in their cheers. "Are you there?"

Mooch lands on the back of her palm, skitters to a cut bleeding on her arm, and stays there, fluttering its wings unhappily.

"I think it's time," Sascia heaves between gasping breaths, "to *attack*."

The moth reacts in seconds: its scaled body ripples, as though magnetized by some invisible force. Its flesh bursts in spikes that transmogrify its soft, hairy wings into smooth, hard onyx. Sharper than a blade, stronger than a rock—in this form, Mooch is a weapon all on its own, yet it folds itself into her hair.

"While I have enjoyed this, pest," Ktren says, turning back to her, "I am eager for a foot rub and a strong drink. Let's end it, shall we?"

Sascia sits back on her haunches, peeking through the curtain of her sweaty hair. Ktren stands a couple of feet away, flicking their dagger into the air. Drops of blood spray the walls each time it lands in their hand—drops of *Sascia's* blood.

Her legs are failing. She can't command them to carry her weight any longer. Her blade trembles in midair, as pathetic as she herself must look, kneeling and bleeding and gasping for air.

With the leisure of a cat waking from a long nap, Ktren stretches their arms over their head, waltzes over, and simply kicks the dagger out of Sascia's hand.

It clatters to the wall with a small, pitiful *clang*.

The spy positions themself dramatically before her, legs spread, chest puffed, dagger aimed at her face. "Human," they say, loud and performative for their audience. *"Yield."*

"Oh, fuck off," Sascia spits.

She and Mooch launch as one. She goes for the hand that holds the dagger; Mooch goes for their eyes. The moth is a sight to behold. Onyx wings spread wide, their edges sharp as a blade, it lunges at Ktren's face, slicing their eyes, their nose, their mouth. The aesin lets out a shriek of panic that is cut short when Sascia buries her fist into their belly.

Momentum throws them both on the ground, hard enough to smart. Sascia has their wrist in her grip, trying to pry the dagger from their fingers, while the aesin rolls them around, tumbling feet over heads. Ktren is too strong, too heavy, too skilled—even with a moth slicing up their face and a human girl wrapped around their torso, the spy comes out on top. They grab Mooch and fling it to the wall, then twist their wrist out of Sascia's grip and pin her hand to the ground.

A sound tears from their throat, less wolf howl and more the harrowing shriek of a banshee. Their cheeks are shredded, strips of flesh peeling off their jaw, one of their lids torn open. They look down at her through those bleeding eyes—

And open their mouth wide.

Their teeth lengthen into sharp incisors, rows upon rows of them, coated with black saliva that drips into the soft column of her neck. Sascia stretches back, away from that maw, those teeth, that hunger, but there is nowhere to go, no way to escape. A sob crawls out of her chest, the whine of a cornered dog.

Ktren is lowering their mouth toward her neck. Sascia can feel their saliva dripping against her collarbone. They will rip into her, tear her to pieces.

A beetle. A gnat. A pest.

Her body reacts. She thrashes with all the strength she has left in her, arcing her torso, kicking her legs, straining against Ktren's hold on her wrists. Out of pure luck, pure frenetic adrenaline, she manages to knee them in the ribs and twist her neck out of the way—

Ktren's fangs bore into the soft flesh of her shoulder.

A cry pours out of her, so hard that it hurts all the way up her throat. The pain is everywhere, pulsing at her ears and darkening her vision. She is consumed by it, by the feel of Ktren's teeth ripping into her flesh, the feel of their wet lips on her skin, the weight of them on her, the *pain*.

It is instinct alone that keeps her going, the vexing insistence of a pest. She snaps her hand out of Ktren's grip, grabs a dagger from the belt across their chest—and plunges it deep into their ear.

The spy slumps onto her.

Their full weight is crushing her chest, but their jaw has grown slack around her shoulder. Sobbing uncontrollably, hands trembling, Sascia grips their chin and pulls their jaws apart.

She screams as her flesh tears anew, but then she's moving, wiggling out from beneath their body, kneeling where Mooch is lying on the floor. She takes the moth into her palm—the good one, because her other arm doesn't seem to be working at all—and crawls all the way to Orran. She studies them, their chest. There. Slow and tortured, but they're breathing.

A few feet away, Ktren is lying face down on the floor, blue blood forming a puddle around their horns. No walls of onyx surround them anymore. The Labyrinth has flattened back into the arena. The third gong must have rung. The Trial is over. Sascia lost. Aesin are trailing down from the sidelines of the cavern, edging toward her with the cautiousness of a tamer approaching a frenzied wild beast.

A figure comes into view. Her hair has unraveled out of its updo. Her face is scored with panic, sweat beading her furrowed brow.

Oh, good, Sascia thinks, mind fogged with blood loss. *Nugau is here*.

Now she can pass out in peace.

32

CRACK

Sascia is sixteen, Danny is seventeen, and the utility closet in their basement is now a veritable map of Dark.

It's an accidental discovery. One day, they find the moth they'd picked up from the lowermost point of Astoria Park flapping its wings frenetically. Not five minutes later, their phones buzz with a citywide alert: a float of Darkcrocodiles has been spotted roving the waters of the East River, right by that park. A couple of weeks later, the same thing happens with a moth from the heart of Jackson Heights, minutes before a swarm of Darkvultures infests the neighborhood's rooftops. The moths, they realize, can detect oncoming attacks.

Little by little, week by week, they secure moths and flora samples from a fifty-mile radius. Danny sets up a camera system to alert them every time one of the moths starts reacting. When the alarm goes off, Danny and Sascia send an anonymous tip to the local authorities. Five times now, their map has saved people's lives.

"I don't like the looks of this one," Danny says one Sunday morning in mid-March. They're standing over an open manhole.

The cover they've just removed has deep claw marks on the inside.

Sascia already has her arguments ready. Whatever made those marks must be gone by now. Their sonar reading shows no Darkcreatures, but it does show a lush paradise of Darkflora—have they ever seen anything like it?

They have not and Danny knows it. His jaw juts out in thought, but he's just as bad as Sascia at refusing his curiosity. Besides, they've got a nova-gun now, bought after three months of saving their busboy wages. It doesn't take Danny long to relent.

They descend the ladder and fall into position: Sascia in the lead, nova-gun across her flashlight, cop-in-movies style, and Danny at the rear, watching their backs. Already, the Dark breathes and coils around them. Vines reach for them and blooms cast their effervescent neon against the walls. They stroll for a long while, in awe of all the strange plants and bugs. Then they turn a corner and pull to a stop, mouths agape.

Before them rises a tree, a proper Darktree, with roots that carve deep into the concrete and branches that hug the entire tunnel. Fruits hang from its thicket of leaves, perfect orbs that look like black glass marbled with sapphire. Neither of them has seen a blooming Darktree before; this Dark has been growing, unperturbed, for a long, long time.

As the tunnel settles into the familiar grinding of Danny's trowel, Sascia lays out the rest of their equipment to host the root sample he's extracting: a collection box, fresh dirt, a spray bottle with clean water. When it's all set up, she reaches into her backpack, scoops a few caramelized almonds into her palm, and waits. The moths trail out of the other end of the tunnel in lazy swirls of bright color. They land straight on the almonds and begin scarfing them down. *Cute little scoundrels*, Sascia thinks—

A snarl cuts through her thoughts.

She and Danny are standing in a second, flashlights aimed at the end of the tunnel. The moths flutter around Sascia's head, almonds and cuteness forgotten.

Two spots of bright red are peering down at them.

The lithe body of a Darktiger lies flat against a thick pipe. Beneath its stripes, its spine juts out in sharp ridges as thick as a kitchen knife. Its mouth is closed, its features tranquil, its eyes deeply intelligent—this is an apex predator.

"Danny, *run*," Sascia hisses, and she's already shooting, blast after blast of nova-light. With every flash, she glimpses images: The tiger lunging. The tiger dashing across the tunnel. The tiger sweeping a clawed paw at her feet.

Glass breaks, moss tears, metal pounds as Sascia follows Danny to the ladder. He's climbing ahead, above her, but the tiger is right there, its lips parted around tusks as thick as her wrist. Logic has fled right out of Sascia's head. She acts on instinct alone, the millennia-old fight or flight. She tears her backpack from her shoulders and launches it at the tiger's snout before dashing up the ladder.

"Go, go, go!" Danny is shouting at her from above.

She tries. She does try. (No one can ever take that away, at least.) Her feet fly over the rungs. Her arms ache with the strain. The ladder reverberates with the stomp of their frantic retreat.

Then claws dig into her calf—she screams.

"Sascia!" Danny cries. He reaches down for her. His foot slips. He falls.

THEY ASK HER AFTERWARD how she killed the Darktiger, but she can't remember.

What she remembers is the impression of Danny's body parting the air. The horrible *crack* as his back struck the concrete. The nova-gun firing shot after shot, a barrage of furious light. Her arms around his torso, trying to help him stand. His trembling voice saying, "I can't feel my legs. I can't feel my legs."

She remembers carrying him up the ladder, her muscles bursting with adrenaline. She remembers his arms digging into her shoulders, her lungs threatening to burst, blood flowing freely down her calf. She remembers riding with him in the ambulance, holding his hand so tight his fingers go white. She remembers Aunt Rania's terrible scream as she bursts in through the hospital doors.

PART III

Harin ye o' skish, o' skish thi haro
(huh·reen yeh oh skeesh, oh skeesh thee huh·roh) *Itkalin saying*

*when met with a blade, with a blade you'll meet;
a popular saying about the principle of reciprocity,
particularly in the context of conflict
or aggression.*

*Colloquial; attributed to General Gryr,
upon seeing the brutal remains in the
final battlefield of the Great Capture, the
hundred-years-long campaign to seize and confine
the Ul'amoon.*

33

POCKET OF SOFT FLESH

Nugau is carrying her.

Bodies flit around them; voices drift from far away. Sascia's heart pounds too loud in her ears. Flames of agony pulse down her shoulder and burn into her chest. It is not right, this heat, the kind of inferno that cannot be survived.

She's placed tenderly on a soft mattress. Orders are barked, liquids poured through her lips. She swallows and coughs, sending a new wave of pain down her body.

Nugau's face reappears. "I'll fix this. Do you hear me, little gnat? *I'll fix this.*"

A new aesin elbows Nugau out of the way, their gloved hands holding small, narrow tools. Sascia holds on to Nugau's wrist and places the moth into the princess's palm.

"Mooch," she breathes, a croak of a word. *Fix Mooch*, she means. *Save Mooch.*

HER BODY HAS BECOME a cage. She lies in that space between dreaming and waking. Tremors shake down her spine, fever sweats through her pores. She cannot move, not even to open her eyes, but she can hear: the aesin speaking and shifting about the room. Sewing her flesh back together.

She thinks, *I want my mom.* Her mother's gentle hands, her father's steady voice, Danny's jokes, Ksenya's smiles, her friends' warmth. She wants to be back there with them, safe, unhurt. Instead, she is a fragile consciousness trapped in failing flesh, her frenzied thoughts her only company. When sleep comes for her, it is a deliverance; when wakefulness returns, she wishes for oblivion.

Then she hears Nugau's voice, close, and feels their hand against her cheek. "Our healers can't treat your fever. You need human medicine. I think Mooch is trying to show me where to find it. I will be gone for a few hours, but I will return, I promise."

Sascia thinks, *Mooch. Mooch is alive. Mooch is leading you away.*

She thinks, *Is it safe to go? Is the Queen angry with you? Will she punish you again?*

But her tongue isn't working. In the end, she doesn't even sense Nugau's departure; sleep has reclaimed her long before she can hear the door close.

IT'S THE FLUTTERING OF wings that brings her to.

Mooch has landed on her face and is traipsing over her closed eyelids, a vexing pest in earnest. Sascia wiggles her nose, to which the moth responds with a nibble at her skin.

"Hey," she whispers, only her parched mouth makes it come out as *erghgh*.

She opens her eyes to find Mooch standing at the tip of her nose. Then she realizes: She *opened* her eyes. She *spoke*, albeit gibberish.

She can feel her body again, head to toes, and it's painful, yes, but it's not hot, nor the kind of heavy that promises death.

The room is an infirmary of some sort. Aesin tools and vials are spread neatly on a desk, heavy aprons hang from hooks. On the bed across from hers, Orran is lying face down on the mattress, their wings held up by a complicated latticework of wires. The wounds on their back are dressed with a swirly neon green poultice and the broken part of their wing has been reinforced with some sort of crystalline cast. Thalla is curled like a cat against them, her nose tucked into their side. Both look asleep.

On the floor by the door lies Nugau. Now sporting purple Darkprints, the prince wears the same organza shirt he had been wearing at the revel, unbuttoned to his midriff, revealing the ridges of his sternum, the long column of his neck. A bandage is wrapped there, stained black with dried blood. He's sleeping right there on the floor, facing the beds, with only a towel tucked beneath his head.

"He refused to let anyone else keep watch," Orran whispers. Sascia twists her head to find him smiling his gentle grin. "But I guess not even the prince of Itkalin can handle four days of zero sleep."

"It's been four days?" Sascia asks.

"Four since your Trial. Two since Nugau came back with your medicine."

At the table by her bed, white-capped pill bottles bearing names like amoxicillin and cephalexin are lined up next to clean bandages. Nugau got her every kind of antibiotic he could get his hands on. "Where did he find them?"

"Your itka showed him," Orran says. "Our healers stitched up your wound quickly, but Mooch wouldn't stop buzzing around Nugau's head, even attacked him at one point. When the healers told him you might need human medicine to fight the infection,

Nugau realized what the itka wanted. He followed it into the tunnels, found a pharmacy in the collapsed station, and grabbed every bottle he could find."

"Did the Queen . . . ?" Sascia's voice trails away.

"She tried. But I don't think the entire army could have held Nugau away from us."

A smile draws on Sascia's lips. "How are you? How is your wing?"

"It will recover. My clan is made for mountain and rock; a spy's dagger will not be what breaks us." He pauses and drags an arm to his side to prop his face off the pillow. Even in sleep, Thalla adjusts herself to remain close to his side. "You could have run, Sascia, yet you stayed and took up the dagger. I will not forget your kindness. You saved my life."

Tears are prickling at the corners of Sascia's eyes. "I only did what was right."

"To do what is right," they say in a reverent tone, "is not a given. It is a choice, every day of our lives, that comes at a cost not all of us are willing to pay. You were. You knew it would cost you pain and you made the hard choice anyway."

"How can you say that?" she whispers. "How can there be kindness in my choice, when my choice was to *kill* Ktren?"

Orran holds her gaze. "Was that your choice?"

"No, I didn't want to—their teeth were in me, their weight on top of me—I didn't think, I didn't plan—I only *acted*, like a trapped animal—"

Dry sobs rattle her chest.

She only acted like a trapped animal, like all those Darkbeasts and Darkcreatures that suddenly found themselves in a world of vicious light. She had acted on instinct alone, all thrashing and hitting and stabbing, with whatever weapon she could reach, in whatever pocket of soft flesh she could find.

A while ago, when Nugau showed her the aesin's mural, Sascia had pleaded for the innocence of humans. *We only sought to protect ourselves*, she had said, and she had meant it then, believed in it wholeheartedly.

Intentions don't matter, Nugau had answered. Then he said—

"When met with a blade," Sascia whispers, "with a blade you'll meet."

Nugau meant this, didn't he? Sascia had all the best intentions in the world, of peace and safety, of a courage that sheds no blood, yet when she was trapped, with those fangs around her shoulder, she had reached for the blade. And the itka had noble intentions, too, but when they opened the door between their two worlds, they set in motion a terrible cycle. The Ul'amoon broke out of their underground cages and into the human world, where they wreaked havoc in human cities. Humans responded with nova-light bombs that traveled through time and space to become the very thing that set the Ul'amoon free in the first place—destroying aesin lands along the way. And so the Ul'amoon broke free, traveled to the human world, and wreaked havoc there. It is an endless cycle, this violence, an ouroboros devouring its own tail.

She looks at Orran for some kind of response—a rebuke, an acceptance, anything that will ease the scorch of this desperate feeling inside her—but the aesin's gaze is trained on the door.

Nugau has woken. He lies still on the floor, but his eyes are open, alert, brilliantly violet.

"You understand now," the prince says.

A cycle of violence between a world of darkness and a world of light, over and over again, with not a spare moment to pause, to think, to understand—to make the hard choice, the choice of kindness.

"I understand."

34

HALF-MOONS

The next time Sascia wakes, the infirmary is cloaked in darkness. Nugau has moved to the floor by Sascia's cot, leaning against its side with his arms resting on his bent knees. Purple marks the Darkprints on his cheeks and deep shadows fold beneath his eyes. Did he sleep at all? Sascia doubts it. He is watching his friends: the slow rise and fall of Orran's chest, the arm Thalla has wrapped around their waist.

He must hear the change in Sascia's breathing, because he looks up at her.

Sascia feels too present in her body: the fold of the mattress beneath her weight, the creases of the blanket over her legs, the pull of the stitches on her shoulder. Under his gaze, every movement is a caress, every heartbeat a confession. She turns onto her good side, tucking her hands beneath her cheek. For a while, they gaze at each other.

"I'm ready now," Nugau says into the quiet.

Sascia knows exactly what he means. She warned him when the Queen raised the Labyrinth around them a second time. The Nugau from the future had told her she would almost die in it. And here Sascia lies, having narrowly escaped death. At long last, Nugau wants to hear the whole story.

"I met you three times," Sascia begins. "The first time, I pulled you out of the Dark near Times Square. Humans had never made contact with aesin before. Your appearance caused havoc. You had an old scar right there." She lifts her finger to the bandage at his neck. "You said I had been judged for my actions in the Battle of Feathers and found guilty of treason. You were sent there to kill me. And that's what you tried to do."

He watches her, still and voiceless.

"The second time is the one you remember," Sascia goes on. "I was with Danny and our friends at the Village Halloween Parade. Mooch appeared out of the Dark and flew straight to you. I thought you had come to kill me. But you had no recollection of the attack in Times Square. You were bright-eyed and full of wonder. You looked younger. Unscarred."

"I was," Nugau says. "After I came back from that year in your world, I could feel nothing but grief and shame. Every night I thought about my parent desperately looking for a way to bring me back, and cursed myself for choosing to stay in your world. I needed to see it again. To decide if it was worth it. Mooch appeared and guided me to that parade. Nan had spoken to me about Halloween. She had thought I'd love it."

He doesn't go on, so Sascia picks the tale up again. "The third time I met you, you stumbled out of the Dark in my closet. You were dying. Mooch was stuck in your throat, poisoning you." Her eyes find the itka, perched on Orran's wounded wing. "I got Mooch out. While I was cleaning your wounds, I noticed your hand. When you attacked me in Times Square, only a month before that in my timeline, I fired a nova-gun on you. But the burn scar on your hand was old, almost completely healed. That's when I realized."

"Ymneen," Nugau whispers. He is staring at his unmarked hands.

"You told me you and the aesin were betrayed. That war would destroy both of our worlds. That I would try to help you, but I would fail. We would all fail. That we never found the reason the itka brought us together. That this was farewell."

She doesn't mention the kiss. The dread of the future presses tight around her. She thought she had changed it, remade it, by winning her first Trial, but now with her near death, with that wound on Nugau's neck... The future is here, and it is unchanged. To speak of kisses right now, of begging for them, feels like defeat.

Nugau lowers his head to the cot, his hair pillowing against her thigh. When he looks at her, his face is a carving of sorrow. "All this time," he whispers, "you jumped into the Dark to save us and made the Heart Claim and tried to convince me to help you and fought and schemed and argued for peace—even though I tried to kill you?"

Heat gathers at her neck. "It sounds far more noble when you put it like that," she teases. "Mostly, I was just a reckless screw-up desperate for a second chance."

His lips quirk into a split-second smile. Then he raises his hand to his neck. "Mooch did this. I don't think it meant to cut me—it was just worried about you. It loves you, just as much as you love it. So why would it bring you here to get hurt, over a peace that you have no chance of achieving? Why would it let you glimpse a future you can't undo?"

Mooch soars back to land on Sascia's arm. It does love her, Sascia can feel that in its every choice, but more than that, it *trusts* her. It trusted her to follow it to an active Maw. It trusted her to protect it from the were-creature in her first Trial. And it trusted her not to land the killing blow when she faced the Darkmanticore. Each time Mooch came to her, it brought her to *where* she needed to be, but also to *when* she needed to be.

"Mooch," she whispers, "did you create the ymneen? Do you choose *when* we end up each time we travel through your doors?"

Atop the knuckle of her index finger, Mooch taps one solitary time: *right*. In the Labyrinth, the instruction meant turn right, but here, in this context, it can only mean . . . *yes*.

"Why?" Nugau rasps at the moth. "Why knot our timelines together? How are we supposed to save each other, when you keep forcing us to meet as enemies?"

Scolded, the moth dives for its burrow behind Sascia's ear, leaving Nugau's question unanswered. Yet some part of Sascia, the part that Nugau calls Ariadne, that never stops trying to understand, knows that Mooch wouldn't have answered even if it could. This is a question she and Nugau are supposed to answer themselves, because it is imperative that they, too, *understand* why the past has been knotted into the future.

"Our choices are still our own," Sascia says: to Mooch, to Nugau, but also to herself. "I do not regret saving you the third time I met you. I do not regret making the Thistha Ren. And I do not regret saving Orran. But Ktren—"

"You were scared. We are all of us scared, and so we make choices out of fear when faced with a threat. *Harin ye o' skish, o' skish thi haro*." His head shifts, his cheek flat against her thigh. Dark eyes bore into her. "But you're right: our choices are still our own. It is time to finally make mine."

Sascia's heart begins to thunder. "You will make the Royal Claim?"

"I have to. The aesin won't all support me, but some will, those who you won over. It will not be a permanent solution, but it will stop whatever punishment the Queen has prepared for you. Without the aesin's full support, she will lose her increased powers, and without her power, the army is weak. She will have to retreat to

Itkalin. We can stop the violence that way, by separating aesin and humans forever, each in their own world."

But what of us? she wants to ask. *What of the future where you beg me to kiss you?* Pressure builds at the base of her throat, squeezing like a noose, but she refuses to let it out. Because Sascia does understand Nugau's choice, even if it breaks her heart.

So she swallows that sob and says, smugly, teasingly, "See? I knew you weren't a coward."

A bark of a laugh spears through him.

Across from them, Thalla opens a heavy-lidded eye to glare at them.

The prince's ears flatten to his head in apology. When Thalla rolls back over, he relaxes against Sascia's thigh. Again, Sascia notices the deep shadows beneath his eyes, the bloodshot tinge of his pupils.

"You can be brave tomorrow," she says. "Tonight, you will sleep."

His mouth quirks up, but he doesn't object. He straightens his legs and crosses them at the ankles, then folds his hands on his lap. A second passes, then another, before his eyes flutter closed. Sascia watches him. The rise and fall of his chest. The dusting of lashes on his cheeks. The swoop of his unruly bangs.

Mindlessly, impulsively, she reaches out and runs her fingers through his hair.

His head snaps up fast—his mouth closes around her hand. Long, sharp incisors press into the soft pad at the base of her thumb. The touch is prickly but not painful. Instead, a current runs up her arm, kindling every nerve in her body into a roaring inferno. Want throbs inside her. It is making her think all kinds of dirty, filthy things. *Harder* and *deeper* and *more*.

She remembers his soft murmur as they danced: *I would like our first kiss to be* as it should, *and far, far more*. What, she wonders, is that far, far more?

He must know. He must see the reaction his teeth cause in her, because suddenly his lips, still around her palm, are curving into a smile. Slow as torment, he digs his fangs out of her skin. He closes his mouth. He leans back against the cot. He shuts his eyes.

Sascia's hand hovers in midair. Half-moons are drawn on her skin. She stares and stares at them. Was this a challenge? She thinks it might have been. She thinks she might have met it. She thinks she might have enjoyed it. Her breaths come out short and hard; she is grinning like a giddy fool.

She reaches out anew and runs her fingers through his hair, again and again and again, until he slips into an easy, fretless sleep.

35

A TEST OF LOYALTY

Footfalls pelt down the throne room. Aesin pour out of tunnels and crevices, more with every minute. They crowd the cavern in clusters on train cars and juts of rock. Once settled, they silently turn their gazes to the dais, before which stand Sascia and Nugau. They know something is about to happen; news that their prince awaits his mother in the throne room traveled fast.

A coil of nerves winds tight around Sascia's rib cage. Her nails flick the gemstone scales of her aesin jacket. Her Doc Martens shuffle against the moss-spotted concrete. Fire licks at the flesh of her still-healing wound where her shoulders have tensed up. She tries to ease them back down, but it's impossible. Fear knows no command.

By her side, Nugau is sculpted marble, a pillar holding up a temple of ancient gods. His back is straight, his neck long, a hand draped casually on the pommel of his sword. Last night, with her fingers in his hair, something shifted between them. He woke her up with a hand against her cheek. He helped her wash her hair, buttoned up her jacket, and laced her boots for her. He didn't speak a word of what's to come and neither did she, the silence growing heavier with every step toward the throne room; if all goes well and Nugau commands the aesin to retreat to Itkalin, these last few moments of tenderness will be their goodbye.

Thalla stands stoic on Nugau's other side, alone, as Orran is still not well enough to move. She glares daggers into the knot of council members gathered around the dais. The tallest—Ktren's parent, Thalla explained—watches Sascia with deathful wrath.

A chorus of steps heralds the Queen's entrance. A dozen guards spill into the throne room, flanking their queen. She is dressed for battle: plated in intricate onyx armor and carrying an antlered helmet beneath her armpit. She does not sit in her throne, but rather walks to the edge of the dais and looks down at them. Before her feet lies the evidence Nugau and Sascia gathered, the newspapers, the video, a few photographs. Nugau showed them to the aesin after Sascia faced the Ul'amoon, and he's displaying them again now to remind them: ymneen rules us all.

Then, to Sascia's surprise, Nugau bows deeply to his mother. When he addresses the army in a loud, authoritative voice, Thalla leans close to Sascia to translate.

"My queen, my mother, you have tried to protect us as best you can. But it is no longer enough. The itka have opened the door and knotted our time with the human world's. We can no longer rely on strength of arms and weapons. We need to find the true purpose of the itka's choices, to save the humans and be saved in turn. If you won't do that, then I will."

His courage stumbles, but only for a moment, as he casts his gaze around the cavern. Then he throws his shoulders back, fists his hand, and raises it to his chest—

Before knuckles can meet skin, before that first *thump*, a whorl of the Queen's power wraps around his wrist, freezing his arm in place. The room replies with the unmistakable sound of blades being drawn from scabbards. Nugau's allies jump out of their seats. The guards position themselves between the crowd and their regent.

The Queen's shimmering violet eyes, so much like Nugau's own, skip over her son and land on Sascia, measuring her up. Whatever she sees, it's not satisfactory—her lip curls.

She speaks, and Thalla translates. "There is no need for the Thistha Ren, my son. You have proven already that you have strength, wits, and heart. I will gladly and willingly yield my throne to you."

This is everything Nugau ever wanted, forgiveness and validation and power over the aesin, and his face reflects the giddy hope in his heart. Even Thalla is smiling while she interprets, but something feels wrong to Sascia. By the dais, Ktren's parent wears a triumphant smile.

It's a trap, Sascia thinks, a second before the Queen speaks again.

Tension seizes Nugau's body. His fingers clench into fists by his sides. Sascia's eyes are tracing reactions: most aesin seem skeptical at first, but then their stance begins to change. Frowns form on their faces. Doubt simmers beneath their gaze.

"Thalla," Sascia whispers carefully. "Why aren't you translating?"

The Queen has stopped speaking. The attention of the whole room is on Nugau.

Thalla doesn't answer, which frightens Sascia all the more. "Please, Thalla."

Teardrops lift off the corners of Thalla's eyes. They float in midair, tiny shimmering beads. "The Queen says that the prince has proven his strength, wits, and heart, but these last few weeks have made his people doubt his loyalty to the aesin. His ability to put his kin first. And so she offers him a bargain: she will make him king if . . ."

The lady trails off, folding her fingers over her lips.

Nugau turns to Sascia then, his features laced with a hundred different emotions. "She will make me king," he says, "if I kill you."

What will you do? Sascia wants to ask. *What will you say?*

But she doesn't need to. She can see the answer on Nugau's face. On the hard planes of his forehead, the resolute narrowness of his eyes, on his lips, pressed close with resolve. Here is everything Nugau ever wanted, a chance for power and bravery and peace.

In one smooth twist of his wrist, he summons his scythe out of the Dark—and lunges at her.

36

WANT AND HUNGER AND GREED

The blade slices through the air.

It is a testament to Orran's training that Sascia dashes to the side mere seconds before the scythe scrapes the floor. It leaves a carved mark on the black rock, deep enough to trace with a finger. Nugau truly meant it; a blow to kill.

Already, Sascia's backing away, palms raised up. "Nugau, please—"

He swings again, this time in a wider, deadlier arc. Sascia ducks away as fast as she can, feet carrying her backward down the vast expanse of the throne room.

"We can find another way," Sascia pleads. "Make a choice of kindness."

"*This* is kindness." His shaggy hair has fallen over his face, completely curtaining his eyes. Sascia can only see the hard line of his mouth and the white grip of his hands around the scythe. "A swift and merciful ending at the hands of an equal."

The words break something in her. The Queen's bargain might have offered him everything he ever wanted, but Sascia refuses to be the price he pays. "I don't want swift and merciful! I don't want an ending! I don't want to be just your equal—I want more. Don't you understand? I've always wanted *more*."

Nugau replies with another fall of the blade, but this time, Mooch is there to meet it. All six inches of its body and wings shift into hard onyx; the scythe screeches against it. The prince's arms reverberate with the contact, yet still he stalks forward. Sascia backtracks, clumsily tripping over her own steps. His eyes cut to something behind her—over her shoulder, the mouth of a half-collapsed train tunnel yawns like a toothless smile.

"Don't run," he warns, but there's something lurid, almost inviting in his voice.

Sascia runs.

The aesin let out a collective snarl as she scrambles over the rubble. Rocks cascade down the debris. Footsteps crunch behind her, slow and measured. From the corner of her eye, Sascia can spot the Dark moving—but it's not Nugau wielding his power. It's moths, dozens of them, slipping out of the shadows to coalesce around her.

Don't hurt Nugau, Sascia thinks to them, a hand outstretched to keep them at bay. *I can fix this. I can turn it around. Just don't hurt him.*

But in the darkness of the tunnel, Nugau attacks in earnest. The first strike is parried by Mooch, the second Sascia just barely evades, the third smacks her in the thigh with the dull flat of the blade. The moths form a vortex around her and Nugau, caging them together. Nugau launches into a breathless attack. A feint to the left, a slice through the right, then a kick at her knees.

Sascia goes down. Before her head can hit the hard rock, there is a hand there breaking her fall, and a body lowering over hers, and a face hovering inches away. The moths are in a rampage, shaping a thunderous funnel that hides them from the rest of the world. But they do not defend her. They do not attack. They only shield her, her and Nugau both, in a cocoon of razor-sharp wings.

"Even here?" the prince grits out, his breath feathering against her cheeks. "You won't fight back even here, when it's only the two of us?"

But she can't. She won't. She hasn't forgotten their promise to each other over stale candy, the forbidden look during the tarant, the tenderness last night, the unspoken grief this morning. The Queen's bargain might have been sweet enough to sway him, but even he can't deny: in another time, in another world, the two of them could have been something brilliant. His betrayal cuts deep, coaxing tears into her eyes. Sascia refuses to make this easy for him. He has made his choice, and so has she.

Panting, she vows: "I will not be your enemy."

"No, little gnat. You're far, far worse."

The words are striking, disorienting—worse still, his hands trace up her arms, pinning her wrists to the ground. His legs press into hers, locking her in place beneath him, their torsos lined up inch for inch. His breath comes out hot and raspy against her cheek.

"*You*," he whispers with difficulty. "You have been my unraveling. All the seams of my being, the stitches I have crafted over my wounds—you have picked at the threads, unwoven the fabric of my essence, and now I am something new, something else, something *yours*."

Sascia's heart roars against her rib cage. "And is it a crime worthy of death?" she gasps out. "To be new? To be mine?"

"No, little gnat. It is an absolution."

Little gnat, he called her.

Absolution, he named this thing between them.

Sascia realizes at last—he wasn't swayed by the Queen's bargain. He will not be her executioner. He is what he has claimed: *hers, hers, hers.*

His fingers around her wrists go soft and tender; he weaves their fingers together. Sascia smooths her body along his, widening her hips, arching her back, stretching her neck to make room for him, for his lips. Nugau lingers there, an inch above the velvet skin beneath her ear. His gaze has become dulcet, dripping with honeyed want.

He whispers, "If I begged—"

Sascia doesn't need to hear the rest. She arcs up and kisses him.

His lips are ravenous; they part her mouth and deepen the kiss. His hand buries in her hair, tugging. Her chest is flush against his, a lightning-bright friction that sends a hum of pleasure down her spine. She is present in her body like she has never been before, in soft and hard flesh, in want and hunger and greed.

Because Nugau was right. She *is* starved, she *is* hungry, she *is* greedy. There is a craving inside her that never had a shape and name, could never be sated or satisfied. But now its name is Nugau, its shape is his lips and hands and body, and she is satisfied, oh so satisfied that she could burst with joy.

Her hungry, hungry mouth moves to devour the hard line of his jaw. He stills beneath her touch, exhaling warm air against her neck. He moves only to give her access: to the soft flesh beneath his chin, the long column of his neck, the crook where clavicle meets shoulder.

Then he shifts, lightning-fast, and takes her earlobe into his mouth. All thoughts slip out of Sascia's head. She becomes only sense. The jittering pleasure of her earlobe in his mouth. The pulsing trail of his fingers beneath her shirt. His grip in her hair. The weight of his body against hers.

There is only travel and discovery, of lips and fingers and flesh upon flesh, and this is what Nugau meant when he named her an Ariadne. This is the true pleasure, the true joy—*exploring*. This is

Sascia's Labyrinth, his touch and his want, and she will gladly be enamored, an Ariadne in love with the Labyrinth itself.

He flips them so that she is sitting on his lap. His hands groove around her ribs. He reaches up and tucks her hair behind her ears. His thumb trails circles beneath the curve of her breast, in a way that makes her warm and aching. His mouth is dark with kissing.

"You wanted the Queen to believe you were going to kill me," Sascia realizes. "You wanted me to run into the tunnel, where we would be out of view."

"I couldn't beg you to kiss me in front of the entire army of the Jagged Blade, now could I?"

A heady laugh bubbles out of Sascia's lips.

Footfalls echo from the end of the tunnel. Nugau sits up, an arm around her waist to keep her close, and peers through the hurricane of moths that surrounds them. They're hidden from view, but not for long. He touches her left shoulder—his fingertip comes away red. Her stitches must have torn during the chasing or the frolicking; Sascia didn't even notice. Nugau looks at the smear of scarlet as though it is the most terrible thing he has ever seen.

"Mooch," he whispers.

The itka springs out of the vortex of wings and hovers prettily between them.

"You can lead her out, can't you?"

In reply, Mooch flutters its wings, the movement endorsed by the dozens of moths around them.

"I'm not leaving you here," Sascia says.

"You can't stay, little gnat. My mother's bargain was clever: killing you would make me the son she wants, the ruthless prince she can support. Letting you live would make me a traitor to my kind and allow her to continue ruling. But in either case, this is not a place for you any longer. She and her council want you dead."

Nugau unfolds, lifting Sascia with him. He pulls the bloodied bandage from her shoulder and smears the red on his scythe, speaking fast as though to convince himself as much as her. "I'll show them the blood. I'll tell them I killed you and that Mooch carried your body into the Dark. They will doubt me, but you'll already be gone, and the Queen won't be able to discredit me without proof. I'll make the Claim and weaken her power and force us to retreat to Itkalin. And I'll—I'll find a way to seal the doors. To keep the Ul'amoon away from you and keep your light bombs away from us."

"Come with me," Sascia breathes.

He begins to shake his head, but Sascia raises her chin, getting right into his face, vexing as a gnat.

"Come with me," she says again. "We'll tell humans about the ymneen and the itka's purpose, and we'll rally the whole world behind us—because we're all scared, yes, but we don't *want* to be. We want to be safe, human and aesin alike. We'll make them draw up a peace treaty that stops the nova-bombs and controls the Ul'amoon and promises whatever kind of help we can offer each other. And with that treaty in hand, Mooch will bring you back here. If your mother is as clever as she sounds, she will sign it."

At his back, the first aesin are visible through the curtain of moth wings, pushing down the narrow tunnel. Nugau must hear them, but he doesn't look. His attention is locked on Sascia. His fingers are clenched tight around the scythe.

"No more blades," Sascia says, clear and decided. "Nugau, *come with me.*"

She offers her hand, palm open, almost juvenile in its theatricality, but something about it breaks him. A quiver passes over his lips, a shine gathers at his eyes.

"I'll come," he whispers, "I'll come, Sascia," and he closes his hand around hers, and Mooch doesn't need to be told or instructed; the black beneath them splits, and they slip through space and time.

37

GOLDEN TICKET

Sascia is still sixteen, but she feels a hundred, achy and weary with hopelessness.

She sits on the hard plastic bench of the hospital's waiting room. Above her, Aunt Rania rages a storm of accusations and insults. Sascia told her everything: How there's a Darkgarden in the basement. How she and Danny have been exploring the sewers. How he had a bad feeling about this one. How she persuaded him to try. A part of her knows she confessed because her guilt needed to be shaped into words, her shame transfigured into someone else's anger. She sits and she listens and she doesn't argue. It *is* her fault.

A doctor comes to announce Danny is out of surgery. The rest of them watch through the window of the revolving hospital doors as the doctor speaks to Danny's parents. Aunt Rania isn't crying—she never did, not once—but Danny's dad, who's flown in from Boston, sheds quiet, glistening tears. Sascia picks at the bandages around her calf where the Darktiger clawed its way into her flesh. When, hours later, the nurse tells them they can see Danny, she stays behind, with a sleeping Ksenya tucked against her side, trying to smother her sniffles.

Aunt Rania doesn't speak to Sascia again, not that day, not the next one, not on the third. On the fourth, she announces into the waiting room, "He's been asking for Sascia."

In his room, Danny lies on his side, eyes closed. His back is a mess of bandages. Plastic tubes hang from the bed. Sascia gazes out of the windows. The hospital has a view of the local park. In the darkness between the thickets stands a figure clad in a black cloak.

(*Not now*, Sascia thinks. *Especially not now*.)

She turns her back to it. She finds Danny smiling.

Sascia wants to ruffle his curls, straighten his blanket, hold his hand, but she doesn't know if she should. She keeps her eyes on the floor as she opens her mouth. She's been thinking long about what she'll say, how she'll apologize, but Danny cuts her off.

"Cuz." He doesn't sound sad or angry. "Please, don't. It was not your fault."

"It *was*—"

"Oh, shut up, will you? Come here."

Sascia goes, right into the arm he's opened for her. She's ashamed to find tears spilling down her cheeks (if Danny's not crying, what right does she have to?) and sheds them as soundlessly as she can. She points to the small TV screen mounted on the wall. "This thing looks decent enough. Should I bring your Xbox over?"

"Now *that*," Danny says, "is the kind of patient care I like."

THEY'RE PLAYING *MARIO KART* when Danny finally asks the question. Sascia has known he would ask eventually; she's been waiting for it. "What did they do to our garden?"

"It's been confiscated. They dismantled the whole thing and took it."

"We were going to do great things with it," Danny whispers. "Save lives."

She's got nothing to say to that. Their parents have made it abundantly clear: no more Darkblooms, no more Darkmoths, no more Dark of any kind for as long as they live.

They continue the game in silence. Danny wins.

The knock comes while they're debating switching to the latest zombie release. The figure that slips in is not family or hospital staff. He's dressed in an impeccable black suit and sports suave rimless glasses that reflect the fluorescent ceiling lights. He introduces himself as Professor Stanley Carr.

The professor speaks in a direct, colorless tone. He tells them about a new initiative he's leading. About the other students, an engineering prodigy from South Korea, a savvy geneticist from Chile, and a young computer genius who goes by the code name Crow. He tells them about what they could achieve under his tutelage; he could have their garden retrieved from Chapter XI, equip it with state-of-the-art technology, and, with hard work and persistence, even secure them a place at an Ivy League of their choice. A xenobotanist and a xenoentomologist, what a pair they could make.

The contracts are deposited soundlessly at the foot of Danny's bed before the professor leaves. The title at the top reads: *Admission to the Umbra Program*. Danny stares at them wide-eyed and open-mouthed, as though they are Willy Wonka's golden tickets.

Sascia takes one look at her cousin, at the *hope* budding like a tender bloom on his face, and goes rummaging for a pen.

38

RUBY-RED SEEDS

Concrete rushes up to meet them.

Sascia barely has time to round her body into a ball before she smacks into hard sidewalk. Nugau lands soundlessly beside her, crouched low like a cat. The street around them assaults the senses: cars speeding past, the spicy aroma of a taco stand, a sea of umbrellas rushing by. It takes Sascia a moment to place herself in the bright, noisy tangles of the human world.

21st Street.

They're standing beneath the raised platform of the observation deck of the Maw. Overhead, the steps vibrate with the stomping steps of tourists. The flea market stretches ahead, packed with vendors and clients. Voices drift beneath the staccato beat of heavy rainfall. The sky is a dark gray, the downpour muting the afternoon light.

"Clever Mooch," she whispers. The rift the moth opened is still visible, a tear of blackness on the base of the concrete barrier around the Maw. Mooch dropped them out of the Maw and right into the shadows beneath the observation deck, where no one would spot them. But the real question is *when* it brought them.

The itka clings to her hair, along with the two dozen moths

that followed them out of the tunnels. Sascia quickly ushers them inside the collar of her military jacket.

Nugau's face tilts to the passersby. "What will happen if they see us?"

Soldiers are posted every five feet around the thirty-foot-tall barrier of the Maw, sleek nova-rifles slung across their chests. A small group of protesters in waterproof ponchos carries placards and banners. Sascia's gaze skips over them—then does a double take.

Her face is on those placards. Her yearbook photo in stark black and white and, beneath it, slogans in bright blue. *No Dark Means No Light. Stop The Darkstruction. There Is No Excuse For Darkcreature Abuse.* A couple of people wear T-shirts printed with grainy camera footage of Sascia in midair as she jumped into the Maw.

"Holy shit," she whispers.

The peace protesters have made her their poster girl. She and the prince need to get out of here before anyone sees her face. Or the Darkmoths crowding her neck. Or the onyx scales of her aesin uniform. Or, well, pretty much anything about Nugau.

A broken umbrella rests on a nearby trash can. Sascia wrestles its prongs into an almost functioning structure and beneath its cover, she and Nugau join the crowd, where she guides them down the street at a hurried trot.

"Where are we going?" Nugau asks.

Where, indeed? Not her family's place—she's not dragging her poor parents into this. Not the Umbra, either—she'd rather chop off a finger than lead Nugau into the hands of Chapter XI. She has no phone and no money, so a hotel room is out of the question. But they need to be somewhere safe, away from people and soldiers and CCTV.

Somewhere a girl who jumped into the Maw and a prince of the Dark would be welcome.

SASCIA SITS ON THE plush sofa of the thirty-first-floor apartment, watching Tae-Suk Ho pace up and down the living room. He buzzed them in only a few minutes ago, instructed them to take off their wet shoes at the door, pointed them to the sofa, and then proceeded to have a very badly timed (albeit understandable) breakdown.

It's unfortunate. Sascia had hoped for any combination of the three roommates besides the one she actually got: Tae, alone. If Andres or Shivani were here, she could count on them to help, but Tae? Honestly, Sascia's surprised the kiss-ass hasn't called Chapter XI already.

Almost as if he read her thoughts, Tae takes out his phone.

Sascia pops out of her seat, causing a riptide of wing-fluttering from her necklace of moths. "Please, Tae, give me a chance to explain first—"

"Danny?" Tae says into the phone.

Sascia pauses mid-step.

"Are you at the Umbra? With Andres and Shiv? Oh, good. I, um, need all three of you to come over as soon as possible." Tae glances over Sascia's head at Nugau. "No, I mean like *right now*. Yeah. Thanks."

He hangs up, stares at Nugau some more, then bends over his phone.

Sascia takes another cautious step forward. "What are you doing?"

"Ordering us pizza. Unless, um, your friend doesn't eat pizza?"

The prince lifts a bemused eyebrow. "I eat pizza. I don't love the little red spicy stuff on it, though."

"Red pepper flakes? Noted. What about pepperoni? That's spicy for some people too."

"Pepperoni?" Nugau asks.

"They're these round slices of meat. Like these." Tae walks over and shows the aesin a photo from the online menu.

"Oh, I like those ones."

"Yeah," Tae agrees. "They're good spicy, not destroy-your-taste-buds spicy."

"Can we also get those little cups of sauce?"

"Dips? Absolutely. What kind?"

"Well, the last time I ate pizza, years ago, there was a white sauce that smelled foul but was incredibly tasty."

The conversation devolves into a long back-and-forth about dips and sides and drinks, and Sascia just stands there, watching them, until Nugau looks up and his face creases with worry. "Little gnat," he says urgently, "what's wrong?"

Sascia is not entirely sure, to be honest. But she *is* crying. Sobs rattle her shoulders, tears crowd her lashes, her nose has gone all horribly snotty. Her moths are angsty, fluttering around her head. Nugau is standing and Tae is wearing a concerned frown, and Sascia is—

She is *here*, in the human world, in her home city, with Nugau and Tae, and Danny is on his way with the rest of the cohort, and they're getting pizzas, and there is something just so simple and yet so all-encompassing in this tiny moment that her heart just can't take it.

That's when the front door opens. Andres freezes with his key in the door. Shivani gapes. Behind them is Danny, *her* Danny, her best friend in the whole wide world.

And Sascia, with all her tears and snot and chest-rattling sobs, crosses the room and falls straight into her cousin's arms.

THE COFFEE TABLE IS a battlefield of cardboard boxes, napkins, and half-empty cups. The cohort is strewn on the sofa and floor, greasy-fingered and happy. Nugau has burrowed deep into the cushions, a hand rubbing his stomach (ten slices will cause bloating for even the most fearsome of aesin warriors). Sascia has eaten only three, too busy narrating the events of the past several weeks to her friends. Mooch didn't bring them to the past or future, but the present, six weeks after Sascia jumped into the Maw.

"Your turn," Sascia says, picking up a crust to feed little bites to the moths. "What happened while I was gone?"

"All hell broke loose?" Danny answers. He's playing with Sascia's hair, as though unwilling to separate himself from her. Sascia feels the same way; she sits on the floor, leaning against his chair, peering up at him every ten seconds to make sure he's still there.

"And that's not metaphorical," Crow adds from Andres's laptop. "It's been almost as bad as First Contact—all shock and confusion and fear."

"There were only a few seconds of footage of the three Darkhumanoids climbing out of the Maw," Shivani explains, "so instead the media focused on *you*. There are hundreds of articles on your childhood, your work at the Umbra, your family—dozens of interviews from your fishing clients."

Sascia winces. All her secrets exposed for the world to see. "I saw my face on protesters' placards."

"Some think you're a spy, working with the Darkhumanoids," Andres says. "Others think you're some kind of witch, because

CCTV caught Big Boy—*Mooch*—leading you to the Maw. But the people that matter believe us."

Us. That means . . . "You told them about the nonlinear timelines?"

Andres nods. "Danny explained what happened the previous night and what you had figured out about the Darknomaly. We didn't know where you'd gone or how to get you back, so we decided to call Carr. He took your theory to Chapter XI."

"What did the Chapter have to say?"

A small pocket of silence descends.

Sascia looks up to Danny for an answer, who says, "We don't know yet. The Chapter has been dealing with a lot of internal strife. Boqin Shen has been forced to step down as director. They're still looking for a replacement. Carr says the Chapter is trying to corroborate your theory with their own research. We've offered to help and for the past six weeks, we've been looking into the correlation between creatures and timelines ourselves and sending all our findings to Carr. But he says the Chapter is holding off making the information public, and that we're not allowed to either. We've been advised to wait."

"Wait?" Sascia bursts out, a thread of anger lacing her voice. "Wait for what? For the aesin to climb out of the Dark and start an all-out war?"

"I think," Shivani says quietly, "they are waiting for *you*."

That makes Sascia pause. "Me?"

"You, the prince," Shivani says, with a polite incline of her head at Nugau, "or whoever might come out of the Dark next. Whether they decide to start a war or broker peace, they need *someone* to do it with."

"That someone is here," Nugau confirms.

"They already know about the ymneen," Sascia says. "Now we

can tell them about the itka's part in it. Their true purpose."

"What does that mean?" Crow asks. "The true purpose?"

"According to the lore of my people," Nugau says, "itka like Mooch split open the fabric of space and time to unite worlds so that they can save each other."

"For a while," Sascia adds, "we thought we were meant to unite to defeat the Ul'amoon, the Darkbeasts, but that's not right. Destroying the Ul'amoon is not the answer—there's some other way we can save each other."

"*Energy*," Tae says without missing a beat, a know-it-all to his core.

The cohort and Nugau are collectively startled. Shivani asks, "Wait, what?"

"Widespread use of nova-lights has been draining us dry," Tae explains. "The industry is keeping it quiet, but data analysts predict we're destined for a global energy crisis within the next three decades."

Rumors of an energy shortage have been circulating ever since the Blackouts. New York was hit the worst, but Shanghai and Rio have had similar malfunctions. And NovaCorp has launched a hundred new products since then, insisting they're the only thing keeping people safe from the Dark—no wonder the world is heading into a crisis.

"What you're describing in Itkalin," Tae goes on, "sounds like an issue of thermal energy. With further study of each other's energy sources, we could solve both problems."

"*Nature*," Danny pipes up a second later. "Climate change was slowly decimating our world even before we met the Dark. Air and water pollution, floods, droughts, storms. But my most recent study on Darkalgae reveals that it consumes waste in water, and there's another xenobotanist in Colombia who just discovered a specific genome of Darkrosewood that produces triple the oxygen most trees do."

Instantly, Sascia's mind jumps to another kind of nature, also at risk. "When we were looking at the vines in my room in the tunnels," she tells Nugau, "you said that they only grow to saplings in your world. But in ours, they flourish."

The prince nods, tight and unhappy. "Kilorn, my other parent, believed that at the rate it is going, Itkalin will become inhospitable to life in a few centuries."

"We can change it," Sascia breathes. "We can fix *everything*. We can ask Carr to set up a meeting with Chapter XI. We can explain everything and help them draw up a peace treaty, filled with every way our world can help yours and yours can help ours . . ." She can't go on, because her voice has gotten all husky again.

Moths perch on furniture and walls, dots of vibrant color in the low-lit room. Mooch stands out among them, four times their size and brave enough to perch right in the middle of the table, near the candlelight.

"This is what you wanted, isn't it?" Sascia whispers. "This is how we save each other."

She expects a single tap on the wood, a *yes*, but instead, the moth flies at her, straight for her nose, and boops it once, twice, three times over, stopping only when she shields her face with her arm and laughs into her elbow, and in moments, everyone else joins in too, relieved and grateful and full of hope.

WHEN SASCIA OPENS THE door, Professor Carr blinks at her as though his brain has short-circuited. He takes her in for a long moment—the leather trousers of her warrior's uniform, the bandages around her shoulder, the Darkmoths perched on her arms—then his gaze glides past her to the Umbra cohort gathered in the living room and the aesin prince sitting among them.

"Miss Petrou," he says, in his usual colorless tone. "You have returned. And brought along guests, I see."

He slips past her into the room and takes a seat in an armchair. Sascia trails after him, feeling a little dazed. They all watch in tense silence as he takes out a handkerchief and wipes his glasses before restoring them to his nose.

"I trust your friends have mentioned that you're somewhat of a celebrity now, Miss Petrou," Carr says. "The xenoscience prodigy that carried out illegal fishing tours. The Umbra funders didn't much enjoy that one, I'm afraid."

God, barely a minute in his presence and Sascia's already annoyed. "You cut my stipend, sir, then you enrolled me in six different remedial courses *at Columbia*. I had to pay for them somehow."

"Precisely what I have argued to both our funders and the Chapter," he says, to her astonishment. "But they are not too keen to trust a girl who so blatantly disrespects the law. It certainly hasn't helped the credibility of your theory. Nonlinear timelines and a special, ancient moth guiding you. An obsession taking root and, finally, an irrational decision."

Laid out like that, in his measured tone and unembellished prose, it really does sound far, far, *far* from rational. She jumped into the freaking Maw, terrified her friends and family, and upended her life because of some hunch. Except that now she has proof, dusted on her arms in wings of glittering onyx.

"I knew what I was doing," she tells Carr. "A war is coming, sir, and it will devastate both our world and theirs—"

Professor Carr's hand reaches out and folds around her fingers, the touch so unusual it stuns her into silence. The rest of the cohort are staring with wide eyes, as shocked as she feels.

Her mentor examines her with steady, unblinking eyes. "I believe you."

Three simple words.

"I believe the Dark sees something in you," he goes on. "I believe there is a reason you are the only human Darkmoths choose to appear to. I believe you are destined for great, unfathomable things that none of us can fully comprehend. And I, Miss Petrou, will not stand in your way as you achieve them." He studies the rest of his students, one by one, until his eyes land on Nugau. "Tell me what you need."

Sascia breaks.

The torrent of a lifetime of pent-up self-doubt unleashes from her chest, like a pomegranate cracked open to spill its ruby-red seeds. Her shoulders hunch over and her rib cage aches with barely constrained sobs. Around her, the moths flutter their wings in comfort. The very words she has sought since she crawled out of that frozen pond in her soggy black velvet dress, spoken by the person she thought understood her the least and hated her the most. It is doubly rewarding, a thousand times more comforting; because if *Professor Carr* believes her, if *he* understands, if *he* chooses not to oppose her, then the rest of the world will follow suit. They will stand not against her but by her side.

She nods at Nugau, and the prince begins speaking, forging the first ingots of a true alliance.

39

THE MAKING OF A UNIVERSE

The professor leaves around midnight, after an excruciatingly detailed note-taking session on the ymneen, the itka, and Nugau's list of terms for a peace treaty. Tomorrow morning, he will present them to Chapter XI and propose the beginning of peace negotiations. Nugau and Sascia will be calling in from an encrypted meeting room courtesy of Crow.

But for now: clean-up and sleep.

As Sascia washes and Danny dries the dishes, he tells her—to her utter shock—about Tae. After seeing the live footage of Sascia's jump, Tae took to the streets in search of Danny. He found him trying to wrangle his wheelchair around the panicking traffic, whereupon Tae barked cars and buses out of the way and got him to the sidewalk. He gripped Danny's shoulders and said, *We'll find her. We'll fix this.* Since then, they've been texting all day every day, about Sascia and the Dark, but also about so much more.

"*Aaaand?*" Sascia asks.

Her cousin's cheeks turn red; he casts a too-wide glance at Tae, who's sitting with Nugau and Shivani on the other side of the big room. "Nothing has happened yet, even though we're constantly alone together. I don't know if there's something actually there or if, you know, he's just being nice."

"Tae has never *just been nice* a day in his life. Trust me, there's something there."

Danny glances at her beneath downcast brows. "I feel so guilty, Sascia. Daydreaming about making out with Tae while you were held captive by creatures from another world."

"Don't be," Sascia replies. "I very much *was* making out while you were freaking out about my well-being."

Danny's eyes go wide. "It happened? Nugau . . ."

Their heads turn to Nugau on the sofa, deep in conversation with Shivani. As the aesin speaks, the Darkprint on their cheeks swirls with color, transmuting from purple to white before settling into blue. Sascia can't help her grin; on Halloween, Shivani had wished she could ask Nugau all her questions, and now she can. The aesin's fluid view of gender, human democracy, and division of government—this could be another way they help each other, couldn't it?

After a moment, Nugau notices Sascia's lingering gaze. A deep mauve crawls over the princess's features. Sascia thinks back to all the little moments when she got the sense she was embarrassing or flustering Nugau. She thinks of Nugau's confession before they kissed. Unraveled and made anew—that's what loving Nugau feels like.

Her own thoughts give her pause.

Love. Is that what she feels? She has always enjoyed flirting and kissing, but she has never thought the actual words before: *I am in love.* They are soaked in dreamful tenderness, drizzled with longing.

When she turns back to Danny, he is watching her with a bemused smirk.

"Shut up," Sascia grumbles affectionately.

"Please," Danny croons. "Just one joke, I beg you."

"Fine. Let's hear it."

He's already sporting a smug grin. "You two are going to take the term 'destination wedding' to a whole new level."

Sascia stares at him, dead-eyed. "That was absolutely terrible. I think it actually hurt my brain. Am I bleeding from the ears?"

He swats the ear she's presented for examination away from his face and breaks into a chuckle. Always eager to join in the fun, Mooch takes flight between them, zapping between her nose and Danny's forehead.

But then Sascia sobers. "Can I call them?"

Danny nods quickly, as though he's been expecting it. He hands his phone over.

Her mother picks up, the sound of pots, pans, and running water in the background. "Danny, baby, I'm busy. Can I—"

"Hey, Mama."

It's apparently enough to break her. Sascia's mother begins crying uncontrollably, babbling half-finished questions, mumbling *you're alive, you're alive*, then screaming at her husband across the restaurant. Sascia tries to answer their questions as best she can, but she's not faring too well herself. Her voice has gone all frantic and high-pitched, and every five seconds she keeps saying *I'm sorry, I'm so sorry.*

Her father manages to wrestle the phone away. "Where are you? I'm coming to get you."

Sascia glances at the living room, where her friends have been (mortifyingly) watching her the whole time. Nugau has gathered all the moths against her chest, trying to keep them from fluttering around Sascia. "I'm somewhere safe. There's something important I need to do tomorrow morning, but I'll come home right after and explain everything."

She expects him to argue, to criticize her—*What could be more important than your family?*—but instead, her father says, "Danny tried to explain why you did what you did. We don't entirely understand it, and we don't like it either, but—we can wait until tomorrow. *At noon.* If you're not back home by then, I'm coming to get you, wherever you might be."

"I'll be there." There's a momentary pause, then Sascia blurts, "Baba, are you angry?"

"Of course I am! You jumped into the goddamn Maw! We thought you were dead!" he snaps, but it's his good snap, the one that she can picture with tears in his eyes and a gruff smile on his lips. "Make no mistake, you will be grounded until you're fifty, but right now, I'm just happy you're coming home."

Home, surrounded by family, fed good food, and swaddled in warm blankets. A short reprieve before the hard part begins: drawing up a peace treaty, stopping a war, loving a princess from a world across time and space.

SASCIA TUCKS HER HANDS beneath her cheek and looks at Nugau.

The two of them are lying on Andres's bed, swathed in the smell of clean sheets and freshly showered bodies. Andres himself has moved to the sofa, Shivani's in her own room, and Danny is in Tae's. The quietude of exhaustion has fallen over the apartment, and Sascia is too nervous to speak. Something has changed inside her, something deep and fundamental, and she's not quite sure what to do with herself.

"How do you feel?" she whispers, the four bravest words she's ever spoken.

Nugau turns on her side. The T-shirt she borrowed from Andres (because Shivani's were too short, which is both ridiculous and delightful) hitches at her neck, exposing the smooth porcelain skin of her collarbone. Thoughtlessly, Sascia reaches out and runs a finger over the groove of her bones.

The princess stays very still and holds her breath for a long time before speaking. "Hopeful and scared at the same time. I worry about Thalla and Orran and all the other aesin who supported me. The Queen cannot openly punish them for my actions, but there will be consequences."

And *Sascia* convinced Nugau to come with her. She lifts her hand from Nugau's neck and hurriedly says, "We can ask Mooch to take you back."

The moths have settled on the pillows and bed frame around them, a dotting of iridescent light against the dark.

"I don't want to go back. I want to try this, here, with you." Her hand closes around Sascia's and returns Sascia's fingers to her skin, the movement so yearning, so craving that Sascia feels set ablaze. "How do *you* feel, little gnat?"

Boldly, Sascia says, "I feel like kissing you again."

Nugau's arm folds around Sascia's waist and moves them both, so that Sascia is sitting on her lap. "Then by all means, do."

Their last kiss was sharp and breathless, piercing as a whetted blade. Now Sascia takes her time. She lets her hands roam over the planes of Nugau's chest. She runs them down her biceps, her elbows, over the jutting bones of her wrists. She guides the princess's fingers to her own borrowed T-shirt, where they climb under the thin fabric to burrow in the grooves of her shoulder blades.

Nugau's hair fans on the pillow. Tenderly, Sascia traces her hairline, her arched eyebrows, the cutting curves of her cheekbones. She lowers herself onto her so that her lips can follow the path her fingers have paved. Small pecks trail from temple to jaw to neck to that wonderful dip between her collarbones.

A shiver runs down Nugau's body. A phantasmagoria of color presses against Sascia's closed lids. When she opens her eyes, the Darkprint on Nugau's cheeks burns bright, changing among colors.

"I feel everything right now, like I *am* everything all at once," Nugau whispers, watching her with hungry eyes. "I know you're not used to it—I can settle into one if you mind."

Sascia takes in the snowflake patterns on their cheeks. The intensity of their gaze. The openness of their voice. It has never occurred to her to *mind*. They are Nugau and they want to kiss her and that's all that ever mattered to her.

"I don't," she says. "I never do."

The smile they give her is breathtaking. They tilt their head up, as though inviting her to explore. Nugau's aesin structure differs from Sascia's in ways she hasn't noticed before. Their bones feel harder, as though made of iron, and the temperature of their skin is far lower than hers. Beneath the shirt, her fingers trail a rib cage that is too short and a torso that stretches and stretches, a smooth expanse of porcelain skin. Their pointed ears keep shivering at her touch. Beneath her chest, Nugau's chest thumps in a slow, steady rhythm.

"The aesin heartbeat is slower," Nugau says. "For every one of mine, your heart beats ten."

"The Heart Claim," Sascia whispers, thinking back to her Trials. "That's why it sounded so slow to me."

"Yours sounds like a hummingbird to me." Suddenly, Nugau flops Sascia on her back and flattens their ear against her chest. They listen for a long time, then prop their chin on her breastbone. Their smirk is devious. "It is faster than usual now. Is that because of me?"

Lying beneath them, with only a thin strip of cotton separating her skin from theirs, Sascia feels much too flushed for words.

She nods—then immediately goes still and breathless. Nugau has lifted her T-shirt and begun their own exploration. Inch by inch they discover, with their fingertips or nose or lips. They spend an inordinate amount of time on her belly button and the jut of her hipbones over Shivani's low-rise pajama pants.

A long time later, Nugau's head pops up again, eyes glazed and heavy-lidded. "Sascia," they say, very seriously, "may I bite you? For us aesin, it's a form of intimacy. I promise I won't make it hurt—"

"Please," she rasps.

Nugau gives her no warning. Their teeth close around the soft flesh beneath her rib cage, shooting licks of flame through her chest. Sascia's eyes flutter closed. She's thinking indecent things again, coarse with want and rough with desperation.

But Sascia has never been too good with self-restraint—she pushes to her elbows and buries her teeth over the closest thing she can find: the soft curve where Nugau's neck meets their shoulder.

The *sound* Nugau makes—a startled sigh of pleasure that could sustain Sascia forever, a godly ambrosia to her hungry mouth. The princet goes absolutely still, in both resolve and surrender. Sascia trails her teeth to their ear. Nugau gasps quick breaths against her neck that make her feel aflame with heady joy. She listens intently; with their every soft exhale, her own body reacts, every inch of her bursting with the need to be touched.

Time becomes endless between them. Their soft sounds stretch an eon. Millennia pass with every exploration of their hands and lips. It is fitting, in a way, for two souls brought together by a knot in time; the meeting of their bodies lasts as long as the making of a universe.

"I HAVE A CONFESSION to make," Nugau whispers later, as they lie on tumbled sheets.

"Mhm?" Sascia is burrowed into their neck, being swept into the lulling waves of sleep.

Their throat vibrates against her skin. "I knew you long before I met you."

"What do you mean?"

"Since I was a young adolescent, I have seen flashes of an image between one blink and the next. It's your face, breaking out of the darkness. Your hand, reaching for mine. When you jumped in the Maw to save us, I recognized you as the face that I've been glimpsing for half my life. That's why I was so hostile at first—I thought you were something evil, come to haunt me. My own guilt, perhaps, for leaving my family when they needed me most. But your hand, it had always felt like an invitation. And your scent . . . it promised a perfect sunny day."

They breathe her in, slow and luxurious, as though she smells intoxicating.

"So in the end, I surrendered," Nugau whispers. "Even now, I cannot give you up. I am a coward through and through, because I would rather bare my throat at your blade than be your enemy."

The words fold around her, warm and snug. Sleep drapes at her eyelids and heat swathes her body, snug and cozy as a childhood blanket. She wants to say *I love you too*, but it is too blunt a statement, too small, too human.

She says instead, "There is no blade. There is only this."

She kisses them, and in that kiss, she bleeds everything: how she feels, how she wishes, how she hopes.

When she leans away, Nugau's face is flushed with color. Their eyes take to the ceiling, where the iridescent marks of the moths cast endless spotlights. "I would like to show you Itkalin sometime, after all this is over."

"Yes, please." She can think of nothing better. Surely, with Nugau by her side, she'll find a way past the unbearable cold of that world. "What does it mean, *Itkalin*?"

"*Itka* is our word for moth, and *lin* is the essence of our world. It is in constant flux, a push and pull, like the black sun in our sky, or the shape of our flowers, or the marks on our skin." Their Darkprint shifts among pulsing colors. "Our world is one of ever-turning change, of endless beginnings. We named it after the first creature that dwelled in it, and after this power that is vast and unknowable, yet always filled with wonder."

They shift to look at her, a hint of a smile on their lips.

"I guess the best translation," they say, "is Moth Dark."

MOOCH WAKES HER.

Around the bed, the moths snap their wings, a flurry of movement and sound. Sascia raises a sleepy hand to pet them, but her touch seems to agitate them even more. Like a swarm, they fly to the window, flapping against the blinds. Something is wrong. She tugs her T-shirt on and rushes to the window. Her every step makes the moths grow louder.

Nugau lifts their face from the pillow. "Sascia?"

But Sascia can't reply. Her eyes are locked on the city below, plainly visible from the cohort's thirty-first-floor apartment. She traces the concrete barrier a few blocks away, with its hundreds of nova-light panels and mortars, its death cannon and trio of helicopters circling above. Beneath all this light, the Maw is a pit of liquid black, vast and bottomless, but . . . its surface is rippling.

No, Sascia thinks. *It's too soon—*

An antlered helmet breaks out of the Dark, then the armor-clad shoulders and three-foot-long broadsword of a warrior queen.

War isn't coming any longer.

War is here.

40

THE JAGGED BLADE

Panic sweeps through the apartment. The cohort crowds the balcony in a barrage of frantic questions. Around the Maw, the concentric nova-light panels flicker on, casting a white glow on the slick surface. Figures are spilling out of the Dark, so fast that at first Sascia can't comprehend what she's seeing. Then she notices their shape, their size, their wings. The aesin are airborne.

Onyx saddles hold them in place atop winged Darkcreatures, wyverns with heads of crimson feathers and long curved horns. Shrill cries leak out of the beasts' mouths; Sascia has heard the sound before, deep within the aesin compound. The Queen must have commanded the aesin to hide these army mounts from Sascia. The army of the Jagged Blade shoots up from the Maw in a torrent of hundreds. At their head flies the Queen in her menacing helmet.

Wearing heavy armor, the army swoops low against the barrier that surrounds the Maw and thrusts their longswords into the nova-light panels, the first line of defense against the Dark. Shards drop into the gaping hole of black below as though in slow motion, a rainfall of fading light.

Nugau steps up next to Sascia on the balcony. Their presence forces Sascia back into her body, standing there against the frigid wind in her borrowed pajamas and bare feet. Moths hover in the air around her, beating wings that have gone hard and lethal.

"The Battle of Feathers," Nugau hisses. "We didn't stop it."

They didn't even have the time to try.

The muscles at Nugau's jaw are tight. Their bare torso shivers with anger. Magic responds to their call; swaths of black are twirling around their fisted hands. "How did they even find a way out?" they ask. "The Queen returned from the tunnels because she couldn't tear one open no matter how she tried."

A riot of clarity blares through Sascia's mind. The Queen's goals have been clear from the very beginning: a way into the human world, an attack, a war to sow vengeance and put an end to the bombings.

"She knew you wouldn't kill me," Sascia whispers. "She knew you would leave with me. She was counting on your choice . . . so that she could use Mooch's rift to tear open a way through. I led the Jagged Blade right to the humans' doorstep."

The realization hits her like an arrow to the chest. All her sacrifices, all her blood and sweat and tears—for this? To be tricked into starting the very war she was trying to stop?

"It is done now," Nugau states. "They are here. The war has begun. The only thing we can do is end it quickly."

The hue of their Darkprint shifts from the many colors of siff into a brilliant blue. That cold mask drapes over the princess's face, only now it is carved into a wrathful, dangerous shape. Dark gathers over her skin. Shadows coalesce into matter. Onyx armor plates lock around her arms and chest. Her scythe crystallizes out of thin air: its long stem, its curved blade, the luminous gemstone of its surface.

Her eyes land heavy on Sascia. "You said our choices are still our own, despite the ymneen. So what will be yours, little gnat? Will you commit treason against my kind?"

"No. Never."

"Will you fight with me to stop this destruction?"

"Yes. Always."

Nugau gives her a grim nod before turning her gaze back to the army. Yet her magic is hard at work; armor pieces are smelted out of the Dark, a breastplate and arm and leg guards that swathe Sascia's borrowed T-shirt and pajama pants. Sascia struggles with the straps at her side, until a new set of fingers takes over. Shivani tightens the breastplate around Sascia's chest while Andres helps her into her Doc Martens.

Danny looks at her, his face paper white. "Are you sure?"

For a moment, Sascia considers. The adults are involved now; she could step back, find a place to hide with the cohort and let Chapter XI deal with this.

On her hair, among the dozens of other moths, Mooch ruffles its wings.

Sascia exhales. Who is she kidding? There has never been a moment in all her complicated, unorthodox life when she has stepped back. She has always marched forward, through successes and failures, through gaping maws and ice-frozen ponds. "I'm sure."

Sharp, muffled blasts of nova-guns permeate the air. Soldiers run along the pathways of the barrier. Beams of light shoot through the aesin formations, sending them scattering left and right. Dark-wyverns are shot out of the air, spiraling back into the blackness.

Yet after every hit, the Jagged Blade comes together again. Fallen warriors are quickly replaced by newcomers. Small groups slip out of formation in quick, efficient attacks. Their focus is on destroying the nova-light panels that guard the perimeter of the Maw and the mortars mounted on the top of the barrier—no doubt to allow the full force of the army to come through. And then it will be war in earnest. Sascia remembers the counterattacks humans launched on Darkbeasts: air strikes, blasters, bombs.

Nugau places her fingers in her mouth and lets out a long, shrill whistle. Seconds pass, then the surface of the Maw splits. A bullet of a creature flies out of it, a Darkwyvern smaller and lighter than all the others. The moment she spots it, the princess hoists herself onto the balustrade of the balcony and flings herself off.

Sascia's stomach plummets. The entire cohort rushes to the edge of the balcony to peer down—a gust of wind throws them back as the Darkwyvern shoots upward. Nugau is atop it, flying parallel to the building, both of them cawing piercing battle cries. Holding her scythe low against her thigh, the princess crouches on her stirrups, her body shifting with every beat of her Darkwyvern's wings. With a swoop, they come to hover before the balcony.

Nugau extends an arm. "Let's end this, little gnat."

Sascia lets the princess's grip hoist her onto the saddle and then—she's flying.

41

ACCESS DENIED

Sascia immediately clutches Nugau's waist, buries her face in the princess's neck, and screams. Air whooshes past at a million miles per hour. The flaps of the Darkwyvern's wings are thunderous, vibrating through Sascia's chest. Beneath her, its spine moves and shifts with every beat of its wings in powerful, teeth-trembling thrusts.

"Easy," Nugau calls over the wind, patting Sascia's death grip around her rib cage. "I've got you."

Slowly and rather unwillingly, Sascia eases her grip. The battlefield stretches beneath them. The billowing cloud of the aesin formation is staying close to the rippling surface, the riders protecting their comrades as they pour out of the Maw. The human forces are lining the perimeter, blasting a steady stream of nova-light at the aesin. Most blasts bounce off their onyx shields and armor, but the few that hit the aesin's soft flesh or the Darkwyverns' paper-thin wings leave ghastly burns behind. On the parapets, soldiers are putting together machine guns, with bullets made of metal and gunpowder that will tear through porcelain flesh as though it is gossamer. Tae's nova-cannon is rotating on its axis, coming to life.

"Hold on," Nugau warns over her shoulder.

The wind snaps at Sascia's ears. The princess drives the Darkwyvern harder around the Maw, where it swoops low and caws the shrill call of its brethren. In mere seconds, dozens of riders break formation to join Nugau: Orran and Thalla and others, too, hundreds of them. The princess is gathering her allies.

Nugau's wyvern plunges into the fray, a vertical drop straight into the heart of the Maw. A scream tears through Sascia's mouth. A current of cold air whips at her face, her arms squeeze Nugau's midriff, her legs clench around the poor creature's back, then thankfully, blessedly, they pull up again, inches above the rippling black. Nugau leans down and swoops a fistful of Dark from the surface of the Maw. Knuckles wrapped with black, she crashes her hand against her breastplate. *Thump, thump, thump*; the drum is a deep, resonant sound, a bell ringing right into the cavities of Sascia's chest.

"*Aesin!*" Nugau calls.

Sascia can't understand the rest of the princess's speech, but the content is obvious: Nugau is finally making her Royal Claim. The princess turns her wyvern in a circle, taking in every aesin warrior in the Maw. Overhead, a CNN news helicopter hovers a few dozen feet away, the light and camera lens mounted on its tip focused on Nugau.

"Hold your fire!" Nugau shouts in English. "Lower your weapons! No more death!"

The drumming beat of the Thistha Ren is echoed through every part of the formation. More and more riders are flying up to join Nugau's allies and stand between the human soldiers and the Queen's army. The sound rises to a melodious cacophony—*Thump! Thump! Thump!*—a trial of the heart in earnest, pumping through their veins.

In her spot at the front of the Jagged Blade, the Queen rises slowly on her wyvern. She doesn't scowl or glare, or even clench her jaw. She only watches her daughter with eyes that shine a little too bright, too wide, too focused. Shadows coil around her wrist, calling forth the immense power of her royal status. Sascia has seen those shadows before. She knows what happens when they reach for Nugau: punishment and pain.

"Watch out!" Sascia warns.

But Nugau has already seen the blast of Dark headed their way. She steers her wyvern aside, barely avoiding the black beam that zaps past it. It lands on one of the skyscrapers surrounding the Maw, raining glass and debris down on the battlefield.

"Mother's anger is showing." Nugau says, quiet and calculating. "I think I can push it right into wrath."

With a tap at the wyvern's stirrups, they are flying again. Nugau takes them on a wide arc around the Maw, keeping close to the concrete barrier. Rivulets of Dark sprout from the princess's fingers. She whips them away and back again, like a cowboy on a rampage. Objects come flying about in their wake, blades and long bows, quivers full of arrows and shields of onyx.

But the princess doesn't stop there. She pushes the wyvern higher around the Maw and focuses on the human army next. Her black whips snatch guns and blasters straight from the soldiers' hands and warp the barrels of mortars and machine guns.

She's disarming them, Sascia realizes. *She's disarming all of them.*

When met with a blade, with a blade you'll meet—but what if there are no blades to speak of? What if the only thing you have left is your voice and your mind? A courage that sheds no blood, just as they promised each other.

"Sascia!" Nugau cries. "Duck!"

No explanation required; Sascia flattens herself against the wyvern's back, right by the stirrups, as Nugau does the same on the opposite side. A blazing fireball of black flames whooshes past where they just were. The Queen is hot on their tail, swinging blast after blast at them.

"Ah, there it is," the princess says. "Mother's wrath."

But she is far less composed than her voice pretends. She keeps glancing behind them, at the onslaught of Darkblasts the Queen is hurling at them. Around them, the battlefield has dissolved into panic: unarmed human soldiers hurry to rearm themselves; aesin dip their hands into the Dark to shape it into another blade. The barrier around the Maw has become a patchwork of rubble and blast marks.

The sky explodes with white.

Beneath Sascia's legs, the wyvern rears on its haunches and lets out an earsplitting shriek. Thousands join it, the sound echoing from every direction. White spots dance across Sascia's vision—one of the other disoriented riders must fly into them, because suddenly they're being thrown off-kilter, bumping into concrete.

Thanks to years of nova-light exposure, Sascia's sight recovers first. The scene before her is horrific. A scorch line has been razed into the barrier, a grotesque scar of absence in the tight lines of the Jagged Blade's formation. The gnarled remains of charred bodies lie in its wake, stark against the concrete, crimson feathers twirling in midair. Both the Queen's mount and Nugau's have been tossed against the wall of the barrier. Sascia's eyes follow the course of the blast, coming to rest at the enormous barrel of the nova-cannon. Wisps of white steam from its mouth.

Holy hell. This thing, Tae's design—it will obliterate everything.

"Nugau," she says, shaking the princess. "We need to destroy it before it can reload."

Trembling, the princess gives a nod. She coaxes the wyvern into the sky again. With a few swipes of her hand, Nugau sends the human soldiers on the parapet back to the walls, trapping them there in nets of pure Dark. She strikes with her scythe, with beams of magic, yet the cannon withstands it all.

"I can't," Nugau groans between gritted teeth. "I doubt even the Queen has the power to destroy this one."

"Get me on there," Sascia says. "I can disarm it."

Nugau nods. "I'll keep the Queen busy. Hurry, Sascia. It looks like it's loading again."

Deep inside the barrel of the cannon, an inner light has started getting brighter.

As the wyvern hovers over the now empty parapet, Sascia slides from its back—Nugau grips her wrist, her eyes fastened on the moths clinging to Sascia's hair and shoulders. "Protect her," she tells them before swooping away.

Sascia climbs up to the control panel of the cannon. Beneath her, she can feel a low vibration as it prepares for another blast. Its design is classic Tae: minimal and straightforward, with only a tiny screen that shows the panels of a recharging battery and four buttons, all unmarked. Sascia will have to experiment.

The first button she taps, on the far left, seems to rotate the cannon left and right. The second moves it up and down. The third makes the cylinders around its barrel spin, calibrating something or other. The fourth she doesn't immediately push, too scared of what it might do. She uses the first two to aim the cannon high in the sky, just in case, then she tentatively tries the fourth button. Words pop onto the tiny screen: TURNING OFF IN 5 . . . 4 . . . 3 . . .

"Yes!" Sascia cries. She glances at the Maw, eager to let Nugau know the crisis is averted.

A strangled scream escapes her mouth.

The Queen and Nugau are locked in battle. Each wields an amorphous throng of Dark. Their strikes reverberate through the concrete barrier. Their wyverns ram together and spring apart in quick, ravenous hits. All around them, the aesin are trying to protect themselves from the barrage of nova-light blasts from the human soldiers.

"Stop!" Sascia cries. Her fingers fumble across the buttons, steering the cannon toward the Queen. She has no intention of firing it, but perhaps it will scare the Queen enough to make her pause. The Queen doesn't hear her, but Nugau does. The princess's jaw goes slack at the sight of the cannon loading up; a second later, the Queen looks up too.

"Look around you!" Sascia calls out, voice laced with desperation. She doesn't know whether the Queen understands her language, but she makes sure to get her meaning across. She points at the death strewn about the barrier, the human bodies strung on the parapets, the aesin and wyverns razed to dust on the concrete walls. "It doesn't have to be this way!"

The Queen is beautiful even in her uncertainty. Her hair wisps like smoke over her shoulders. Her powerful chest rises and falls with deep breaths. Beneath her helmet, her mouth is pressed into a solemn line.

And then, horribly, impossibly, the cannon roars to life. Its cylinders spin so fast that they become a blur. Light gathers in the depth of the barrel, a growing inferno of white.

"*Sascia!*" Nugau cries, pulling her wyvern up.

Panic jostles Sascia into movement. She hits the off button immediately—

Two words appear, in a tiny font: ACCESS DENIED.

Mooch and her other moths intuit her desperation. They lift off her shoulders and land on the mouth of the cannon, one by one, forming a shield of onyx wings.

No, don't, she thinks—but she has no time to speak it.

She can only watch as the cannon erupts.

The light consumes her moths first, their tiny bodies evaporating into black dust. Then it travels across the expanse of the Maw and blazes through the Queen.

Her onyx-plated armor melts off.

Her flesh singes. Her hair catches fire.

Her mouth parts in a soundless scream.

And where a queen once stood, now ashes scatter.

42

CRIMSON FEATHERS

Time slows, as though Sascia is experiencing the world through cold water.

Nugau and her wyvern dive to catch the remains of the Queen's charred body in midfall. The princess is askew, nearly out of her saddle, pulling her mother's shriveled corpse close. Aesin riders crowd around the pair, both Nugau's faction and the Queen's, in a blur of armor and wings.

A wail rises from Nugau's lips, the mournful sound of utter devastation. The aesin throw back their heads and howl, not a war cry this time but a searing lament, torn from the throat, shredding the vocal cords. When the howls ebb, Nugau gives a sharp command.

At once, her allies separate from the crowd and begin rounding the army to form a funnel. Numbed with shock, the aesin simply follow instructions, diving back into the Maw in a steady stream that widens and widens. In mere minutes, all but Nugau have disappeared back into the Dark. The humans are holding their fire, satisfied to see their enemies retreat.

Nugau is the last to go. The princess's gaze rises to Sascia on the parapet, where she is frozen atop her machine of violent death. The sharp features of Nugau's face are chiseled into pure, deathful wrath.

Sascia opens her mouth to speak, to explain, but—

"You *promised*," Nugau calls out, voice breaking. "We could have had peace and unity, but you—you chose the blade. The next time we meet, I will choose the blade too."

Then, with a flick of the reins, she dives into the Maw.

You have been judged for your actions in the Battle of Feathers, Nugau had said the very first time they met in the alley on 53rd Street, *and you have been found guilty of treason.*

Even through the tangle of time of the ymneen, Sascia thought her choices were still her own. She tried to make the right choice, to stop the coming war. But she ended up doing the very opposite: She led the army of the Jagged Blade here. And by killing the Queen—however unintentionally—she has started the war between humans and aesin. There is no stopping it now, no changing what's to come.

She has failed, yet again, in a way so spectacularly foolish that there can be no coming back from it. No second chance, no forgiveness, no hope.

Beneath her lies a wasteland of corpses and shattered glass.

Crimson feathers drift across the sky, dotting the skyline in a snowfall of death.

43

THIS ISN'T A LIFE

Sascia is eighteen. Technically an adult, although she doesn't feel like one right now.

She sits in the center of the sofa, with Ksenya on her left and Mama on her right. In front of them, Baba paces back and forth. The TV is on behind him, on mute. Hollywood is producing a big-budget film of the Darkgriffin attack and its cast was just announced. Public opinion is split; some welcome the production, others say it's too early. Sascia's eyes are locked on the screen, but there's nothing to shield her ears from her father's disappointment.

"How did this happen, Sascia?" he asks, again. "We let you enroll at the Umbra, to spend your time and effort there, because we thought you were making something out of it."

She was—she *is*. It's just that her effort can't be quantified in a GPA and SAT scores.

"You knew the conditions of your provisional acceptance to Columbia from the get-go. You had two years to get your GPA up and study for the SATs. Yours"—he brandishes Columbia's rejection letter—"are not the scores of someone who's been doing the work."

"Isn't my work with the moths more important?" Sascia asks. "I've developed an entire surveillance system that will allow us to use the moths' movements to predict Darkcreature attacks in New York. If I keep expanding my map, we could have an attack alarm system more accurate than any invented before."

"How are you going to keep expanding your map if you're kicked out of the Umbra?"

"I'm not going to get kicked out—"

"I spoke with Professor Carr, Sascia. He told me he made it clear to you that without furthering your education, it would be impossible to convince the Umbra funders to keep providing you with a stipend. Isn't that true?"

Sascia gives a begrudging nod. Yes, it is true, and yes, it's ridiculous. Scholarship doesn't require an Ivy League education. She can educate herself just fine if she keeps furthering her education the way she does now: with the books she reads, the experiments she conducts. This is not about scholarship. It's about *money*. Umbra students need to constantly prove their genius so that Carr can constantly ask his funders for more cash.

"I can keep working on my moth map on my own," she says now to her father. "I'll get a job and in my free time I'll recreate the moth garden. I can easily refurbish my closet to host the garden safely, and I can get all the software I use with my friend Crow's help. I don't need the Umbra, or Carr's funding—"

"Sascia, be real."

The severity of the statement must startle him too, because he stops his pacing and comes to perch in front of her, on the edge of the coffee table. His features ripen into something sweet and concerned. "You are still young, but you have seen exactly how the world can turn our life on its head in an instant. You have seen me and your mother work sixteen- and eighteen-hour days to keep the restaurant afloat. You and Ksenya both know better than most kids that life doesn't always give us the luxury of choice."

Ksenya stares straight ahead at the soundless TV, her jaw locked tight. She's back from Greece for two weeks, for what was supposed to be quality family time—instead, she gets this.

"Honey," their mother tells her husband, "it's not all so hopeless as that. They might be limited, but we do have choices. We made plenty of them in our time, and the girls will too. It's just that," she adds with a soft smile at Sascia, "we have always hoped you'd make better choices than we did."

The back of Sascia's nose is burning. She'd rather stab herself in the foot than cry, in front of her father, during this particular conversation, so instead she grits her teeth and lets her anger take over. "Isn't it the better choice, always, to do what you love?"

"Kardia mou," he whispers gently. *My heart.* "I know you love your moths. I know you're passionate about protecting the Dark and its creatures. But love doesn't put food on the table. Passion doesn't keep a roof over your head. Loving the Dark, protecting the Dark, dedicating your entire life to the Dark—that is not a life."

And isn't that the saddest thing you've ever heard? All that she has loved and worked for, discredited with a simple sentence. Because, if that isn't a life, if Sascia hasn't been living, what has she been doing?

Her father reaches for her face, cupping it in his rough palms. "You are the smartest, kindest person we know. Isn't that right?"

Mama and Ksenya nod emphatically.

"You can do so many wonderful things," he says. "But first, you need to get your life together, kid."

THE NEXT MORNING, SASCIA pleads her case to Professor Carr.

Another year at the Umbra, during which she will get her grades up and ensure a spot at Columbia. She promises to enroll in whatever remedial courses he chooses for her, and promises to excel in them. There's nothing Carr can do about the loss of her stipend, but she'll figure something out.

"I can do this," she tells Carr. "I'm a clever girl, after all."

How wrong life proves her.

PART IV

soron mola (soh·ron moh·lah)
compound noun

true purpose; an intent that drives
one's actions to their most genuine essence, or
purposeful truth; a truth that is acted upon with the
most honest, deliberate intent.

Archaic; from the extinct tribe of Uslu, who
dedicated their life to the care and study of itka and
are believed to have been allowed by them to leave
Itkalin and explore new worlds.

44

THE RUINS OF DELUSION

There's a knock on her door.

As soundlessly as she can, Sascia pulls the covers over her head. Her ceiling lights, three floor lamps, and two bedside lamps create a supernova amount of brightness. It seeps through her comforter, bathing her closed lids with a soft peach color.

The door creaks open. "Sascia?" her mother whispers.

Sascia makes sure her chest rises and falls in slow, rhythmical breaths, as though she is deep in sleep. It is eight in the morning on a freezing early-March Tuesday. Normally, Sascia would already be dressed and heading out the door for class, or Umbra work, or fishing tours.

There's no class to go to anymore. She hasn't been expelled, but only because she was never an actual student to begin with. They recommended independent study from home; the presence of the Queen-killer is too distracting for her classmates, apparently.

There's no Umbra either. The whole program has been put on hiatus. Shortly after the Battle of Feathers, Professor Carr was elected the new director of Chapter XI.

And there are no fishing tours. Her tour-guide email has blown up with requests, but she reads none of them. Her fishing gear has been confiscated. Her bank accounts suspended. A slew of her former clients are enjoying their fifteen minutes of fame, their only claim to it that they hold the spoils of her first insurrections in plastic cups.

Sascia has nothing to get out of bed for. It doesn't matter. She likes it here in her fort of pillows and blankets, where it is warm and cozy and swathed in bright light.

After another minute, she hears the door close.

CONTRARY TO THE OPINION of half the internet, Sascia is not heartless. She knows exactly how much pain and panic she has caused by starting this war. She is the harbinger of fear; for the entire world, for her friends, but most importantly, for her family.

When her father knocks on her door hours later, she forces herself to get up and throw on a hoodie to join them at the dinner table. It is the only comfort she can give them right now: watching her take care of herself by eating.

Her parents have brought up a pot of dolmadakia from the restaurant today, a minced pork, rice, and mint mixture wrapped in vine leaves and drizzled with avgolemono sauce. Sascia chews fast. (She might have a heart, but she does not have patience. The sooner she's done with her plate, the sooner she can retreat to her room.)

They've turned into full family affairs, these dinners. Her aunt comes down from her apartment upstairs, Danny drives home from Princeton whenever he can, her parents take a break from work. The five of them sit at the cramped table in the kitchen, conversing about their day. They try to catch Sascia's eye or ask her a question she will grace with an answer longer than a couple of words, and Sascia tries, she really *does try*, until the weight of it becomes unbearable and her failures, her world-altering mistake, come crushing down.

In the first few weeks after the Battle of Feathers, whenever the floodgates opened, her family would wrap their arms around her and comfort her; she would last a minute, maybe two, before disentangling herself. She does not deserve their comfort and so now, after nearly two months, she has learned to run and hide at the first hint she's about to start sobbing.

She does it now, scraping her last dolmadaki onto Danny's plate. Her chair pushes back with a screech.

"Come play video games with me," Danny blurts before she can leave the room.

And because she has never been able to say no to Danny, never fathomed she'd be the cause of so much of his pain and worry, Sascia draws a smile on her face and nods.

They play. It does bring her some joy to be lost in a world of kick-ass warriors for a few hours. Her mind quietens. Her muscles unwind. She's only the shift of her fingers, the *click-clack*s of her control, the colorful settings of mountains and lakes and evergreen fields.

Danny talks while they play. About his college classes and his hangouts (emphatically *not* dates) with Tae. Then he slowly steers the conversation to Nugau. Sascia answers every question he asks. She has screwed up *so much*, but she will not screw up this too, the only honest relationship left in her life.

Bit by bit, over the course of these miserable two months, Danny pries the whole story out of her. He snorts when she tells him Nugau has a sweet tooth. He whoops when she tells him their first kiss was while Nugau held a blade against her throat. He only asks about the fun stuff, the happy memories, and he never pushes her with suggestions and solutions and ways to make this right.

After a while, she realizes. It's because he knows there's no fixing this.

Around midnight, Sascia shuffles back downstairs and into her room. She leans against her closed door and looks around her with glum resolution. Drawers lie open; closet doors swing wide, sagging off their hinges. The big floor lamp from the dining room sits in her closet. Two flashlights shine beneath her bed.

After she was released from Chapter XI's interrogation and instructed to remain at home until further notice, she arranged her room like this, ordered dozens of nova-light fixtures and plastered them around the apartment, then made her parents vow they would never turn them off.

There is not a dot of darkness in the entire building. No place where anything could crawl out of the Dark, not a Darkcreature, not a Darkhumanoid, not even a Darkmoth. (God—she can't even think about that. About Mooch, its body dissolving against the onslaught of the cannon blast.)

She shuffles to her window and pulls the curtain aside, just a sliver. On the street below, the beige van has not moved an inch in the past two months. A team of Chapter XI agents are sitting in it right now. Sascia imagines them slumped low in their chairs in front of their monitors, hands folded over their laps, drowsy after devouring takeout from Athena's Yard. (Typical Greek that she is, her mother insists on feeding them.) The screens in front of them are blank, revealing no activity in the Dark.

She refuses to be the reason for any more hostilities against Darkcreatures. The Battle of Feathers has left the world trigger-happy. Nova-light mortars have been distributed and stationed around every Darkhole in the world, army presence has tripled, and the peace movement hasn't been able to recover from their poster girl committing a very publicized murder.

At least the news channels are gone now. They finally realized they were never going to get the exclusive they longed for. It only took two months of never allowing them a glimpse of her face, never leaving her house, never contacting anyone she knows.

This doesn't matter either. She deserves all of that and worse.

THE SWEET RELEASE OF deep slumber is nearly impossible when your room is as bright as the surface of the sun. Sascia lies ramrod straight on her bed, palms facing the ceiling, lids closed, counting her inhales and exhales as per the instructions on the sleep meditation podcast she has on.

If she allows herself to think about it, really, truly think about it, she can trace the source of her downfall to the very beginning. That moment in her grandparents' house in suburban Queens, watching the Darkdragon wreak havoc through Shanghai. She had seen its scales and believed that was what her savior's cloak had looked like when she almost drowned. She had thought that they had come from this new world to save her because she was special, worthy, made of magic herself.

That's what led her to ruination: the delusion of being more than she is.

She convinced her cousin to enter that damned sewer because she thought she was more than just a scared kid. She jumped into the Maw because she thought she was more than just another bystander waiting for others to protect her. She made the Heart Claim because she thought she was more than just a powerless human. She carved her way out of the Labyrinth, kissed Nugau, promised them that together they would change the course of history, because she thought she was more than time itself.

In the end, she is what she always has been.

A girl made of impulse and longing, too foolish to ever get her life together, not even when the fate of the world depends on it.

A screw-up through and through.

Sascia folds the covers over her head. Sleep doesn't come, not for a long time, and when it does, it is barren of dreams.

45

A STORY OF PERSEVERANCE

On the three-month anniversary of the Battle of Feathers, Sascia wakes from a midafternoon nap and finds a note on the kitchen table: *Dinner upstairs today*. Aunt Rania must be trying a new recipe for the restaurant. Sascia takes a whiff of her armpits, then forces herself to take a long, scalding hot shower. Wiping a palm on the bathroom mirror, she stands there and looks at herself as the steam slowly reclaims the edges of the glass.

She is a splinter of her old self. Her usually neat short bob has grown almost to her shoulders. The scars left by Ktren's teeth have taken on a dark gray quality against her olive skin. If she stares too long, her reflection becomes someone else, a fragment of essence that lives only in the sheen of a looking glass.

She throws the cupboard open and fishes out the comb and scissors. She begins cutting in neat straight lines, as she's done for the past four years. By the end, the white sink is marbled with tufts of her sandy brown hair.

There. Much better. At least she knows who she's looking at now.

Ruffling a towel through her hair, she shuffles to her room and pulls on a pair of black jeans and her oversized "home" sweater. She doesn't bother with shoes; she climbs the stairs to her aunt's apartment in the pitter-patter of her slippers.

Danny opens the door.

Behind him, on the mismatched furniture of Aunt Rania's living room, sits a whole array of people. Her parents and aunt are on the sofa, Andres is slumped in the armchair while Shivani perches on its arm, Tae rests cross-legged on the floor next to a laptop from where Crow must be watching. Even Ksenya is here, leaning against the far wall with her arms crossed over her chest.

Sascia drags her gaze down to Danny. "Is this an intervention?"

"Damn right it is," he answers, closing the door behind her. "Long overdue, in my opinion."

"Fantastic," Sascia says tonelessly, and takes her clearly assigned seat on the dining chair pulled into the center of the room. *She. Is not. Heartless.* She knows they're here because they care, because they worry, because they think something is wrong with her. Sascia just has to listen and appease them and it will all be over in a jiffy.

This isn't her first rodeo, after all. There was another intervention, almost a year ago now, the dreaded *get-your-life-together* shebang, and Sascia very much doesn't want to repeat that.

"Andres," she says, "is that a new tattoo? And Shiv, you wear glasses now?"

Shiv gives her a smile and Andres nods, rolling his sleeve up. A lithe Darkbloom is inked around the tight muscles of his forearm.

"Hiya, Crow," Sascia says to the screen.

"Hiya right back at you, S."

"Mom, Dad, do you know everyone?" Sascia asks, forcing chirpiness into her voice.

"Yes, we've been introduced," her mother replies. "Lovely kids. They all care about you very much."

Oh no. Sascia doesn't want to hear about that. She wants to keep things light, calm, reassuring, the smoothest intervention there ever was. She swivels her attention to her sister at the back of the room. "When did you get here, Ksenya?"

"This morning," Ksenya replies, uncharacteristically icy.

"Don't you have exams in like a week?"

"I do." Two short, clipped words.

Oh god. Even her sweetheart of a sister is upset?

Sascia falls quiet. Let them do the talking, as per the rules of intervention.

Danny wheels himself next to Tae. "As I tried to mention yesterday," her cousin begins, "Chapter XI is holding a board meeting this week. Insiders are saying the purpose of the meeting is to set up the first global action to limit the Dark. They're calling it border control."

Yes, Danny did say something of the sort during *Final Fantasy VII* last night. Sascia didn't reply because it was an entirely unnecessary conversation. Chapter XI is going to do what Chapter XI is going to do. The world will keep turning (an endless ouroboros devouring its own tail and all that), but Sascia is not a part of it any longer.

"We think," Danny says, emphasis on the *we*, "you need to talk to them."

"I have talked to them. Six whole days of interrogation, to be exact. It was very successful, as you all know, and I even came away with a little parting gift." She waves her hand to the window, outside which the monitoring van is always stationed.

"No snark," her father gruffs out from the sofa. Then, softer: "Listen to your friends, kardia mou. They're here to help."

"I know that," she whispers. "I just don't think there's any help to be had."

"Sascia, the Chapter is discussing sending a nuclear apocalypse worth of missiles into every host of Dark in the world," Andres says. "It would obliterate everything: fauna, flora, all the harmless creatures we've been fighting for all these years."

"All the big beasts too," Shiv adds, "the ones that just don't know any better."

"And according to you," Crow adds, "some of these bombs will end up in Itkalin."

Sascia presses her lips together. "And how exactly do you expect me to stop them?"

"Tell them what you told me," Danny says passionately. "About the aesin and their culture, their history and customs, their values and beauty."

"They already know. I told the Chapter everything I could think of that would convince them the Battle of Feathers was not an act of aggression but of defense, and they didn't care to listen—"

"Tell it to the rest of the world, then. News channels have been reaching out for months for an interview. Go on TV and convince the rest of the world the Dark is worth saving."

"Danny," she snaps, getting worked up now. "I can't. I'll just make things worse, like I always do—"

"Oh, will you get over yourself, Sascia!"

The outburst comes from the very back of the room, where Ksenya has unfolded from the wall. It is so unlike her—the raised voice, the scowling face, the finger stabbing in Sascia's direction—that the entire room swivels to gawk at her.

"You sit there and roll out your little snarky comments and dismiss your friends when they're literally begging you to help stop a war," Ksenya continues, "when all your life *you*'ve been the one begging, *you*'ve been the one caring for every Darkcreature you come upon. *You*'ve been the one marching into every host of Dark you can find, with not a care in the world about the people you leave behind worrying if you'll ever come back or if you're lying in some pit, torn and lifeless."

"*I know*," Sascia snaps, because now she's angry too, livid with the unfairness of it all. "Do you think I don't know, Ksenya? Do you think I didn't hear our parents argue about the stress I was putting on the family, on Danny, on you? Do you think I don't know I'm the reason you left home to live in sunny, safe Greece?" Her chest rattles with crackling breaths, like logs left too long in a too-hot fire. "I have tried to be different, Ksenya. I have tried to be what you guys wanted, what you needed from me, but I failed every single time. Dad is right: I can't get my life together, so I might as well stop trying, because then, at least, I will cause no more pain."

From the sofa, her father whispers, "When did I say that?"

"You said that," Ksenya snaps at him, "in that horrid speech you made after Sascia got her Columbia rejection. All that *that-is-not-a-life* nonsense, because god forbid your kids ever do something you don't completely understand, right? Like move to another country and turn their passion into their work and fall in love with someone they weren't supposed to. Right, Dad? Right, Mom?"

Sascia's mouth hangs open. Never before has she heard her sister raise her voice at their parents, and never before has she heard a callout so *on point*. Because that's exactly what her parents did, isn't it? They fell in love, her mother dropped out of law school to turn her passion of cooking into a job, her father moved here to the US to be with her, and they secretly eloped despite their families' explicit objections.

"That's different—" their father starts, but his wife lays a hand over his.

"Honey," their mother tells him, "hush. Listen."

Ksenya's voice sugars into gentleness as she turns back to Sascia. "I can see you carry those words on your shoulders, day after day. But, Sascia, it was just a foolish thing our fool of a dad said in a moment of worry. It is not who you are."

The words hit Sascia like a fist to the stomach. Out of nowhere, her lashes are filled with tears, thick and briny with salt.

"But it is," she whispers to her sister. "I'm the girl who couldn't deal with her grandma's death and made up a hallucination for years and years. I'm the girl who risked her life and her cousin's life to build a moth garden. I'm the girl who had a golden ticket to an Ivy League education and wasted it all because she preferred to care for her moths instead of study. I'm the girl who jumped into the Maw to stop a war yet ended up doing the exact opposite. I'm the girl obsessed with the Dark, in love with its princet"—god, is this really the first time she's said it out loud, in front of her parents, no less?—"and still, I betrayed them."

She stops to heave a few panting breaths, then whispers, "I have tried to be more, to be better, all my damned life. But nothing ever changes. No one ever believes in me."

Her plea falls heavy into the quietude of the room.

They don't move, eight somber statues of pity.

But then the silence is broken—by Tae, of all people. "When have you ever cared, Sascia?"

The question is so startling, she can only mouth, "What?"

"I said," Tae repeats, raising a haughty eyebrow, "when have you ever cared about what people think of you?"

Sascia is too stunned to speak.

"Over the past two years, I've sat in countless meetings at the Umbra where Professor Carr dismissed your research and belittled your wits. You never faltered. Never backed down. I used to judge you for it. But when Nugau first came out of the Maw, I watched you jump right in to save them, unafraid, armed only with *my* sword, one of the dozens of weapons I have crafted, yet never had the courage to wield myself. It made me think of what it means to truly fight for what you believe in."

His gaze tenses, wrinkling at the corners.

"What we just heard," Tae says, "all the things you and your family have gone through and survived . . . They don't make up a story of failure, Sascia. Life has knocked you sideways in a hundred different ways and yet, every time, you get back up again. Yours is a story of *perseverance*."

The whole room watches, breath held, as Tae unfolds from the floor and thrusts a hand at her.

"So get over yourself," he says, "get back up, and let's save the goddamn world."

46

DARK-SHAPED WOUNDS

Of course, Sascia takes his hand.

She takes his hand because it was a damn good speech, and because she can see it now, see herself through Tae's eyes, and the eyes of the people she loves most gathered in this room to pull her out of her own misery. She thinks of Professor Carr saying *I believe you*. Of her father saying *All this studying, all this work. Don't think I haven't noticed*. Of Nugau saying *Your Mooch* and the thrill she felt to be chosen by the itka, to be made into magic by proximity to it. She thinks of coming out of the Labyrinth the first time, awash in the glow of her victory, an army of aesin thumping their approval.

Every step of her life she has fought for that approval, for *validation*—from her parents, Carr, the aesin, Nugau, even Mooch and the Dark itself. But she never truly needed it, did she? Her story is one of perseverance. She has failed, spectacularly, desperately, but each time, she has gotten back up and tried again. She will always try.

So now she stands and folds her fingers into Tae's, and asks him, "*How?*"

"Let's start with getting you into a room with Chapter XI," Tae replies, and there's barely a half-second pause before the rest of the room springs into action—as if they all believed in her in the first place and were just waiting for her to catch on.

"I'll use my contacts to arrange a meeting," Andres offers, pulling out his phone.

"And I'll put all our evidence together in a nice PowerPoint," Shivani adds.

Danny says, "I'll see if the Chapter goons in that van can help—"

"They're gone," her mother blurts from the sofa.

The room stares at her, causing a deep red to creep up her cheeks. "I went out with, um, their usual lunch order three days ago," she explains in a hurry, "and they were just gone. They haven't been back since."

As one, the cohort rushes to the windows. The street across from the apartment building is empty, no beige van in sight. Confused glances ping-pong around the room. Three months of surveillance and suddenly Sascia's security detail just packs things up and disappears?

"Crow?" Danny calls out urgently.

"On it!" Crow's voice chirps from the laptop. "I see there's a security camera on your restaurant's entrance . . ."

Sascia's father answers fast. "Go for it."

They wait in silence, listening to the clickity-clack of Crow's keyboard.

"*Oh shit*—" Crow gasps. "Sending over the footage now."

Nine bodies squeeze together for a clear view of Danny's laptop. The footage shows the steps of Athena's Yard in the night, the neighborhood cars parked in front of it, and on the other side of the street, the front half of the beige van. The night is quiet, perfectly still, until some disturbance shakes the sides of the van. Agents pour out, half a dozen of them, disappearing from the frame. They return minutes later and shove what looks like a sack of shadows into the van—Sascia can't tell exactly what it is, because the back of the van is out of the camera's range. The driver rushes ahead to hop into his seat, swatting at the dark shadows buzzing around his head. In moments, the engine is revved up, the lights are turned on, and the van is speeding away. Only the shadows remain, tiny dots of black swirling in the current created by the car's frenzied getaway.

As the shadows steady themselves on the breeze, a couple fly closer to the camera. Sascia recognizes their shape: small bodies, short wings, bright neon blues and purples and whites. Her heart steadies into thundering resolve. *Darkmoths.* That's what the Chapter agents were carrying away.

"Shivani," she says, glancing at where the girl stands closest to the wall. "Turn off the lights."

When darkness falls, it feels like a welcoming.

"This is far too many moths," Sascia's father complains from the front seat.

He is not wrong.

About a hundred moths are plastered on every surface inside her dad's old Toyota. Most perch on or around Sascia, like worker bees around their queen, but others line the top of the car, the dashboard, the windows. The moment Shivani switched the lights off, Mooch popped out, battering Sascia's face with what could be interpreted as either kisses or slaps.

Mooch, *alive*—Sascia laughed and sobbed and just burst with emotion. Three months of keeping herself away from her moths had been so damn lonely. When it was sated, the itka zoomed across the apartment, driving its body into every light switch and plunging them into deeper darkness. Within seconds, the place was abuzz with the beating of wings.

To their credit, none of the passengers in the car seem the least bit concerned by tiny Darkcreatures crawling over them. Her father is driving, her mother is in the passenger seat, and Ksenya, Sascia, and Andres are crammed in the back. Danny is driving his own car, just a stone's throw behind them, bringing Aunt Rania, Shivani, and Tae.

They refused to let her go alone, even though she has zero clue where exactly Mooch is taking them. The moths had just poured out of the apartment, almost carrying Sascia on their velvet wings, and would have continued dragging her along if she hadn't put up her hands and cried, *Enough, enough! Where do you want me to go?* The little scoundrels didn't answer, of course, but they did pour into the car when her dad threw the door open, and they did calm down after he started driving according to the directions Mooch tapped onto Sascia's skin.

So they're going . . . somewhere. In the security footage, it looked like the Chapter agents were abducting the moths, so Mooch must be leading Sascia to them. But why? The others are regular Darkmoths, but Mooch is an itka; it could just tear open the world and get the moths out, or drop Sascia exactly where she needs to be. So why this?

On Sascia's left, Ksenya is a fidgety ball of nerves, a panic attack waiting to happen, but her jaw is squared and her fingers clasped tight around Sascia's.

It's still hard for Sascia to wrap her head around how much her little sister sees her, how well she understands her. *It was just a foolish thing our fool of a dad said in a moment of worry. It is not who you are.* These simple lines soothe a deep ache in Sascia's core. Someone knows her, someone believes her, *understands* her, a sister with the same bright-colored memories, the same Dark-shaped wounds.

"It looks like there might be a structure up ahead," Crow says from the phone. "I'd suggest killing the lights and finding a hidden place to park, Mr. Petrou."

When they went off the interstate and into upstate New York, Crow had pulled up a map and started analyzing potential destinations, but even the mighty hacker had guessed wrong. Now, after nearly an hour on an inconspicuous dirt road, all bets are off.

"Well, damn," Sascia's father mumbles from the front seat as he pulls the car to a stop and kills the lights.

Nestled amid oaks and birches, the sprawling compound consists of concrete smokestacks surrounded by high-security fencing. Bold military signs indicate restricted access and warn against trespassing, while guards in dark-colored camouflage patrol the grounds, carrying heavy military-grade nova-weapons.

"Where are we?" Ksenya whispers.

From the speakerphone, Crow chirps, "Former power plant. Discontinued in 1994, acquired by a private company in 1997. Records about it have been erased and satellite map images are blurred, which makes me think it's a top-secret facility. Army, perhaps."

A silence follows, during which they all stare at Sascia, who in turn stares at Mooch, resting on her shoulder. "Little guy, why are we here?"

A shiver starts at its body. In a wave, its form shifts from its head to the tips of its wings, velvet giving way to hard onyx. On the windows and the dashboard, the rest of the Darkmoths follow suit, as though Mooch is a general raising a war banner. The moths are preparing to fight.

"You want us to get in?" Sascia asks.

Yes, Mooch taps.

"Is this where the Chapter agents brought the other moths?"

Mooch taps three times. In the Labyrinth, that meant not right, not left, but *straight*. Here, with the binary of *yes* and *no*, it means—what? *Not applicable?*

Sascia glances up at Andres, at her family. "I don't know what is in there, but Mooch wants me to go, so I'll go. I think it's best if you guys stay here—"

"Andres," Crow says from the phone. "Tell her to shut up."

"Shut up, Sascia," Andres says dutifully.

"Tae," Crow goes on, "have you got one of my remote hacking ports on you?"

"Of course I do," Tae says on the group call, sounding almost offended.

"Danny, Andres, between some pollen and some Darkmold, could you create something that causes a micro allergic reaction?"

"Yup," Andres says at the same time that Danny blurts:

"Sure—*ow*! Mom! It's not going to be deadly!"

"And, Shiv," Crow asks, "how would you feel, from an ethical point of view, about enraging a swarm of Darkrats, then unleashing them on the patrols?"

"Not great," Shiv mumbles. "But a girl's gotta do what she's gotta do."

"Then," Crow concludes, "I think I can get us in."

"Kids," Sascia's mom says from the front seat, where she's gone a particularly alarming shade of pale. "This sounds a little drastic. Should you really be planning a heist on a private facility patrolled by armed forces?"

"I don't like it either," Aunt Rania pipes up from the other car.

"You don't have to be a part of this," Sascia says. "You've done so much already, you can turn around and—"

"Sascia," her father interrupts. He's looking at her through the rearview mirror, like he used to do on long drives when they were children. She braces herself for one of his earth-leveling looks, but when she meets his gaze in the mirror it is gentle, full of warmth. "We're not leaving you kids alone. If this is the only way, then whatever your hacker friend needs, we'll do it."

"Hell yeah, Mr. Petrou!" Andres sings.

Cackles of nervous laughter break from every mouth.

"Well," Crow says in a wicked voice, like a supervillain rubbing their hands together, "if we're all on board, the hacker friend has a plan."

47

MOTH GIRL

Crow's plan turns out to be as bananas as one would expect.

First, Shivani disappears into the woods with a pack of power bars from Danny's glove compartment and returns looking frazzled and wild-haired to announce the army of Darkrats is ready. Then Danny bosses Andres around to collect Darkpollen allergens. Tae is cooped up in the back seat of Danny's car, coordinating with Crow on the hacking side of things. The poor adults and Ksenya are on reconnaissance, all four of them huddled over a phone, marking the times of the patrol's comings and goings.

During the whole time, Sascia paces back and forth among them, checking their progress like a busybody. She has a bad, bad feeling about this. For three months, the security detail was stationed outside her home. What called them away from her?

Once the team is ready, Crow's plan goes into action. They all crouch in their designated spots, ready to spring at Crow's signal. Sascia kneels next to Ksenya in the thicket of trees, waiting for the first step in the plan.

The guards don't notice them at first.

They are darting shadows in the night, there and gone again before you can blink. But eventually the soldiers notice; they begin to yelp small, undignified curses. The scene erupts with movement.

The three figures outside the security booth start hopping from foot to foot. Another two, farther into the compound, blast beams of nova-light into the ground around them. A whole wave of Shivani's Darkrats darts over gravel and concrete, their impossibly long scaled bodies spilling between legs and vehicles like a river of black. Commands are barked, patrol cars revved up, guards flood out of the buildings.

"Ah, the symphony of chaos," Crow chirps in Sascia's earbud. (In lieu of proper army earpieces, they're using their own earbuds on a group call.) "Such beauty, such grace."

"You're ridiculous," Danny whispers on the other side of the line.

"And you, my dude," Crow says, "are a mastermind."

He really is. He and Andres have concocted a cocktail of pollen and Darkmold, ground it to powder, then sprinkled it on the fur of the rodents now rushing through the compound. It only takes seconds for the highly irritative dust to radiate off their spiky fur. The soldiers are not truly dying (Aunt Rania made sure of that), but it sure looks like it. Black gore drips from their nostrils, streams of snot that writhe in the air like liquid shadows.

"My turn," Ksenya whispers.

She makes to stand, but Sascia reaches out. "You don't have to do this."

"I know." In the darkness, Ksenya's smile beams with warmth. "I want to."

She flicks her hood on and sneaks through the woods, crouching low for cover. A flurry of moths follows in her wake, their Darkprints casting the foliage in eerie neon hues. Keeping to the shadows, Ksenya flattens herself against the side of the security booth and props open the electrical panel by the door. With swift, focused movements, she plugs in Crow's port, which will get the hacker into the facility's systems.

"Hey, you!" a guard calls.

Ksenya has just enough time to close the panel and make a dash for the entry gate—she's caught as she's slipping through. Guards grab her by the elbows, batting the surrounding moths away.

"It's her!" one of them calls to the others farther inside. "It's the moth girl!"

Because to them, it *is* the moth girl.

Sascia and Ksenya have always looked like two sides of the same coin, one sharp-edged, one sunny and golden. But now, her long hair tucked in the collar of her shirt, wearing Sascia's black hoodie and telltale Doc Martens, with moths clinging to her like bees to sweet nectar, Ksenya is the spitting image of the so-called moth girl.

Early on, as Crow explained her plan, Danny had interrupted. *They're going to assume it's Sascia, coming to save her moths.*

And that, Crow had answered, *is exactly what we want.*

Sascia watches, breath held, as the soldiers carry her sister away. The only balm to her rising dread is the assured *click-clack*s of Crow's keyboard in her ear.

After a few, endless, minutes, Crow says, "I'm in."

Sascia looks at Danny through the woods, his wheelchair stationed by the car. His laptop is propped open on his lap, his fingers paused between furious typing. He, their parents, and Shivani are staying behind to be their eyes and ears. Their gazes hold; there was another moment like this, on the precipice of change. He had held her gaze then, while fire roared toward a nest of helpless larvae.

He holds it now, and says into his phone, "Go get your moths, cuz."

Sascia runs. Tae and Andres break into a sprint behind her, all three of them keeping to the shadows of the woods. The northwest security booth lies abandoned, the guards either occupied by the rats or Fake Sascia's arrest. At Crow's command, the green dot of the camera stationed at the post blinks off. The door of the fence buzzes open.

Sascia and the boys swoop inside and dart for the wall of the closest building. While Crow works the security system, Danny whispers directions to them. Left, right, right again. Every camera they meet momentarily goes dark. Every door they come across is instantly popped open. They find their way to the center of the facility and slip into an empty corridor. The space is brighter here, all white linoleum and fluorescent lights. It feels exposed in a dangerous kind of way.

"The guards are escorting Ksenya in through the security barracks," Crow says. "You'll have fifteen minutes, maybe twenty, to locate the moths before her cover is blown. Sascia, tell me where you need to go and I'll make sure you don't run into someone unpleasant."

Sascia glances down at Mooch, the one moth she didn't give to Ksenya, sitting daintily on her palm. "Which way, buddy?"

It flies ahead, taking them on a sprint through the facility. They stop only when Danny alerts them that a guard is moving ahead or when a door takes a bit longer for Crow to hack open. Then they turn a corner to find Mooch hovering before a set of double doors.

"Crow?" Sascia asks.

"Done," the hacker replies.

With a beep, the doors slide open.

It is a sprawling space, wider than a stadium and taller than a twenty-story building. The top is capped with a metal grate, but above it, the walls spiral up and up—they're standing inside the old factory silo. One end of the room is dark, packed with the metal shadows of machinery, but the other is awash with light. Glass panels of nova-lights of low lumen have been propped up to make three walls and a low ceiling.

In the center of the nova-light structure is a figure. Handcuffs chain their arms to metal posts. Their legs are folded beneath them and their head hangs unnaturally between their shoulders. Plastic tubes are wedged into their back, bulging their flesh; through them runs a river of black.

Sascia is already running. She skids on her knees before them and gingerly cups that face up, pushing their hair away, hoping, hoping, hoping for a sign of breathing, for a heartbeat, for clear, open eyes.

"Nugau?" Her voice echoes across the empty space, as though a beast of fury is unsheathing its fangs and claws. "Nugau, *who did this to you?*"

48

MENDED WITH POWDERED GOLD

Nugau's stillness rips through Sascia, a profound, lethal silence.

Her fingers shake as she traces the white swirls of their Darkprint to tilt their face up. Slow, labored breaths rasp through the princet's chapped lips. Their eyes are closed, their whole body slack against the chains.

A desperate whimper shoots out of Sascia.

In her ear, voices are rolling over each other, flushed with worry. She can only focus on one of them—Danny's. "Sascia, what's going on? There are no cameras in the silo for Crow to hack into. Are the moths hurt?"

It's not moths, it was never moths—Mooch told her, didn't it? When she asked if the facility is where the Chapter agents brought the abducted moths, it had tapped three times: not a yes, not a no, but something in between, because the agents hadn't captured the moths, but they had someone else.

"Chapter XI has Nugau," Tae mutters from where he's come to stand above Sascia.

"It can't be the Chapter," Andres says from Sascia's other side. His eyes are big and round on Nugau's half-broken form hanging from the posts. "The board wouldn't approve of this . . . mistreatment. I need to make a call. I'll be right back."

As he retreats to the corridor outside the silo, Danny asks, "What does Andres mean, *mistreatment*?"

"Nugau is chained to a cage of some kind," Sascia whispers. "A nova-light cage."

"It's not a cage," Tae breathes. "Can't you see? It's your and Danny's . . ."

Sascia follows his gaze to the glass walls around them, panels strewn with tiny nova-light bulbs, identical to—

"Oh god. It's our latest project, Danny." Her head spins with shock. "The walls of our garden that we've been working on turning into anti-Dark shields—they've used them to create a nova-cage."

"What the hell," Danny whispers. "Tae, if I guide you through it, can you dismantle the cage?"

"I can do you one better. This cube design is based on one of my own blueprints for—" Tae stumbles, suddenly going red. "For you, Danny. So that you can put up entire greenhouses for your botanic garden."

"Oh," Danny whispers. (It is a very meaningful *Oh*.)

"Like all my designs," Tae goes on, "it's meant to be remotely controlled. If you and Crow get me to the server room, I can turn the whole thing off."

"On it," Crow chirps. "Unless you guys want to moon for a little longer?"

"*Shut up*," Danny snaps.

"I, um, I'll go—" After some more incomprehensible stammering, Tae turns on his heel and disappears through the doors.

"Sascia," Danny instructs, "find a way to get those chains off Nugau."

Sascia's eyes are narrowed almost shut against the glaring lights of the cage. Long tubes sprout from the princet's back and run across the floor toward the shadowed end of the silo. Black seeps through them, like a blood transfusion—only aesin blood is dark blue, so what exactly are they siphoning out of Nugau? She can't wait for Tae. She needs to get Nugau out of here as soon as possible. She rushes to a row of storage shelves against the far wall and grabs the first piece of metal she spots, a crowbar of some sort.

Back in the cage, she covers Nugau with her jacket—and begins smashing.

Glass shards explode as panel after panel comes crashing down. Her sneakers crunch on the debris. The muscles of her arms are burning. She stops when the three walls are hollowed out, because she can't risk destroying the ceiling—any debris might hurt Nugau. She focuses instead on the cuffs. Once, twice, she wrenches her crowbar against the links, but all she causes are scratches.

Mooch flies out of her hair to hover over the shackles.

Fright shoots through Sascia's veins. She plucks Mooch out of the air and hides it against her chest. "You can't," she rasps. "The light will hurt you."

She remembers the Battle of Feathers all too well. The small bodies of her moths silhouetted against the barrel of the nova-cannon. Their wings disintegrating, shadow swallowed by light, when the nova-cannon blasted beneath her hands. Those moths are forever gone, but Mooch is here, alive, and she's never risking any moth's life like that again.

Yet Mooch has other ideas. It wiggles through her fingers, wedges itself between the cuff and Nugau's skin, then ... *bursts*. There's no other way to describe it; one moment, its wings are small curves of glass, the next, they're slabs of hard rock, twice their normal size. Mooch's wings crush through the cuff, tearing it in two, and Nugau's arm drops to their side.

Sascia is already there. In the time it takes her to brace her arms around Nugau's chest and hoist them up, Mooch has broken the princet's other hand free as well. Sascia half carries, half drags Nugau over a sea of shards and into the safety of darkness.

She collapses on her back, Nugau sprawled between her legs, the long tubes tangled in their limbs. For long moments, she lies there, gasps spearing through her tired lungs, ignoring the ruckus of questions in her earbud, until she hears a faint cough and then—

"You are a menace, little gnat."

Their eyelids are still closed, but their lips are crooked in a smile. Sascia's heart sings a litany: *they're alive, they're alive, they're alive.*

"I have been looking for you," Nugau whispers through barely parted lips.

"Hush. Save your energy while I figure out how to get these tubes off of you."

"No. I need to tell you now, while I still can."

Their eyes flare open, wide with intensity. Time slows, and dread settles onto Sascia's bones. What can be more important than getting out of here?

"After my mother's death, the aesin rejected my Royal Claim. The Queen's council seized control and held a tribunal—to decide your punishment, but also mine. Killing you would be the only way I could atone. I set out to find you with anger in my heart, with vengeance and hatred. Mooch led me to you. You pulled me out of the Dark in that foul-smelling alley. I thought that nothing would satisfy me more than revenge. That your death would make up for all the hurt and injustice of the Battle of Feathers."

Those terrible moments before the Jagged Blade retreated to

the Dark come back to her. The hurt in Nugau's eyes, their voice breaking. In her sleepless nights, Sascia had thought of the princet emerging from the sewer on 53rd Street, of their hate and anger, and she had thought, *Perhaps I shouldn't have fought so hard. Perhaps I should have yielded instead.*

"But you lay beneath my feet, defeated and weak," Nugau whispers. "My scythe was at your throat. Your gun was at my chest. You didn't know me. You didn't care for me. And yet, you didn't strike, little gnat. You faced a blade and chose to lower yours instead."

Yes, Sascia remembers that. Fear colors the memory, but the outline forms another shape, the brushstrokes soft and soothing. A person had climbed out of the Dark that day. An elf from a fairy tale, a nymph out of a heartland forest. And Sascia, who has loved the Dark all her life, could not destroy them.

"I never meant to hurt you, or the Queen, or the aesin. I swear, Nugau."

"I know. I have seen it. Your love, your kindness, your want—I have seen it all."

Sascia waits, breath held.

"I returned to Itkalin, but I couldn't stop thinking about that moment. I needed to understand why you let me live. Why you chose to be my ally. Why you betrayed us. So finally, one day, I asked Mooch to lead me to you." Nugau's chest trembles. "The first time it did, you were in a schoolyard. You were a child, playing with your cousin. The second, you were even younger, nestled in the back of a passing car. The third, you were in a snowy driveway with your family. Dozens of little snippets I've seen of your life, and each time, I kept to the shadows, watching, trying to understand why Mooch brought me to a time you didn't even know the Dark existed."

Her first thought, her most immediate, is *of course*.

Of course it was Nugau.

All this time, the figure in black, standing in the distance beneath a thicket of shadows, was never a trauma-induced hallucination. The truth shatters her—then puts her back together, like broken pottery mended with powdered gold. She is not the girl who believes in delusions. It was real and it was Nugau, angry, desperate, curious Nugau, trying to understand even through their grief and fury. The itka brought the princet to Sascia, as it always does, weaving them together through the tangled mess of time and space.

It feels both an injustice and an inevitability, to be thrown together and ripped apart.

"Why?" she whispers to the moth hovering between her and the princet.

Nugau answers for Mooch. "I think it knew I wanted to understand and it tried to help me. But I still don't understand, little gnat. If their soron mola is to save us, why do the itka keep tossing us back and forth in time? Why have they knotted our timelines? Instead of salvation, they have created an endless circle: violence and loss, and violence again. Who benefits from that?"

Crystal tears drip at the corners of Nugau's eyes. Sascia wipes them with a knuckle and lowers her forehead to the princet's. She has no answer to give them, nothing to make this impossible hurt go away. *No one* benefits from an endless circle of violence—

But that's not quite true.

When met with a blade, with a blade you'll meet: humans and aesin both have been taught that's the only way to survive. But it isn't always so; when Danny found his first Darkblooms, he chose to nourish them instead of rooting them out. When Shivani encountered her Darkrats, she chose to train them instead of kill them.

When Orran and Thalla met a human girl who caused trouble for their friend, they chose to embrace her instead of shun her. And Sascia herself, when faced with a blade, chose to lower hers instead. There are other ways to live, other choices to make—but humans and aesin have both been taught to fear, and to make choices out of fear, and who benefits from that, from the never-ending meeting of blade against blade?

The blacksmith.

The answer strikes her like a slap to the face: the blacksmith benefits. The industry that has thrived on threat and fear and promises of safety. The industry that profits off war.

Like the Queen's council: weapons builders, breeders of war mounts. The financers of the Jagged Blade.

Like human corporations: NovaCorp, producer of all nova-light weaponry. LIHT, the manufacturers of the strongest security systems in the world, used in every household, store, and street corner. Hyanzi, supplier of electricity to power all of the above.

All of them, funders of the Umbra.

Sascia's arms around the princet go slack.

"Nugau," she whispers, "how did you end up here?"

"Mooch led me to a new you," Nugau says. "I stood across the street from your house and watched your shadow drift across the curtain. All your lights were on, a blinding white. And somehow, I knew this was the right you. The you of our strange, looping present. But before I could come to you, figures appeared out of nowhere. They put these shackles on me that nullified my powers. They threw me into this cage. They—" Their eyes drift to the tubes running out of their back. "They use these horrible things to draw my power."

We were betrayed, Nugau said while they lay in Sascia's bed, delirious with poison. *I was trying to find you. But they found me instead. With their light-woven chains. Their ray-sharp arrows. Their mortars of white ash.*

The chains—Sascia recognizes them now: an early prototype of Shivani's to track her Darkrats' comings and goings. The cage: Danny and Sascia's design, based on their garden walls. The tubes: one of Andres's ideas to separate a Darkcreature's energy from their blood. All of them inventions of the cohort, created for Chapter XI after Nugau first appeared in Times Square.

Only they were never meant for Chapter XI, were they? *Is this where the Chapter agents brought the other moths?* Sascia had asked Mooch, and the itka had tapped three times: *Not applicable.* Its objection didn't have to do with the moths. It had to do with the Chapter. Because these inventions, like all work produced by students within its facilities, are the property of the Umbra Program.

The truth strikes her like a blow, fogging her mind.

"*Carr*," Sascia says. "It's Carr."

And this too feels like inevitability. Of course it was Carr, the consummate scholar, the acclaimed xenoscientist, excellent by all accounts except one: next to Boqin Shen, he would always, always be second best. And so, when he wasn't elected director of Chapter XI six years ago, he had collected the biggest corporations with an interest in the Dark and promised them a boon: all the strange, unlikely young talent in the world, studying and researching and creating for them, product after product. When Nugau came out of the Dark that first time, it was like a goose had laid a golden egg. A new threat, bigger and scarier than ever before, and a *war*—what better way to sell billions of guns, sonars and sensors, security systems, and every weapon necessary to keep humans safe?

Carr had tasked the Umbra cohort to create inventions he

could later use for this exact purpose. Instead of taking Sascia's theory and the cohort's evidence to the Chapter, he had stalled for precisely what she unknowingly delivered on a plate: an army of Darkhumanoids. A devastating attack. The beginning of war. With this new threat, he had finally managed to instate himself as director of the Chapter and pass the new anti-Dark laws that would benefit his investors the most. *Border control*, he called it, but Sascia knows better now. It is *greed*—for power, for profit.

I believe you, he had told her. *I believe you are destined for great, unfathomable things that none of us can fully comprehend. And I, Miss Petrou, will not stand in your way as you achieve them.*

And Sascia, fool that she was, desperate for his validation, had believed him too. He hadn't even lied, not really. He did not stand in her way. He stood to the side and watched, without ever interfering, and eventually, he had gotten what he wanted: the princet of Itkalin.

"The bastard," Sascia hisses, and reaches for her earbud. "It's Carr. Danny, can you hear me? *It's Carr—*"

Electricity zaps overhead.

The lights flicker on one by one, nova-panels strewn on the curved walls, beaming their vicious brightness around the silo. Through the blinding white, Sascia can make out figures flooding in from every door, carrying guns and nova-blasters.

One of them wears a pristine dark gray suit. He marches straight through the open space and comes to a stop a few feet from Sascia and Nugau. With his index finger, he pushes his glasses farther up his nose. The bright reflection conceals his eyes.

"Well done, Miss Petrou," Professor Carr says. "A clever girl, after all."

49

A GOOD SCHOLAR

In an instant, Nugau has unfolded to their full height. The patterns of their Darkprint swirl with colors, then settle into purple. He staggers weakly, yet pushes Sascia behind him, shielding her with his body. Spittle sprays from his lips as he barks, "Stay back."

In response, Professor Carr lifts his palms leisurely. "Let us not resort to violence, Prince Nugau. It is unseemly."

Sascia responds by flinging the crowbar straight at the professor's face.

It hits him in the shoulder, sending him stumbling back. In unison, the soldiers raise their rifles on their shoulders, barrels aimed at her.

"Unseemly?" Sascia cries. "*We* are unseemly? What about you? What about all this?"

She throws an arm out to gesture to the tubes leaching power from Nugau's back, the wreckage of the nova-cage, the dozens of armed soldiers, the thousands of light panels around them.

She taps her earbud. "Crow, Danny—"

"Don't bother, Miss Petrou. My staff interfered with the signal several minutes ago."

She had been so caught up in Nugau's confession, in the earth-shattering revelation that he was the figure in black, that Carr was his captor, that she didn't even notice there were no longer voices in her ear.

"Your family and Miss Kaur have been apprehended, and Mr. Ho and Mr. Matthei will soon be too. I expected this brazenness from you, Miss Petrou, perhaps even Miss Crow. But I must admit, it is immensely disappointing to see the rest of my students fall into your trap."

Brazenness. That's a new one to add to the long list of Carr's thinly veiled insults. Yet Sascia finds she doesn't mind this one at all. Brazen is the pigheaded man's word for bold. For defiant.

For brave.

She positions herself before Nugau and throws a hand out. Mooch gets the drift immediately—it bursts out of her hair and rips the world for her. Her nova-sword drops out of thin air and into her waiting palm. The rift lingers—she needs only to distract Carr long enough for Nugau to slip into the Dark. She nudges at Nugau with her head, a voiceless command to *go*, then closes both hands around the sword's hilt and aims its tip at Carr.

"I am not made of Dark," the man says. "That toy will not hurt me. But I must admit, *that* was remarkable to see in person. A door through time and space . . ."

He takes a step toward Mooch—Sascia swipes. The sword barely catches Carr's sleeve. But Nugau didn't use the distraction to jump into the rift. Instead, he steps forward and buries a punch in the professor's stomach. His violet eyes glint with fury—and then, suddenly, roll back into his skull.

A soldier behind Carr is tapping into a tablet. The tubes in Nugau's back come alive, sucking him of energy. The prince's spine arches and he collapses back into Sascia's arms.

"Stop!" she screams. "Please, stop!"

Elegantly, Carr straightens and watches with indifference as

Sascia helps Nugau to his feet. "There is no need to be upset. My methods might have caused the prince some discomfort, but I assure you, my goals are benevolent. I am a scholar, first and foremost. My only goal is knowledge. Acquired through research, perfected through study. That is the essence of science, not whatever naive notions of kindness you have."

"Science," Sascia mocks. The truth has been laid bare to her; she's done pretending. "This is not science. It is profit and power and control: the war industry churning out its products of destruction so that the many scared, desperate people of the world can protect themselves—and in the meantime, you gain wealth and power. Do these soldiers even know your research is not actually sanctioned by Chapter XI?"

Judging from the subtle glances and shuffling in the room, some didn't.

But Professor Carr seems unaffected. "Very good," he says, and he even sounds, to Sascia's horror, genuinely impressed. "I see you're finally applying that brain of yours to something useful. Let me accelerate your efforts: even knowledge is beholden to subsidizing. It is the way our world works. You would have realized that sooner had you spared even a single thought for what goes on beyond the confines of your own obsessions."

"My *obsessions*," she hisses, "are ancient gods that can tear a hole into space-time."

"That, they can. It was the entire reason I let you find us."

Her face slackens with surprise.

"Please, Miss Petrou. Did you think I wouldn't know the moment you stepped out of your house? I wanted you here, with your moths and the doors they can open."

Her muscles clench, dread clamping at her shoulders. She is aware of Nugau sagging against her side, of Mooch buried in her hair, its legs pawing the soft skin behind her ear. If Carr wants her here, if he needs her moths, then this was a trap, and why would Mooch willingly bring her right into it?

Carr clasps his hands behind his back. "I meant what I said before the attack at the Maw, Miss Petrou. I have always believed in you. I was merely waiting for you to do the same. To unlock the power I first glimpsed in you two years ago."

Years ago—the meaning behind his words makes her breath catch.

Her mind flashes back to that hospital room, the smell of antiseptic, the crisp white linens, the condensation gathered on the window. She remembers listening to the soft beeps of the machines keeping Danny alive. Glancing out the window to spot a figure clad in black looking up at her. Turning her back to it, annoyed by it haunting her even in the worst moments of her life. Then, a few hours later, the knock on the door. Professor Carr's tall, oppressive presence. His smooth words. The contract that sealed her and Danny's fate.

"You knew," Sascia breathes. "All this time, *you knew*."

"I told you. A good scholar is constantly on the lookout for the bizarre, the unusual, the unexplainable—such as two kids injured while building a map made of Dark. A good scholar investigates prospective students before inviting them to join his program."

She inhales sharply, the sound echoing in the vast silo.

"At first," he says, "I thought it was as your medical files suggested: the hallucinations of a traumatized child. But your recollections were always consistent. The figure wore a cloak of black scales. It came out of the darkness and disappeared into it. I decided to have your cousin's hospital room monitored. Imagine my surprise when my people called with an urgent report. There was a figure clad in a black cloak stationed outside the building. It had appeared straight through the Dark. I saw the footage myself, the scans and readings. Then I got into my car and drove to you."

I believe you are destined for great, unfathomable things, he had said. Not because she had convinced him through her work and talent, but because he accessed her medical records and had her watched. He had signed her and Danny on to the Umbra to keep them close. In every meeting, he drilled her relentlessly on her findings, treating her as a disappointment. Because her moth alarm system wasn't what he wanted from her. He wanted the figure in black. He wanted Nugau.

And then, when Sascia had jumped into the Maw, he had positioned himself as an ally to the cohort to keep their discoveries on the Darknomaly secret. When they invited him over after Sascia returned from the Maw, he had believed them instantly and without a doubt because he had always known they were telling the truth.

The betrayal cuts through flesh and sinew, deep into the pit of her belly. He had never been a teacher, never a true mentor, and yet somehow, Sascia had still believed she could trust him. But he had kept her under his thumb for years, honing her passion with his rejections, whetting her skill with his doubts, until it was finally time to wield her.

Now that time has arrived.

"What is it that you want from me?" Sascia asks, deathly quiet.

"I want what you want. A door into the Darkworld, to traverse as we choose, free of the whims of brainless bugs. Isn't that precisely what you have always wished for?"

Seven months ago, the answer would have been yes, in a heartbeat. She would have chopped down the tree herself, carved out the door from its wood, and propped it on its hinges. The answer is still yes, in a way. But now, after knowing Nugau, after living with the aesin, after understanding their joys and troubles and the ouroboric curse of knotted time, what Sascia wants is not a door to barge through, but a door to knock on.

"A door should not be forced open," she says. "There should be an invitation."

"Just like the invitation *they* got to burst through the darkness, I suppose?" Carr says. "Just like the thousands of Darkbeast victims, millions in damages, entire city blocks obliterated?"

This has always been one of Professor Carr's greatest skills: he has an argument ready at all times, and he can articulate it in such an infallible manner that Sascia becomes stumped. He nods, as if he expected her silence, and gestures at an assistant.

Energy crackles through the tubes attached to Nugau's back. A choked cry tears from his lips. His arms seize as the tubes fill with black. The liquid Dark flows out of Nugau's body as though it is blood through a vein. Snaking across the floor, the tubes feed Nugau's magic to a structure of metal on the other end of the silo.

It is a ten-foot ring, composed of several cylinders. As Nugau's magic funnels into them, the cylinders come alive. An otherworldly glow begins to pour out of the center of the ring. Faster and faster they turn, casting an eerie breeze around the room. Around it sit weapons ready to be wielded: mortars, howitzers, another nova-cannon—artillery that could annihilate an army.

"For six years, my research has focused on how humans can enter the Darkworld. We believed that the Dark was too cold for us, but I have recently discovered that it is only the *passage* between our world and theirs that gets dangerously frigid. With the prince's power—his magic, as you so love to call it—my machine can shape a permanent door that will eliminate this issue," Carr says. "A Darkgate, if you will."

A whine of pain trickles through Nugau's clenched teeth as his magic is siphoned out of him. Trembling, Sascia struggles to keep the prince upright.

"But despite my best efforts, the prince's power alone does not work," Carr continues. "Like any door, it requires a key. You and your moths are that key, Miss Petrou. You will open the door for us. You will show us the way into the Darkworld. And in exchange, I will let your family and your friends leave this place unharmed."

The nova-sword shakes in her hands. She glances down at Nugau—he warned her, just minutes ago: violence and loss, and violence again. She might not have chosen the blade in Times Square, but someone else will always be right there, to choose the blade instead. On and on, a circle with no ending in sight.

But what else can she do? What other choice does she have, if not the blade?

She holds Nugau's gaze and whispers, "Forgive me."

His eyes grow wide. "Sascia?"

Her movements are fast, focused. If she pauses, she'll rethink. She'll cower. She lets go of him. She marches through the silo to the Darkgate. She splays her palm.

Mooch extricates itself from her hair and lands on her fingers. Sascia studies the shape of its wings, the swirling patterns of its Darkprint, the now familiar way its feathered antennae nibble at her skin.

"We have come far, you and I," she whispers, low enough that only Mooch can hear. "But we need to go a step further. To become a key that opens the door between worlds. But you and I, we're a pair. If you refuse, I will not force you. If you find another way, I will follow you. What do you want, little guy? What do you choose?"

On her palm, Mooch taps once. *Yes.*

Sascia takes a step forward, her index finger extended. Mooch dives into the Dark.

Before them, the Darkgate begins whirring in earnest. Black spins in its center. It has begun. The door is opening—

"Stop!" Nugau cries out. He's on his knees, shaking with the effort of keeping himself upright, his features raw with emotion.

"Please, little gnat. It's not knowledge he wants. It's not research and study. Scholars do not march into a new world clad in military uniforms and armed with weapons. Look around us—that right there is a cannon identical to the one that killed the Queen!"

"I know," Sascia says, dragging her gaze to the nova-cannon facing the Darkgate. "I was the one who fired it in the Battle of Feathers. The Queen-killer, the Darkhumanoid-lover, traitor to humans and aesin alike. Right, Professor?"

Carr's composure is infallible. Yet Sascia doesn't need to see the emotion on his face any longer. She knows, and for the first time, she trusts herself: before her lies evil.

This cube design is based on one of my own blueprints, Tae said a few minutes ago. *Like all my designs, it's meant to be remotely controlled*. It was such an offhand comment in such an anxious moment that it had barely registered. But now Sascia knows what it means. Remotely controlled, like all of Tae's designs. Like the cannon.

"It was never me, was it, Professor?" she calls out. "It was never a mistake. *You* had remote control of that cannon. *You* shot the Queen. Because it's not knowledge that you want, or study, or research. What you want is *war*. The kind that will make you and your funders rich. The kind that will make you the most powerful man in the world."

Carr pushes his glasses farther up his nose. "You have always been obsessed with fairy tales, Miss Petrou. But I assure you this is not one of them. I am not the villain of this story. My decision to fire the killing shot that day ensured the survival of an entire city. And my actions tonight will ensure the survival of humankind."

There it is, clear as day. It's not just war he wants. It's annihilation.

But this is the thing: Sascia really is a clever girl. If it's war he wants, war is what he will get.

She plunges her hand into the gate of writhing Dark and pulls them out, one by one. Orran, framed by his enormous wings. Thalla, arrow already notched in her bow.

And behind them, the entire battalion of the Jagged Blade.

Let blades meet blades.

50

A SONG OF TRUST

"Open fire!" Carr screams.

In one move, Orran clashes their shield into the floor and sweeps Sascia behind it. Its hard gemstone surface vibrates with bullets and nova-light blasts. Orran crouches low, their face close to hers.

"Hello there," the aesin says. A dangerous smile draws on his lips, one that she imagines the fiercest warrior in the Jagged Blade might often wear in battle. "I had a feeling I would see you again. I was the only one unsurprised when the itka appeared to rally us up."

Mooch happily flaps its wings against her cheek.

Orran folds his fingers around her hand, where she is still gripping the hilt of her nova-sword. "Go get our prince, will you? We can handle the rest."

They move before she has time to process their command. The battalion steps as one against the onslaught of fired shots, their shields interlocked to form an impenetrable barricade. Aesin stride around Sascia, more and more of them flowing out of the Darkgate.

Sascia's palms are slick with sweat. She stands on shaking legs and surveys the scene: the humans are raining bullets and nova-blasts on the shield formation. Every few seconds, the battalion's defense parts to allow the archers to shoot their arrows. Human soldiers drop here and there, aesin crumble to the ground around their comrades' feet.

Thalla has remained by Sascia, firing arrow after arrow on the nova-light panels. Glass rains down all around the silo, enfolding the space in the sharp sound of shattering.

"I'll cover you," Thalla bellows. "Go!"

Sascia launches through the soldiers locked in battle, jumping over fallen weapons and bodies, ducking beneath wings and blasts of light. In the center of the room, Nugau is on his knees. His fists are braced against the floor, trembling with the force of keeping him upright.

A body slams into her, knocking her off-kilter. The soldier, a human, casts her a panicked look, but before they can aim their gun at an approaching aesin, Sascia kicks it out of their hand. The aesin pauses, scowling at her over bared fangs—it's one of the council's lackeys, Sascia realizes, who mobbed her on her first day in the dining tunnel.

"Traitor," they hiss. "Killer."

"I didn't kill your queen!" Sascia cries over the ruckus. "Her killer is the same human who kidnapped your prince and has bound him here to fuel the gate." She points to the nova-cannon at the end of the room. "You want to avenge your queen? Destroy the cannon. Destroy all their guns."

The aesin's eyes fasten on the display of firepower across the silo. The urge to distrust Sascia seems to be rooting them to the spot, but then Mooch darts out to land prettily on their nose. The aesin drinks in the presence of the holy itka. Something within them changes. Blue flames flare around their fists. When Mooch drifts toward the cannon, the aesin breaks into a sprint after it, calling others to join them.

Sascia takes off in the opposite direction. Amid the fray of soldiers locked in combat, Nugau is a bundle of shivering limbs. She slips to her knees by his side and traces the ridges of his back. His flesh is raw around the circular plugs rammed into his spine. Tubes protrude from them; his power oozes out in a trickle of pure Dark. Both plugs and tubes are hot to the touch, singeing Sascia's fingertips.

She needs to cut them.

"Nugau, can you hear me?" she says as she raises the nova-sword over her head. "I need to get you free. Brace yourself—"

Pain tears through her arm. The force of the shot throws her sideways to the floor. A scream bursts out of her. Ksenya's white T-shirt is stained red where the bullet tore through Sascia's bicep.

A few feet away, Professor Carr lowers his gun. His expression is unreadable no longer: his brows are stitched with barely contained fury. His voice rings over gunshots and the grinding of metal. "Will you never learn, you stupid, stupid girl?"

But Sascia is made of courage, of passion, of perseverance. Carr is no match for her.

"I guess not!" she screams, taking great joy in being obstinate one last time, because the bastard shot her, he really shot her, but he didn't think to aim for her sword-wielding arm.

She throws all her strength into it and just *flings* the sword straight at him.

The blade soars through the air and buries itself deep in Professor Carr's shoulder—not the part of its tip that is made of light, but the frame beneath that is a razor-sharp thin blade. Blood drips from the blade, painted a shimmering pink against the power of the nova-light. Carr blinks once, twice, then collapses against the shattered walls of the nova-cage.

Cradling her injured arm to her side, Sascia walks over to where he's propping himself up. His glasses are cracked, his lip is quivering, but she doesn't care. She steels a boot against his torso and wrenches the sword from his body. He cries out, a gargle of curses that Sascia barely hears—she's already walking back to Nugau, raising the sword high over his back.

She brings it down on the tubes.

Plastic shatters, black tar seeps out, and Nugau heaves a shuddering breath. Sascia is already there, her good arm around his waist, and she helps him stand. He tilts but doesn't fall. Beneath the curtain of his bangs, his eyes are hooded and unfocused, as though he is a breath away from unconsciousness.

"We need to get you back to Itkalin," she whispers. "Orran! Thalla!"

But she can't even spot her friends in the throng. The lines between the aesin battalion and the human soldiers have been erased. A mass of wrestling bodies and clashing weapons lies before Sascia, any identity the soldiers might have now concealed behind armor, weapons, and war cries.

"Mooch!" she calls, but the itka is on the other side of the silo, helping the aesin hack the nova-cannon into pieces.

She is alone. She is not afraid.

She never quite figured out the soron mola, the itka's true purpose, but she has purpose enough of her own: she's going to get Nugau to safety, to the Darkgate on the other side of the silo, and into the Dark. Fabric tears as she shreds the bottom of her T-shirt into a makeshift bandage to wrap around her bleeding bicep. She places Nugau's arm over her shoulders and takes a few steps, testing her strength; when she's certain she won't collapse beneath Nugau's weight, she shoves the nova-sword into a loop of her jeans and picks up an abandoned onyx shield.

A strangled cry tears through her teeth as she props the shield before them with her injured arm, but she doesn't stop—she can't stop, not with Nugau's back bleeding against her arm, with his head lolling against her shoulder. She starts walking, a straight line to the Darkgate. Bodies are locked in battle around her, barely sparing her a glance, but the errant bullets are too dangerous. Twice already, shots have bounced off the shield. She's almost in the middle, where the fight is thickest, when a human soldier notices her.

"Hey!" he cries, shoving his opponent off him and striding in her direction. "Stop!"

He reaches to his waist for his pistol—

A deep *pang* rattles his skull. He drops like a stone. Behind him stands Tae, gripping the thickly rugged military tablet he just used to knock the guy out. He grabs an abandoned shield and rushes to flank Sascia and Nugau's backs, screaming all the while, "Oh shit! Oh shit! Oh shit!"

They begin moving again almost compulsively, because standing still amid the blasts of magic and bullets around them is by far the worst choice. They make slow progress through the throng, but they're safe behind their shields. They would be moving faster if Tae would just drop the tablet and pick up Nugau's other arm instead.

"Tae," Sascia cries out, "get rid of the damn tablet and help me!"

"I can't," he shouts back, turning the tablet's screen toward her. It shows the scene unfolding around them, with a red dot blinking at the top right corner—he's recording this? "They jammed *our* signal, but they didn't jam their own. I hid in a closet while the soldiers looked for me and I hacked this tablet to call Crow, who told me to come here, to record, to get proof. She's broadcasting this live to every social media she could access. CNN picked up the feed just a few minutes ago."

A message appears on the screen. Sascia can't focus enough to read it, but Tae can. "BBC, too, apparently, and Al Jazeera and CNC World. Crow says she's estimating ten minutes before this place is flooded with Chapter XI agents and the military."

"And who are they coming to help?" Sascia gasps out.

Her gaze locks with Tae's. It doesn't matter whether they're coming to help Carr's mercenaries or the aesin battalion. They'll still barge in here, guns a-blazing, to get things under control first and ask questions later, and meanwhile, the two armies will keep fighting, keep dying, and Nugau will bleed and bleed—

"Screw that," Sascia says. "Screw all of this."

She drops her shield, hands Nugau's frail body to Tae, and *calls*.

It is soundless, her call, and yet it vibrates in her throat, fills her mouth, and unleashes itself, ringing like a tidal wave across the space.

Out of every crevice of darkness in the silo, every corner and shadow and pocket of black, moths pour. Not hundreds, not thousands, but millions. And all of them, every single one, is an itka. They burst out of the Dark in their shimmering whites and blues and purples, shooting through the air as fast as bullets. Their hard onyx bodies connect with guns, swords, and shields, with armor and bulletproof vests. The moths grab every soldier, human and aesin, off their feet and flatten them against the rounded walls of the silo.

Her hand outstretched, Sascia holds them there, hundreds of soldiers held captive at the mercy of her moths. Their faces are slack with surprise—and fear. They're waiting for her to say something, even Tae, who's taken a few steps away to better position the camera, but Sascia is not one for great speeches. She is all spur-of-the-moment, whatever-comes-tumbling-out-of-her-mouth, consequences be damned, but this is *about* consequences, about the fear people fall prey to, the blades they pick up, the endless cycle of violence.

She lets her fury settle, her mind sharpen, and speaks from the heart, from her own soron mola: awe, respect, love, and perseverance.

"I am no more and no less than you are," she calls out. "Not an expert, like Professor Carr claims to be, not a prince, like the Darkhumanoid behind me. Not a poster girl for peace or a Queen-killer. But I have something to say, nonetheless, and I hope you hear it."

She turns in a circle, grabbing the scared gaze of every soldier pinned to the walls. Thalla is among them, her nose bleeding into the collar of her uniform. Sascia holds the lady's gaze and at once, Thalla begins translating in a high timbre that carries around the silo.

"The Dark has hurt me too," Sascia goes on. She points to her arm, where blood stains her makeshift bandage. "Human weapons have hurt me too. But hurt is not our nature. It is a choice, one we make when we're scared or angry or confused, so today, I'm asking you: make a different choice."

Against the walls, the soldiers writhe, trying to get free.

"Choose to lay down your weapons. Choose to negotiate peace. Choose to be allies—because our worlds were not brought together by chance. You have all seen what my moths can do. They are gods of the Darkworld. They can open the door between our worlds, but traveling through it is not straightforward."

She pauses for Thalla to translate, and gestures at the Darkgate across the silo. Without Nugau fueling it, it has begun to power down.

"Our timeline and that of the Dark are not linear. When you travel through the door, you might end up in the past, or the future.

The nova-bombs we dropped into Darkholes traveled to the past of the Darkworld and liberated the Darkbeasts from their cages—the same Darkbeasts that we created the nova-bombs to destroy in the first place. This man," she says, pointing at Carr, "the esteemed director of Chapter XI, has known this truth for a long time. He chose to hide it from you, because this is more profitable: fear and hurt and war."

Thalla's translation takes a few minutes, which Sascia spends watching, studying. A wave of whispers tides over the silo, hued with accusation—but not at her. At Carr.

From where he's holding Nugau a few feet away, Tae turns the tablet toward her. A notification from Crow has popped up at the top of the screen: I hope you all enjoy attention, because I just sent a copy of our theory on knotted time to every major news company in the world.

Whatever happens here tonight, the rest of the world will know the truth. They'll make an informed decision, one that Sascia hopes is of courage that sheds no blood.

"The moths," she says, "bridged our worlds together and made a tangled knot of our timelines because they want us to save each other. Our worlds are slowly dying—think about the environment, the climate, energy sources, overpopulation. But together, we can find *another way*."

"The way," a voice whispers, "of the Moth Dark."

Slumped against Tae, Nugau props up his head. He is a sore sight: pale skin, cracked lips, trembling legs. Yet he speaks in a voice that carries through the vast space, resonant and regal, repeating his words in the aesin tongue.

"The tenets of the Moth Dark are about ever-turning change. About endless beginnings. About growth and progress and inclusion," the prince says. "But in our fear and fury and grief, we forgot—death can only ever be an ending. And we, my friends, cannot let this be our ending."

No one is struggling against the moths' holds any longer. They are enraptured and dutiful, because they can see the truth of Nugau's statement on the floor before them: death is only ever an ending. If they keep fighting, battle after battle, nothing will change, nothing will begin anew.

It starts as a *thump*, soft and distant.

Thalla has wiggled an arm free of the moths' hold and beats it now against her breastplate.

On the other side of the silo, Orran picks up the beat. An aesin warrior bleeding from his temple follows. Then comes another—a human, who knows nothing of the Thistha Ren, nothing of the aesin culture, yet can understand this heartbeat means agreement. He thuds a gloved fist against his bulletproof vest, and soon others join, human and aesin alike. Fist by fist, chest by chest, the beat of the Heart Trial echoes from every corner of the chamber, the sound almost lyrical, a song of trust woven into their flesh and bone.

Nugau's head tilts back.

At his side and over Tae's shoulder, his palms unfold. Sascia can't see it with the naked eye, but she can *feel* it—power gathering at the prince's fingertips, seeping into his flesh, filling him up. The Royal Thistha Ren is complete, Claimed and proven, and so now it is time for Nugau to receive its gift: his magic increased a thousandfold.

Now it is time to crown a new king.

Sascia thinks, *You can let go now*, and the soldiers drop from the walls like sacks.

She thinks, *Take them home*, and the world around her splits, hundreds of nicks beneath or behind the aesin, living, injured, and dead. They are sucked back into Itkalin without preamble, except, when they go, they place the knuckles of their index and middle fingers against their lips, the sign of respect Orran made to the itka.

The chopping sound of helicopters echoes from outside the silo. Chapter XI is here.

"Nugau," she says across the room to him. Mooch is hovering in front of him, a door to the Dark waiting for the prince. "Go home. Tend to your injured, bury your dead. And when you're ready, Mooch will help me find you, and we will figure this out."

But Nugau doesn't go.

He only opens his eyes and turns them to her—they are wholly black.

"No," he says.

He opens his palm to Mooch; the moth lands on it.

"You were right, little gnat," he says. "A door should not be forced open."

What door? Sascia thinks, her pulse raging at her neck. The itka's rifts are all closed, except the one that stands before him. At his back, the center of the Darkgate is empty once more, powered down.

"And I," the king says, "will make sure it never happens again."

Then he flings Mooch into the Dark.

51

A KISS FAREWELL

The rift stitches itself together, sealing their worlds apart.

Sascia's heart is a sledgehammer pounding against her ribs, frantic and scared, shattering the hope she's gathered so carefully, so painfully within her chest.

Nugau opens his palms and the Dark rushes to him.

From every crevice in the silo, thin veins of darkness meet into arteries. Black spiderwebs over the walls and floor, drips from the ceiling, uncurls itself from the nooks and crannies beneath equipment. Even their shadows lean toward him, hers and every other human's in the room, reaching for him with long, disfigured limbs.

The Dark gathers at Nugau's feet and climbs up his legs, his torso, his shoulders. It gathers at his hands, thick as tar, and it seeps through his skin, clouding its porcelain color, darkening and bulging his veins.

"What is he doing?" a soldier asks, his confusion reflected on every face in the room.

Carr's soldiers are just standing around, their weapons scattered on the floor, untouched. Only three are moving, medics from the looks of it. They go from body to body, checking their pulse, propping them up, tending to wounds.

"I don't know," Sascia whispers. She is looking straight into

Nugau's eyes, the black, depthless pools of them, but the king doesn't see her, not truly—his attention is elsewhere, focused solely on his task.

"Look out!" a soldier bellows.

A moment later, a net of Darkvines drops from the ceiling. Its onyx branches are charred, smoking like embers, and when they hit the ground, they shatter into ash. More Darkfauna slithers burnt and dead from the shadows of the tall silo. Creatures, too, hundreds of little bugs and smaller rodents, thumping onto the linoleum like black hail.

Nugau is doing this, Sascia realizes. He is gathering the Dark, pulling it from corners of this world and secreting it beneath his skin, but this is not an empty darkness—it is filled with life, plants and creatures big and small. With the Dark stripped away, this life becomes exposed to the light and withers away in seconds.

The silo gleams white and gray, bare of the Dark, but still the black torrents to Nugau's body, a continuous flow that thickens instead of thinning out. Sascia turns in a circle, tracing its source—there, beneath every door. The Dark comes and comes, a never-ending stream, and Sascia feels her stomach drop, her dread turning to acid, but she still doesn't understand, not until a voice speaks it aloud:

"He's pulling the Dark to him. *All* of the Dark."

Professor Carr stands before the monitoring station by the shattered nova-cage. The right side of his suit is soaked through. His arm hangs limp at his side, blood dripping from his fingers. But his good hand is flying over the keyboard, punching in commands, and on the dozen screens before him, there are readings, graphs, data, pulled live from the many sensors at his disposal. On the biggest screen is a wireframe globe in grayscale, with green dotting the most active hosts of Dark in the world: the Maw, the Shanghai

Pit, the Rift of the Baltic Sea, the hundreds of smaller Darkholes in the world.

And from each, the green is leaking out, to gather instead at a point just north of New York, the very spot they're all standing in now.

All of the Dark. Nugau is pulling all of it into himself, so that there may never be a door forced open again, for creatures and weapons to come through, to hurt and be hurt in turn.

The doors of the silo bang open. The soldiers in front of them startle and dash out of the way. Dark is pouring in, rivers six feet wide, rushing to Nugau from every direction. His body quakes with the force of it. He hitches a breath—like a thief, the Dark finds the narrow opening of his mouth and barges in. He chokes, a horrible sound, but the Dark forces his jaws wider and pours itself into him. The veins at his neck bulge, black against his gray skin.

In two strides, Sascia is with him, but she doesn't know where to touch him, how to help. "Nugau," she says, "you can't—"

"Let him, Miss Petrou," Carr says. He leans back against the monitoring station, his face drained of color. "It is the only kindness his world can offer: separating itself from ours."

"But it's not," Sascia whispers. "There are countless kindnesses. That they can offer us, and we can offer them."

Her fingers hover inches from Nugau's face, where the Dark writhes over and under his skin, until finally, she swallows her fear and cups his cheeks. She eases his jaws closed with her thumbs, cutting the Dark's access into his chest, and she lowers his head to hers, brow to brow. His eyes flutter closed, almost in relief, and hers are dusted with tears. She blinks them away quickly, because there's no room for despair or fear, no room for anything but saving him.

"You have to stop," she says. "It's killing the Darkcreatures in our world. It's killing *you*."

"I'm sorry," he whispers. "But it's the only way. I'll seal the doors. None will come in, none will come out. You will be safe, all of you."

She shakes her head, furiously, against his brow. She won't accept that, won't accept making his death the price of everyone else's safety, because it is not fair. They found each other through worlds and across timelines, and they've only just started. They should have a future together, however long they choose to make it. A beginning, or endless ones, just as the Moth Dark promises.

"I'm so sorry, little gnat," he whispers again.

Her tears fall hot and salty, sticky between her skin and his. They push at each other, temples and cheeks and noses, as though desperate for a touch that will soon be gone forever. *Kiss him*, she thinks, but she can't, because she knows what it would be: a kiss farewell.

She hugs him instead, wrapping her arms around his waist, and after a moment, she feels him strain against the Dark flooding into him, fight to reclaim his body, and soon, his arms are around her, too, and his nose is buried in her neck, gulping down the smell of her. They shift in place, pivoting around each other, pulling each other closer, and as they turn around themselves, a cosmos spinning on its axis, Sascia opens her eyes and looks.

Around his body, the Dark has begun to sour. Bubbles of air pop at its surface, hissing dangerously. The room is in pandemonium, soldiers running around the scattered carcasses of Darkcreatures and Darkplants. Tae is at the monitoring desk, typing furiously, and the tablet is propped against a fallen shield, facing Sascia and Nugau, this doomed embrace of darkness and light. And perhaps this is what the itka wanted, their soron mola: a whole world bearing witness to the ultimate sacrifice, the deepest of griefs, so that it may learn some kindness itself.

But Sascia can't accept that. A courage that sheds no blood, that's what they promised each other. Sascia will keep her promise and will not allow Nugau to shed his own blood.

She cups his cheeks again and brings his face to hers. "You asked me once, *What gives you the right to want?* I didn't have an answer then, but I have one now. I need you to hear it."

His skin is ashen, his veins stark black.

"There is no right to wanting," she whispers. "I'm not entitled to it, nor has some grand authority granted me its privilege. I want because I *wish*, because I *dream*, and perhaps that makes me just as greedy and vexing as you once said, but I will not be ashamed any longer. I will not apologize. I want magic and I want the Dark and I want you to *live*."

His eyes have fluttered shut. "Sascia . . ."

Before he can speak, she whispers into his lips, "If I begged—"

"You need never beg."

His hand tugs her hair, tilting her chin to him, and her arms tighten around his waist, pulling him closer. Their mouths meet softly, tenderly, as if they are trying to memorize each other's touch.

As though this is farewell. One last kiss before the end.

Deep in Sascia's throat, something tingles. Wings flutter against the roof of her mouth. Mooch, she thinks—then, again, with clarity, *Mooch*.

The itka is between her teeth.

The itka is across her lips.

The itka is in Nugau's mouth.

All the pieces of their knotted story have folded into place, except one: Nugau in her bedroom, poisoned, delirious, and awash with Dark.

"What—" Nugau leans away, but Mooch is already inside his lips.

His eyes bulge and his hands move to his face, but Sascia clamps a palm over his mouth. He doesn't struggle—he goes utterly still beneath her touch. There is no moment to speak, to reassure him. Darkness explodes all around him, a great avalanche of black pouring out of his nose, his ears, his eyes, swathing him in a cocoon of Dark, and between one moment and the next, he is no longer there.

Sascia stares at the cracked linoleum where he just stood. People are calling out to her, a dozen different voices that Sascia can't tell apart. They think she killed him, but Mooch was never the poison. Mooch was the cure that saved Nugau, that *will* save Nugau, in that strange knot of time that is both past and future.

And there, alone in a packed room, after the very last of the ymneen has unveiled itself, Sascia buries her face in her fingers, because this is the end, isn't it? That night in her room, when she asked Nugau why this was farewell, they answered, *It has to be. Separation is the only way to keep our people safe. I understand that now.* When she asked them when she loved them back, they answered, *I don't know that you ever do.* Nugau is alive, and that is all she wished for, but there is no future, not for them, not for their worlds.

"Sascia," Tae calls out.

She can't bear to glance at him, at anyone, but he insists, calling out emphatically, "Sascia, *look.*"

Closest to them, a soldier kneels before a Darkwildcat. Its fur is charred and clouded with blue blood, but it is still breathing. The soldier picks it up tenderly and unzips her jacket, folding its injured body within the darkness of her uniform. A few feet away, a group of soldiers is running from Darkplant to Darkplant, covering each one with their own clothes: their Kevlar vests, their jackets, their shirts. Another group has taken to ripping the wiring of the nova-panels, dampening the light in the room.

And before the monitors, there is Tae, pulling up dozens of live feeds from all over the world: tourists on a busy street in Tokyo holding their umbrellas over a badly singed flock of Darkbirds. Young men on bikes, pedaling fast down a suburban street, smashing every nova-light in sight. Sightseers on the observation deck of the Maw, kids climbing over the barrier and lying flat on the nova-panels, shielding the glow to protect an entire forest of half-burned Darktrees that has appeared in the bottom of the Darkhole.

Everywhere, everywhere, humans are coming out to help, to protect, in whatever way they can. Sascia was already crying, but now she starts sobbing, her chest rattling, her eyes blurry and lips stretched with joy, because these people—they're doing exactly what she begged them to:

Making a different choice.

52

WHEN SHE'S COLD

Sascia is ten.

The gossamer veil of half sleep has draped over the world, casting a starlight glow on her surroundings. Her grandparents' house is always cozily warm, and so Sascia has rolled the comforter into a body pillow, hugging it with her arms and legs. Lying on her side, she can look straight out the window.

She likes this view. The house sits at the end of a dirt road, far from town. There is no source of light to hide the stars overhead or the woods below, where the narrow trunks of the birches grow close together, as though they are friends weaving their arms around each other. The wind makes them sway as if loping in and out of some bucolic dance.

Between the tree trunks stands a figure.

Sascia knows it well by now. A figure clad in a black cloak of lustrous gems. A hallucination, according to the doctors. She's supposed to tell her parents when she sees it, and they're supposed to take her to the doctor. Dr. Diaz is a kind enough woman, funny even, but Sascia doesn't like visiting her. She always feels like she's there to *choose*, between things that are real and things that are not.

It is warm as a furnace in the house, but outside, the temperature has dropped. Grandpa Panos said there might even be snow tomorrow. When Sascia is cold, and her parents are feeling indulgent, she gets a piece of chocolate. She likes to place it on her tongue and work it against the roof of her mouth until it is a warm, melting, delicious goo.

She disentangles from her makeshift body pillow and tiptoes down the hall. When his grandchildren visit, her grandpa keeps a bowl of candy on the dining table with no restrictions whatsoever regarding when they can have a piece. Sascia chooses her favorite among them and hurries back to her room.

Cold air assaults her face as she props the window open—from the bed opposite hers, Ksenya lets out a disgruntled noise. Sascia places the candy on the sill and shoves the window back down.

Back in her nest of sheets and pillows, she watches the view. Waits for a glimpse of the figure in black. Sleep claims her long before she has a chance.

When she wakes, the sun glistens bright and eager across a blue sky. There'll be no snow today; perhaps tomorrow. Her sister's bed is empty. From the kitchen, Sascia can hear Ksenya and Danny and Grandpa chatting over cereal. She's almost to the door when she remembers.

Her feet rush soundlessly over the carpet. The candy is no longer on the sill.

But there, beneath the window, by her grandma's rosebushes, lies the wrapper, golden and emblazoned with a red-and-white *Twix*.

53

NECESSARY TENET

"The end of an era," Danny says, his chin propped on a fist.

His wheelchair is stationed at the door of the Umbra meeting room, facing the expanse of open office space where Chapter XI agents are tearing down the facilities. Computers are confiscated, equipment dismantled, ongoing projects carefully placed in black cases. Five empty cardboard boxes await the cohort's personal belongings. The fate of their work is as yet undecided, but one thing is for certain: the Umbra is no more.

"And good riddance," Tae says drily. He's leaning on the doorframe next to Danny, a finger playing with the curls at Danny's nape. (Sascia would find the casual touch endearing if she hadn't experienced so much of it in the last two weeks. Since the events of the silo, he and Danny have been—and Sascia can't stress this enough—*inseparable*.)

She won't lie; it's still hard to reconcile the image of a teacher's pet that she had of Tae with what he actually is: a proper rebel. All this time, he had been collecting details on each and every single one of the cohort's inventions that went on to become patents for NovaCorp, Hyanzi, and LIHT products. His meticulous record-keeping proved instrumental to Chapter XI's case against Carr and his benefactors. Their trial is set to begin later this month.

"Right on," says Andres, clamping a hand on Tae's shoulder.

Andres, too, had a part in Carr's downfall. Sascia had been right to suspect he was a little too good for the Umbra to begin with. It turns out Andres was a spy all along, working closely with the Latin American division of the Chapter to infiltrate what they (rightly) suspected was the insidious underbelly of Carr's research. That call he'd run off to make was to his parents, who had gone on to call Boqin Shen (now reinstated as director), who had in turn called his allies in the Chapter. An hour later, the Umbra funders had been arrested in a massive global enterprise.

"Crow," Shivani says, "is asking if Tae's mountain of empty coffee cups is being confiscated too."

The five of them share a quiet chuckle.

But when the phone buzzes again, four times in quick succession, Shivani releases a deep sigh. Crow has been texting incessantly. She was the only one whose actions two weeks ago (aka all the hacking) could get her in actual legal trouble. Fortunately, she got off with a warning and a six-month probation period, during which she's forbidden from using any electronics except for an old internet-less flip phone.

"Come on, then," Andres says, grabbing a cardboard box from the pile.

They fall in line, navigating the crowded office to get to their lab rooms. Danny pauses at the corridor, his lips drawn down. "Aren't any of you just a tiny bit sad?"

He gets four identical scathing looks, to which he responds with a blabbering, "I mean, obviously we all want the bad guys to rot in jail forever, but this program was just as much *ours* as it was Carr's. Without the Umbra, we'll just have to be normal college students, scattered around the world, and who knows when we'll be in the same room together again."

For a moment, standing before their ransacked lab rooms, cardboard boxes in their arms, their shared fear finally spoken aloud, Sascia feels it: this is the end.

But then Shivani says, "Well, you'll be seeing me quite often. I've been offered a position at Chapter XI here in New York. Liaison to 'Darkgifted youth'—it's what they're calling us now. Young people with connections to the Dark that can't quite be explained."

Thanks to Crow's hacking skills and Tae's talent with a tablet camera, the whole world knows about what Sascia can do with Darkmoths now. In the two weeks since, several people have stepped forward to claim similar strange Darkgifts. A liaison is a good first step. God knows she and Danny could have used a mentor when they were younger.

"Wait," Andres says, "*I've* been offered a job at Chapter XI, in their xenogenetics team."

"Me too," Tae grumbles. "Head engineer."

"Me three. Darkflora preservation." Danny cocks his head at her. "Sascia?"

She nods, and Danny's face goes all bright and happy, moments away from shouting *Avengers, assemble!* Sascia doesn't have the courage to tell him right now that she hasn't accepted yet, doesn't know if she will, that she has no idea what she's going to do, college or research or fishing tours or something else entirely.

As the cohort chats away, she slips into her lab and sets the box on her desk.

The lights are on for the first time in perhaps ever, the garden safe beyond the lumen-blocking glass. It's not much of a garden currently. The wall is bare cement, with only the tiniest Darkmoss growing here and there. No bugs whatsoever.

Nugau sucked the Dark out entirely in an eighty-mile radius, and reduced it acutely all around the world. The Maw and the other Darkholes in the world still stand, albeit nearly half their original sizes, but the small pockets of Dark in basements, closets, and woods are barely hanging on. They would have disappeared entirely, taking their Darklife with them, if it hadn't been for all those thousands of people who saw a wounded creature, a dying plant, and made the choice to save it.

Sascia still can't think of it without choking up. She wipes her tears on her sleeve and proceeds to carefully transfer the Darkmoss patches to her box. But when that's done, she looks around the room, at a loss. There's nothing here for her now that the moths are gone. Well, not gone, technically. According to Danny's estimates, it will take a few weeks for the Dark to recover enough to host Darkflora, and then another few weeks before Darkfauna can come crawling out. Sascia hasn't tried to call Mooch—she was not built for patience, but she's learning.

Darkmoss packed and safely covered, she trails to Danny's lab, adjacent to hers. Her cousin is in a similar state of dissociation, staring at the barely-there stalks where his Darkplants used to be. She grips his shoulder and says, "Go help Tae. I've got this."

When he's gone, she switches the lights off and goes from pot to pot, transferring them into her box—which is no small feat, considering her right arm in still in a sling, healing from her gunshot wound. Danny's desk has much more personality than hers: funny Post-it notes and framed photos, bobblehead toys of his favorite video game characters, three different pairs of sunglasses, and his missing smartwatch. Sascia tucks them all away. As the box fills and the desk empties, she thinks it again: *this is the end, this is the end, this is the end.*

The last frame contains a photo of their family at their grandpa's birthday last year. It's spring and the sun is out, refracting against the camera lens. The seven of them are packed close together in the backyard, captured in complete spontaneity. Grandpa Panos had cracked one of his foul-mouthed jokes and the rest of them had broken into shocked guffaws. Mama has gone red, Baba and Aunt Rania have thrown their heads back in laughter, Danny and Ksenya are sharing a mischievous look, and Sascia is bent at the waist, her smile so big you can see all her teeth.

Behind them, the woods seem to have turned jovial too, the long trunks of the birches sloping into each other like old friends reuniting after years apart.

Sascia stares and stares, but she can't unsee it. The trees, tall and skinny, gathered together like friends, like—

I stood in a thicket of trees—birches, I later found out—with long, spindly trunks that seemed to lean on each other for company.

The first time Nugau had come out of the Dark, they were a young adolescent fleeing a swarm of vicious bats. Mooch had opened a door for them to a thicket of birches, to a house, to an old lady sitting on the porch, almost as if she was waiting for them. A lady who had looked at Nugau and had not been afraid. A lady who had taught them English and history and art. A lady who had insisted Nugau, with their love of stories, would enjoy Halloween. A lady who had removed all photos of her family when Nugau arrived—as though, perhaps, the princet might recognize the hue of their skin or the sharp points of their ears.

Nan, Nugau had called her, because that's the name her family used, but her name was never Nan.

Her name, if Nugau had asked, would have been Sascia.

That woman is herself, in the future, living in her grandparents' house, waiting for the day she knows a princet will step out of the Dark in need of saving.

Because that is the point, the soron mola: to save and be saved.

The itka will bring them together again, in Sascia's distant future but Nugau's past—because *that* is the most important part. The knotted time. The ymneen.

Sascia understands now, everything and all at once, with perfect, desolate clarity.

Two worlds exist, separate and dying.

Perhaps not soon, not for centuries, but their death is inescapable and they know it, which makes them desperate and violent. If a door appeared, to another world where what they lacked was plentiful, these two worlds wouldn't even hesitate: they would pick up the blade and claim that new world for their own.

But what if the door opened not to the present, but to the past and future? What if time became a tangle, knotting them together? And what if there was a human girl from one world and a young princet from the other who could teach each other how to lay down the blade?

The itka had opened the door and thrown them together, again and again.

The young princet fell into the new world afraid and injured, and they were met not with a blade but with a helping hand. They learned and understood and fell a little bit in love with this new world. They returned to find their own world in chaos. And when the princet found the new world again, and a vexing human girl, they chose to offer a hand themselves. Slowly, the two of them learned and understood and fell a little bit in love too, and when their worlds came into collision, the princet and the girl knew what to do: abandon the blade.

But all of it, all of the itka's mad plan, hinged on a single detail, a necessary tenet.

The girl had to be unafraid.

And she was, almost foolishly so, but that too was a thing she had learned.

In that very same thicket of the woods, where the birches leaned into each other like old friends. Where she had once fallen into a pond, and the water had closed in heavy and cold, and a hand had plunged in and dragged her out, and a figure in a scaled cloak had saved her, the very scales she saw a few years later on a terrifying beast, except she knew not to be afraid, because that figure had saved her. They were not evil, and so this beast couldn't be evil either.

"Mooch?" she whispers, tugging on the thread that connects them.

Beneath Danny's desk comes a fluttering, then the itka is there, alive and whole and looking up at her from the knuckle of her index finger where she holds the photo.

"Nugau saved me as a child, didn't they?" Sascia asks. "That was the first knot in the ymneen. If they hadn't, if I had drowned, none of this would happen."

Mooch taps, once.

"But for Nugau, it hasn't happened yet."

Mooch taps once again.

"What happens if they decide it's not worth it? If they would rather have their family whole, and their cities intact, and the Ul'amoon shackled again?" Sascia's chest rattles with a sob, her eyes are blurry with tears, but she keeps going, keeps speaking, because she knows what she has to do now and the itka got it all wrong: she *is* afraid, she is terrified. "What if a slow, inescapable death is better than all this hurt?"

Mooch lands on her cheeks.

It kisses her skin where it's sticky and salty with tears, and more itka come out of the shadows beneath Danny's desk, big and lustrous and powerful, and settle on her face, on her hair, on her shoulders, soft and gentle and ever-changing, their emergence an affirmation and a comfort—a hug of gods, of time, of the Moth Dark.

Because they know Sascia has already decided. She will offer Nugau the choice, for it is Nugau's choice to make, the soron mola in its true essence. The moths brought them together so that they may *choose* to save each other, again and again and again, even when they are enemies, even when they cast each other away, even at the cost of their own lives, because only then will they know how to save their worlds in turn.

"Sascia?" her cousin asks from the doorway.

He sees her on the floor, in an embrace of moths, and he wheels himself to her, Tae and Shivani and Andres right behind him, and they close their arms around her, with no need for proof or explanations, and the five of them press close, hearts beating in tandem, a Heart Claim of their own making: *together, together, together.*

54

A HAND THROUGH THE DARK

Together, they make a greenhouse.

They put it up in an abandoned warehouse in Jackson Heights, which they rip apart, replacing tin with light-blocking glass, iron with wood, and cement with soil. Tae designs and installs the most beautiful flower-patterned low-exposure nova-windows. Andres refurbishes the foundation, Sascia sets up the pots, and Shivani strings soft lanterns between the pillars. Crow is still on probation; she reads them her favorite book series over the phone as they work. When the greenhouse is ready, Danny begins to fill it: small patches of Darkgrass and Darkmoss at first, a Darkshrub here and there. Darkbugs arrive on their own, vexing little scoundrels, but with every week there's a new species of Darkrodent and a new kind of Darkflower. Then, almost five weeks in, they open the doors to find a Darktree at the heart of the room, and three Darkravens perched on its branches.

Next month, after they get their Chapter XI–approved license, they're going to open it to the public.

But tonight, it's just the six of them.

They sit on two of the benches strewn around the Darksycamore tree, munching on popcorn (Crow's idea; she said both visitors and inhabitants will like it). Around a dozen Darkcreatures are gathered around them, *Snow White* style: squirrels, mice, ravens, a strange four-eyed fox. Mooch is perched on Sascia's knuckles, expertly stealing every other bite of popcorn from her fingers. They talk for a long time, lost in the rhythm of effortless chitchat, until Shivani starts yawning like a sleep-deprived cat, and between one moment and the next, they're all gathering their stuff and bidding their good nights.

Sascia stays behind.

Halfway to the doors, Danny raises an eyebrow at her.

She gives him a soft smile. "It's time."

He wheels himself back and takes her hands into his. "Are you sure?"

"Yes. I've been sure for a long while. I just wanted to see your greenhouse first—"

"Bap, bap, bap." He raises a finger. "Don't say *first*, as though there won't be a *next*."

There might not be, but Danny doesn't want to hear that. He thinks he knows what Nugau will choose, because for him, love has been blissful and unburdened, the only logical choice. Sascia hugs him, inhaling his familiar smell, memorizing the feel of his arms around hers. When he leaves, he switches the soft lights off.

Sascia is alone, with the squirrels and the ravens and the Dark.

Mooch dips and dives around her, a flurry of neon white against the black. It follows her chirpily to the heavy trunk of the Darksycamore, where the darkness is thickest. All is tranquil, but the silence grates against Sascia's nerves, like an overture before the inevitable crescendo.

She lifts her hand.

The fight in the silo has unlocked some new skill within her. Her awareness has spread, languid as a dream. She can feel the power she exerts now when she dips her fingers into the Dark. It feels like a call, spoken not with the vibrations of her vocal cords but with her essence.

Something soft and cold meets her fingertips. She splays them wide in invitation—a hand folds into hers. She pulls.

An arm, a shoulder, a head, then Nugau is right there, half in, half out of the Dark of the sycamore. His Darkprints are purple above his soft jawline. His hair drapes long over his shoulders. A soft linen shirt hangs from his body. Fear rims his eyes with white—he jolts away from her and Sascia lets him, dropping him back into the Dark.

This was not the Nugau she's seeking. He was young and frightened, no hint of recognition in his gaze.

Again, Sascia plunges her hand into the Dark. Moments pass indolently before her skin prickles. This time, Nugau is clad in armor sleek with gore. Her Darkprints blaze blue, stark against her pale skin. The jagged scar marks her jaw, but her forehead is empty of wounds. When their gazes meet, Nugau's eyes sear with hatred.

Heart battering a drumbeat against her ears, Sascia snaps her hand away as though scorched. The Dark swallows those hateful eyes, that wrathful sneer.

This was a Nugau of vengeance, thirsty for justice for her mother's death.

The third time, she pulls out a startled Nugau, small and round-cheeked, on the cusp of adolescence. The fourth, she pulls out a Nugau reeking of some acrid smell, their eyes glazed with what can only be drunkenness. On and on it goes, navigating the knotted timeline of their worlds through the tips of her fingers.

I knew you long before I met you, Nugau confessed the night before the Battle of Feathers. *Since I was a young adolescent I have seen flashes of an image between one blink and the next. It's your face, breaking out of the darkness. Your hand, reaching for mine. When you jumped in the Maw to save us, I recognized you as the face that I've been glimpsing for half my life. That's why I was so hostile at first—I thought you were something evil, come to haunt me.*

But Sascia has never been a haunting. She has just been a girl on a mission, determined to a fault. Want is her hook, grit her fishing line. She dips her hand in again and reaches out. A face emerges through the pool of Dark that does not cower or sneer. A gaze that is steady, measured, unflinching.

This time, Sascia doesn't drop them back into the fold of darkness. She tugs.

Out Nugau comes, drawing themself upright amid the roots of the sycamore.

A jagged line stitches across the skin of their jaw. Red welts dot their hairline. Their lips, Sascia notices, are marked with a single line of black, right down the middle, where the poison left its brand. Their Darkprint is a constant flux of color, of siff, of *all*. They watch her with the intensity of a person who knows too much and still not yet enough. It reminds her of the mask they wore beneath the Maw, the pretense of aloofness that they donned like armor.

But then Nugau looks past her. They see the greenhouse in all its wonder. Their jaw dips slowly, until their lips are parted ever so slightly.

"*You* did this?" they whisper.

"Danny mostly. The rest of us just helped."

"That's what he dreamed of. A botanic garden."

"Yes!" It comes out like a happy sob; that Nugau remembers, that they care.

The two of them stand there, a few feet apart. You could fit a whole world in the distance between them, a whole millennium come and gone in the blink of an eye.

"You didn't come," she says.

"You didn't call."

Nugau's eyes flash to Mooch, resting at her ear, and return to her face.

"I didn't think I should try," Nugau says. "When I last saw you, in your bedroom while I was poisoned, you were unscarred, unhurt. I watched you realize what was happening to our worlds, what the ymneen truly was. You were afraid and I didn't—I *don't* want that for you."

"I *was* afraid," she says, remembering. "But I didn't make a choice of fear. I saved you and I kissed you and when you left, I wished that you hadn't."

"Little gnat," they whisper, "don't make this harder. There will be no more attacks on your world, and no Ul'amoon as far as I can control them. Isn't it better like this, separated and safe?"

Sascia tinges her voice with tease. "*Coward.*"

The soft exhale of a laugh leaves their lips.

It thrills her, that sound, and makes her hope. "You were never the enemy," she says, "nor were the Ul'amoon. The true enemy is time; it ticks past, bringing us closer to a day where our worlds will not be able to undo the damage. But for you and me, time has always been an ally."

The mask drops from their features and Nugau emerges, the real Nugau, her Nugau: as ravenous as she is, as awed and curious.

They take a step toward her. "You figured it out. The sorun mola."

Sascia gathers her courage, every ounce she Claimed and proved true, and says, "I found the first knot. The moment that could unravel the entire ymneen. Undo the pain we've caused each other, or let it come to pass, or something else entirely. It will be up to you."

Nugau watches her for a long moment, the gears of their mind working. "Why me?"

"I think that perhaps the itka saw in you, in me, wonder where there should be fear. Like an Ariadne in love with the Labyrinth itself. They opened the door to save us both. But we had to go through this tangled mess of a time together, so we could understand what it takes to save each other."

"What does it take?"

"A hand, I suppose. A hand instead of a blade. A hand through the Dark." She breathes a laugh, almost to herself. Time is funny that way, always coming full circle. "I have made my choice—I do not regret it. But you have to choose too, Nugau."

"Between the hand and the blade?" Their voice is barely a whisper. They can feel it too, perhaps: that this will not be a simple choice, black and white, obvious and harmless.

"I think it's best if I showed you. But . . ."

She's not sure what to say. She won't plead for her life, because if she asked, if she begged, she thinks that Nugau would not refuse her, and this choice needs to be theirs and theirs alone. But she *wants* something, that insatiable hunger gnawing at her insides.

"Before you go," she whispers, "can I—"

The rest is stolen by their mouth. In a flash, Nugau has crossed the space between them and taken her into their arms. She hovers inches off the ground, snug against their chest, safe in their lean arms, and her fingers are in their hair, her lips are on theirs, caressing, easing open, tongue around tongue. They rasp hungry breaths and pull each other closer and deepen the kiss, ravenous and sated and ravenous again.

Parting is an effort, as though trying to force a galaxy apart.

Beneath the sycamore, dozens of itka somersault in the air, a veritable kaleidoscope of beating wings. Nugau's eyes widen at their presence, at the very obvious truth that this is about to lead to the moment, the first knot, the soron mola, but they turn back to Sascia, catching her face in their fingers.

"Tell me to stay," they whisper.

She won't, because she has made her choice, a hand through the Dark, and that hand only invites, never forces.

And Nugau must realize, must understand, in that way Sascia finds both wonderful and terrifying, because they bend low and press their forehead against hers. Their eyes close, their lashes dusted in the nebular colors of their Darkprint.

Behind them, the Dark has come alive, reaching black tendrils to Nugau's back and shoulders, tugging at their hair. They will be gone in an instant.

"I asked you a question," Sascia says against their lips, "the last time you saw me. You weren't sure of the answer."

When do I love you back?

Oh, little gnat, I don't know that you ever do.

"*I* am sure," Sascia whispers, "and Nugau, I *do*."

Nugau's eyes flare open, that brilliant violet, and the corners of their lips curve up in a smile, there for an instant and gone the next, because the Dark has wrapped around them and snatched them away.

Sascia stands beneath the Darksycamore, alone once more.

Nugau will arrive in a thicket of birches, Sascia knows. It will be winter, fresh snow on the ground. The ice will be shattered, the pond rippling with frantic movements. Nugau will see her in that pond, drowning, and they will understand. They can let her die and undo the damage of the ymneen. They can wake up back in Itkalin, a child again, with their mother and their parent, and their world will still be broken and dying, but not under attack. Or they can save her, so that they might meet her again in the future—her future, his past—and understand her and trust her and love her. Learn to be unafraid together. Find a way out of the cycle of violence together.

Sascia shuffles backward to the bench and drops onto it, her breath fogging the air, her eyes trailing the shades of darkness in the greenhouse, and after a moment, she throws her head back and laughs, a short stab of a laugh, because she does not know, she really doesn't know what Nugau will choose, but she hopes and she wishes and she wants, and there is no shame in that any longer, not ever again, for what she longs for is the most shameless thing in the world:

A future, of darkness and lips and the fluttering of moths.

PART V

AN ENDING AND A BEGINNING

itkalin (eet·kuh·leen) *compound noun*

moth dark; the principle of constant flux and ever-turning change that lies at the heart of the aesin way of life; also, the name of their nation.

Archaic; from itka, *the first creatures to populate the world, and* lin, *the essence of malleable darkness. In recent years, the word has become synonymous with growth, progress, and hope, with the promise of a new beginning.*

ACKNOWLEDGMENTS

This book was born out of a question: What if there was magic in our world, dangerous, scary magic, and a girl who wasn't afraid of it but enamored?

I'm incredibly lucky to be surrounded by people who aren't afraid of magic either—who love it instead.

My biggest thanks to my US editor, Gretchen Durning. I will forever be in your debt for nurturing this story's strangeness and ambition, for your in-depth thoughts and brilliant notes, and for being a fantastic advocate in every way. To my UK editor, Amina Parchment-Youssef: your wisdom and support are deeply appreciated—as is all your swooning during the romance scenes. This is my proudest work yet and I owe that to both of you: thank you.

My utmost gratitude to my extraordinary team at Putnam and Penguin Random House US: Felicity Vallence, Shannon Spann, Astrid Rojas, Lizzie Goodell, Christina Colangelo, Bri Lockheart, Jessie Clark, Natalie Vielkind, Madison Penico, Rye White. This was a complex story in every aspect, and I'm incredibly grateful for the meticulous work of the amazing copyediting and proofreading team, Krista Ahlberg, Marinda Valenti, Christine Doran, and Lauren Riebs. It is also, in my humble and completely unbiased opinion, a stunning edition—I'm beyond thankful to Rebecca Aidlin for the interior design, Kaitlin Yang for the cover design, and the incredibly talented Kim Myatt for the stunning cover art. My deepest thanks to Kim Ryan for being the fiercest warrior.

To my wonderful team at Penguin Random House UK: Jess Dunne, Stevie Hopwood, Sarah Doyle, Elsie Regan, Minnie Tindall, Becki Wells, Lauren Maxwell, Adam Webling—I deeply appreciate your dedication and hard work on this book. To Chess Vincent: thank you for being my plus-one in one of the greatest moments of my career.

To Mike: How can I ever adequately express my gratitude? You are the best agent, best supporter, best fan, and best person. If you'll allow me to get a little cheesy: you are the Danny to my Sascia, throwing a sword in my hands and telling me to go for it. To the rest of my team at DG&B, Lauren Abramo, Michael Bourret, Gracie Freeman Lifschutz, Nataly Gruender, and Masie Ibrahim: I'm honored to be one of your authors.

I'm so incredibly thankful to my street teams: the Fated and the Umbra Cohort. Your openhandedness with your love, your enthusiasm, your work, and your time amazes me. Running these street teams has been one of my very best experiences as an author—thank you for being a part of it.

To the authors who read and blurbed this book: Claire M. Andrews, Kiera Azar, Natasha Bowen, Alexandra Christo, Bea Fitzgerald, Rachel Greenlaw, Alwyn Hamilton, Esmie Jikiemi-Pearson, Pascale Lacelle, Angela Montoya, A. B. Poranek, Ava Reid, Allison Saft, Sarah Underwood, Leslie Vedder and Amélie Wen Zhao—I deeply appreciate your kind words and generosity. The biggest thank-you and my deepest love to Kat Dunn, Anna Meriano, and Words & Thai, the most thoughtful champions.

To booksellers, librarians, bloggers, and reviewers: your support means the world. To my readers: I can't properly express my gratitude. There have been lots of great moments over the past three years, but whenever someone asks what my favorite is, it's always meeting you, hearing your thoughts, chatting about books, gasping at twists, swooning over love interests. I wrote Sascia for you, because we lovers of books would all be that person if someone dropped us into a fantasy story, right? Walking around with our mouths open, marveling at the pure *magic* of the world?

To my family and my friends: I write characters surrounded by love because of you. Thank you.

And to George, always: thank you for making the different choice with me.

ABOUT THE AUTHOR

Author Photo © Kostas Amiridis

Kika Hatzopoulou is the bestselling author of *Threads That Bind* and its sequel, *Hearts That Cut*. She is a native Greek and current Londoner and holds an MFA in writing for children from the New School. In her free time, she enjoys urban quests and gastronomical adventures while narrating entire book and movie plots with her partner. Find Kika on Instagram and TikTok @KikaHatzopoulou and on her website KikaHatzopoulou.com.